SUSAN KRINARD
Luck of the Wolf

HQN™

Recycling programs
for this product may
not exist in your area.

ISBN-13: 978-0-373-77469-2

LUCK OF THE WOLF

Copyright © 2010 by Susan Krinard

This edition published by arrangement with Harlequin Books S.A.

For questions and comments about the quality of this book
please contact us at Customer_eCare@Harlequin.ca.

® and TM are trademarks of the publisher. Trademarks indicated with
® are registered in the United States Patent and Trademark Office, the
Canadian Trade Marks Office and in other countries.

www.HQNBooks.com

Printed in U.S.A.

Luck of the Wolf

PROLOGUE

March, 1882

"WE MUST HURRY!"

Franz grasped Aria's arm and tugged, his sheer determination winning out over her stubborn strength at last.

It didn't happen often. Aria was used to being stronger than even the strongest woodsmen in the mountains, and it had been a long time since anyone had tried to make her do anything she didn't want to do.

Franz was only a little old man. He had been old from as far back as she could remember, when she had toddled about his cottage on stubby, awkward legs. And he had always been worried about her, even when he wouldn't tell her why.

Later, when she had been old enough to understand, she had begun to ask questions. "Where are my mother and father, Franz?" And later still, when she first learned how to become a wolf: "Were they like me? Why am I so different from everyone else?"

Franz had never really answered any of her questions, not to her satisfaction. He had told her that her parents were dead, though he hadn't used exactly those words. He had said that he wasn't really her uncle, though he loved her like one, and that friends of her parents had brought her to him when she was a baby.

But he had said he didn't know if her parents were like her. Only that he would always take care of her, that she would always be safe with him, that she must never forget she *was* different, and never go down to the big, shining town at the foot of the mountain.

"I am twenty years old, Franz," she had told him just a week before, when she had decided to go beyond the village and into the valley, where the big town's pitched roofs and spires glittered with a fresh crystalline blanket of late-winter snow. "I am no longer a child."

He had begged her not to go. "You know how the rumors have spread in the village since you came of age," he told her. "It will be far worse in the town. If you should reveal yourself, even for a moment…"

But she had ignored him. And her adventure had not turned out quite as she had expected. The town had been filled with people crowding and pushing and talking all at once, and the streets had stunk of dung and spoiled vegetables. Everything was much too big, too bright, too loud. She had been quick to turn and flee back to the mountains.

And now, as they prepared to leave the only home she had ever known, the real fear in Franz's eyes stopped her final protest before it could reach her lips.

Franz had turned her world upside down when he'd first announced that they were to leave Carantia, to abandon the woods and mountains that were as much a part of her as the wolf she could become.

"You are not the only one of your kind," he had said. "I led you to believe that you were unique, but my deception was meant to protect you. People are afraid of what they do not understand, and there are many humans in Carantia who would hurt you if they knew your true nature."

And that, he had explained, was why he had kept her in isolation for so many years, forbidding her to venture beyond the village. Far away there was an even bigger town where a king ruled Carantia, a king just like in the storybooks Franz had given her as a child. But he was not a good king, and his people were angry and unhappy. That made them dangerous.

Aria hadn't been interested in kings. She had begged Franz to tell her more of the others like her, where they lived and how they survived in a hostile world.

"It is not my place to tell you," he had said. "And there is much I do not know. We will go to the men who first brought you to me, men who now live far across the ocean."

"But who are they?" she had asked.

"Those who, like me, wish to keep you safe. They will welcome you as one of them, and tell you everything you must know.

"We will go to America."

America.

Aria knew little of that country, only a few stories Franz had told her about the men who had founded it, and the fact that they had no kings or queens. In America, across the vast ocean, there were many *wehrwölfe* who walked quietly among humans, free to live as they wished so long as they were careful.

Werewolf, they said in English. She knew how to speak English. Franz had taught her many languages. When she got to America, she would not be mute.

And she would finally meet her own kind.

"Even in America," Franz had warned, "you must not advertise that you are not human. Fear will drive the ignorant to violence, and most Americans know nothing of *wehrwölfe*. Until we find the Carantian exiles, you will call yourself the name you have always used here."

When Aria had asked why, he had only shaken his head and promised her an explanation when they reached America.

And now they were on their way. The wind moaned, laden with a burden of fresh snow. Franz pulled himself into his pony's saddle and breathed sharp puffs of mist from within his fur-lined hood. He kicked the pony forward. Aria mounted her own pony and rode up beside him.

"We must ride far this day," he said, his voice so soft that even her wolf's ears had to strain to hear him. "If I fall…"

"You won't fall!" she said angrily. "You know these mountains better than anyone."

He turned his head toward her. "You are young and strong. No matter what happens to me, you must ride on to Trieste. I have given you all the money you will need to take a ship to Italy, and thence to America and the city of New York. You must go on to San Francisco by train."

"Not without you," Aria said. "How will I ever find my way?"

Franz reached out to touch her sleeve. "Your instincts will guide you." He patted his coat pocket. "I carry the documents that will make your introduction to the Carantians in San Francisco. Should I fail, you are to take these documents and—"

"Hush," Aria said, stroking his hand, the joints stiff and swollen even through his thick woolen gloves. He could not heal himself as she could. "You can give them to me when we reach San Francisco."

He lifted his head and met her gaze, and she saw the tears in his eyes.

"*Ja,*" he said, and kicked his pony into a trot. Aria twisted in the saddle to catch one last glimpse of the cottage. It was already gone.

A new life lay ahead. A life where she would no longer be alone.

She clucked to her pony and followed Franz into the forest.

CHAPTER ONE

San Francisco, May 1882

CORT RENIER GLANCED one last time at the girl on the stage and spread his cards with a flourish.

"Royal Flush," he drawled with a lazy smile. "It seems the luck is with me tonight, gentlemen."

They weren't happy. The game had been grueling, even for Cort. The players were the best, all specially—and secretly—invited to the tournament, all hoping to win prizes no legitimate game could offer.

Prizes like the girl, who stared across the room with a blank gaze, lost to whatever concoction her captors had given her. She was most definitely beautiful. Her figure was slender, her face, even beneath the absurd white makeup, as classically lovely as that of a Greek nymph, her golden hair begging for a man's caress.

She couldn't have been more than fourteen.

Cort's smile tightened. It was her youth, as well as her beauty and apparent virginity, that made wealthy, hard-hearted men fight to win her.

Many girls could be bought in the grim back alleys and sordid dives of San Francisco's Barbary Coast. But not girls like this one, who so clearly was no child of San Francisco's underworld. Who was of European descent, not one of the unfortunate Chinese immigrants who routinely fell victim to unscrupulous traffickers in human flesh. Someone had taken a risk in offering her as a prize, if only the secondary one. The organizers of this contest were no doubt confident that she would simply disappear, hidden away by the winner until anyone who might look for her had given her up for dead.

Cort's gaze came to rest on the man whose hand had lost to his. Ernest Cochrane wasn't accustomed to losing. His lust for the girl had been manifest from the moment they'd sat down at the table. He had a bad reputation, even for the Coast, even if he deceived the high and mighty with whom he associated in his "normal" life. If he'd won her, she would have suffered a life of perpetual degradation as a sexual plaything for one of the most powerful men in California.

Until he tired of her, of course. Then she might, if she were lucky, have been sold to another man, less discriminating in his desires.

Or she might have ended up in the Bay. Cochrane wouldn't want to risk any chance that his wife and children and fellow entrepreneurs might learn what a villain he truly was.

The others were no better. Even those Cort didn't know stank of corruption and dissipation. They were dangerous men, and every one of his instincts had rebelled against becoming involved. He wasn't some gallant bent on protecting womankind from a fate worse than death, however well he played the role of gentleman. If she hadn't been so young, he might have ignored the girl's plight. Yuri had urged him not to be a fool.

But it was done now, and Cochrane was glaring at him with bitter hatred in his eyes.

"Luck," Cochrane said in his smooth, too-cultured voice, "has a way of turning, Renier." He nodded to one of the liveried attendants. "We'll have another deck."

Cort rose from his chair. "I do thank you, Mr. Cochrane, gentleman, but I am finished for the evening, and I believe this game has been won in accordance with the rules of the tournament." He tipped his hat. "Perhaps another time."

"Another time won't do, Mr. Renier. And I have doubts that this game was played honestly."

"If I were a less reasonable man, Cochrane, I might choose to take offense at your insinuation." Cort inclined his head. *"Bonsoir, messieurs."*

He knew it wouldn't end so easily, of course. He heard Cochrane's hatchet man come up behind him before the hooligan had gone a foot beyond his hiding place behind the curtains on the left side of the stage. Cort casually hooked his thumb in the waistband of his trousers. The man behind him breathed sharply and shifted his weight.

"Now, now, Monsieur Cochrane," Cort said. "We wouldn't wish this diverting interlude to end on an unpleasant note, would we?"

"Another game," Cochrane said, less smoothly than before.

"I think not."

The hatchet man lunged. Cort turned lightly, caught the man's wrist before his fist could descend and twisted. The man yelped and fell to his knees, cradling his broken limb to his chest.

Cort sighed and shook his head, flipping his coat away from his waist. "As you see, gentleman, I carry no weapons. However, I find it quite unmannerly to attack a man when his back is turned." He bowed to Cochrane. "I bid you good evening."

His ears were pricked as he walked away, but no one came after him. They'd been at least a little impressed by his demonstration, though how long that would last was another question entirely. It would be the better part of valor by far to leave this establishment as soon as possible.

And he would have to take his prize with him, even if he didn't want her and had no place to put her. He was threading his way among the gaming tables toward the stage when Yuri came puffing up to join him.

"Why did you do it?" Yuri whispered, his accent thick with distress. "You have lost us half a million dollars and made enemies we cannot afford. Have you gone completely mad?"

Oh, yes, Cort thought, recognizing the true height of his foolishness. He could avoid Cochrane's henchmen for a while, but he didn't want to spend the rest of his time in San Francisco watching his back, and fighting was always a last resort. His strength and speed had a way of attracting too much attention. And the kind of attention he liked had nothing to do with being *loup-garou.*

"Don't fret, *mon ami,*" he said. "Has my luck ever failed us yet?"

The question was sheer bluster, of course. He had not always had such luck. In fact, he and Yuri had been nearly penniless when they arrived in San Francisco. He had won just enough over the past several months to pay for room and board, and to get himself invited to the tournament, which had been intended only for the wealthier patrons of San Francisco's gambling establishments.

But he had chosen to compete in the secondary match for the sake of a sentimentality that should have been crushed long ago, like all the other passions he had discarded over the years.

"Would you have me leave a child to such a wretched fate?" he asked.

Yuri had just opened his mouth to make a sarcastic reply when a tall, thin man with a crooked nose rushed up to them. His gaze darted from Yuri to Cort and then warily over Cort's shoulder to the table he had left.

"Cortland Renier?" the newcomer asked.

Cort bowed. "At your service."

"You're ready to claim your prize?"

"I am."

"Come this way."

The thin man scurried off, and Cort strode after him. Yuri rushed to keep up.

"I think you'd best stay behind," Cort said over his shoulder. "The girl may be frightened if both of us approach her."

Yuri snorted. "And you care so much for the feelings of this girl you have never seen before?"

"I intend to protect my winnings," Cort said.

"I am not going back into that room," Yuri said, gesturing behind him.

"In that case, I would suggest that you go home."

Yuri muttered a curse in his native language and stopped. The thin man went through a door at the left foot of the stage, which opened up into a small anteroom. A second door led to a larger room, empty save for a few broken chairs, a table laden with various prizes and a quartet of rough-looking characters Cort supposed must serve as guards.

The girl sat in the only sound chair in the room, utterly still in her white nightgown, her hands limply folded in her lap. The smell of laudanum and some sickly perfume hung over her in a choking cloud. She looked like a doll, which Cort assumed had been the point of dressing her to appear the waif, innocent and pliable and ready to be used. What she might be like free of the narcotic was anyone's guess.

His guide disappeared and the guards glowered at him as he approached the girl. She didn't look up.

"Bonjour, ma chère," he said softly.

Her fingers twitched, but she continued to stare at the floor some three feet from tips of her small white toes. Cort moved into her line of sight.

"It's all right," he said. "No one will hurt you."

Slowly, so slowly that the movement was hardly visible, she lifted her head, her gaze sliding up the length of his body. Her eyes, when they met his, were remarkable, even clouded with the effects of laudanum or whatever else they had given her. Their color was neither green nor blue but some intermediate between them, the color of the sea on a clear, still day.

The knowledge struck him all at once, stealing his breath. He had been more of a fool than even he had realized. This girl wasn't merely some unfortunate who had run afoul of the most vicious elements of the Barbary Coast. It was remarkable that she had been taken at all.

For she was *loup-garou*. And he understood then why he had been compelled to rescue her.

There were a number of very colorful curses Cort had learned in childhood, before he had become a gentleman. He swallowed them and smiled.

"Come," he said. "It is time to leave this place."

Her tongue darted out to touch her lips, but she didn't acknowledge his words in any other way. Her shoulders slumped, and her chin fell to her chest.

Werewolf or not, it was clear that she couldn't walk without help. Gingerly Cort reached for her arm. It was firm under his fingers, not at all like that of the passive doll she appeared to be.

Taking hold of her shoulders, he raised her from the chair. For a moment it seemed that she might stand on her own, but that moment was quickly gone. Her legs gave way, and her head lolled to the side. Her eyes rolled back under her eyelids.

"*Cochon*," Cort growled. "You have given her too much."

Only the guards were there to hear him, and their indifference couldn't have been more obvious. Cort lifted the girl into his arms, looking for a door that didn't exit into the main room. There was another narrow doorway at the back of the room that Cort's nose told him led outside. He strode past the guards, shifted the girl's weight to the crook of one arm while he opened the door and walked into an alley heaped with rubbish and stinking of urine.

Early morning fog was rolling over the city, bringing with it the damp chill so familiar to San Francisco's residents. Knowing that he was more vulnerable while he was carrying a helpless female, Cort moved quickly into the street, listened carefully and continued at a brisk pace away from the saloon.

The cacophony of smells—exotic spices, liquor, unwashed bodies, brackish water and things even Cort couldn't name—nearly choked him, even after so many months as a regular visitor to the Coast. Inebriates and opium-eaters crouched at the sides of the street, some so lost in their foul habits that they didn't notice him pass, others stretching out their hands in a pitiful plea for money. Shanghaiers, lingering in the shadows, followed Cort's progress with calculating eyes. On more than one occasion he heard footsteps behind him, too regular and furtive to be those of a drunkard.

But his stalkers refrained from attacking him, no doubt recognizing that he would not be easy prey, even with the woman in his arms. Still, Cort released a sigh of relief as he turned onto Washington Street, where he shared a two-room apartment with Yuri. The woman who ran the boardinghouse never asked questions of either of them, and she wasn't likely to begin now, no matter what strange cargo Cort brought home with him.

The girl still hadn't stirred by the time he walked up the creaking stairs and passed down the hall to his room. He kicked the door, wincing at the idea of possible damage to his highly polished boot, and waited for Yuri to answer.

Fortunately, the Russian had taken his advice and gone directly home. Yuri opened the door, grimaced and stepped aside. Cort carried the girl to the moth-eaten sofa that graced what passed for a sitting room and laid her down, taking care not to jar her.

"Chyort," Yuri swore. "What are we supposed to do with her?"

Cort took off his hat and hung it from the hook on the wall by the door. "That is my concern."

"It's as much mine as yours as long as she is here. I trust that will not be long."

"I do not intend to keep her," Cort said, returning to the sofa.

"Even a day is too much. Cochrane is not easily thwarted. He will have no difficulty in finding us."

That was indeed a danger, but Cort was in no mood to cower in fear from a man like Cochrane. "You are free to move on if you wish, Baron Chernikov."

Yuri drew himself up. "I am no coward."

"*Bien*. If she has any family in the city, we shall find out soon enough."

"Family? What family would allow this to happen?"

Indeed. There were few enough werewolves in this part of California, and those of any honor would hardly permit one of their own young females to roam alone on the streets or be exposed to the rough elements of San Francisco's less polished neighborhoods. Yet it was also true that most of the *loups-garous* with whom Cort was personally acquainted were hardly models of virtue— lone wolves all, making temporary alliances with each other only when circumstances demanded it.

"I don't know," Cort said, "but as she is *loup-garou,* I do not believe she can be completely cut off from her own kind."

The Russian's eyes widened. "She is *oboroten?*"

Cort gave a curt nod, and Yuri breathed a laugh. "Ah. Now I see why you saved her."

"I would have done the same had she been human."

"Would you?" Yuri brooded as he looked the girl over. "Werewolf females don't usually wander about in the city unescorted, do they?"

"Not as a matter of course. The men who took her could have had no idea what she was."

"Then—" Suddenly Yuri grinned, showing his even white teeth. "Someone must want her back very much."

"Naturally. There are only two established *loup- garou* families in San Francisco. If she doesn't belong to them, we will inquire—" He broke off, struck again by his own stupidity. It should have occurred to him the moment he recognized what she was—hell, he should have thought of it when he first set out to win her.

"We could get back some of what you lost," Yuri went on, recognizing Cort's comprehension. "*Most* of it, in fact, if we handle this correctly."

"You do realize that we are speaking of *loups-garous?*"

"You are one of them. Have you lost confidence in your ability to charm anyone you wish to?"

He had certainly not charmed Cochrane. There were limits even to his abilities.

But Yuri was right. There was no reason why they shouldn't benefit from Cort's act of charity while restoring the girl to her own people. It would, indeed, have to be handled carefully, and it would be necessary to make the girl fully aware of what he had done. A little gratitude on her part would go a long way.

Rubbing his hands, Yuri paced across the room. "As soon as she is well again, you must visit these families. I will look out for Cochrane."

Cort turned back to the girl. "She has been given far too much opium. The fact that she is *loup-garou* means she is likely to recover with rest and care, but she must be watched carefully."

The Russian clapped his hands, in high good humor. "I will leave that to you."

"After you make yourself useful by fetching water and a cloth."

Yuri shrugged and went into the bedroom. Left in peace for the first time in hours, Cort studied the girl as he had not had the chance to do before. The vividness of her eyes was hidden, and her virginal gown had seemed opaque from Cort's place at the table, but now he could see that the cloth, molding as it did to the curves of her body, concealed nothing at all.

And what it did not conceal almost brought him to his feet. She was most decidedly not a child. Her breasts were small and firm, the nipples pale brown and delicate. But her body was very much a woman's, down to the soft triangle of blond hair between her thighs.

"Ha!"

Yuri's triumphant shout brought Cort around in a movement so sharp and swift that the Russian was forced to skip back several feet to avoid Cort's clenched fist. Cort quickly lowered his arm, but he knew what Yuri had seen: the rough, hot-tempered, uncivilized boy Cort had been when he'd left Louisiana. The boy who still refused to be silenced after all the years Cort had worked to bury him.

The grin on Yuri's face broadened. "Well," he said, "I believe this is the first time I have ever been able to catch you unaware."

Cort relaxed. "Should I be on my guard against you, *mon ami?*"

Yuri harrumphed, offered Cort a towel and basin of water from the washstand in the bedroom, peered at the girl and frowned. Cort recognized the very moment when he saw what Cort had seen. He glanced at Cort, eyes narrowed.

"Perhaps it is not *I* whom you should guard against," he said.

Cort set down the basin, strode into the bedroom, and returned with his pillow and the tattered blanket that served as his sole bed covering. He dropped the pillow at one end of the sofa and spread the blanket over the girl, touching her as little as possible.

"You should go to bed, Yuri," he said coldly.

"She is no child."

"She is young enough."

Pursing his lips, Yuri stepped back. "Just as you say." He turned again for the adjoining room, his expression thoughtful. Cort felt an unaccountable burst of irritation, which he quickly suppressed. He picked up one of the cloths Yuri had brought, dipped it in the basin and hesitated.

She is young enough. He'd said that not only for Yuri's benefit but for his own. How young—or not— might be revealed when he cleaned the paint from her face.

Cort wrung out the cloth and brushed it over the girl's cheek. The paint came off on the towel, and the water made streaks across her face like the tracks of tears. Her lips, gently curved, parted on a moan.

When she subsided into silence again Cort finished cleaning her face as best he could, allowing himself to pretend that his hand was separate from the rest of his body and that his eyes saw nothing but a girl in need of rescue. When he was finished and her clear ivory skin had been stripped of the obscene "adornment," he rocked back on his heels and blew out a long, slow breath.

The question of her age was not entirely solved, but now that he could see her face, he knew she was at least a half-dozen years older than she had appeared in the saloon…and far more beautiful than even he had guessed. Her lips, no longer smeared with some pale tint designed to give her a more childish appearance, were softly rounded and womanly in a way no child's could be. Her eyes were framed with long lashes, darker than her hair, and her features were mature and defined, with high cheekbones and a firm chin.

Cort closed his eyes to shut her out. She was still help-less, and the last thing he wanted was to feel anything more than a detached interest in the girl's usefulness to him and his empty wallet. He certainly had no desire to acknowledge any attraction to her, even of the most primitive physical kind.

She was nothing to him. And while he could reluc-tantly accept that he had been instinctively drawn to her because she was *loup-garou,* she could not be as helpless as she appeared. If he'd let matters take their natural course and allowed Cochrane to win her, she would have been able to defend herself once she recovered from the influence of the opium. Her potential buyers were all human, and no match for even the smallest female werewolf.

Unless she came from a family like the New Orleans Reniers, the *loups-garous* who ruled all the werewolves in that city and much of human society besides. They seldom Changed, and when they did it was only for ritual occasions and to remind themselves why they were superior to mere humans, and other werewolves not as privileged as they were. Madeleine had been delicate, sheltered, never expected to take wolf shape in defense of her life or her honor.

If this girl were like Madeleine…

Cort laughed. He was constructing a life for her that might bear no resemblance to reality whatsoever. He had never made any effort to learn how the San Francisco families lived, whether or not they hewed to their animal roots or preferred to ignore them altogether. Until the girl woke up, it would all be fruitless speculation.

With a quick glance at her face, Cort crouched over her. Her breath, still tainted with laudanum, puffed against his face. He lifted her head.

The contact sent a wash of sensation almost like pain through his body. The last time he had felt anything like it had been when he was with Madeleine. He had assumed then that it had sprung from his love for her, and that such feelings could never come again.

And of course they had not. That was impossible. Whatever he felt now was merely a pale imitation.

Cort quickly tucked the pillow under her head, adjusted the blanket once more and got to his feet. He pulled the room's single chair close to the sofa and sat, stretching his legs and leaning as far back as the rickety chair would permit.

Think of the reward, he told himself. Yuri had been correct; they could be comfortable again, perhaps more than that, if they played their cards right. If *he* did.

And then, at last, he might find the means to take his revenge.

He closed his eyes again, focusing all his senses on the girl. He could safely rest for a time, knowing that he would be aware of any change in her condition and would be fully wake long before she was.

And then, in a matter of days, she would be gone from his life forever.

CHAPTER TWO

ARIA WOKE SUDDENLY, her head pounding and her eyes stinging. Her mouth was dry and her tongue leaden, coated with a foul taste that made her gag.

For a moment all she could do was lie still, listening to her pulse boom behind her ears. She was afraid to open her eyes, afraid to see what might lie on the other side of her eyelids. Memories fought a furious battle in her brain, some so unbearable she tried to force them away.

But she couldn't. They were too strong, etched into her senses in sound and scent and taste. Hunger. Confusion. Harsh, mocking voices, and a rag soaked in bitter poison slapped over her mouth.

Had those been the last memories, she might not have struggled so hard against them. But there were others far worse.

She tried to swallow the bile in the back of her throat. She didn't know where she was, but it might be somewhere even worse than the last place she had been before they had forced her to take the potion.

You must face it, she told herself. Hiding from her fear would gain her nothing, and knowing the truth would allow her to make a plan to escape. How many others were here? She had a hazy vision of many men looking at her, and the low hum of many voices. There had been one man in particular, though she could not recall his face. Someone who had touched her gently.

Open your eyes.

She did, and the room swam into focus. Peeling paint on a low ceiling. A few scraps of mismatched furniture. A wall covered with torn and faded paper. She was lying on some sort of couch, and a blanket covered her up to her chin.

She breathed in slowly. Mildew, dust, stale cooking. Bread and cheese closer by, setting her stomach to rumbling.

And another scent she recognized, cool and clean and masculine.

The room spun as she turned her head. The man sat a few feet away, long legs stretched before him, his head resting on the back of his chair. He was tall, well formed and elegantly dressed; his hair was deep auburn, and what she could see of his face was as handsome as that of any man she had seen in her long journey west.

He was not one of the men who had captured her. But she knew his face.

Cautiously raising herself on her elbows, Aria pushed the blanket aside. Sickness spiraled up from her stomach, and she had to sit still for several minutes. She watched the man's face for any sign of waking, but he seemed completely unaware of her. Once again she tested her strength. This time she was able to sit up, and after a moment the hammer beating inside her skull fell silent.

Wherever she was, it wasn't what she had expected. Despite the voices she could hear outside the room, she felt no sense of threat. She still wore the gown they had put on her, but when she touched her face she realized that it was clean again.

They meant to sell me, she remembered. They had spoken of it when they were certain she couldn't hear. She was to become the "property" of the man who won her in some sort of card game, like the ones she and Franz had sometimes played on snowy evenings. Property just like the sheep who belonged to Matthias the shepherd, or the pony she had left behind in Trieste.

She looked hard at the man. Had he been the one to win her? Was he waiting to do the kinds of things to her that she had seen men doing with women in the back alleys of New York and San Francisco?

Even if he was, he seemed to be alone. She had some chance of escape.

Biting her lower lip, Aria pushed the blanket below her knees and swung her legs over the side of the couch. Her feet touched the bare, pitted floorboards. She put a little of her weight on them, testing her steadiness and the surface beneath her soles.

The boards made no sound as she pushed herself up. Another wave of dizziness caught her, and she stopped, half crouched, her heart drumming under her ribs. There was a door across the room, not far. All she needed to do was open that door and find her way to freedom.

Aria straightened, ignoring the protest of her stiff muscles. She took a single step. The man didn't move. She took another step, and another, until she was passing him and only a few feet from the door.

"You had best stay here, *ma petite,*" the man said behind her. "You are not well enough to leave just yet."

The words were as soft as lamb's wool, the English touched with the pleasant lilt of an accent, yet she was not deceived. There was steel behind the voice, and she knew she would never escape without a fight.

"You need not fear me," the man said, getting to his feet. He turned, and she could see he was indeed very handsome...and very dangerous. Though his face was almost expressionless, his eyes, more yellow than brown, seemed kind—but Aria did not believe for a minute that this man was kind.

"Who are you?" she demanded.

"One who means you well."

She retreated until her back was against the door. "You're one of *them*," she said.

"You remember?" he asked, arching his dark brows.

Aria curled her hands into fists. "You were with them," she said. "You were in that place."

"If you remember so much, you know that I took you away from those who would have harmed you."

She knew no such thing. She thought this was the man who had touched her during the few brief seconds when she had fought her way free of the mist that filled her head. She thought he might have lifted her up in his arms.

But that meant nothing. She bared her teeth.

"If you want me," she said, "you will have to kill me first."

The man sighed. "I do not *want* you, and I have no intention of killing you. Come sit down before you fall."

Taking stock of her body, Aria realized that she might very well lose her strength at any time. The mist was gathering behind her eyes again, and her legs felt far less steady than they had when she first stood up.

"Stay away from me," she warned.

The man sighed. "What is your name?"

"What is yours?" she retorted.

"Cortland Beauregard Renier, at your service." He

bowed deeply, then walked to the couch and picked up the blanket. "And as I am a gentleman, I recommend that you cover yourself."

Aria stared at the blanket and glanced down at her dress. Heat rushed into her face. She had not been aware enough until now what the gown revealed, and though she was not ashamed of what nature had given her, she had seen the look in the eyes of the men who had handled her. The same look she saw in the stranger's eyes.

With a burst of courage, she darted forward to snatch the blanket from the man's hand. As soon as she grasped it she lost her balance, tottered and began to fall. He caught her, lifted her up with a strength she could not resist and returned her to the couch. She scrambled away from him to the end of the sofa, drawing up her knees and pulling the blanket over them.

"Bien," the man—Cortland Renier—said, and sat down in his chair. "Now we will talk like civilized people."

Civilized. How she had come to hate that word. Franz had used it to refer to the world she was about to enter, as if it were a good thing. But "civilized" meant you went hungry because there was nowhere to hunt, nothing to do but root through heaps of discarded food along with the stray dogs. It meant asking questions no one could or would answer, and most of all it meant people who looked nice but proved to be otherwise.

"Let me go," she said.

"You can hardly leave until you are properly dressed." He settled back as if he meant to reassure her. "I have no suitable clothing at the moment, but if you will be patient—"

Aria wanted to laugh. "I can make you let me go. When I am stronger—"

His brows arched higher still. "I do not plan to keep you prisoner," he said mildly. "It is my intention to restore you to your family, a plan I will set in motion when I know your name."

"My family?" The laugh burst out of her, thick and wrenching. "I have no—"

The look in his eyes stopped her. They were piercing and sharp, as if he already knew everything that had happened to her since Franz's terrible accident in New York.

"What is your name?" he asked again

She wanted to tell him. She wanted so desperately to trust someone, anyone, and he had not restrained her or tried to hurt her in any way. She could almost believe he meant her well.

But she had believed that before. Believed because she had to think that she would find the people Franz had said would welcome her in San Francisco. Her own kind. The ones who could answer all her questions. She had thought then that she couldn't make it all the way to the West Coast without help, not in this strange and unknown country with its unfamiliar customs and terrible cities, and seething crowds of humans.

Still, she *had* made it here, though she had quickly learned that it was better to be alone than to rely on any stranger.

"I don't need your help," she said.

"The Hemmings?" he asked, as if she hadn't said anything at all. "The Phelans?" He shifted his weight on the chair. "Did you run away?"

Aria jerked up her chin. "I didn't run away from anyone."

"*Ma chère,* this bickering will do neither of us any good. I saved you from a terrible fate, and—" He stopped abruptly. "Did those men do anything that…" His gaze shifted to her waist, then below.

A great rush of heat made Aria feel as if the blood was boiling under her skin. "No," she said. "They didn't hurt me." She looked away quickly, but not before she saw the relief on Cortland Renier's handsome face.

"Thank God for that," he said. "But you might not be so fortunate next time. That is why I have no intention of allowing you to return to the streets. Your people—"

"I don't *know* my name!" she burst out.

The silence lasted so long that Aria had to look at him again. Renier was still frowning, but now she could see that he was bewildered, as well.

"How is that possible?" he asked.

Now that she had decided to lie, she had to do everything she could to make the lie seem true. And in the most important ways, it was. She slumped against the cushions. "I don't know," she whispered.

"The drugs," he said. "You are obviously not well." He began to rise. "You must eat and rest. Tomorrow, when your mind is clear—"

"It wasn't what they did to me," she said. "I don't remember *anything.*"

His eyes narrowed. "Forgive me if I find that difficult to believe, *chère.*"

"I don't care what you believe. I don't know where I came from." She shivered for effect. "I remember the water. It was cold. And then I was walking, and I didn't know anyone. I was hungry. A man said he would give me food and a place to get warm."

"What did this man look like?"

"He was…" She screwed up her face. "I don't know.

He was one of *them*. They gave me something that made me sick. That's all I remember."

"Were you on a ship?" he asked. "Did you fall into the water?"

"I don't know!" She buried her face in her hands. "Can't you leave me alone?"

He got up. "I am afraid I cannot, *chère*," he said. "If, as you claim, you remember nothing, you will face certain ruin if you return to the streets."

"Why do you care?"

"I am not like those who took you. Any honorable man would feel bound to protect a woman in your position."

"I don't want protection," she said, meeting his gaze. "No one will ever trick me again."

"Your naiveté is touching, *mademoiselle,* but misguided."

"I told you, I can *make* you let me go."

"Ah." He nodded with revolting smugness. "Forgive my discourtesy, but how do you propose to do that, *chère?*"

It was foolish, and she knew it. If there had been any other way, she would have taken it. But she had nearly lost herself after Franz's death, forced to pretend to be human during the weeks that followed. She had almost forgotten what she really was. But once she showed Renier, he would never trouble her again.

Tossing the blanket aside, she began to pull off her nightgown. Renier started in surprise, and that gave her such satisfaction that she almost didn't mind that he would see her naked.

The Change was as swift and easy as it had ever been. Aria felt new strength flowing into her body as the transformation drove the last effects of the poison out of her. Her senses grew so keen that the smells and sounds of the place were almost painful. In a handful of seconds she was no longer naked and vulnerable but powerful and unafraid.

She grinned, showing her teeth. No words were necessary, even if she could have spoken them. Renier would be just like the men who had seen her Change in New York. His shock would soon give way to horror. He would scramble away in terror, and she would knock down the door and make her escape.

But it didn't happen as she planned. Renier didn't try to run or collapse into a gibbering puddle. He was as cool and collected as he had been since she'd awoken, his head slightly cocked as if he found her performance amusing.

"Bravo," he said. "You have made your point. Unfortunately…" He rose, turned his back to her, removed his coat and hung it over the back of the chair. He loosened his tie and removed the studs in his collar. His waistcoat came off, and then his shirt. His fine shiny boots and stockings followed, and finally his trousers.

Aria knew what was coming. She hadn't guessed. She hadn't met a single *werewolf* since the ship had landed in New York. When Renier Changed, it was like looking in a mirror for the first time in her life. His fur was auburn instead of gold, but he was everything she had imagined when she had come to San Francisco, so full of hope and dreams.

He was her kind.

Shaking out his fur, Renier sat on his haunches and stared into her eyes. She thought she might be able to dodge around him; he was bigger than she was, but her smaller size might make her faster.

If she'd had the will. If she hadn't been paralyzed with wonder and a fearful, dangerous joy.

Renier wasn't paralyzed. He Changed again while she hesitated, turned his back to her and put on his clothes. When he was fully dressed, he returned to his chair.

"So, *chère*," he said softly. "You didn't know I was *loup-garou*."

Loup-garou. That was a word she hadn't heard, but she could guess what it meant. She couldn't very well deny that she hadn't known that Cort was a werewolf.

He didn't wait for her to answer. "Now," he said, stretching out his legs again, "there can be no secrets between us."

No secrets. Franz had promised that she would learn important things when they got to America, things only the *wehrwölfe* in San Francisco could tell her. He had even hinted that he himself knew more than he had ever let on.

But he had never had the chance to explain. He had taken all those secrets with him in death, and his special documents with them.

Maybe Cortland Renier *could* help her. If he knew about werewolves in San Francisco, it seemed possible that he would know about the Carantians, too. And he had mentioned families. Was that what Franz had meant? Was it possible her family wasn't dead after all? Would she find cousins, uncles, brothers or sisters among those who waited for her?

She licked her lips. Franz had said the Carantian colonists in San Francisco were good people, honorable and steadfast. But he had said there were bad werewolves, too, just as there were bad humans. How was she to distinguish one from another, when she couldn't even be sure when a man was human or not?

You don't have to tell him everything, she thought. *You can wait and see if he really means what he says.*

Moving quickly, Aria grabbed the blanket in her jaws and raced to the door. She Changed, snatched up the blanket and wrapped it snugly around herself. Renier crossed his legs casually and smiled.

"Now that we understand each other," he said, "you can have no further doubts that I wish to help."

Aria pretended to relax. "Did you know what I was all the time?" she asked.

"Long enough. The fact that you could not recognize me, however, greatly complicates your situation."

"Why? The people who took me…they weren't werewolves, were they?"

"It seems unlikely."

"Then I could have escaped as soon as the poison went away."

"Perhaps. But where would you have gone?" he asked. "If you have no memory…"

"How many others like us live in San Francisco?" she asked quickly.

"A dozen, perhaps."

"You said there were families.…"

"Two that I am aware of, and various lone wolves."

Any of whom might know or even *be* the Carantians she was seeking. "Do they hide what they are from humans?" she asked.

He regarded her with new interest. "Why do you ask, *ma chère?* Surely you know that all *loups-garous* conceal what they are, even as they move in human society. Was it different with your people?"

"I don't remember." But of course that was exactly what Franz had told her, that werewolves had to hide what they were, and she had seen what had happened the one time she'd been careless in New York. "Does anyone know what *you* are? Humans, I mean?"

"One man only, in this city. But—"

"Is it the man in the other room?"

"Baron Yuri Chernikov. You will meet him later."

Yuri. It was a Russian name. Aria could speak fluent Russian, but she had never met a man from that country. "He is your…friend?" she asked.

"You have no more to fear from him than you do from me."

But what did that really mean, given that she had no real idea whether she could trust Cortland Renier or not? Why should she trust this Russian, when he was human like the men who had taken her?

She had much more to learn before she could decide.

"You asked me if I ran away," she said, circling around the room. "Wouldn't someone be looking for me if I was lost?"

"One would presume so." He watched her progress with keen yellow eyes. "I will make inquiries of the families I mentioned before."

The Hemmings and the Phelans. She couldn't keep the hope and yearning out of her voice. "So you know them?"

"Not personally, but that is no object." He stretched his arms, and joints popped. "You must strive to regain your memory, beginning with your name."

Aria stopped. Should she tell him her name? There must be a reason why Franz had warned her never to tell anyone what it was, why he'd made her go by another even in Carantia.

"What kind of name is Renier?" she asked.

"It is of European derivation."

"Where do you come from?"

"From another part of this country, to the east." He raised a brow. "Why do you ask?"

"It's the way you talk. It's different from most of the people I've met here."

"Your manner of speech is also a little different, *mademoiselle,* though I can't place the accent."

Aria rubbed her arms, though the room wasn't cold and she seldom felt uncomfortable even in freezing temperatures. "Where are we?"

"In the rooms I share with Yuri. You are quite safe." He rose. "You obviously need other clothing. I will buy a minimal wardrobe for you until we determine what course of action to take."

In all their time in the mountains, Franz had bought everything they had needed. She'd almost never had money of her own. After Franz had been robbed of the papers and his money, then killed by the thieves, she'd had only what Franz had given her for herself. When she'd used it up getting to San Francisco, she'd quickly learned just how necessary money was to survival.

"I haven't any money to give you, Mr. Renier," she said.

"I have sufficient funds to cover what you will need. And you may call me Cort."

Cort. So much easier to say than Cortland Beauregard Renier.

"Will you give your word not to attempt to leave while I am absent?"

She would be foolish to do so. But Cort was still her only possible connection to the other *wehrwölfe* in San Francisco.

And she wanted so badly to trust him.

"I will stay," she promised.

He nodded and strode toward her. She moved out of his way, and he went through the door to the other room. The Russian's voice, his speech heavily accented, rose in question. Aria could understand every word he and Cort spoke, and she knew Cort was perfectly aware of that.

"She's awake," Cort said, "and well enough, but she doesn't remember her past."

"*Chyort.* I don't believe it."

"Believe as you choose. Whether or not she is telling the truth, we must help her."

There was a long pause, and then the Russian said grudgingly, "I suppose you are right. But if she remembers nothing, how do you intend to find her people?"

Cort went on to tell Yuri the same things he had told Aria. When the discussion ended, the two men emerged from the adjoining room.

The human, Aria thought, was nothing special. He was a little round in the belly and plump in the face, but he carried himself like Cort, straight and proud. He walked into the room, paused and looked Aria up and down. His gaze came to rest on her face, and he stopped breathing. A moment later he seemed to remember that he could not live without air.

"So," he said, and clicked his heels together. "Baron Yuri Chernikov, at your service."

It was the same thing that Cort had said, but Aria didn't believe it this time. There was something about the Russian she didn't like, even if he was Cort's friend. He had doubted that she was telling the truth about losing her memory. He was right, of course, but every instinct told her not to trust him.

"I don't know my name," she told him bluntly.

"So I have been told." He glanced at Cort. "You are going to buy her clothes?"

"I was about to leave," Cort said. He smiled at Aria. "She has given her word to remain. You will have a chance to get acquainted."

"It will be my pleasure," Yuri said. "And I will be certain that the young lady receives whatever she needs to make her comfortable."

"There is bread and cheese in the cupboard," Cort said. Aria's stomach rumbled again, too loudly for him to miss. "You must be hungry," he said.

"Yes. Thank you."

"I'll bring more to eat when I return," Cort said, exchanging a glance with Yuri—a glance Aria knew she was not supposed to understand—and retrieved a hat from a hook on the wall. He turned at the door. "Trust me, *chère,*" he said. "We will uncover your past, whatever it may be, and restore you to your people."

He left, and Yuri went to a cupboard that stood against one of the otherwise bare walls. He removed a wooden platter with the bread and cheese, and set it down on the table in the corner.

"It is true that you remember nothing?" he asked, taking a seat on the couch.

Aria hesitated, sat in the chair at the table and sniffed at a piece of cheese. She remembered, with a pang of sadness, the fresh, pungent cheese she had eaten nearly every day in the mountains.

But there was no returning to that life, even if she had wished it. And instinct, even when it went against her desire to believe what Cort had said, told her to continue to withhold information about that life.

"It's true," she said, biting into the cheese.

"So." Yuri rubbed his knee. "You can be sure that Cort will learn the truth about you and your origins."

It felt almost like a threat. "You have known Cort a long time?" she asked, as she swallowed a bite of stale bread.

"*Da*. A long time." She caught him staring at her, and he quickly looked away. "I know more about him than anyone else in this world."

"Did you always know he wasn't human?"

"Yes."

His grimly amused expression made Aria shiver. After she had eaten all her shrunken stomach would accept, she struggled with a fresh wave of exhaustion. She might have risked sleeping with Cort present, but she could not feel comfortable doing so with Yuri in the room. She retreated to the couch, settled in one corner and wrapped the blanket tightly about her body.

She had given her word. And it was true that she had nowhere else to go, and no real understanding of this country and the people in it. But still she watched the door, half anticipating and half dreading Cort's return.

CHAPTER THREE

THE MAN WHO CALLED himself Hugo Brecht stared unseeing at the curtains that separated the private dining room from the peasants outside and sipped his wine. It went down sour and bitter, though it was said to be of the finest French vintage.

He had lost her. After years of fruitless searching, she had escaped him again.

Hugo swallowed the last of the wine and set down the glass. He remembered every day, every hour, of those years of seeking the lost princess. He had gone through hell and crossed the world to find her. Alese di Reinardus—the sole surviving heir to the throne, daughter of Hugo's cousin twice removed, the King of Carantia—spirited away from her enemies in infancy and transformed by her protectors into Lucienne Renier of the New Orleans werewolf clan.

When at last he had found her in New Orleans and taken her captive, he had been patient, waiting for the day when she would be old enough to marry him. She would become his bride and give him the throne he had coveted long before he had engineered the coup against Carantia's king.

Alese's escape had altered all his meticulous plans. It was as if she had vanished from the face of the earth. All the rogues and investigators and lawmen he had hired to find her had returned empty-handed. Even he had begun to lose hope.

Until he heard of the tournament and the beautiful girl—golden haired, with eyes the rare blue-green of the finest turquoise. Subtle inquiries had convinced him. It had to be Alese. He'd been sure of it once he'd seen her.

How she could have been overpowered by humans and become a prize in San Francisco's most notorious underground poker tournament he couldn't guess. What had she been doing since her escape? Why hadn't she returned to New Orleans? Had she been too ashamed? Afraid he would find her there?

The fact was that it made no real difference what had happened to Alese during the past four years since she had escaped his custody. He had her at last.

Or so he had believed.

Hugo's hands clenched and unclenched on the table-top. He had not dreamed it possible that Cochrane could fail to win the match. The man was said to be the best in the city, perhaps in all the West, and yet he had lost to a common gambler.

No. Cortland Beauregard Renier was very far from common. He was *werewolf,* and that was the one circumstance Hugo had failed to prepare for.

Cortland Renier. A man of great skill—or luck. By all accounts an inveterate gambler, one of that class of men who considered themselves gentlemen but haunted the Coast seeking the easy life they hoped to acquire by the most dubious of means.

But this one, they said, could be very dangerous if crossed. That was hardly a surprise, given his inhuman nature.

Still, it was not his nature that troubled Hugo at the

moment. The name Renier was not uncommon in parts of the United States. It was held not only by the most powerful werewolf clan in the country, but by lesser breeds scattered through the South and West.

The question was which clan and family claimed the man who had stolen Hugo's prize, and whether or not his being here at such a time was more than mere coincidence. Most of all, Hugo had to find out whether Renier knew he had just taken custody of his own missing relation.

Hugo rang for another bottle of wine and scowled at his empty glass. If the New Orleans Reniers had heard of the tournament and the girl who stood as one of the prizes, it was not so incredible that they would have sent a family member to see if she could be the missing Lucienne. Discreetly, of course. The New Orleans Reniers had not widely advertised Lucienne's kidnapping, and Hugo suspected that few in the family actually knew her true name and origins.

The name "Cortland" was not one Hugo recognized from his time in New Orleans. Even if the man was one of the Western Reniers, unconnected with the aristocratic lineage, he must quickly have realized that the girl was a werewolf.

Such females were not easily acquired in the West, especially not by lone wolves, and lust could be a powerful motive.

Lone wolf or New Orleans Renier, Cort was not likely to be an easy mark. Hugo's clear advantage was that Cortland Renier, whoever he was, would not be likely to recognize him.

Hugo allowed his thoughts to simmer as the waiter brought another bottle, held it for his inspection and poured the wine. When the human was gone, Hugo's mind was a little clearer. Assuming Cortland Renier was a free agent and didn't recognize his prize as "Lucienne Renier," she might be desperate and frightened enough to disclose her name.

How would Renier respond? Would he choose to help her? That would be only a little less problematic for Hugo than if he were a direct agent of the New Orleans Reniers.

Slapping a few coins down on the table, Hugo rose. It was only a question of getting the facts and making his plans accordingly. He would get Alese back. There was no question of that. He would set his men to watch the boardinghouse where Renier lived, and the gambling halls and dives he frequented. He would send a telegram to his contacts in New Orleans. By tomorrow or the next day, he would know if Cortland Renier had the backing of the clan.

If he did not, Hugo would approach Renier directly. He might simply take her by force, which would seem to be the easier path, but there was always a risk in using violence against a fellow werewolf. Alese might escape again.

No, Hugo thought as he walked toward the saloon door, he would take the somewhat lesser risk of offering Renier a substantial reward for the girl's return.

One way or another, Alese would become his bride, the bride of Duke Gunther di Reinardus. The weakling cousin who now held the Carantian throne, ruling at the whim of the noble houses, would be far more easily deposed than Alese's parents had been. And those who would change the ancient Carantian way of life, the human-lovers and rebel egalitarians who wished Carantia to become part of the corrupt modern world, would suffer the fate they deserved.

It couldn't be.

Cold logic told Yuri that the girl in the other room couldn't possibly be the one she so vividly resembled. It had, after all, been eight years since the duke had stolen her from New Orleans, and there was no guarantee that a woman grown would resemble the child of twelve she had been then. Especially a woman who had so clearly suffered since her abduction from a pampered, aristocratic life.

He paced the narrow boarding-house hallway, shaking his head with every step. What were the odds that she could have escaped Duke Gunther di Reinardus, the ruthless traitor, the very man responsible for the deaths of her parents, and ended up in San Francisco at the very same time he and Cort were here? And she *must* have escaped, because the Gunther he had known eight years ago would never have let her go.

Yuri sat down on the steps and fiddled nervously with the unlit cigarette dangling from his fingers. It must be the same woman. He had seen the birthmark below her shoulder blade when her blanket had slipped. As fantastic as the whole thing seemed, he had never been one to doubt his senses. That very pragmatism had originally allowed him to accept the existence of werewolves and join the duke in his scheme to claim the Carantian throne.

A scheme that, apparently, had failed at some point in the years since he had left the duke's service. Given the way di Reinardus had abandoned him in New Orleans once he'd taken the girl, Yuri couldn't help but take a great deal of satisfaction in that fact.

He pushed the cigarette between his lips and tried to strike a match. His fingers trembled too much to keep it steady.

Think. If this girl had in fact lost her memory, it might explain why she hadn't gone straight back to New Orleans. Perhaps she'd been on the run ever since.

But *when* had she left Gunther? Weeks ago? Years? Gunther would have begun grooming her for the throne as soon as he took her, and that would not have been a difficult task, given her upbringing among the New Orleans Reniers. Raised to be accomplished and cultivated, accustomed to every luxury due a girl of breeding, she would have needed little refining.

Where had that refinement gone? The way this girl had eaten, spoken, behaved…none of that suggested an aristocratic background. What had Alese di Reinardus, also known as Lucienne Renier, become?

And where in God's name was Gunther?

Casting an uneasy glance toward the door, Yuri finally managed to light the match and nearly burned his fingers. He threw the blackened stick to the floor. Unless Gunther's death or complete incapacitation had set Alese free—and Yuri didn't believe anything short of the wrath of God himself could kill the bastard— the duke must be looking for her. Perhaps the girl's amnesia was merely an embellishment to a desperate masquerade.

Gunther would certainly never rest until he found her. But if he had tracked her here to San Francisco, Yuri would soon know. The duke would quickly have learned the name of the man who had taken possession of his missing prize.

He would be on this doorstep momentarily, if he were not here already.

Sucking in a deep lungful of smoke, Yuri closed his eyes. Perhaps, for once, the duke had failed. Perhaps Alese had well and truly eluded him. And that left a whole wealth of opportunities for Yuri and Cort. Dangerous ones, perhaps, but if they acted quickly...

Without even knowing who she was, Cort was fully prepared to find her people and restore her to them for a price. Once he knew the girl was Lucienne Renier, he would see the beauty of Yuri's scheme. There was little the New Orleans Reniers wouldn't pay to get their lost "cousin" back.

And if or when Gunther discovered what had become of her, Yuri and Cort would be long gone.

Yuri dropped the cigarette and ground it out with the toe of his boot. Timing was everything. They needed to get the girl out of the city, just in case Gunther tracked her to San Francisco. And there were other things that would have to be done. It wouldn't be necessary for Cort to know all the details to play his part in the plan.

Especially now that they had a princess on their hands.

Knees creaking, Yuri got to his feet, painfully reminded that he was no longer young. Soon he would need the money he had as yet failed to acquire and keep. This might be his final chance, and he was determined to take it. And if he got his revenge on Duke Gunther di Reinardus in the meantime, so much the better.

Cort was just approaching the door to the rooms he and Yuri shared, precariously balancing several boxes in his arms, when the Russian walked into the hallway.

A jolt of alarm shuddered through Cort like an unexpected earthquake. "Where is she?" he demanded.

"Inside, asleep."

Cort relaxed. "She's well?" he asked.

"The *devochka* has many questions, but she shows no signs of distress." He grabbed Cort's arm and pulled him back along the narrow hall. His eyes were bright and calculating.

"What are you up to, Yuri?" Cort asked, recognizing that look all too well.

The Russian lowered his voice to a whisper. "Do you not recognize her?"

Cort set the boxes down. "What are you talking about?"

"The girl!" Yuri shook his head impatiently. "She resembles Lucienne Renier in every detail, even given the difference in age from the time she was abducted."

Lucienne Renier. The name startled Cort, and it took another moment before he remembered the story. He hadn't known the child stolen away from the grand manor of the New Orleans Reniers eight years ago. He had courted Madeleine in secret and had never visited her openly at Belle Lune until the last time he had seen her. If he had ever glimpsed Lucienne Renier, it had been briefly and at a distance.

Yuri, however, had been for a time a guest at the Renier plantation just outside New Orleans—an exotic but impoverished nobleman who, despite his human nature, was of interest to the Reniers because of his aristocratic bloodline. Though the Reniers had not widely advertised the abduction, Yuri would likely have heard about it firsthand.

It was his connection to the Reniers that had brought the two of them together at a French Quarter tavern shortly after Cort had won enough money to leave Louisiana. The Russian had taken Cort's side in an after-game brawl, and once Cort learned that Yuri had recently parted ways with the Reniers himself, they had fallen into earnest conversation.

That, in turn, had led to a mutually beneficial

agreement: Yuri would teach Cort to be a gentleman equal in every way to the Reniers of New Orleans, and Cort would support them both with his gambling skills. But if Yuri had spoken of the abduction when they'd met, Cort hadn't been listening. He'd had far more personal things on his mind at the time.

"They never learned who took her?" he asked.

The Russian snorted. "Obviously they did not." He rubbed his hands like the disciple of Midas he was. "Eight years. It is a long time. But I swear it is the same girl. No other could have such eyes."

Cort sat heavily on the stairs that faced the building entrance. It seemed too incredible to be believed, and the implications were staggering.

Lucienne Renier. A girl who bore the same surname he did, but only the most distant connection by blood. Like Madeleine.

Yet this girl was nothing like Madeleine. She had none of Madeleine's refinement or manner of speech, and for all her radiant beauty, her behavior was as rough as an uncut diamond. Could the offspring of such a family forget everything she had been taught before her abduction, all the graces, mannerisms and expectations of her station?

She had pride enough, true, but it wasn't the sort the Reniers displayed. There was no arrogance, no pompous expectation of fealty from lesser beings, human or *loup-garou*.

How could she have lost so much? Where could she have been all this time?

She doesn't remember. If she had been alone on the streets for any length of time, she would have had to fight for survival. It could have changed her beyond all recognition.

And yet…

"She was only a cousin, of course, not one of the central line," Yuri said, "but she was regarded as a daughter by Xavier Renier."

"What of her real parents?"

"I presume they were dead, though nothing was ever said of them. Regardless of her relationship to the New Orleans clan, they would have spared no expense in searching for her." Yuri paced from one end of the hall to the other, his breathing sharp with excitement. "You spoke of finding the girl's family and claiming a reward. This could not be more perfect! Of course we must make careful preparations. We will—"

"What if you're wrong?" Cort interrupted.

Yuri stopped as if he had walked into a wall. "I cannot be. I would know if she—"

"Memories can deceive."

A calculating look replaced the exultation on Yuri's face. "Not only *my* memories. The Reniers remember her as she *was*. They will not expect to see what she is now—a wild, unschooled guttersnipe fought over by gamesters. You and I, however…we can make her into what they *do* expect."

Cort rose and gathered up the boxes. He understood Yuri completely. The Russian recognized that he might be wrong, that the girl might only be a fluke of nature, a perfect duplicate no more real than the reflection of a face in a pond.

But it didn't really matter. Yuri's plan could work. The Reniers could be persuaded to accept her if they wanted her badly enough. So many, human and werewolf alike, lived in a world of dreams, blind to what they didn't wish to see.

Just as *he* had lived, once upon a time.

"You must see that it's worth the gamble," Yuri said. "Their gratitude would be immeasurable if they were convinced of her identity. She—"

"You forget one thing, Yuri," Cort said. "She may refuse. If she regains her memory…"

"Her memory will prove us right. You will see." Yuri smiled, sly as a fox. "And what a coup for you. They may not even recognize you as Beau Renier, at least not at first. And when they do…" He rubbed his hands together. "The swamp wolf will have the pleasure of restoring a child of the noble Reniers to those who spurned him."

After all their years together, Yuri knew exactly where Cort was most vulnerable to persuasion. Cort hadn't forgotten a single humiliation, a single curse, a single blow he had suffered at the hands of the New Orleans Reniers. He'd been no more than a temporary amusement for a bored girl in search of adventure, briefly titillated by the prospect of rebellion against her autocratic father.

Because of her—because of all of them—he had transformed himself into the very image of the gentleman Madeleine might have accepted. When he made his fortune and could look her father and brothers in the eye, equal in every way, then he would go back and show Madeleine what she had cast aside.

His fortunes had proven more fickle than he had anticipated, and he had almost given up on the idea of returning. Now he had the opportunity that had eluded him.

And what if she has another family searching for her? He would be robbing her of a life she might have forgotten, but it would still exist, waiting for her return.

There was no earthly reason why he couldn't make

other inquiries, as he'd promised the girl. Such an investigation might take weeks, if not longer. But he could set it in motion immediately, and in the meantime make whatever preparations were necessary to groom her for her role as Lucienne Renier.

Oh, she might resist at first. She certainly had a mind of her own. But more than once he'd seen yearning and sorrow in her eyes, especially when he'd spoken of other *loups-garous* in San Francisco or speculated about her family. She wanted to belong to someone.

Perhaps he could win that sense of belonging for her as he had never been able to do for himself. And profit in the winning.

"It is a reasonable plan," he said to Yuri. "But you must contain your eagerness, *mon ami*. She is like a wild animal who must be coaxed into the cage little by little. We must begin by discovering what she does know. With rest, safety and careful cultivation, whatever she was before may emerge on its own."

"We can't keep such a girl hidden long," Yuri said, "even if Cochrane makes no attempt to steal her back."

"Then we'll keep her confined until such time as we can find a safer place to put her."

Yuri fingered his short beard. "A safer place," he murmured. "It should be outside the city. Leave it to me." He nodded to himself. "She will need a complete transformation, and you and I cannot do it alone. I have thought of someone who would be ideal to teach her subjects on which you and I are not qualified to speak."

"Is that not somewhat premature?" Cort asked.

"Not if we wish to move quickly."

"Who is this person?"

"An old acquaintance from New Orleans, from a time

before you and I met. She is well educated, has excellent taste and is familiar with New Orleans Society."

"How familiar?"

"She is not *loup-garou,* but she has had frequent dealings with the leading families in the city. She knows your kind exist."

"And you trust her?"

"As much as I have ever trusted anyone."

"How do you expect to pay her? Until I've won a few more games, we'll have barely enough funds to cover the girl's basic necessities."

"Babette has fallen on hard times. She is widowed and currently resides in Denver in a state of near poverty. I am certain she will settle for a modest salary and a cut of the reward."

"How much do you suggest we tell her?" Cort asked.

"She can't do her job unless she knows as much as possible," Yuri replied.

"Say nothing of my previous association with Lucienne's family."

"Naturally."

"How long will it take to get Babette here?" he asked.

"I can telegraph her immediately. She could be here in a few days."

"Then do it."

"At once." Yuri examined Cort from under half-closed lids. "You'll have plenty of time alone with the girl while I'm gone. Are you certain you have no… personal interest in her?"

"My tastes hardly run in that direction," Cort said with a cynical lift of his brow. "And even if they did, I would not act on them. The girl claims that no one touched her. She may or may not be a virgin, but she must be guarded from anyone's amorous intentions from now on."

With a curt nod, Yuri removed a silver case from inside his coat, tapped out a cigarette and left the boardinghouse. Cort felt the uncomfortable weight of the half-truths he'd told Yuri, pretending he'd never felt any physical attraction to the girl.

But the fact that he had felt such attraction in the past hardly meant he couldn't ignore it in the future. He shifted the packages, returned to their rooms and walked through the door.

The girl was bundled up on the sofa, her chin on her knees, her body taut under the mantle of her deceptive calm. Her nose twitched. Cort set down the packages and bowed.

"Mademoiselle," he said, "I trust rest and a meal have improved your health."

She glared at him from under the mane of blond hair that had fallen over her face. "I am very well, Cort."

"Did you enjoy your visit with Yuri?"

"I don't like him."

It surprised Cort that Yuri hadn't tried to make himself agreeable, given his ambitions. "Perhaps you will like this better," Cort said. He unwrapped one of the packages to reveal half a ham and another that held a loaf of bread, butter and jam.

The girl's nose twitched again.

Cort set the food on the table. "You are free to eat as much as you like," he said.

"I can get my own food."

"By stealing it? That would be unwise, *ma chère.*"

"Stop calling me *ma chère.*"

"As yet you've given me no alternative," he said.

Pretending to ignore his comment, she eyed the other packages. "What are those?" she asked.

"Clothing for you. Proper attire for a lady." He put one of the boxes on the table and began to untie the ribbon.

"A *lady?*" she echoed.

Her voice held a note of scorn that surprised him. "Certainly. Is that not what you are, *mademoiselle?*"

She tucked her chin against her chest. "No. And I don't want to be one."

Cort let the half-untied ribbons fall back onto the lid. "I beg your pardon?"

"I've seen many ladies. They can barely move in the clothes they wear, and they act as if they are weak and helpless." She sniffed. "I don't have to be like them. I don't *want* to be."

The contempt in her voice startled Cort into silence. The situation was far worse than he had imagined. She had not only forgotten that she had been raised as a lady, but she felt no desire to become one. What in God's name had given her such a low opinion of her own sex?

In truth, was his opinion any better?

"When did you decide this, *mademoiselle?*" he asked.

"Before I came to—" She stopped, looking at him warily from under her lashes.

Before she came to San Francisco? Had she begun to remember? "If you were not a lady, what were you *before?*"

"Just…" She averted her gaze. "Just what I am now."

"You are a woman, are you not?"

She seemed to struggle with an answer. "Not every woman is a lady."

If Cort had been prone to despair, he might have felt it then. "That is true," he said. "Some are—"

"A lady would never go to the places those men took me."

"You are hardly at fault for what they did. If you come from one of the families I mentioned, you are a lady by birth and breeding. And not all ladies are as you described."

"They all wear those awful dresses, don't they? The ones with the…" She gestured at her blanket-clad body with eloquent distaste. "The stiff things they wear on top, and the bottoms like hobbles for ponies, and the pointed shoes and the silly hats and—"

Cort raised his hand to stop her. "The dress I have brought you is quite plain, *mademoiselle*," he said with all the patience he possessed. "It was purchased ready-made and can be put on without the help of a maid. You need have no fear of resembling the fine ladies you speak of."

One of her feet emerged from under the blanket, as if she were dipping her toes into frigid water. "But I've never worn a dress before," she said plaintively. "At least…I don't think I have."

"How were you dressed when the men took you?"

"Like you."

He barked a startled laugh. "Like me? You were wearing a man's clothes?"

"Yes. Is that so funny?"

Appalling, Cort thought, but hardly funny.

"No," he said, attempting to soothe her agitation. "It was a wise precaution if you were alone on the streets. Someone must have told you to disguise yourself."

"I don't remember."

That refrain was rapidly becoming tiresome. "You have no clothes of your own. Wherever you come from, whatever your past, society has certain expectations of any young woman."

"Even *loups-garous?*"

"Even *loups-garous.*" He took the lid off the box, unfolded the paper in which the dress was wrapped and draped the garment over his arm.

"Surely you have no objection to this," he said.

Her cheeks flushed. "How can I run in something like that?"

"As long as you remain under my protection, you'll have no need of running."

He could see her preparing to remind him that she didn't need protection, but she seemed to think better of it. "Can you take it back?" she asked in a small voice.

As he had guessed, she wasn't nearly as confident as she pretended. "I suggest you try it on before you make any decisions." He laid the dress over a chair and glanced at the other boxes with a frown. One contained sensible but attractive boots, another stockings and undergarments and the last the corset no lady did without. The shoes and undergarments would surely not be objectionable, but the corset?

He left that box aside and opened the others, leaving their contents in place. "I will wait in the other room while you dress," he said, and walked into the bedroom, closing the door behind him.

For what seemed like hours he paced the small room, twice bumping into the beds with uncharacteristic clumsiness. He imagined her letting the blanket fall, standing naked as she examined the dress. He envisioned her slipping the drawers over her strong, slender thighs and easing the chemise over her head. The thin lawn was just sheer enough that her nipples would show pale brown and tempting through the fabric.

Cort wiped the image from his mind. He heard the rustle of heavier cloth, noises of frustration and the clatter of shoes. When he could bear it no longer, he opened the door.

The girl was standing in the center of the room, the dress in place, balancing on one booted foot. She was very red in the face.

"Here," she said. "Are you happy?"

Happy was not the word for his feelings at that moment. The dress was very plain, as he had said, intended more for a shop girl than a well-bred lady. But she…she made it look like the most expensive French couture. Her figure needed no corset, nor could her stiffness and embarrassment hide her natural grace. His body stirred in unwelcome rebellion.

"Parfaitement," he said in a half-strangled voice.

She gave him a suspicious glance and suddenly lost her balance. Cort was beside her in an instant, but she shoved him away.

"I hate these shoes," she said, kicking off the one she had been wearing.

"But you like the dress, yes?" he asked.

She pulled the sides of the skirt away from her body. "No."

He took a seat in the chair and rubbed his chin. "How can I help you, *ma chère,* if you refuse my assistance?"

The girl bristled. "What do you want in return for this 'help'?" she demanded.

He had already given her an explanation, but apparently she had yet to accept it. Once again Cort wondered what she had suffered before he had found her. What had she seen on the streets? Had she been living under circumstances where men routinely used women as objects of pleasure and convenience?

"I regret if I have given you the impression that I want anything from you," he said stiffly.

Her face fell, and she stared down at her bare feet. "I'm…sorry," she said. "I'm just not used to…"

She didn't finish the sentence, but he couldn't doubt her contrition. It was a step toward gratitude, in any case. And gratitude was exactly the emotion he wished to arouse. That, and unquestioning trust.

He would have to work very hard to earn that particular prize.

"Whatever you have suffered in the past," he said gently, "not all men are like the ones who abused you. There are motives other than…" He stopped, unwilling to put his thoughts into words. They seemed far too dangerous when he himself could not quite control his physical reaction to her. "Have you known no kindness in your life?"

"I…"

Don't remember, of course. "If that is true," he said, "I regret it deeply."

She met his eyes. "I believe you."

Another small step. "You do me honor, *mademoiselle*," he said.

All the yearning he had seen before filled her face again. "Do you really think you can find my family?"

"I am certain of it."

"There is so much I don't understand. Everything is so strange."

"I will guide you."

Something in her seemed to give way, and she

stumbled back against the table. Cort jumped up to support her, and this time she didn't push him away. All the resistance went out of her body, and she looked up, vulnerable and frightened and trusting. Her eyes were like the sea at its most tranquil, right before a storm.

He didn't intend to let that storm break. He held her, feeling the warmth and suppleness of her body, taut with the kind of muscle built by vigorous exercise. If he had ever doubted that she had experienced something very different from the soft, easy life of a Madeleine Renier, he had no such doubt now.

And yet she was so beautiful.

"Ma belle," he murmured.

Her eyes half closed, dreamy and inviting. Her lips parted. She could not have offered a more appealing invitation.

He lowered his head. She made no move to stop him. With a staggering flash of insight, Cort recognized that she didn't fully comprehend what he was about to do. She had understood enough to realize that the men who had taken her had planned something unpleasant for her.

But in this matter of a kiss her expectations were only half-formed, like those of a child who has heard snatches of conversation between her elders about things no youngster should know. Cort was certain now that she had never been touched.

A string of bitter curses ran through his mind, each one more profane than the last. He had lied to Yuri when he'd said he had no interest in this woman. He might tell himself so, but his resolve was not nearly so firm as a certain part of his anatomy, which had quickly developed the troublesome habit of demanding his attention whenever he was near her. And even when he wasn't.

Perhaps if he had never seen her body in that diaphanous gown, or witnessed her Change, he might have dismissed such unwelcome sensations more easily. But he *had* seen it. All he wanted now was to feel her flesh touching his, taste her lips and her breasts, hear her eager little cries of joy when he introduced her to a world of pleasure he was certain she had never known.

And that would make him no better than the others who had lusted after an innocent girl. Would turn him into a barbarian who would use her for the sake of his own satisfaction. Destroy the very trust that was so essential in what was to come.

Slowly he released her. She swayed a little and found her balance again. The protective stiffness returned to her body. She edged away from him and toward her safe harbor on the sofa.

The sound of ripping fabric made Cort wince. She started, glanced at the shoulder seam of the bodice and bit her lip. He no longer doubted that she had little experience with dresses.

At least the garment hadn't been *too* expensive.

He smiled at her. "Would you feel more at ease in a shirt and trousers?"

"Oh, yes." She grinned, all embarrassment forgotten, then her shoulders slumped again. "But if you really think I need to wear a dress to see my family…"

"I do. In spite of your doubts, I remain convinced that you are of good family. I am certain that they would be deeply dismayed if they had any suspicion that you had suffered as you have. Dressing properly will help ease their worries. That is what you would wish, is it not?"

She hung her head. "Yes," she said. "I will learn to wear a dress."

She was so earnest that Cort almost felt ashamed.

Her loneliness was like a wound in his own body. Whatever companionship she'd had before he had won her, it couldn't have been enough. She would do anything to ease that emptiness inside.

Once he would have done the same.

"I promise," he said, "that I will not ask more of you than you can give."

Her smile was radiant, giving without holding back any part of herself. "Thank you," she said, glancing down at her updrawn knees. "I have remembered something."

Cort braced himself. "And what might that be, *mademoiselle?*"

"My name," she said. "It's Aria."

CHAPTER FOUR

ARIA.

Not Lucienne, as Yuri had hoped, but something far more enchanting.

Aria. A song. She *was* a song, as enticing as a waltz, as earthy as an Acadian air, as full of fire as a Beethoven symphony.

God forbid that he should learn that melody too well.

"Aria," he repeated. "A lovely name."

"You won't tell anyone, will you?"

The tone of her voice brought Cort to attention. "You wish to keep it a secret?"

"I...I just don't want anyone else to know."

Which was most peculiar. Was that the name she had been using since her abduction, the name her captor had given her? But why would she want to conceal an assumed name? Had she remembered something she didn't want to share even with him?

"You can confide in me, Aria," he said. "Why don't you want anyone to know?"

"I don't know why!" she said, her voice rising. "It must be important, but—"

"Do you remember ever having gone by any other name?"

She frowned. "I remember someone calling me 'Anna.'"

Anna. Not an inspired name for a woman like her. "Would you prefer that I call you by that name?"

"Yes," she said, then lowered her voice. "Except when we're alone. But I still don't want you to tell anyone else about Aria."

Cort saw no good in pushing her too far. "I will not share your name with anyone without your permission," he said. "You have my word."

"Thank you," she murmured.

"Have I permission to tell Yuri your real name?"

"I...I suppose." Her eyelids began to droop, the fringe of long lashes brushing her cheeks. She quickly opened them again, but Cort knew she was losing the battle to stay awake.

"You will have my bed tonight," he told her. "Yuri and I will sleep in this room."

"I don't mind sleeping here," she said.

"There is no need." *And I would prefer you sleep well away from the door.* If Cochrane should send someone after Aria, it would be at night. Cort would spend the dark hours in the hall, watching for intruders. Yuri could guard the inner door.

"I will find you other clothes," he said. "Yuri will remain with you while you rest."

Aria made a faint sound of protest. "Why does anyone have to stay with me?"

"Because the others who...wanted to take you when I found you may come looking for you."

"Here?"

"They are dangerous men, and I won't take any chances with your safety."

"Very well." She sighed and closed her eyes. In seconds she was asleep.

Innocence. That quality seemed to radiate from her

face like the gentle light of a candle burning bravely in the darkness. Whatever she had experienced, it had left no real mark on her.

Why should he find that appealing? He hadn't been attracted to innocence since he'd courted Madeleine, and in the end, she had proven anything but innocent.

Yes, indeed. They would have to acquire new lodgings very soon. Lodgings that would allow for more distance between him and Aria.

At least her feelings about him would not be likely to proceed any further unless he encouraged her.

And he wouldn't. No matter how much she provoked him.

Cort took hold of himself and went out to see if Yuri had returned.

The Russian was smoking in the hallway. "Well?" he asked.

"She's sleeping again. I have a few more errands to attend to."

Yuri gave him a long look. "What is it?" he asked. "What has happened?"

Cort told him briefly about her reaction to the dress.

Yuri rolled his eyes. "This will not be easy."

Feeling an unaccountable desire to defend Aria, Cort glared at Yuri. "She has remembered her name."

"Lucienne?"

"Aria," Cort said.

Yuri eyed him askance. "You do not seem disappointed."

"*I* never assumed she was Lucienne Renier."

"You were confident enough to agree to my plan. In any case, she might not remember her real name. Or she might be lying about not remembering."

"You think she is feigning her amnesia?"

"It is possible, is it not?" Yuri took a drag. "Have you changed your mind about our plan?"

Cort considered telling Yuri that he had decided to place advertisements in local papers and thought better of it. Yuri wouldn't be pleased. "I believe we must be cautious," he said.

"I am still confident that she *is* Lucienne. We must proceed on that basis, or we cannot proceed at all."

Yuri was right. Yet a little prick of unease kept Cort silent. By the time he had finished his errands, however, he was thinking clearly again. Night was falling, and for once the sky was clear. He returned to the boardinghouse in far better spirits.

Yuri met him in the hall.

"She is going to need a great deal of work," he grumbled.

Cort's good mood began to fade. "Have you had an argument?" he asked.

"What makes you think that?"

"She doesn't like you."

"So? That means nothing to me. She trusts you, and that is enough."

"Did she tell you so?"

"You can try to turn a Russian bear into a pussycat if you wish. " He shook his head with a sigh of resignation. "We will have to begin as if she were a peasant child from some backward *derevnia* in Siberia."

Cort began to grow angry. "A peasant?" he repeated softly.

"She eats like a peasant, behaves like one and speaks like one."

"As I did?"

Yuri threw up his hands. "You are one no longer. Nor will she be when we are finished."

Damn Yuri. It would be the same discussion all over again if he let this continue. "I have things to give her," Cort said. "You're free to go out."

"*Spasibo,* Your Highness," Yuri said, bowing with an ironic snap of his heels. "When have I your permission to return?"

"Before nightfall, Baron Chernikov. And bring back a proper dinner and a bottle of wine, *s'il vous plaît.*"

Growling like the Russian bear he had spoken of, Yuri strode out the door. Cort went on to their rooms, knocked lightly and waited for Aria to answer.

She opened the door a crack, her face pressed to the jamb, a single turquoise eye visible in the narrow gap. The eye widened, and Cort almost thought he caught the edge of a grin.

"Oh. It's you," she said with an air of indifference, and opened the door. She was wearing a sheet from one of the beds, gathered and tied around her waist with what looked like one of Yuri's suspenders. She glanced at the packages, skipped out of his way and took her accustomed place on the sofa. Beside her lay the damaged dress. She picked it up and began industriously stitching the shoulder seam.

"I asked Yuri for a needle and thread," she explained. "I will have this mended very soon."

Cort set down the packages and watched her, careful not to reveal any of his thoughts. Her skill was evident in her deft motions and the painstaking care she put into the task. Ladies of good family might embroidered handkerchiefs or antimacassars, but few made or mended their own clothing.

"Where did you learn to sew so well?" he asked.

Aria looked up, and Cort could see the pleasure she quickly concealed. "It isn't difficult. Anyone can learn to do it."

Especially anyone who didn't have the luxury of replacing worn clothes with new ones.

"I've brought you a few more items you'll need," he said.

Aria set down her sewing. "My shirt and trousers?"

"Among other things."

"Thank y—" She wrinkled her nose. "Something smells awful."

Cort couldn't have agreed more. He knew better than to give a *loup-garou* female perfume, no matter how subtle, but the paper the shop girl had wrapped the items in was scented.

"It will fade," he said. He laid out a selection of hair combs, a mirror, a brush and other toilet items. Aria slid off the couch and approached, real interest in her expression. She picked up and examined each item in turn. The mirror she held a little longer, staring ferociously into the glass as if she could make no sense of what she saw in it. After a minute she put it down.

"Thank you," she said.

Cort was unaccountably pleased by her gratitude. *"Voilà,"* he said, opening the last package.

As soon as she saw the trousers she gave a crow of delight and nearly knocked Cort over in her eagerness to take them from him. She held them up to her waist.

"They are perfect!" She danced like a foal kicking up its heels as he displayed the shirt and cap and shoes. "How wonderful!"

Bemused and reluctantly charmed by her antics, Cort considered how mortified any respectable mama would be to see her daughter in such bliss over a secondhand, outgrown set of common boy's clothes. But Aria was unaware, or simply didn't care, how she must appear or who might disapprove.

With a little bob of her head, she dashed off into the bedroom. The sounds that followed told him that she was obviously in some haste to remove her makeshift robe and change clothes. Cort did his best not to listen or imagine her appearance between the shedding of one garment and the donning of another. He was studiously examining one of many threadbare spots in the ancient, dirty carpet when she reemerged.

Aria *might* have passed for a boy if she had taken the time to bind her breasts and tuck her hair under her cap. As it was, with her tresses tied back in an untidy queue, she looked once again a full five years younger than the twenty or twenty-one years he judged her to be.

It would be easier, much easier, for him if she wore such clothes for the remainder of his time with her. But that wouldn't be possible. Soon enough she would be accustomed to wearing proper garments again. Perhaps, given the many layers with which modern women armored themselves, that would make things easiest of all. Her flesh would be confined, untouchable.

But that wasn't going to happen soon enough. Her warm body fell against his. "*Thank* you," she said, wrapping her arms around his waist.

Cort closed his eyes, working desperately to suppress his instinctive response. The smell of her hair filled his nose. Her heart thumped against his ribs. She broke away, and he realized with relief that he had been able to stay true to his resolve. She was only expressing her gratitude as a child would, oblivious to the consequences. His body remained under his control.

His emotions were another matter. He was in another kind of danger now. The danger of becoming fond of her. He could so easily step over the line from a certain admiration to something like affection. And he had given up such feelings many years ago. Any personal interest in her could only lead to disaster.

"De rien," he said, setting her back. "It's nothing."

"Au contraire," she said, speaking with a distinctly European French accent.

"You speak *français* very well," he said.

"Do I? I wonder where I learned it."

From a teacher whose employers considered it an essential skill, he was sure. But why that, and not an appreciation for other pursuits essential to the American rich?

"Well," he said casually, "it is an ability not everyone can master."

She plopped down in the chair and gazed at him as if he were a demigod and she his acolyte. "You are very kind," she said.

Yuri would have laughed. Cort would have done the same if he hadn't seen in her eyes what he had hoped to see: complete and absolute trust.

Will you betray that trust? he asked himself, then shook off the thought. "Yuri will be bringing dinner presently. Is there anything more you need?"

"I want to go outside."

She had managed to startle him yet again. "Surely, after what has happened—"

"I'm not afraid."

"Nevertheless, it would not be wise, especially after dark. Those men—"

"They won't come around if you're with me, will they?"

Not openly, perhaps. But the type of scum Cochrane would employ would use any tactics to get her back, and Cort had no more desire to fight now than he had before.

"I can't stay in this room forever," Aria said.

"It has only been one day. For the time being…"

She hopped off the chair. "But you're like *me!*" she said. "Why can't you understand? Werewolves weren't meant to be confined like—" She broke off and glanced toward the door, jaw set. "You can come and go as you please. Why should you care if I go out, too?"

The girl was stubborn, yes. And apparently used to getting her way. That was certainly a Renier trait. But her insistence that being *loup-garou* should allow her to run free was not.

Cort listened to the quickening of her breath and observed the high color in her cheeks. It was as if she remembered racing through wood and over meadow, hunting the marshes and tasting the raw, steaming flesh of a deer or rabbit.

He remembered. Once he had relished such barbarities. But he had only Changed a half-dozen times since he'd left New Orleans, and one of those times had been today.

"You must be patient," he said. "Your time will come."

Aria's shoulders sagged, and she retreated to the sofa.

It was an unpalatable victory. Cort knew better than to leave her alone in such a mood, but he could at least give her privacy to overcome her anger. He went out into the hall and sat on the stairs, counting the minutes until Yuri's return.

The Russian came bearing a generous dinner and the

requested bottle of wine. Cort and Yuri shared the wine without offering any to Aria; she seemed indifferent to the slight. The three of them ate in near-silence. Yuri looked between Cort and Aria with suspicious curiosity. Cort saw no reason to enlighten him as to the cause of the tension.

That night was not an easy one. Aria had finally agreed to use Cort's bed, while Yuri slept on the sofa. Cort spent the night pacing back and forth in the street, every sense straining for the approach of footsteps or the smell of the men who had played against him in the tournament. No one came. When he went back inside a few hours before dawn, he could hear Aria tossing and turning in his bed, her warm body tangled among the sheets.

It was not only Aria who would have to be patient.

THERE WAS ONLY ONE SMALL, dirty window in the sitting room, and Aria spent nearly all the next three days planted in front of it, watching the parade of men and women in the street below go about their business. She had seen almost every kind of American in her journey west, from the fine ladies Cort so admired to the most common folk, like those she had been accustomed to in the mountains.

This part of the city, however, had no "real" ladies or gentlemen, except for Cort himself.

Aria had become very familiar with the dark, stinking streets of the Barbary Coast. When she'd first arrived in San Francisco, she had quickly learned that this city was almost as vast and incomprehensible as New York had been. She had discovered how difficult it was to find anything when you were alone, and how important money was when you didn't have any.

She had managed to survive on her own for a while, moving from the brighter areas of the city into the grimy, fetid alleys where she could find food and shelter without having to pay for them, using her hunter's senses and instincts to win her small advantages over the untrustworthy folk who knew and understood this terrible place so much better than she ever could.

But Cort had been right. She had assumed everyone she met was human because she didn't know how to recognize one of her own kind. In the mountains, she had always known that she was stronger and faster, and could smell and hear better, than anyone else she met. Franz had finally told her that all *wehrwölfe,* at least those of pure blood, had such advantages over humans. She had been able to use them in the human world, but she wouldn't have known a Carantian werewolf if she had bumped right into him.

Aria sighed and leaned her chin on the window frame. After weeks of keeping to herself, she had made one mistake. The mistake of letting hunger drive her to trust a stranger because she had not been able to fill her stomach in three days.

Now she had everything she needed to eat, and a quiet, safe place to rest. She knew she shouldn't be so ungrateful and troublesome, but she couldn't help it. Her feet were beginning to itch with the need to run, and her nose longed to smell the ripe scents of wood and mountain.

If only Cort could understand.

Someone shouted in the street, and Aria leaned closer to the filthy glass to see what it was. A wagon had turned over, and two men were shaking their fists at each other as the overripe vegetables were crushed on the ground beneath their feet.

The sight didn't distract her for long. She was too busy trying to decide who Cort Renier really was. After she'd gone to bed last night, when she'd really taken the time to think, she had remembered all the expectations she had carried with her from Carantia.

She had always assumed that the *wehrwölfe* she met would be like her. Any werewolf would prefer the freedom of the wild to a human city with its high brick walls and crowds of people, even if they had to live among humans some of the time.

But Cort *liked* this place. He felt at home in it. He didn't understand why she wanted to get out, even if it was dangerous.

Were the werewolf families, the Hemmings and the Phelans, like him? Cort had made very clear that they would want her to be a lady. Were they happy to stay in small boxes like this one, in a world where you couldn't smell anything green or hear anything but the clatter of wheels and loud voices and clashing metal?

The itch in Aria's feet became a nagging pain. She moved around the room, and examined each stick of furniture and the faded paintings as if she hadn't already memorized every inch of them.

No, she couldn't make any sense of Cort. What was worse, she couldn't make any sense of herself. She'd never had such feelings as she had when she was with him. Unease, annoyance, frustration, confusion.

But those were not the *only* feelings. Nor even the strongest ones. She had been so glad when he had offered to help her and when he'd agreed to bring her the boys' clothes. She had basked in his compliment about her French. She had wanted to tell him so much more than just her real name. She had wanted to surrender the last of her suspicions.

Maybe that was why she had embraced him. Because she finally wanted to let go. She'd wanted him to…

Her face went hot, and she touched her forehead with her fingertips. Franz had told her about men and women when she was sixteen. Humans and werewolves weren't so different from the wild animals she'd seen mating in the woods, he'd said. They wanted to be together, male and female, and make children in the same way the forest animals did.

She had wanted to see that for herself and had gone to the edge of the village to watch the people there. What she'd observed had only confused her more. Some of the villagers spent a great deal of time kissing each other, not at all the way Franz kissed her on the forehead. It had looked very nice indeed.

But once they were in New York, she noticed something very different…men and women in shadowed alleys, the men grunting and groaning as they pushed themselves into women with paint all over their faces. Franz had turned very red and finally admitted that those men didn't want to make babies. They enjoyed what they were doing, even if the women did not. Franz had warned her to be very careful around such men.

She hadn't given any real thought to his warning. When the evil men had taken her, she hadn't realized what they wanted at first. But when she listened to the things they said about her, everything fell into place.

They didn't want to make children, either. They wanted to sell her to someone who would take his pleasure with her, just as those other men had done with those women in the dark streets. Whether she wanted to or not.

Cort hadn't tried to do that. But when he had held her and looked down into her face, his mouth so close to hers, she had remembered what she'd seen in the village, the gentler things those people had done, and had known something wonderful was about to happen. Something she wanted with all her heart.

The sound of footsteps climbing the outside stairs pulled her out of her pleasant dreams. She ran to the door. The scent was unmistakable, like the rhythm of the footsteps themselves.

Not Cort, but Yuri. Aria backed away from the door and waited for him to come in.

He gave her a cursory smile that she didn't quite believe, though she knew he wanted her to think he was her friend.

"Hello," she said warily. "Where is Cort?"

Yuri eased himself into the chair with a grunt. "He is conducting necessary business." He stared at her in a way she found disconcerting, and she stared back, trying to make him look away.

But he didn't. He seemed to be weighing his thoughts, getting ready to say something important.

"Do you remember nothing more of your past?" he asked at last.

Aria shook her head.

Yuri stroked his beard. "Well," he said, "we may have discovered something of interest. Cort did not want to tell you until he had made further inquiries, but…"

"What have you found?" she demanded, circling his chair.

Once again he made a show of hesitating, as if he enjoyed keeping her in suspense. "We believe we have located your relations, but they are not here in San Francisco."

Not in San Francisco. That meant they couldn't be the Hemmings or the Phelans or the Carantian exiles.

"Where?" she asked, refusing to give up hope.

"My dear, prepare yourself for a shock. Your kin are the Reniers of the city of New Orleans in the state of Louisiana."

CHAPTER FIVE

HIS LUCK HAD most definitely changed. Cort laid out his winning hand, and the other players accepted in silence, grimaced or threw down their cards in disgust.

Two thousand dollars. It wasn't much, but, added to his winnings during the past few days, it would be enough to make a serious start on Aria's "education."

Nodding to the other players, he gathered up his chips and went to cash them in. This was a decent establishment, aboveboard and free of the dangers that lurked in the worst of the gambling dens on the Coast. But after his recent run of luck, his reputation was beginning to make him less than welcome at the better places. If he intended to keep earning what he and Yuri needed, he would have to return to the less savory locations.

As he collected his money and secured it under his coat, he heard someone coming up behind him.

"Monsieur Renier?"

The voice held the cadences of a foreign tongue. Cort had never heard it before.

He turned and sized the man up quickly. Expensive clothes, a taut, proud bearing, a lean face punctuated with icy blue eyes, graying hair under a spotless top hat. Cort judged him to be in his fifties, and of an educated background.

He was also *loup-garou.*

"How may I assist you?" Cort asked.

Removing his gloves, the man bowed. "I have a business proposition for you, Monsieur Renier. One I think you will find interesting."

Cort smiled, but he wasn't amused. San Francisco was full of "businessmen" of every sort, many far from legitimate. "What sort of proposition?" he asked, leaning back against the bar. "Are you a gambling man?"

"Forgive me." The man bowed again. "I am Hugo Brecht. What I propose would be no gamble for you, *monsieur.* It would be, as they say, a 'sure thing.'"

"You intrigue me, sir," Cort said, "but I am content with my winnings." He tipped his hat. *"Au revoir."*

He got no farther than a few steps before Brecht laid a hand on his arm to stop him. Cort didn't so much as give him a glance.

"I will kindly ask you to remove your hand," he said in a pleasant voice.

Brecht declined to cooperate. *"Monsieur,* you must listen. It is in regard to the girl you won during the tournament."

All thoughts of dismissing the man drained out of Cort's mind. He swung around, tense and ready to fight. "What about her?" he asked softly.

"Please join me in my private booth and I will explain."

Damned right he would explain. The primitive part of Cort was tempted to drag Brecht into the alley behind the building and beat the answer out of him.

But he hadn't yet fallen so far, and Brecht was already moving away. Cort strode after him, his heart beating fast. Brecht didn't look like an errand boy or a hatchet man, and few *loups-garous* would consent to being a human's agent. Still, it was possible that Cochrane had sent him without knowing what he was.

Possible, but not likely.

Cochrane almost certainly didn't know that were-wolves existed, or he would have behaved very differently with Cort.

Brecht's private booth was one among several others located down a short hall. Brecht swept back the curtains and ushered Cort inside. He took a seat. When Cort didn't follow suit, he poured himself a glass of the wine that sat on the small table in the center of the booth. Cort's nose told him that the wine was of excellent vintage and had probably cost a small fortune.

"Since this is to be a gentlemen's conversation," Brecht said in a clipped voice, "I would prefer that you make yourself comfortable."

Cort leaned over the table. "I would prefer that we get to the point," he said.

"As you wish." Brecht sipped his wine with a casual air, but there was nothing casual about the way he watched Cort. "I presume you still have the girl?" he asked.

"She is safe and well."

"Excellent." Brecht studied the contents of his glass. "You have done me a great service, *monsieur,* and I intend to reward you for it."

"Indeed?" Cort settled into the vacant chair at last and pretended interest in the label on the wine bottle. "Perhaps you ought to explain your interest in the girl."

"It is very simple, Monsieur Renier. She was lost to her family some time ago, and I have been seeking her ever since. When I learned of the tournament and the prize for the second-tier match, I planned to enter the contest. Alas, I was too late." He met Cort's eyes. "It is essential that I restore her to her family."

A sharp chill of shock raced up Cort's spine, and he bought time by making a show of considering what Brecht had said. His first thought was to wonder if Yuri had been wrong all along and Aria belonged to some local werewolf clan.

His second thought was more lucid. *Lost some time ago,* Brecht had said. But how long? Eight years, perhaps?

Cort picked up the second glass that stood empty on the table and filled it. "Strange," he said. "She has said nothing about being 'lost.'"

The other man raised a brow. "Indeed? What *has* she said?"

Cort had no intention of providing more information than he had to. He certainly wouldn't tell Brecht about Aria's loss of memory.

"She has said very little," he said. "She has not even revealed her name. What is it?"

A tic jumped in Brecht's cheek. "I am not surprised she failed to tell you. After what has occurred, she is doubtless afraid and ashamed to go home."

He'd deliberately dodged Cort's question. Brecht, too, was bent on revealing as little as possible. If he was an agent of the New Orleans Reniers…

Did they know *who* had won the girl? It seemed unlikely, or they wouldn't have hesitated to approach Cort directly and demand her return. Brecht was either employed by the Reniers and was bargaining in more-or-less good faith, or he was simply a mercenary, like Cort himself, who believed he had recognized Lucienne Renier and saw a chance to claim a reward from the *loup-garou* clan.

Yet if *he* was not working for the Reniers, how could he be certain that Cort himself was not?

"The family's name?" Cort repeated.

"You have no idea, *monsieur?*"

Cort gave him a taste of the truth. "I have heard nothing of any local family missing a daughter."

"The family wishes to remain anonymous."

"What makes you certain that she is the one you seek?"

"I was able to obtain a good description."

"Descriptions can deceive."

"Nevertheless, I am sure." Brecht took another sip from his glass. "I must ask…have you touched her in any way?"

Cort began to rise. "I am a gentleman, *monsieur.* Your insinuations…"

"Forgive me," Brecht said, waving his hand. "Naturally I take you at your word. I presume your intention in winning her was to help an innocent girl escape a terrible fate. The family in question has authorized me to be very generous. You may ask any price for her return."

Any price. Cort was almost torn between asking more than Brecht could ever expect to receive from the New Orleans Reniers or rising to his feet in great offense and claiming to be a member of that very clan.

But that was too great a risk when he knew so little of Brecht or his true purpose. He settled for mild reproach. "I think you mistake me, sir," he said.

Brecht reached inside his coat. "I am sure that we can reach some sort of agreement."

"Are you not interested in learning if she has been used by those who put her up for auction?" Cort asked.

"That would be most unfortunate." Brecht's mask

slipped, and Cort could see the wolf in him struggling to emerge.

Cort finished his wine and rose. "I am afraid that you have provided too little information for me to accept your offer. The girl is an innocent, and I do not intend to cast her out into the world until I am certain she will be protected."

"Very admirable," Brecht said, barely showing his teeth, "but your concern is unnecessary. Since you have no personal interest in the child…"

She is no child, Cort thought. But he only shook his head. "Pity has been my sole motive. Nevertheless…" He moved toward the curtains. "I must in good conscience decline until you are able to provide evidence of your honorable intentions."

"Perhaps this will ease your doubts." Brecht pulled out a fat leather wallet, withdrew a large number of bills and laid them on the table. The amount was staggering.

"This will surely recompense you for your time and sacrifice," Brecht said, smugly certain of victory.

He had some reason to be. Such a sum would recompense Cort a hundred times over. He would never have guessed that he would ever turn down such an offer.

"Monsieur," he said, "you are generous indeed, but again, I must decline." He bowed. "Good day." He bowed again and pushed his way out through the curtains.

Brecht released a harsh breath, and Cort fully expected the man to come after him. But by the time he reached the street, he knew he was not being followed.

That didn't set his mind at ease. It was remotely conceivable that Brecht was telling the truth. Aria might be lying about everything, from her name to her amnesia. If Brecht was in fact honorable and Cort refused to cooperate, the man could simply tell the Reniers that Cort had her.

Yet if Aria hadn't lost her memory, why wouldn't she tell Cort right away that she had been kidnapped and ask to be returned to her family? Could it be that she didn't want to go back to them? But why, then, would she appear to be so eager to find someone, anyone, to whom she belonged?

If he had to choose which one was the liar, Aria or Brecht, Cort wouldn't hesitate. Brecht stank of deception. Cort had felt the simmering emotion beneath that cultured speech, and it was not merely concern for the girl or relief at the prospect of restoring a wayward daughter to the bosom of her family. There was something too personal in his interest.

Cort reached the boardinghouse in ten minutes. He stopped in front of the porch steps, his mind working furiously. *He* had made his position clear enough, but it was evident that Brecht wouldn't give up easily. If he wasn't able to bribe Cort, Brecht might very well take the kind of action Cort had expected from Cochrane.

The danger to Aria hadn't diminished. If Cort wanted answers, he would have to speak to her and gauge her responses carefully. He had expected her to trust him. If *he* couldn't trust *her*...

His body strangely heavy, Cort went into the house. He wasn't ready to talk to Aria yet, and he didn't believe that Brecht would send anyone to the house in daylight or so soon after their conversation. He would tell Yuri what had happened, but not now. The next few hours would be devoted to questioning the locals about Hugo Brecht.

He spoke briefly to Yuri, warning him to be vigilant, and slipped away before Aria could claim his attention. He couldn't afford to have anything on his mind but his newest enemy.

"Do you understand what you must do?"

The men—two werewolf, two human—nodded without quite meeting his eyes. They were rough fellows, but they had been in his employ long enough to understand the consequences of failing Duke Gunther di Reinardus.

He sent them on their way and strolled out of the saloon, nodding and smiling to the proprietor, who had good reason to appreciate his taste in fine wines. The smile was a mask, of course. He felt nothing but contempt as he walked out into the street, stepping over sewage and horse droppings and the bodies of men too drunk to sit up, let alone stand.

All humans were scum, hardly worthy of treading the same earth as any werewolf. But even among his own kind there were those no better than the most loathsome dregs of this city. Cort Renier was a perfect example.

Gunther's lip twitched as he made his way through the mud and filth. He brushed off a whining, dirty child begging for pennies and recalled the conversation. The risk had been considerable, but he had learned much of what he needed to know. He had little doubt now, even before he received the expected reply from New Orleans, that Cort Renier was an independent agent, not a member of the New Orleans clan. His trace of an accent and perfect French told Gunther that his origins were almost certainly in Louisiana, but everything else about the man pointed to inferior blood and breeding.

If Alese *had* told Renier her assumed name and the location of her relatives, or if he had already guessed who she was, he would now be doubly on his guard. That was only to be expected. Renier had certainly done an excellent job of pretending disinterest in the money Gunther had offered.

But pretense it was. Gunther did not for a moment believe that the man was honorable, nobly and unselfishly committed to guarding an abused girl's innocence. One of his kind would never act simply out of altruism. It had been far too much money for such a rogue to turn down—unless he believed he could obtain more directly from the girl's family.

The dirty human whelp stumbled and fell as Gunther pushed him away a second time. His thoughts returned immediately to Renier. Either the man was playing a deeper game than even Gunther could imagine, or he was simply stupid.

That, too, Gunther did not believe. Underestimating the man would almost certainly be a mistake.

Gunther turned the corner into an even more fetid street, attempting to close his nostrils against the stench. Perhaps Renier would think over their conversation and decide to accept the money after all, but Gunther wasn't taking any chances. His men would dog the rogue's footsteps and watch his boardinghouse every hour of the day and night. They were under strict orders not to act unless there was a certainty of success. Once a decisive move was made, there might very well never be another opportunity.

Pondering the obstacles that still lay ahead, Gunther slowed his pace. Renier's boardinghouse was another block along the street, squeezed amidst a row of equally decrepit houses, saloons and bordellos. He cut into a back alley, turned and continued parallel to the street, then turned back again toward the main thoroughfare when he was across from the boardinghouse.

The porch sagged, the colorless paint was peeling from all the walls, and the roof looked on the verge of collapse. A pitiful domicile for any werewolf, especially one who fancied himself a gentleman.

There was no reason why Gunther himself should keep watch; his men would be along soon enough. Still he lingered in the shadows, leaning against the pitted brick wall beside him, and waited to see if anything interesting might happen.

Nothing did. The girl remained hidden, and there was no sign of Renier. Dusk was settling over the Coast and Gunther was preparing to leave when a man emerged from the boardinghouse, plumpish but unmistakably arrogant in his bearing. He looked right and left as he stood on the porch, pulled out his pocket watch and straightened his overcoat.

Even in the gloom of evening, Gunther's keen wolf eyes picked out the details of the man's face. He stiffened.

Yuri Chernikov.

Gunther watched the Russian stride away from the house in an obvious hurry. There was something furtive in Chernikov's movements, in spite of his fast pace. But then, he had always been more rat than man, scurrying from one foul nest of schemes to another.

The wolf in Gunther urged him to pursue, relishing the image of Chernikov cowering at his feet. But he knew better than to give in to instinct without the balancing influence of intellect.

Intellect told him that the seemingly bizarre coincidence of finding the Russian in San Francisco, leaving the very boardinghouse occupied by Cortland Renier, was no coincidence at all. Yuri had been in New Orleans with Gunther eight years ago. Cortland Renier almost certainly came from Louisiana. The two of them might have known each other for years; Gunther had never bothered to vet all of Yuri's connections once he had found those useful to him.

Gunther chuckled grimly. It was almost amusing. Had Yuri urged Cort to enter the game because he had guessed the girl's identity, or had he recognized her afterward? He would certainly have known her as soon as he'd seen the birthmark on her back.

He would have realized that she must have escaped his former employer, but he obviously hadn't suspected that Gunther was also in San Francisco. He would have seen an unprecedented opportunity in her fortuitous appearance.

But had he told Cortland Renier the full truth?

Smiling coldly, Gunther walked back to his hotel. Perhaps it would not be necessary to use violence after all.

YURI WAS GONE.

Aria pushed away from the window and circled the room, counting her steps for the hundredth time. It seemed years since the Russian had told her about her real family, and ever since then she had been able to think of nothing but talking to Cort.

But he hadn't given her the chance. He'd come home briefly to speak with Yuri—a conversation she hadn't quite been able to make out—then had left again immediately, as if he wanted to avoid her. She could guess his reason for running away. He didn't want to explain why he'd kept something so important a secret.

Yuri had claimed they'd just found out who she was, but that didn't make any sense. Didn't she and Cort have the same surname? Why, she'd asked, hadn't he known her identity right away?

Because, Yuri had explained, she and Cort were

related in only the broadest sense of the word. The first Reniers had come from Europe centuries ago, but the various clans spread across the United States shared little more than the name itself.

She had wanted to ask more about those clans, but Yuri had shaken his head and changed the subject. He'd told her that she'd been "taken away" from her cousins in New Orleans many years ago, and that they had been looking for her for a very long time. With a terrible hope, she had begged to know if her parents were still alive.

He had told her what Franz had always claimed: that her parents were dead. After that he'd refused to answer any more of her questions.

Aria hugged herself as if she might burst into pieces if she so much as breathed too deeply. She had a sur-name now, a real identity. She was finally beginning to find out who she was. Who she truly was.

She stopped in the middle of the room and tried to quiet her soaring thoughts. There was still so much she didn't understand. Franz had told her she had come to him when she was a baby. In her earliest recollections she had been too small to reach the pretty carvings Franz always kept on the highest shelf of the big glass case in the cottage parlor. She could see herself reaching and reaching, tears running down her cheeks when the exquisite figurines remained beyond the grasp of her chubby hands.

So clearly someone had taken her away from her family—her cousins—when she was only an infant, sometime after her parents had died. When she and Franz had left for America, Franz had said she would meet the men who had first brought her to him. He had said they wanted to keep her safe. But New Orleans was very far from Carantia, and Franz had told her that there were many in Carantia who would want to hurt her.

So why would anyone have taken her from her family in America and sent her all the way across the ocean?

And why would Franz have kept her past a secret? Why had he kept her isolated in the mountains? Why had he waited so long to tell her about her own kind and bring her to America? Why had she and Franz headed for San Francisco instead of the city called New Orleans, where her family had been looking for her?

None of it made any sense, but there must be some explanation. Franz must have had very good reasons for doing what he had. He was no longer here to explain, but soon she would know. Soon she would know everything.

Torn between sadness and exultation, Aria tried not to let her wild suppositions overwhelm her. But when night fell, tugging at her senses like the sweet smell of fat deer grazing on the thick summer grass, she could no longer bear it. She had to speak to Cort.

You must wait, she told herself. It was what Cort wanted. It was the safe thing to do.

But she didn't want to be safe anymore. She wasn't stupid enough to let another stranger on the street fool her with promises, and fill her with poison that made her blind and deaf and dumb. Even in this ugly city with its stench of rot and machines and thousands of conflicting odors, she could track a familiar scent.

Twisting her hair into a knot on top of her head, Aria secured it with one of the pretty, fragile ribbons Cort had brought and planted her cap on her head. She found the stuff Cort used to polish his boots and shoes, and smeared it over her face so it looked like smudges of dirt.

With only a twinge of guilt, she slipped into the hallway, paused to listen and then crept out the front door.

No one was paying any attention to the house, or to her. People came and went on their own business, heads down, dragging their scents behind them. She was just another boy to them, and that was the way she wanted it.

There were no lights on this street like the ones she'd seen in other parts of San Francisco, but she didn't need them. There was still a trace of Cort's scent, very faint, lingering just outside, as if it had been trapped in a bubble that burst only as she walked through it.

Concentrating with all her might, Aria followed the scent as she would follow a days-old deer track in the mountains. It wove in and out of a thousand other distracting smells, most unpleasant, but she grasped it tightly and moved deeper into the noxious maze of the Barbary Coast.

She was so focused on Cort that she only smelled the men when they were almost upon her. Metal caught the light from an open doorway, flashing down in an arc near Aria's shoulder. Rough hands snatched at her shirt, and a rope slapped against her face. She broke free and ran into a small street squeezed between two ugly brick buildings. All she needed was a minute to get out of her clothes.

But her attackers didn't want to give her any time at all. While one of the men swung the rope, the other came at her again, too fast and strong to be human.

CHAPTER SIX

ARIA DODGED OUT of his way, furious at her own stupidity. Cort had been worried about her going out alone. She had assumed he was concerned about the men who had taken her the first time.

But these weren't the same men at all. She might not have Cort's ability to recognize *wehrwölfe* just by looking at them, but she couldn't mistake the way this man moved, or how easily he countered her attempt to escape.

It was almost funny that the second werewolf she'd met wanted to hurt her. But he did, and there was no point in trying to warn him off, or ask him and the other man what they wanted.

And no one was going to help her. She'd learned in her first week on the Coast that the people here knew better than to get in the way of bad men.

Backing deeper into the alley, Aria swept off her cap, dropped it on the ground and ripped open the front of her shirt. The man with the rope waited while the other werewolf began to remove his own clothing. Aria tore her trousers open with one hand and threw them aside. Cold, damp air wrapped around her arms and legs as she flung her underthings away.

The strange werewolf finished undressing a moment later. He was big all over and very hairy, and when he Changed his shoulder stood as high as Aria's head. She closed her eyes and let her own wolf take her. Her enemy went straight for her front legs and knocked them out from under her.

But Aria was fast, and strong. She had spent years running and riding up and down mountain slopes, and along treacherous trails that wound through dense forest and beside sheer cliffs. Her muscles reacted instantly, propelling her to her feet again. She snapped at the stranger's nearest foreleg, her teeth sinking through fur, and into flesh and bone.

Her enemy yelped and snarled, swinging his big head around to seize the ruff on Aria's neck.

"Don't hurt her!" the other man cried. "He wants her alive and well!"

But the wolf didn't seem to hear. He bore down on Aria, smothering her with his far greater weight. She realized that he could crush her without even trying. She struggled beneath him, gasping for breath, her tongue lolling and her ears flat against her skull as she scrabbled at the mud with her nails and tried to get a grip on the stranger's belly.

"Baldwin!" the man yelled. "Stop! If you—"

His voice cracked on a cry of pain. Aria made a feeble attempt to lift her head.

Cort, she thought. And suddenly she was free, the massive body on top of her tumbling sideways with a grunt of surprise. Aria leaped up, her whole body protesting the sudden movement, and sprang toward her attacker. A warm, thickly furred shoulder brushed hers. Together she and Cort fell on the stranger, who snapped and snarled but proved no match for the two of them working together. He rolled on his back in a grotesque posture of submission, and the stink of urine mingled with the foul carrion odor of his breath.

Cort stood over him, bristling and growling. Aria couldn't laugh, not in this shape, but she grinned and danced with joy. She had never felt anything like this before, not even when she brought down the fleetest and noblest of stags after a long and exhausting hunt. She and Cort had won. Together.

But Cort didn't seem interested in their victory. He Changed and stood over their enemy, clenching and un-clenching his fists.

"Get out of here," he said, something cruel and rough replacing the usual smoothness of his voice. "Tell your master he won't have her, even if he sends every *loup-garou* in California."

He aimed a kick toward the other werewolf's belly, but the beast dodged away and fled. The man who hadn't Changed was already gone.

Cort turned to her. "Stay as you are," he said harshly. He went to the mouth of the alley, glanced left and right, and gathered up the clothing he had dropped there. He had torn his clothing off when he'd Changed, and the garments were badly mangled. He examined them with obvious disgust.

"Ruined," he said. He pulled on the trousers, which were ripped lengthwise from knee to hem, and fastened the two remaining buttons. He drew the equally torn shirt over his head, ignored his once-shiny vest and finished with his stained and dirty coat. His feet were bare and covered with mud. He looked so unlike his usual self that Aria wanted to laugh again.

That would not be a very good idea, even if she could have managed it in wolf form. He glared at her, prom-ising reprisals for her disobedience, and picked up the rope the men had left behind.

"There is no point in collecting what remains of your

clothes," he said, "and it wouldn't be advisable for a young woman to be seen walking the streets in a state of complete undress. You will pose as a dog until we get home. As for me—" He examined himself and made a sound of disgust. "I will doubtless be considered just another inebriate emerging from a fight in some den of iniquity." He made a loop out of the rope. "Come here."

The freedom she had claimed for so short a time, the warm rush of victory, could not be taken from her so easily. She laid her ears flat and bristled.

Cort sighed. "If you knew how much trouble you have caused…" He dropped the rope. "Stay close to me. If you stray more than an inch—"

He left the rest of the threat unspoken, but Aria heard the real anger in his voice, in the flat cadence of his words and the slight but noticeable change in his accent. She realized that she had seen him annoyed, even short-tempered, but never angry. Never so furious. Not with her.

Lowering her head, she crept toward him. He spun around and strode out of the alley, pausing once to study the ground.

"Someone seems to have availed themselves of my best pair of shoes," he said.

With a grimace, he took a handful of Aria's thick ruff in his fist and began walking. The feel of his hand in her fur was not in the least uncomfortable. In fact, it felt warm and strong and wonderful.

She realized he hadn't been angry with her just because she had disobeyed him and taken a stupid risk. He was upset because he had been *afraid* for her. He had always claimed to care what happened to her, but now she was certain he had really meant it. He must have had a reason not to tell her who she was.

They were back at the house in five minutes. Cort let her go when they were safely in the hallway, and opened the door to their rooms. She darted inside, shook out her fur and Changed.

Something in Cort's expression made her rush to find the hated dress. She put it on in the bedroom and came out again.

Cort was hunched in one of the chairs by the table, his elbows resting on his knees, staring at the carpet.

"You could have been hurt," he said, not looking at her. "You do understand that?"

She climbed onto the couch and drew up her knees. "I was looking for you," she mumbled.

"Where is Yuri?"

"He went out. I don't know where."

Cort cursed in fluid French. "Now perhaps you understand why you must do as I say." He raked his hand through his hair. "Damn Yuri. If I'd only told him—" He cursed again. "We can't stay here tonight. They must have been watching the house."

Aria was almost glad. She had come to hate this place, this prison, even though she'd only been here a few days. The only thing that had made it bearable was Cort himself.

"They weren't the same men who took me before," she said. "What did they want?"

He was quiet for a long time. "There is someone else who may be after you," he said. "A man came to me this afternoon. He claimed he knew you."

Aria sat up straight. "Who was he?" she asked. "What did he say?"

"Hugo Brecht," he said slowly. "Do you know him?"

She shook her head, disappointed and relieved at the same time. "I have never heard his name before. Not that I can remember," she added, recalling her supposed amnesia. "Why would he want me?"

Leaning back in the chair, Cort blew out his breath and closed his eyes. "Do you remember anything about the place those men took you after they gave you the drugs?"

"There were lots of voices. And smoke," she said, trying to sort out the sensations that had made so little sense at the time. "I couldn't see much at all."

"Do you know anything about gambling?"

"I know it has something to do with playing cards. That was what you and those men were doing, wasn't it?"

"For money, yes. And prizes. You were one of the prizes. And I…" He laced his fingers behind his neck. "I was trying to win you so the other men couldn't have you."

Bad men, he meant. Men who would use her. Not gentlemen, like him.

"And you did win," she said, feeling her nose clog up with tears she didn't want him to see.

"Yes." He opened his eyes and met her gaze. "But the men who lost were very angry. Some of them still wanted you, for…" He coughed. "Do you know you are very beautiful, Aria?"

She knew what the word meant, of course, and she sometimes thought the face she saw in the reflection of a lake or pond was pleasant. But no one had ever called her beautiful before.

"Men appreciate beautiful things," Cort said. "Some

will go to any lengths to get something they consider rare and special. That was why those men wanted you."

His words made her feel warm inside, even though she didn't know why she should be "rare and special." But she began to understand what Cort was talking about.

"This man Brecht…" she began.

"I am reasonably certain that he is the one who sent those blackguards after you."

"But one of those men was a werewolf."

"So is Brecht. He would have even more reason for wanting you, since you are *loup-garou,* too."

She blinked. "But you don't know him?"

"I have never seen him before. There are *loups-garous* in the city, lone wolves, who are not affiliated with any family here."

He had said something like that before. Aria had a sudden disturbing thought. "Brecht" could be a Carantian name. What if he were one of the exiles she'd been seeking? One of the men who'd brought her to Franz?

"Were other werewolves gambling for me, too?" she asked.

"Not openly. Still, it is quite possible that one or more were doing so through human agents."

Had Brecht been one of them? Even if he had been, she couldn't see how he could be Carantian—or not one of the good Carantians, anyway—when he had sent bad men to take her. And how would he even know that *she* was Carantian? If the men had only seen her when she was a baby…

And that brought her back to the most disturbing thought of all: Why had they taken her from America in the first place?

"We can't wait any longer to move you to a safer place," Cort said, completely unaware of her gnawing questions.

"I'm not afraid of them," Aria said. "They couldn't win when you and I were fighting together."

"For God's sake, Aria, your naiveté—"

"That werewolf was bigger than you, but you didn't have any trouble defeating him."

"I fought only to stop him," Cort said, "not because it gives me any pleasure."

Suddenly the conversation had turned again, and so had Aria's thoughts. "What do you mean?" she asked.

"I never Change unless I have no choice."

"But why?"

"It's barbaric and primitive, not fit for civilized people."

Aria flinched as if he'd slapped her. She had seen him in wolf shape twice, and both times it had seemed natural for him, like exchanging one familiar set of clothes for another. Just as easy and natural as it was for her, as necessary to her existence as breathing.

Wouldn't it be that way with every werewolf?

She squatted where she was, not caring if the seams of her dress ripped all over again. "I don't understand," she said. "How can you believe that?"

"Wolves are animals, bound by no law or principle. They act on instinct, not rational intelligence. Their emotions and behavior are savage."

As his had been in the alley? But he hadn't truly hurt the men who had tried to capture her. He had always been in control.

That didn't seem to matter to him. She understood what he really meant, and the knowledge made her sick to her stomach.

Cort was ashamed of being a werewolf. It seemed a ridiculous idea, like being ashamed of having blond hair or brown eyes. In all her years of solitude, Aria had never regretted being what she was, only that there were no others like herself.

But Cort had always known there were others. And still he was ashamed.

That meant he must be ashamed of her, too.

"I *like* Changing," she said quietly. "You must think I'm a barbarian."

"*Non.* I didn't mean…" He trailed off. "I'm sorry. I shouldn't have spoken as I did."

"Maybe you wish you hadn't said it," she said, "but it's what you believe, isn't it?"

"*Chère,* I—"

"What about all the other werewolves in San Francisco? In America? Do they think Changing is primitive and barbaric, too?" She jumped to her feet. "Do all of our fa—all Reniers hate what they are, like you do?"

All at once he was staring at her, his muscles as hard and tense as they had been just after he had Changed into a human again. He examined her face intently. "Have you remembered something, Aria? If you know who you are, you must tell me."

She lifted her chin. "Yuri told me," she said. "He said I belonged to the Reniers of New Orleans." She swallowed. "Did you know all the time?"

In spite of her careful study, Aria could no longer tell what Cort was feeling. He held her gaze as if he had nothing to hide.

"No," he said. "It was only after I had already begun searching for your kin that I realized how closely you resembled the New Orleans Reniers and made a few inquiries."

"Yuri said you didn't know who I was because you and the other Reniers are only very distant cousins," she said.

"That is true."

"But Yuri said you come from the same place, this 'Louisiana.' You *must* know them."

Maybe she wouldn't have noticed if she hadn't been watching him so carefully, but Aria saw Cort's jaw clench and the skin twitch ever so slightly above his upper lip. "My family is…not of the same branch," he said, looking away. "We seldom dealt with the New Orleans clan."

"But you *have* met them?" She jumped up. "What are they like, my family?"

"We will discuss that at a later time. There are other things—"

"But who *am* I?" She started toward him, almost too excited to speak. "Yuri told me I was taken away from them when I was very young, and that they have been searching for me ever since."

"You were kidnapped, stolen from the Reniers by a stranger."

It took a moment for Aria to swallow her shock. Kidnapped? Had the Carantians kidnapped her? Why would anyone want to steal her from her family?

"Who was he?" she asked faintly.

"No one knows."

She was almost too dazed to continue the conversation. "Did I have another name…before?"

"Lucienne," he said in a strange, sad voice.

Lucienne. It had a pretty sound to it, but it didn't feel right, no more than Anna did.

"You said you didn't want anyone else to know that

your name was Aria," Cort said, looking at her again. "Have you remembered why?"

It would be so very easy to tell him now that she'd never lost her memory. She trusted Cort, didn't she? He had a right to know. She would be able to tell him all her fears and hopes and dreams.

And he'll think you're a liar and a cheat. He'll believe you never trusted him at all.

She backed away from him and sat on the couch again. "Please," She said. "Tell me about my family."

The corners of his eyes squeezed together. "They are *loups-garous.*"

"I know that. Yuri told me. But are they like *you?*"

He rose and smoothed his coat as if there were something left of it worth tidying. "You should rest, Aria. As soon as Yuri returns, we will find new lodgings until something more permanent can be arranged. A good hotel, somewhere those men won't dare accost you again. I'll begin packing." He walked toward the bedroom and turned in the doorway. "Do not stir from this room."

Aria sprang up, feeling as if she might jump right out of her skin even without the Change. Even though he hadn't said much about them, the way Yuri had spoken of the New Orleans Reniers made her certain that they must be like Cort. There would be ladies in tight, fancy dresses and gentlemen in embroidered vests, speaking in soft, pleasant voices.

Only Cort isn't always a gentleman, she thought. He hadn't been soft or pleasant in the alley. She wasn't afraid of him when he was angry. In many ways, she understood him better when he lost his temper. When he was cool and calm and spoke in that easy drawl, she didn't really know who he was. Just as she didn't understand how any werewolf could despise the Change and the other half of himself.

Caught between emotions she couldn't untangle, Aria took off the dress, picked up her needle and thread, and set about repairing it all over again.

"DAMN YOU, YURI," Cort snapped, the accent of his birth thick in his words. "First you tell Aria she's a Renier, and then you leave her by herself after I warned you to be vigilant. Are you mad?"

Cort's scowl was so grim that any human would have cowered instinctively in atavistic terror rather than face such a dreadful sight. Any human but Yuri.

It was not Cort's justified anger that affected Yuri now, but the realization that they had come so close to losing the girl. That was his own fault. His business had been urgent enough, it was true, but he had made a very serious mistake in believing she had sense enough to remain in the house. And in thinking that, because no one had tried to find her yet, they would be safe a little while longer.

"Calm yourself, my friend," Yuri said, though he was anything but calm himself. "I told the girl because you refused to do so. We could not afford to wait until you were satisfied that she was Lucienne Renier." He glanced toward their boardinghouse across the street. "In any case, you were victorious. You have certainly increased her trust in you by rescuing her."

"Rescuing her?" Cort's voice dropped to a growl. "She fights like a demon."

Or a wolf. Yuri rubbed his arms. The heavy late-spring fog almost made him forget how much more miserable he would be in Russia at this very moment without the resources to which he was entitled. The resources he might lose even before he gained them.

"These men," he said. "Did you know them?"

"I may have seen the *loup-garou* in passing," Cort said. "I didn't know the human, but—" He broke off and glared after a man scurrying along the street as if daring the unwitting interloper to notice his ragged suit.

But. Yuri grimaced. He thought he knew what Cort must be thinking. They had always assumed that it would be Cochrane looking for the girl. But it would take a human fully aware of the existence of werewolves to hire one for such a job, and there were very few such men in San Francisco. What if another werewolf had been behind the attempted abduction?

An even deeper chill numbed Yuri's body. *Di Reinardus.* What if di Reinardus were here in San Francisco and had known about the tournament? What if he had hired Cochrane to play for him? What if he'd been biding his time ever since, waiting for just the right time to take the girl from the man who had won her?

If that were true, he would have made it his business to learn all about Cort. And that meant he would know that Yuri was with him.

Yuri's mouth was so dry he felt as if he hadn't taken a drink in weeks. "You had no clue as to who might have sent them?" he asked Cort.

Cort continued to scowl after the disappearing figure. "We are not the only ones who know of the missing Renier girl."

Yuri's stomach heaved. "Who?" he said, choking on the word.

Cort explained in clipped sentences what had happened at the saloon. When he had finished, Yuri was forced to lean against the nearest wall for fear that he might topple into the mud.

"Hugo...Brecht," he said heavily. It wasn't a name he knew. But it was German, like many Carantian surnames, and Cort had said the man was *loup-garou*. "Why in God's name didn't you tell me before?"

"I intended to," Cort said, too preoccupied to notice Yuri's reaction, "but I wanted to see if I could learn anything more about him first. He seems to be something of a cypher, but I'm convinced that he believes Aria is Lucienne. Whether he's in this for himself, or working on behalf of the Reniers, he doesn't want her identity to be made public." He slammed his fist into the wall. "*Maudit imbécile.* He is more desperate than I believed."

Yuri worked to steady his voice. "What did he look like, this Brecht?"

"Blue eyes, graying hair. A hard face." Cort looked at Yuri through half-closed lids. "Why? Does he sound familiar to you?"

Familiar, yes. Too familiar. Except for the hair. But hair color could be changed.

"I...I am not sure," Yuri said. "It is possible I met such a man in New Orleans." He cleared his throat. "Yes, I believe he was one of those criminals who deal in extortion, and the secrets of the rich and powerful."

A startled look crossed Cort's face. "Could he be the man who kidnapped Lucienne?"

Yuri laughed hoarsely. "Him? Impossible. Such a man would have claimed a ransom long ago. No, the man I remember would be just the sort to see the profit in—"

"Doing exactly what we plan to do?" Cort finished, apparently satisfied with Yuri's hasty answer. "In other words, he is not the kidnapper, and he is not likely to be an agent of the Reniers."

"*Nyet.* I cannot imagine how he could be."

"Then his actions were those of an opportunist who hoped for an easy win with one swift strike," Cort said. "He didn't achieve his goal, and he seems intelligent enough to cut his losses. Nevertheless—" He pulled out his pocket watch. "We must get Aria away within the hour."

"Yes. Yes." Yuri released his breath. "What did you say to the girl?"

"She didn't know him, of course. I told her he was *loup-garou,* one of the men who wanted to win her in the game."

Tell him, Yuri thought. *Tell him everything.*

But he couldn't. There hadn't been any need for it when they'd first met in New Orleans, because di Reinardus had left with Lucienne and Yuri's part in the abduction was over. If he said anything now, Cort would never trust him again. He certainly wouldn't go along with the plan as Yuri had conceived it.

There is no plan. How could there be? There was no standing against di Reinardus. He was ruthless and utterly without scruples. Nor could he easily be deceived. Cort might—*might*—be a match for him, except for one thing.

Cort *did* have scruples. He might pretend he didn't, but it was all a sham. He played the cardsharp and trickster when necessary, but he had an honorable streak that Yuri had never been able to eradicate.

And yet that honor could give way to something much less civilized. Yuri understood just what it had meant for Cort to Change and fight as a wolf. If he were to return to what he had been when Yuri met him, the situation could become very complicated.

Yuri ground his teeth with such force that his head exploded with pain. He had a decision to make. The wisest course for him would simply be to leave San Francisco. Forget loyalties he had never expected to run so deep.

"We can take her to a hotel for the time being," Cort said, oblivious to the depth of Yuri's distress. "The Palace, I think." He lifted his head to sniff the air. "If Brecht should try to abduct her again, he's likely to find that there are hardly unlimited numbers of *loups-garous* available for such employment in San Francisco." He watched another man shuffle along the street. "Have you secured us a place outside the city?"

"An isolated hunting lodge in the Sierra Nevada. Its owner is conveniently out of the country and will hardly notice temporary tenants."

"And the woman?"

"Babette is on her way from Denver."

"How much have you told her?"

"She knows the girl is Lucienne."

"But not that she goes by the name 'Aria'?"

"No. But I see no reason—"

"I suggest that we allow Aria the decision about whether or not to tell Madame Martin."

Yuri shrugged. "As you please."

"Then finish your arrangements quickly. I'll take Aria to the Palace. Brecht's men won't take me by surprise again."

Yuri could only hope that was the case. He might decide to abandon Cort and everything he had worked for, but he sincerely hoped the werewolf would find a way to outwit di Reinardus.

If he were to be honest, though, he was forced to admit that was as likely as finding five aces in an honest deck.

"You have enough money for the hotel?" he asked Cort.

"Enough to begin. I will get more, once we know Aria is safe." Cort lowered his head, and Yuri could sense the wolf bristling under the other man's skin. "There can be no more mistakes, Yuri. Next time…"

"There will be no next time," Yuri said. "The girl is too valuable a commodity to risk."

For a moment Yuri was convinced that Cort was about to strike him. His eyes had gone cold, and his lips had curled back from his teeth. Something very like hatred burned in his face.

The moment passed, but it left a sour taste in Yuri's mouth, sourer even than the taste of his fear.

"I will go," he said. He set off at a brisk pace, fingering the tiny, bejeweled Derringer in his trouser pocket.

It was too late to warn Babette off now, of course. She would arrive in San Francisco very soon, and the best Yuri could do was meet her and send her right back to Denver. Hell, he would go with her. Anything to avoid what was surely coming.

If he had any sense, he wouldn't wait at all. When no one came for Babette at the station…well, she was a clever and resourceful woman. She would find a way to—

There was no sound at all, no warning. A hand closed over Yuri's mouth before he could even think of drawing the Derringer.

"Take care, my friend," a familiar voice whispered. "No harm will befall you if you come quietly."

CHAPTER SEVEN

A HARD, MUSCULAR ARM locked around Yuri's chest, pulling him off the street. Yuri let himself go limp, knowing there was no use fighting. San Francisco's alleys were endlessly convenient for trysts, clandestine meetings—and ambushes. There was little chance anyone had seen what had just happened, or would have cared if they had.

All he could do was pretend a confidence he was far from feeling.

"There," the voice said. "We shall have privacy here." Di Reinardus removed his hand from Yuri's mouth. "I apologize for the violence, old friend. I have urgent matters to discuss with you."

Yuri turned to face the duke, bile in his throat. The Carantian had hardly changed in the eight years since he had abandoned Yuri in New Orleans.

"Gunther," Yuri said, deliberately using the duke's Christian name. "It has been a long time."

In New Orleans such familiarity would have offended di Reinardus's dignity, though he and Yuri had already known each other in Russia for a number of years before the abduction.

Today, the duke merely shrugged. "So it has," he said coolly. "I confess, I did not imagine we would ever meet again."

I'm sure you did not, Yuri thought with an inward sneer. But he didn't let his contempt show on his face.

"I do regret how things turned out in New Orleans," Gunther said, stepping back. "When the opportunity arose to take Alese, I had no time to consider anything but an immediate departure."

"Of course," Yuri said, smiling icily. "You could not have been expected to send for me afterward. Your great plan was far more important. I completely understand."

"I am glad to hear it."

Yuri bit back his laugh, knowing the duke was quite indifferent to his feelings one way or another.

"We had good times together, didn't we, Baron?" Gunther said. "You were a loyal ally, coming ahead of me to America and confirming the girl's identity. If it had not been for you, I might never have learned that Lucienne Renier was in truth Alese di Reinardus." He shook his head. "The queen was clever in those last hours of her life. Sending her daughter to live with distant cousins in the United States, to be raised as one of them, protected from those who might use her to win the throne." He smiled. "Her Majesty's plan did not go quite as expected, however."

Yuri's anger made him reckless. "Yet Alese is no longer with you," he said.

The duke's good humor vanished like the sun behind an eclipse. "I had her for four years, Chernikov. She was sixteen, nearly ready. But she—" He broke off, his upper lip quivering with rage.

"She escaped," Yuri finished, unable to forgo the dangerous pleasure of seeing di Reinardus admit failure.

Gunther didn't answer immediately. He struggled

with his emotions as Cort had struggled, wolf contend-
ing with man.

"Ja," he said at last. "But I have found her again." His
arm snapped out, and his fingers snagged Yuri's collar
with vicious force. "What have you planned, Chernikov?
To return her to the Reniers for a price?"

It would do no good at all to lie and tell the duke
that he had no such plan. "You spoke to Cort Renier,"
he said.

"An *honorable* man," di Reinardus spat. "How did
you come to be acquainted?"

"We met in New Orleans soon after the abduction,
when I found myself at loose ends."

"Ah. A mysterious character, this Cort Renier. What
are his origins?"

"He is not one of Alese's close kin, as you surely
know by now. It was merely coincidence that we met at
all, and I did not ask about his background. It was unnecessary." He shrugged. "I found certain of his skills
to be advantageous to my future."

"Advantageous? He has some ability as a gambler,
but you hardly appear to be enjoying a life of luxury."

"Yet he won the girl." Yuri smiled spitefully. "I presume you had a man playing for her?"

The duke examined his spotless fingernails. "Did he
recognize the girl when he entered the game?"

"Even I didn't know who she was until afterward.
Renier had no knowledge of her origins."

"What drove him, then? Lust?"

"Occasionally his motives escape me, even after eight
years."

"And has she told him who she is?"

Yuri could see no way of avoiding the apparent truth.
"She claims not to remember who she is."

"What?"

"She says her name is Aria, and that she has no memory of her past life."

"I find that very difficult to believe."

"Nevertheless, she has resolutely abided by her claim. She behaves nothing like a lady of the New Orleans clan. There is no telling what may have happened to her in the four years since she escaped your tender care."

The duke stroked his chin. "You have of course told your associate who she is."

"I haven't told him that Lucienne is a princess."

"That was wise of you." Di Reinardus dropped his hand. "Renier has agreed to your plan to sell the girl to the Reniers?"

"He has. You will not find it so easy to try for her a second time."

The duke's fist tightened, digging into Yuri's skin. "Do you presume to think you can stop me?"

"I presume nothing," Yuri whispered, no longer able to draw a full breath. "I am…leaving San Francisco."

"Because you found out I was here?"

There was no need to answer that question. "Monsieur Renier…is no weakling. He—"

"You call him a friend," the duke said, "yet you would betray him to save your life."

"For the sake of my life? Yes, I would betray him. *I* am not an honorable man."

"True enough." The duke released him again. "But you will certainly be useful to me, honorable or not."

Yuri straightened his collar. "And what recompense will I receive for risking my life against my former colleague?"

The blow caught Yuri full across the mouth. "You said it yourself," di Reinardus said. "Your life."

Yuri wiped the blood from his lips. "Is that all?"

The duke examined his right glove for rips. "You are not indispensable to me, Chernikov. Never forget that fact."

There was no doubt as to what Yuri ought to do now. Grovel on his belly and beg for mercy. But his blood was running hot with the pride of Russia's ancient aristocracy. He had not forgotten what he had been, what he might become again. He was Gunther's equal in birth and breeding. He would not cower like a slave. Not this time.

"I cannot simply take the girl from him," he said. "He defeated your mongrels handily. He could kill me as easily as you can."

Gunther's face was granite sheathed in ice. "You will have to choose, Baron, whose wrath you prefer to provoke—mine or Renier's. If you make the error of telling him of our little discussion, you will not have another opportunity to make the same mistake."

Yuri probed a loose tooth with his tongue, checking his rage behind a soft voice. "What do you want me to do?"

"You need only continue to keep Renier's trust. I will let you know when I need you."

Then the duke turned and disappeared into the fog. Yuri fingered his neck. He knew he would have bruises there for days to come, and he would have to hide them from Cort. He couldn't afford to lie about how he'd come by them.

For he had no doubt that Gunther di Reinardus would be watching him. Watching him and Cort and the girl. Having been defeated once, the duke would not take immediate action. He would wait patiently for the right moment to strike again.

The Russian language had many excellent words for cursing, and Yuri used them all as he walked out of the alley. Just as Gunther had said, he would have to decide, knowing full well that the duke would use him again without paying for his "loyalty." Di Reinardus might even find it convenient to destroy his tool once it had ceased to be useful.

Cort wouldn't so easily turn on Yuri, even if Yuri admitted something of the truth. But Yuri knew he was a hopeless coward. If he was lucky, he might aid Cort a little longer before he surrendered to the necessities of self-preservation.

THE PALACE HOTEL was a marvel of architecture and elegance. Aria knew it because Cort had told her so. But it was not the outer edifice, rising seven stories above Market Street, that impressed her most. When the carriage entered the Grand Court and stopped behind the other vehicles, each with its cargo of ladies and gentlemen, she couldn't help but gape. At one end of the court stood dozens of potted plants the likes of which she'd never seen before, with broad, waxy leaves curving gracefully toward the floor. A band was playing just out of sight, and fountains bubbled on every side of the courtyard.

When she had come by train from New York to San Francisco, she had found shelter wherever she could while the other passengers went to hotels near the station. She hadn't been able to see inside them, but from the way they had looked on the outside, she doubted they were this grand.

"Aria."

She glanced at Cort, half-dazed. He stood outside the open carriage door, offering a gloved hand with an impatient gesture. He was wearing a brand-new suit he had bought to replace the one that had been ruined during the fight, and he looked as handsome, as elegant, as ever. Though she had never seen him wearing anything but a gentleman's clothes, he seemed like a stranger to her. As strange as this foreign world she would have to learn to understand.

Trying and failing to crush the gnawing doubt that refused to go away, Aria tugged free the hem of her cloak, which had caught on the carriage seat, and hopped down. Cort pulled the wide brim of her hat lower over her eyes, adjusted the cloak around her shoulders and tilted her chin up with his fingertip.

"Are you afraid?" he asked.

"Of course not."

But now that she was on her feet again, she wasn't quite so certain. She felt as if she were standing in one of the vast cathedrals Franz had once described, in this cavernous space with tier upon tier of white-columned balconies from which guests looked down, appearing hardly larger than ants. The ceiling above the court was made of glass, and sunlight streamed down with a soothing warmth that almost eased her fear.

Almost. She fingered the shiny clasp Cort had given her along with the cloak, wishing she were back in the old boardinghouse in her shirt and trousers. The much-mended dress chafed her skin. Cort had said she had to wear the cloak to cover it up, because where they were going people would notice her too much if she went just as she was.

I don't care if they notice me, she thought. But as she watched the men and women parading through the wide, glass-paned doors that led into the hotel proper, she knew she *did* care. Because Cort did.

He had called her beautiful.

"Remember," he said, offering his arm, "keep your hat low, and let me do the talking."

"I haven't forgotten," she mumbled, hooking her arm through the crook of his elbow and hoping he wouldn't feel her shaking.

Cort strolled along as if he had always lived in this place, tipping his hat to the ladies and nodding to the gentlemen. Aria shut out the overwhelming sights and smells, and remembered the things he had told her before they left the boardinghouse for good.

"You will need to become reaccustomed to the finer things in life," he'd said, as she'd tucked the last of her new belongings into a carpet bag. "The Reniers of New Orleans are wealthy and spare no expense in their luxuries. They are highly educated, and wear clothing designed and made by the best English and Parisian tailors. They have considerable power and influence in politics and commerce, and they own large blocks of the best real estate in the city. They move in the highest circles of society."

"With other werewolves?" Aria had asked.

"Most of their dealings are with the human elite. Of course they don't display their dual natures except among a select few." He had given her a very serious, almost admonishing look. "If you are to present yourself as their lost kin, you must be what they expect you to be."

It was the same lecture he'd given her when he had thought he would find her family in San Francisco, but worse. It didn't matter how long she'd been missing or where she'd been. The Reniers might not accept her if she didn't have all the graces demanded by good society.

She would need proper speech, proper manners and pride to go along with her position.

"Maybe I don't want them if they don't want me the way I am," she had said.

Cort had caught her under the chin, forcing her to meet his gaze. "Would you live the rest of your life in the gutter, with no money and no prospects, when you could have every comfort for the rest of your life?" His mouth twisted. "Believe me, Aria. Such comforts are few and far between for most in this world. To reject them would be the height of folly."

She'd wondered if that were really true. The Reniers were wealthy, and she knew money was very important in the world outside the mountains. She supposed that she and Franz had been poor, but she had never lacked for anything she needed: food, shelter, clothing—even a pony.

If I stayed with Cort, she'd thought, *it wouldn't matter if I was rich or "proper."*

The idea was so startling that she didn't dare follow where it led. She'd said the first thing that popped into her head.

"Would *your* family expect me to be perfect?"

He'd given her a narrow glance, as if he had never expected such a question. "My family…they are not as powerful as the New Orleans Reniers." His lip twitched again. "They would expect…" He trailed off, staring at the carpetbag with no expression at all. "You belong to the New Orleans Reniers, and their opinion is all that should concern you."

She hadn't dared to ask any more questions, and he'd gone on to tell her about the Palace and the "safe" place outside San Francisco to which they would soon be traveling. That was where her lessons would begin.

"It is in the mountains and will provide a change of scenery for you," Cort had said. "In the meantime you'll have a taste of your future at the Palace."

And now she was getting her taste. She gripped Cort's arm as they walked through the tall doors into a large room where people were milling about and many voices talked all at the same time. There were men and boys in clothes that all looked the same, rushing around with every kind of bag and trunk.

Cort pulled Aria along and stopped at a long table, where he spoke with one of the several men stationed there. He pulled out his wallet and gave the man money. The man gave him two keys in return, smiled at Aria and signaled to one of the uniformed boys. The boy took their two carpetbags, and soon they were walking across the big room, through another set of doors and into a hallway. Cort stopped before a grilled gate, and the boy slid it open.

Behind it was a tiny room, and at first Aria was afraid to go in. She had never liked small places. But Cort gave her a gentle push, and they joined another boy inside the box. The second boy pulled a lever. The floor lurched under Aria's feet. She gasped, and the first boy smiled apologetically.

"Many of our guests are surprised by our hydraulic elevator," the boy said. "It was the first one installed in San Francisco. I assure you that it is perfectly safe."

Aria glanced wildly at Cort as the "elevator" began to shake and vibrate, but he didn't look at all worried. She felt her legs turn rubbery, and the sense of motion became stronger. It seemed to take forever before the elevator stopped with a little bump, and the second boy slid open the grill. It opened onto another hallway, wide enough for two people to walk abreast and decorated with more potted plants.

"Your floor, sir," the boy with the lever said. Cort tossed him a coin and followed the first boy into the hall. They stopped again at another door, and when it opened, Aria could only stare.

"Anna," Cort said, gesturing her ahead of him.

They had agreed to go on using that name in public. She was still convinced there must have been a reason that Franz had insisted she keep the name "Aria" hidden.

She walked into the room. The boy and Cort followed her, and the boy set their bags down on a low table between two chairs and a couch that was itself shaped like a very long chair. He waited while Cort gave him a coin, and then left with a bow.

"Well?" Cort asked.

He was asking how she felt, but she still didn't know. She wandered around the room, pausing to examine the couch and its heaps of velvet pillows, several tables holding vases with bunches of flowers and the intricately patterned carpet. A door led off from one side of the main room. Hesitantly, Aria opened it. A huge bed dominated the smaller room. A lacy canopy hung over it, white and delicate. The furniture, pretty as it was, looked as though it would break if she used it.

"This is your bedroom," Cort said behind her.

"But it's much too big! I don't need—"

"Everything will be different from now on, Aria. It would be best if you accept that quickly."

"Where are you going to sleep?"

"In the room next door, with Yuri."

In a place like this, so strange and different from anything she'd ever known, that seemed very far away.

"I wish you would stay here," she said softly.

His body went as stiff as a shepherd's crook. "That will not be possible. A lady does not share her accommodations with a man to whom she is not—"

"But we *did* share accommodations at the boardinghouse."

"This is different." Cort cleared his throat. "You are soon to rejoin your family, and they would not approve. There are certain rules."

Rules. Always more rules. "I don't understand," she said.

"When Madame Martin arrives, she can…"

Aria was fascinated to see the reddish color come up into his face.

"I'll ask her to explain," he finished.

"Does it have something to do with what those other men would have done to me if they had won me instead?"

"Aria! You *know*—"

"I know that people mate the same way animals do. It looked as if the men enjoyed it, but it didn't look as if the women did."

Cort grew redder still. "Where…where did you see this, Aria?"

"In the alleys away from the big streets, usually when it was dark. They were always in a hurry."

Cort pulled at his collar. "That was not… Aria, what you saw—"

"Have *you* ever done it?"

It didn't seem possible that Cort could turn even redder than he already had, but he did. "Aria, this is not a fit conversation between us."

"You wouldn't try to do those things to me if I didn't want to, would you?"

"No! Aria—"

"Then if you wouldn't hurt me, why should my family care?"

He pulled at his collar with such force that one of the little fastenings popped off. "This conversation is over, Aria."

But the thought wouldn't go away. Cort might never try to do those things with *her,* or hurt anyone he *did* do them with, but if men enjoyed the act so much, he must have done it.

She had felt very good when he had held her in his arms. Would joining with him that way feel as nice?

Kissing the way she'd seen the villagers do would surely be very nice indeed. She looked into his eyes and stood up on her toes, breathing in his scent. His mouth was so close, his body so warm. If only...

Cort hopped back as if she had poured snow into his trousers. He raked his hand through his hair and went to the window, pushing the heavy curtains aside to look down at the street far below.

"Yuri will be arriving soon," he said, his words coming quickly. "I'll be going out again. You do understand that you must stay in this room unless one of us escorts you?"

She could see he was going to pretend they hadn't spoken at all since they'd come into the room, and she began to wish she really had poured snow down his trousers.

"I understand," she said. "I'm to be a prisoner again."

CHAPTER EIGHT

CORT GLANCED IN her direction and quickly looked away. "Must we have this discussion again?" he said.

"No. I understand."

"*Bien.* And don't answer the door unless you're sure it's one of us."

"I won't." She tugged at a ribbon at the front of her bodice, nearly pulling it loose. "How long do we have to stay here?"

He let the curtain fall and leaned against the wall, arms crossed and brows drawn.

"Until Madame Martin arrives, as you very well know." The set of his jaw made it clear that he would not be pushed any further. "As soon as Yuri returns, he'll have a meal sent up to you. Follow his instructions at all times."

Cort was silent after that, and Aria couldn't get him to talk again. After a while Yuri came and Cort went out. Yuri ordered the promised meal, which she ignored.

While he thumbed through a book, no more interested in conversation than Cort had been, Aria engaged herself with the magazines Cort had bought on the way to the hotel. *The Delineator, Woman's Home Companion* and *Harper's Bazaar* were filled with color fashion drawings, which Aria examined with a skeptical eye. Nothing about the pictures, pretty as they were, made "modern" fashion seem any more attractive to her. There were articles about cooking and cleaning and all sorts of other things "proper" women did that she couldn't bear to read, because they only confused her more. She didn't see how she could ever be like the ladies in those pages.

She threw down her magazine and glared at the pages sprawled open on the carpet. She could still change her mind, couldn't she? Forget her family and try to become what she wasn't?

After all Cort has done for you? He'd bought her things, protected her, cared for her, and it seemed all *she'd* done was make it more difficult for him by complaining and questioning everything. He was so often irritated with her now, and yet he had never suggested that she find someone else to help her.

A strange, nagging little doubt nudged the back of her mind. He had said the very first day they'd met that "Any honorable man would feel bound to protect a woman in your position."

But she knew not just any man, honorable or not, would have done what he had. Cort was different, not only because he was *loup-garou*. He cared about her, even if he didn't want to kiss her. He wanted her to be safe and happy. It should have been enough to know that, and not have to understand the reasons.

But it wasn't. Not anymore. She still knew almost nothing about Cort except that he came from Louisiana, played cards and didn't seem to want to talk about *his* family. She had no idea what he did when he wasn't with her, or what he wanted for *himself*.

Aria pressed her face into the back of the long sofa, breathing in the smell of the hundreds of bodies that had lain there before her. The future had always seemed a little unreal to her, but now it seemed to have turned

into a bottomless abyss. Why was she only now beginning to realize how little she knew about both Cort and
herself?

Yuri had begun to snore, but Aria hardly heard him.
She felt as if she were looking up at the sky through
a pall of fog, trying desperately to see the stars. They
seemed so close, and yet they remained invisible. A
mystery.

There was only one thing she was certain of, one
truth that left all her uncertainties behind. She wanted
to be with Cort. Not only here, but wherever they went.
Not just now, but as far into the uncertain future as she
could see, and beyond.

She groaned into the musty fabric. Cort certainly
hadn't behaved as if he wanted to stay with *her*. He
wanted to give her away to someone else. The way he
had talked, he didn't even plan to see her once they went
to New Orleans.

With a sniff, Aria picked up the fallen magazine,
smoothed it carefully and opened it to an article about
the silly undergarment called a "corset." When Cort
returned, she would be ready. Just not in the way he
expected her to be.

THE SALOON WAS nearly empty of customers. Cort's
first thought was that the patrons had heard rumors
of a certain attack on Cortland Renier and anticipated
trouble as a result.

Of course, that was unlikely. But those few patrons
who hugged their drinks along the bar or at the tables
took one look at him and quietly left the premises.

Cort walked up to the bar. "Where is Brecht?" he
asked the barkeep in his softest voice.

The man picked up a glass from the bar and began to polish it. "Don't know anyone by that—"

The last word was cut off, neatly strangled at its source by Cort's fingers around the man's throat. A glass dropped from the barkeep's hand and shattered at his feet behind the counter.

"I think you do," Cort said, pulling the human down across the bar. "I met him here yesterday. He bought some rather expensive wine. Does that refresh your memory?"

Rolling his eyes, the barkeep gurgled in protest. Cort tightened his grip.

"If you're afraid of Brecht," he said, "you might consider the fact that *he* is not the one holding you by the throat. Your danger is more immediate now, I assure you."

The man's chin bobbed. "I…" He swallowed, his face going red. "I'll tell you."

Cort released him. The man hugged the counter with outspread arms as he sucked in several deep breaths. "Brecht…ain't here," he rasped. "He left. Didn't say where he was going."

Cort drummed his fingers on the scarred wood inches from the barkeep's flushed face. "You can do better than that, *mon ami.*"

Slowly the barkeep straightened, carefully avoiding Cort's stare. "I can't tell you no more."

There was too much fear in the man's voice to suggest he was lying. "What about his hirelings?" Cort asked. "The men he sends to do his dirty work?"

This time the man didn't bother to pretend he didn't know what Cort was talking about. "There's some men in the back room," he said. "I've seen 'em with Brecht. That's all I know.'"

"If it is not," Cort said, "I shall certainly learn the truth soon enough." He smiled at the barkeep, slapped down a few coins and walked away from the bar. He knew word of what he was about to do would be on the streets within hours.

He felt absurd satisfaction at the prospect. Ever since he'd left the hotel, he had been tossing in a storm of emotions, each and every one bringing him closer to the reefs.

Aria had asked him to stay with her. He'd been so sure she didn't know what she was saying—until she'd talked about mating, and what men and women did together in dark alleys, and then he'd known he'd grossly underestimated her knowledge of such intimate matters.

Oh, she still didn't understand the half of it, not in the sense an experienced woman would. She wasn't even sure a woman could enjoy the act of love. But the instinct was there, just as it had been when she'd almost let him kiss her. In fact, he would have sworn she'd been trying to kiss *him* after that very troubling conversation.

Both of them—she from ignorance, he from sheer lack of self-control—were in danger of giving way to something that could only end in disaster.

Cort knotted his fists and strode toward the back room. Just the thought of the fight ahead relieved his confusion. It was necessary, yes, but it would also be a pleasure.

He smelled the stench of hard liquor even before he caught the scent of the men themselves, an odor strong enough to dull any *loup-garou*'s senses, and he knew his quarry wouldn't be prepared when he walked into the room.

Heads lifted and bleary eyes tried to focus on him

as he opened the door. He recognized two of the men at once, and after a moment of confusion they clearly recognized him. The *loup-garou* had healed his wounds when he'd Changed back to human form, but he looked no less alarmed than his human partner. Two other humans were with them, just sober enough to pull their knives before Cort had closed the door behind him.

"Gentlemen," Cort said, "I do regret this interruption of your celebration, but I believe we have unfinished business." He glanced at the two armed men. "I presume that you also work for Brecht?"

The taller of the humans, marked with an ugly scar from forehead to chin, waved his knife. "You made a mistake coming here, Renier."

"I believe your associates would tell you that it is they who made the mistake in acting on Brecht's behalf. I wonder if your judgment is as poor as theirs."

The *loup-garou* tried to stand, lost his balance and toppled over the table in front of him, spilling the contents of his glass. It wasn't often that werewolves could become so drunk; the man must have been going at it for hours. His partner had already begun to edge toward the back of the room and the door that led outside.

The other two humans, however, had decided that they would not be cowed by a single man, even though they undoubtedly knew that man was not human. The one who'd spoken tossed his knife from hand to hand. His companion didn't bother to show off. The two men separated, intent on making it more difficult for Cort to attack them both at once.

Cort didn't even try. He went straight for the drunken *loup-garou,* caught him by his frayed coat and threw him headfirst at the wall. The man slid to the floor unconscious, blood spilling from a cut in his forehead. Not dead, but not about to get up anytime soon.

The man who'd been so eager to display his skill with a knife lunged at Cort's back. Cort spun and slammed his fist into the scarred face. The knife flew across the room. As the werewolf's partner slipped out the door, the other human attacked.

Cort finished with him quickly, leaving him bloodied and beaten but still alive. Alive enough to report exactly what had happened.

Cort bent over the man who'd threatened him. "I have a message for your employer," he said. "I'll kill any man he sends after the girl."

The thug groaned. "I...I can't give him no message. He's gone."

"Gone where?"

"Left San—" The thug spat out a gob of blood. "He said...he didn't need us no more."

Cort let him go. He couldn't be sure the man was telling the truth, but no matter how much Brecht offered in payment, few men would willingly put themselves in Cort's way after this little demonstration.

And if Brecht really was gone, it would solve all their problems completely.

A pair of young gentlemen were standing just outside the door when Cort returned to the main room. They stared at his bloody face, looked beyond him through the open door and quickly walked away. Another pair of eyes and ears to regale the Coast with tales of the carnage.

Cort lowered his head and stalked through the saloon, aware of eyes following his progress to the front door. He'd never wanted the kind of reputation he would have now—or at least he hadn't before he'd let his anger and frustration overcome his sense.

An ability to fight like a common sailor would hardly lessen his reputation in the eyes of a large portion of the Coast's population, and it would certainly achieve what he intended, but *he* knew just how far he had sunk. No cool, dispassionate manner could alter the fact that he had fallen back into the pit.

But he need not fall any further. Not if he was careful. Not if he remembered why he'd spent so many years remaking himself. He'd gone after Brecht's men to protect Aria, but this was as far as it went. He'd come far too close to losing himself completely. From now on, he must focus solely on what he wanted and how he planned to achieve it. Nothing but cold, calculating resolve.

And just to prove he was capable of it, he wouldn't go out of his way to keep his distance from Aria or try to avoid touching her. He would test himself in the fire until he was well tempered and completely invulnerable.

He laughed at himself, and a sailor half-hidden behind a table cringed. Cort saluted him and walked out the door.

CORT RETURNED TO Aria's room a few hours later. The first thing she noticed was that he had a few little spots of blood on one white cuff. The second was that he was most emphatically *not* in a good mood.

Yuri was certainly aware of his friend's ill humor. He looked Cort up and down without noticing the blood spots, shook his head and left without a word. Painfully conscious of all the bewildering thoughts that had been going through her mind in Cort's absence, Aria set down the book the Russian had given her.

"War and Peace," Cort said, reading the title from across the room. "It's in Cyrillic. You can understand it?"

This wasn't at all the way she'd wanted their next conversation to begin. She shrugged and closed the book. "I must have learned when I was a child," she said.

His eyes were very sharp. "Odd that you remember languages when you have forgotten so much else."

"Why should I forgot how to read?" She was angry, though she didn't know why. "Do you think I'm stupid?"

"Aria." He sat down on the long sofa beside her and laid his hand on her shoulder. "I have never thought you stupid. You are an enigma, to be sure, but no one could doubt your intelligence."

His hand was warm and firm on her shoulder. She bent her head to rest her cheek against his knuckles, rubbing her skin gently over his. He drew in a sharp breath and abruptly dropped his hand.

"You haven't eaten your supper," he said.

"I'm not hungry," she muttered.

"You will eat."

"I will if you answer one question."

He regarded her warily. "What is it?"

She waved at the room around them. "Doesn't this cost a lot of money?"

His shoulders relaxed. "You need have no worry about the cost, Aria. It will be taken care of."

"But the dress and all the other things you bought…" She fingered the cloak she'd laid over the back of the couch. "There's a lot I don't know about money—"

"That is clear," Cort grumbled.

"—but I know the difference between a place like this and that nasty old boardinghouse." She spread her arms. "Why did you stay there? This is the kind of place a gentleman should live in, isn't it? Like the other Reniers?"

He was on his feet before she had a chance to blink. "Leave such matters to those who understand them."

"I *want* to understand." She caught his gaze again. "You said the other Reniers had a lot of money. Do *you?*"

"Aria," he warned, "that is none of your—"

She followed her instincts. "I don't think you do. I..." She stiffened her resolve. "I don't want you to spend any more money on me if you don't have it."

Muscles rigid, Cort walked back to the window. He gripped the curtains so hard that Aria thought he might tear them apart. "I earn what I need," he said.

"How?" she asked. "What things do gentlemen do to get money?"

He ran his hand down the edge of the drapes. "Do you remember what I told you about the card game?"

"Of course."

"That is how I earn my living," he said. "I'm usually very good at such games, and men will bet a great deal of money if they think they have a chance at winning."

"And you usually win?"

"Since you..." He stopped again. "Yes. Enough to cover any expenses related to getting you home." There were so many different emotions on his face that Aria couldn't make heads or tails of them. "It's vulgar to talk about money, Aria. You'll have to learn to—"

"I'll pay you back," she said.

"That isn't necessary."

"I *want* to. And if my family is happy to see me, won't they want to give you what you—"

"I want *nothing* from them," he snarled.

His anger didn't scare her. Not nearly as much as what his words might mean.

"You don't like them, do you?" she asked. "You said your family hardly ever met with mine. They aren't rich like the New Orleans Reniers, are they?"

"They—" He sucked in a deep breath. "They have what they need."

Maybe that *was* the truth, or at least part of it. But there was much more, and Aria was determined to discover it.

"What made you hate my family?" she asked.

Aria heard the curtains rip. He stared at the torn fabric in his hands as if he couldn't imagine how it had happened.

Aria sat up on her knees so she could watch his face. "What did they do, Cort?"

He smiled…lazily, the way he used to when they'd first met.

"You wouldn't find it an interesting subject, *chère*. It's long in the past."

"Is that why you don't live in New Orleans anymore?"

The curtains fell with a clatter, rod and all. "That had nothing to do with it," he said, breathing fast. "I preferred to explore the rest of the country rather than remain in Louisiana."

Aria could smell the lie as she could smell a stranger passing in the hall. Her mind jumped wildly from one thought to another, drawing little strands of meaning together into an untidy knot of comprehension.

"You were looking for something," she said. "Just like me."

Cort walked away from the window with sharp, jerky

steps. "I came west to make my own life. And that is what I have done."

Just like I will, Aria thought. *But I'll be going east. Not into the future, like Cort, but into the past.*

And that left her with the most important question of all. But her throat went dry, and once again she couldn't ask it. So much still lay unresolved between them.

The smell of meat and potatoes and a dozen other good things wafted through the door, interrupting any chance of further conversation. A man brought in a rolling table covered by plates heaped with food, and in spite of everything, Aria found that her appetite was undiminished. Cort picked at his meal and left most of it untouched. At midnight he went to the room he shared with Yuri, offering only a quiet good-night.

Aria put on the heavy nightgown Cort had bought her, lay down in the big bed and tried to sleep.

But the bed was too soft, the room itself too alien in its refinement. She almost longed for her plain little pallet in the cottage, or even the sprung mattress in the boardinghouse. At least *that* had smelled of Cort.

Far too restless to stay still, she got up and went to the door of the sitting room. No sound in the hallway, except for the scratching of a mouse and snores from nearby rooms. No voices. Even Cort and Yuri must be asleep.

She wandered back to the window, gathered up an armful of the abused curtains and breathed in deeply. Cort's scent still lingered in the fabric. She tore a piece free of the rest and curled up on the couch the way she used to do at the boardinghouse. Wadding the curtain under her head, she closed her eyes and pretended that Cort was still with her.

But he wasn't. In many ways she felt more alone now

than she had in the mountains, when she had truly believed she was the only one of her kind in the world.

Maybe Cort felt the same way. He hadn't only been angry when she'd asked him about his family and the other Reniers. She had seen something else on his face, too. Pain. Sadness. It was almost as if he had lost something dear to him when he'd left his family to seek his "own life." Just as she had lost Franz.

Aria lifted her head and gazed at the moonlight streaming through the window. Cort kept his secrets as well as the moon. Or herself.

But not forever. When she found out why he was so angry and hurt, then she would know she could share everything with him. Maybe it wouldn't just be her needing him. Maybe *he* would need *her,* too.

"YOU ARE TOO kind, *monsieur,*" the woman's voice said.

Aria sat up, suddenly aware that she must have slept far longer than she had intended. A path of sunlight lay stretched across the carpet where moonlight had been before, and the bare window glittered like crystal. She brushed her hair out of her face and listened again for the voice.

"My pleasure, *madame,*" Cort said on the other side of the door. Aria scarcely had time to jump to her feet and smooth her nightgown before the door opened, and Cort walked in with the stranger.

The first thing Aria noticed was that the woman had a flowery scent about her, though it was a pleasant fragrance, instead of the overwhelming stink humans called "perfume." The second thing was that the strange female was wearing exactly the kind of fashionable clothing she'd seen in the magazines and in the courtyard: a straight, snug skirt bedecked with flounces and ribbons, with a ridiculous bow of some sort right on the rear, and an equally tight bodice with a lacy panel down the front. Her hair was dark, and tucked under a hat covered with more bows, flowers and feathers, and she carried a frothy parasol in a dainty white-gloved hand. She wore the dress as if she had been born in it.

She was also beautiful. And when she smiled at Cort, Aria's heart fell straight down to her feet and through the floor underneath.

Cort smiled at the lady in return and looked at Aria. The good humor in his eyes faded along with his smile.

"Madame Martin," he said, "this is Anna, your pupil. Anna, Madame Babette Martin."

Babette Martin beamed at Aria. *"Que belle!"* she exclaimed. "How charming!"

Her voice was low and rich, like the deepest notes Franz had played on his fiddle, and it held an accent much stronger than Cort's. Aria thought of her own voice, and how coarse it must sound in comparison.

"Anna," Cort said, "kindly go and dress."

Had Aria been in wolf shape, she didn't know if she would have growled at Cort's bossy manner or slunk away with her tail between her legs. Half-afraid to leave Cort and Babette Martin alone together—though she really didn't know why—she rushed off to change. Her fingers trembled on the buttons of her bodice as she dressed. The skirt almost tripped her up when she raced back into the sitting room and skidded to a stop.

"Good morning," she said, essaying a half curtsy and feeling very foolish as she made it. She comforted herself with the fact that Cort surely would have to approve of her attempt.

But he didn't. He merely regarded her with a frown, and looked her up and down.

"You can see that she needs considerable instruction," he said, as if Aria were one of the prize rams Berthold the shepherd had brought to show her after he had won a competition in the village.

"You are too hard on the girl, *mon ami,*" Babette said with a throaty laugh. "Such a beautiful child will surely be a delight to teach."

"I am *not* a child," Aria said.

Cort ignored her. "If anyone can do it, *madame,* I believe you can."

Aria detected something like sympathy in Babette's eyes. "We will need a little time to get acquainted. Perhaps you might leave us alone for a while?"

"I don't want to be left alone," Aria said.

"Anna!" Cort snapped.

"It is nothing," Babette said. "We shall grow to understand each other, *c'est ça?*

"Are you certain you wish to do this?" Cort asked her.

"I would not refuse Yuri. We are old friends. And I do love a challenge."

"You have my sincerest admiration, *madame,*" Cort said. He bowed over her hand and kissed her gloved fingers. "I will leave you, but should you require anything…"

"Tea, perhaps, if it is not too much trouble."

"I will see to it immediately." Cort cast Aria one last, assessing look and walked out the door.

Babette glanced around the room with obvious pleasure. "What a lovely room," she said.

Aria plopped down on the sofa. "Is it?"

"Very fine indeed. Monsieur Renier must have great faith in you, *mademoiselle*."

Her manner was so pleasant that Aria found it difficult to maintain her resentment. "Did he tell you everything?" she asked, sitting up a little straighter.

"You are fortunate enough to belong to one of the most influential families in New Orleans."

"Is that where you come from?"

"I am originally from France, but I lived in New Orleans for many years."

"Do you know *what* I am?"

"If you mean do I know you are *loup-garou*, like Cort and the other Reniers, then yes, I have that privilege. There are many such as you in New Orleans."

That was something Cort hadn't told Aria. "You aren't afraid?"

"Why should I be? A woman is a woman and a man a man. I have never known your kind to be more dangerous than anyone else."

Her calm acceptance didn't comfort Aria nearly as much as it should have. "Have you known Cort for a long time?"

"Only since I arrived. He is quite charming himself, *n'est-ce pas?* And so handsome."

Aria fidgeted, not liking Babette's tone when she talked about Cort. "You are good friends with Yuri?" she asked.

"We knew each other in New Orleans." For the first time since she had walked in the door, Babette lost her smile and the light went out of her eyes. "I have not seen him in a very long time."

They way she spoke of Yuri intrigued Aria, but she had more important things on her mind. "Do you really want to teach me?" she asked.

The lady joined her on the sofa, folding her delicate hands neatly in her lap. "Of course I do, *ma petite*. I have never met a more promising student."

"You have done this before?"

The other woman hesitated, though her smile never wavered. "In a manner of speaking," she said.

Madame Martin was hiding something, Aria was sure of it. And she needed to know much more about the woman before she'd come anywhere close to trusting her as much as she had learned to trust Cort.

"What if I don't want your help?" she asked.

"I was under the impression that you were eager to return to your family."

Her gentleness made Aria feel ashamed. "I'm sorry," she mumbled. "It's just…since I don't remember, sometimes I am a little afraid. I didn't mean to seem ungrateful, *madame*."

"*Ce n'est rien.*" Babette laid her hand over Aria's. "You need not be formal with me, Anna. I believe we shall become good friends."

Aria looked away. The door opened, and a uniformed man entered with a tray of steaming tea and biscuits. He laid the tray down on the table near the couch and left with a bow.

Babette rose to take charge of the tea things, pouring with an easy grace Aria couldn't help but admire.

Maybe it was possible that they would become friends after all. After spending so much time with Franz and Cort and Yuri, it might even be nice to have a female friend. Someone she might confide in. Someone who might "explain" the things Cort hadn't wanted to talk about.

And teach her how to make Cort really *notice* her, the way he had noticed Babette.

Aria took a teacup from Babette and thanked her. "When you lived in New Orleans," she said, "did you know my family?"

"Certain members of it, on occasion," Babette said. She sipped her tea, watching Aria over the rim of her cup.

"Were you there when I was kidnapped?"

"Yes. A terrible thing. But it is over now, and soon you will be with them again."

The tea suddenly tasted very bitter on Aria's tongue. "Why would anyone want to steal a little baby?"

Babette's delicate brows drew together. "A baby?" Her expression cleared. "Oh, yes. You have forgotten." She set down her cup and touched Aria's arm. "You were not an infant but a child of twelve when it happened. I have no doubt that time spent with your family will restore what you have lost."

With great effort Aria kept her body perfectly still. A child of twelve. At that age, she had been living in the mountains with Franz.

She could not be Lucienne Renier.

ANNA WAS, INDEED, a delightful girl. Rough around the edges she might be, but Babette was not in the least put off by that small flaw, or by the girl's tragic loss of memory. The child was beautiful, with the natural grace of all her kind, and was clearly as smart as a whip. Perhaps even perceptive enough to recognize that Babette, too, had something to hide.

Oh, it was not entirely a secret. At least not from Yuri, though Babette was certain that Cort didn't know who she really was. The naive country girl, who had been born Mathilde Babin in a bare, tiny cottage in Auvergne, had risen from common prostitute to become the most celebrated courtesan and madam in New Orleans. Her brothel had become a watchword for gracious hospitality, and she had been content enough in her life.

Then she had met Baron Yuri Chernikov at an exclusive party and fallen in love. She had been ready to give up everything for him: fortune, comfort, pride.

But Yuri, who had once claimed to love her in return, would never marry a whore. He had ambition. She could have no part in the life he planned to create.

Babette smiled sadly and looked at the girl sleeping on the chaise longue, her hand trailing over the side and her astonishing golden hair draped across her face. Babette had trained girls before, but they had been intended for a very different fate. She must be careful never to step over the line. Anna must never learn what Babette Martin had been.

And Yuri must never learn that she still loved him.

Leaning her chin on her hand, Babette looked more carefully at Anna's recently mended dress. It might have been appropriate for a country girl or a servant with no expectation of improvement, but it was hardly suitable for the lady Anna had been and was to become again. Especially without corset or petticoats. Cort had bought foundation garments for the girl but had been wise enough to hold them in reserve until Babette arrived.

Babette's first task would be to teach Anna, the once and future Lucienne Renier, how to wear them. That might not be easy, for Yuri had been right. Anna was wild. But that would only lend her a certain fascination when Babette was finished.

Fascination, indeed. Babette remembered Cort's gruffness when he'd dealt with the girl, as if she could do nothing to please him. It seemed an unnecessarily harsh attitude when one considered that Cort and Yuri planned to make money from returning her to the Reniers. True, the girl would ultimately benefit from their scheme, but Babette couldn't help but feel that there was more going on than met the eye.

For if there was one thing she had learned in her decades of pleasing men, it was the range of male emotions. Which was quite limited, really. They were driven by two basic feelings: lust and pride. Lust, under the right circumstances, could become something much more noble. But it must always contend with pride. Cortland Renier had plenty of both.

There was no doubt in Babette's mind that he lusted after his charge and was holding that lust in check with great difficulty.

And unless she was very much mistaken, Anna felt the same way. Babette had been convinced from the moment she'd walked into the room that Anna was a virgin, but virginity was hardly an obstacle to sexual desire. Anna had only just begun to recognize the urges, and power, of her own body.

Such power unleashed without understanding could lead to tragedy, and Anna's interests would not be best served if she acted without realizing the consequences. Still, it seemed highly unlikely that Monsieur Renier would indulge his lust or allow the girl to do so.

Did Yuri know what was brewing between them? He had given no indication of it, but she would not necessarily have expected him to notice unless the attraction became far more blatant than it was now. He would certainly not approve of any possible threat to their plans, no matter how remote it might seem to him.

It would be very interesting to see how things played out in the weeks ahead. Very interesting indeed. And if Babette could do just a little to help Anna recognize and tame her woman's power—power she would need for whatever lay ahead—she would feel that she had done something of worth besides exchanging her experience for money.

With a smile of satisfaction over a decision well made, Babette poured herself a cup of cooling tea.

CHAPTER NINE

"WE WILL LEAVE San Francisco tomorrow," Cort said.

He, Yuri and Babette had gathered in Cort's sitting room, tension bubbling among them like an overflowing pot of scalding soup.

Cort wasn't entirely certain of its source; Babette seemed perfectly composed, and if Yuri was glowering, that was hardly unusual. Once he'd seen them together, Cort had quickly surmised that they had been lovers sometime in the past, but Yuri wouldn't have invited Babette to be part of their scheme if he had considered their relationship to be problematic.

On the other hand, the fact that Aria had thrown Cort so completely off balance again gave him a strong desire to tear his own curtains from their rods, but he thought he was doing well enough in concealing the urge.

"No sign of observers?" Cort asked.

"You would know better than I," Yuri said.

And, indeed, Cort hadn't seen any sign that Brecht's men, or Brecht himself, had come anywhere near the hotel. He had made subtle inquiries on the Coast and haunted the backstreets while Yuri watched Aria, and he had come to the conclusion that Brecht's hatchet man at the saloon had been telling the truth. Brecht was gone. With any luck, gone for good.

That was a powerful relief. There would be no going back once they left San Francisco. Provided there were no further complications or attempted abductions, the solution to Cort's current problem was finally within his grasp. In a few months' time Aria would be a different girl. She would no longer be a hoyden blurting out whatever came into her mind, scrambling about in shirt and trousers, fighting like a street urchin and making propositions that would lead to her own disgrace. She would have learned control and discretion, and how to behave with a man.

Wasn't that exactly what he wanted?

"We are wasting time," Yuri grumbled.

Cort glanced at Babette. "Are you ready to leave, *madame?*"

The Frenchwoman inclined her head. "I might have wished to take greater advantage of this city's better purveyors of fashion, but…"

"You knew we wouldn't be here long enough for that," Yuri said.

"There are tailors and seamstresses in Sacramento," Cort said. "They should be adequate until Ar-*Anna*," he corrected himself, "is ready for New Orleans."

Babette snapped open her fan. "Such a primitive place it sounds, this Sacramento," she said, "yet I suppose it cannot be helped." She cocked her head. "I presume you still wish to be discreet in our departure?"

"It would be foolish to take any unnecessary risks," Cort said. "I am confident that Brecht has given up his pursuit, but…" He looked from Babette to Yuri. "We must take every precaution."

"What do you suggest?" Yuri asked.

"I propose that that we split up. We will proceed as if Brecht is watching us, and make him believe he's following Anna when in fact he'll be chasing somebody else."

"Ah." Babette tapped her chin with one gloved finger. "It occurs to me that I am approximately Anna's size. Is that perhaps what you had in mind?"

"A *loup-garou* will generally rely on scent rather than sight," Cort said. "If you dress in Anna's clothes, Brecht or any werewolves in his employ will follow you instead of her."

"Out of the question," Yuri said, starting up from his chair. "If there is the slightest chance that Brecht has not left San Francisco…"

"I think it is a good idea," Babette said, reaching toward Yuri as if to ease him down again. "I see no reason to believe that this scheme will be particularly perilous."

The Russian snorted loudly. "I presume *you* plan to accompany Anna while I escort Babette," he said to Cort.

"Is it not the most sensible approach?" Babette said before Cort could reply.

"Sensible!" Yuri said. "Convenient, you mean." He glared at Cort. "If I did not know you better, I would assume you were trying to preserve your own skin at our expense."

The bitterness of Yuri's accusation cut Cort far more deeply than he could have expected. Yuri had no idea how little he wanted to travel alone with Aria.

"If I believed you would be in any danger," Cort said stiffly, "I would find another way. This is only—"

Rising with an abrupt, angry motion, Yuri circled the room. "What is the rest of this plan?"

"You will take the ferry, then board the train bound for San Jose. Anna and I will travel by steamboat and rail to Sacramento."

"And should anyone follow us and discover their

mistake," Babette said, "they will simply get off at the next stop and resume their search for the real Lucienne Renier."

"I am reassured," Yuri said, his voice heavy with sarcasm. "But you have not considered the possibility that they may wish to question us as to Cort's intentions."

The force of Yuri's protests seemed more than a little out of character to Cort. The Russian had certainly been willing to take risks in the past when the reward was great enough, and this scheme was far less dangerous than many they'd attempted.

"I suggest that we arrange a public falling-out," Cort said. "Anna can pretend that she wants nothing more to do with me, and you'll have ample reason to claim that we have broken off our partnership."

"Why should Brecht or his men believe that she wants to leave you," Yuri said, "after you fought beside her against them? She has obviously made no attempt to run away before. And Brecht will have realized that you don't work for the Reniers any more than he does. Why should you let Anna go with me?"

"C'est facile," Babette said. "Yuri and I shall conceal ourselves somewhere until the morning after the fight, making it appear as if Anna has fled, and Cort will appear greatly angered to anyone who may be watching. Then Cort and Anna, posing as myself, can reveal an intention to search for the runaway, delaying while Yuri and I go on to the ferry."

"You make it sound simple," Yuri said with a sneer.

"I do not see why it should not be."

"My dear Babette, I never realized that your intellect was as well developed as—" Yuri looked her up and down, his gaze coming to rest on her bosom, and made a gesture that took in her entire body.

Cort got to his feet. "Your behavior toward Madame Martin is unacceptable," he said. "I was under the impression that you were friends, but regardless of your past relationship, I will tolerate no more of this disrespect."

"Or what?" Yuri said with a mocking smile. "You'll challenge me to a duel?"

"It doesn't matter," Babette said with a sweet smile. "I have always known Baron Chernikov had a foul temper."

"Ha," Yuri muttered.

Cort inclined his head to Babette. *"Merci, madame,"* he said. "If you are quite certain…"

"I trust your judgment with regard to this Brecht. In any case…" She shrugged eloquently. "I have lived far too dull an existence since I left New Orleans."

"You will be recompensed for this additional service."

She lifted her glass to him. They, at least, seemed to understand each other well enough, but Yuri continued to burn up the room with his stare.

"Let us assume," the Russian said, "that Brecht's men, should they follow, do leave the train immediately upon discovering that they have been led astray. What then?"

"Once you're certain they've gone," Cort said, "you will continue south a few more stops, leave the train and make arrangements to join us in Sacramento."

Yuri said nothing more, and after a while Babette rose gracefully and excused herself. Yuri sat down again and fingered the stem of his wineglass, spinning it around and around in its puddle of condensation.

"I have my own proposition to make," he said at last. "*I* will take Aria, and you will go with Babette. Brecht is more likely to follow *you* if he believes Babette is Lucienne."

"Do you think I hadn't considered that?" Cort said. "The fact remains that the one most in danger is Aria herself. Can you best a *loup-garou* in a fight? You're far more likely to face the threat of harm if you are with her, and you will not be in a position to defend her."

"There was a time when you would have done anything to avoid a fight yourself."

Cort remembered the fierce joy that had come over him for the brief time he had fought the men in the saloon—before he'd had the sense to be disgusted with himself. "I will, of course, do what is necessary." He caught Yuri's gaze. "I would almost believe that you consider Brecht a much greater threat than you have indicated. Is there something else you should be telling me?"

"*Nyet.*" Yuri rose. "I presume you will inform the girl of our plan. I will await further instruction."

He bowed with mocking formality and walked out of the room, leaving Cort to brood over what the Russian had said. There *was* no risk. Perhaps he should show his confidence by abandoning the plan altogether.

But if there was even a one-in-a-thousand chance that someone would come after them…

Cort growled at his own foolishness. He'd made sure of Brecht's men. They wouldn't dare make a move on the German's behalf. It was over.

THEY PUT THE ESCAPE PLAN into effect the next morning. Aria had vociferously protested the whole affair, unwilling to pretend to fight with Cort in public and determined to persuade them to abandon the masquerade. Madame Martin had gently but firmly convinced her that the plan, however flawed, was their best course.

In spite of her doubts, Aria proved to be an excellent actress, so convincing that Cort himself half believed that she hated him. They staged the performance in the hearing of several hotel employees, not quite public but effective enough. The argument was left deliberately vague, so that the eavesdroppers couldn't be sure of the reason for the fight.

When Aria went with Yuri, parting from Cort and Babette in a flurry of feigned curses and threats, Babette returned to her room, where she put on one of Aria's dresses, saturated with her subtle scent. Aria, in turn, wore Babette's simplest gown. Both women were to wear hats with veils of heavy netting.

Yuri and Babette "departed" the hotel a short time later. Cort made a show of anger at their betrayal in front of the boy who came to take his bags, while Aria remained hidden. Cort had already purchased tickets for the steamboat departing for Sacramento from Pier Three. They would disembark at a point along the Sacramento River and continue by train.

They reached the pier without incident, and by the time they boarded the boat, Cort had abandoned any last-minute concerns. Aria said very little as they crossed a string of bays and entered the river. Only when they changed over to the train and found their seats did she speak again.

"I'm sorry I had to shout at you," she said.

"You did just as you we asked to do," Cort said, not quite able to forget the fire and loathing in Aria's eyes when she had played her part with such apparent enthusiasm.

"I hated it," she said. She looked up, anxiety plain in her eyes. "Do you think Yuri and Babette are all right?"

"I have no doubt of it."

"But Madame Martin...I don't want anything to happen to her."

"She is in no danger."

She searched Cort's face. "I like her very much. You like her, too."

Cort shifted uncomfortably. "I respect her," he said. "She is an intelligent woman who understands the world as it is."

"Do you like her...better than me?"

Good God. Aria was jealous. He'd thought her attitude toward Babette had been unusually defiant, but he hadn't considered all the possible implications of her behavior.

He'd been a damned fool not to, after their very uncomfortable conversation in the hotel room. What was going through that busy little head of hers? She'd asked him if he'd ever done "it." Could she possibly think he'd had sexual relations with Babette?

He groaned silently. One moment he was convinced Aria was entirely ignorant of the most basic aspects of male and female relationships, and the next that she understood everything all too well.

The train rocked sharply, and Cort's stomach rattled with it. "I am saddened that you feel it necessary to ask that question, Anna," he said, barely remembering to use her public name.

Aria sank down in her seat and tucked her chin against her chest. Cort was greatly relieved that she wasn't inclined to continue the conversation, but the relief didn't last. She was so close that their arms touched, and Babette's slightly perfumed scent was giving way to Aria's very natural but alluring fragrance.

Like Babette better than Aria? A beautiful, charming, sophisticated woman over this…this…

This equally beautiful, honest, fearless, extraordinary girl.

"We will be in Sacramento soon," he said abruptly. "The hotel we'll stay in is modest, on the edge of town, but I don't expect to be there long. We will wait for Yuri and Babette, and then go on to the mountains."

Even the thought of new surroundings far away from the city didn't seem to cheer Aria. She folded her arms across her chest and stared at the seat back in front of her.

"Would you…" She swallowed audibly. "Would you be very disappointed if…if things didn't go as we plan?"

The question was entirely unexpected. Cort sat up in his seat. "What do you mean?" he asked.

"I mean if—" She looked up, meeting his gaze. "I mean if I don't turn out the way you want me to? If I can't be a lady?"

Only her usual fears after all. "What makes you ask now, Anna?"

She shuffled her feet. "Madame Martin is so elegant. I don't see how I can ever be like her."

"Madame Martin is very sure of you. And so am I."

Her eyes were too bright, as if she were close to weeping. Something hard and painful settled in Cort's throat. She was unhappy, and *he* was responsible.

When he'd first spoken of her family, she'd seemed

excited enough, or at least pleased at the prospect of being reunited with them. When had that changed? Had she lost her enthusiasm when he'd rejected her tentative advances?

He thought through her questions again, the ones probing into his past and the state of his wallet. She had asked if they could go to *his* family instead of the New Orleans Reniers. Her ignorance would have been amusing if it hadn't been so sad. As if the bayou Reniers would have anything to give her.

As if *he* did.

"You have nothing more to be afraid of, I promise you," he said.

"But if…if I couldn't do it…would you be very disappointed?"

He permitted himself to pat her hand. "You won't disappoint me."

The reassurance didn't seem to help. Aria continued to stare out the window, presenting a blank surface he couldn't penetrate.

That was all to the good, wasn't it? If she kept her distance, he could keep his. If she felt uncertain about him, about herself, she wouldn't approach him with her innocent desire.

His cock began to harden. If it were not for that innocence, he might have given her what they both wanted. He would take great care with her, unlike most other men.

If only…

An idea came into his head, both terrible and enticing. He glanced at Aria, who was pretending to sleep. So easy, and so satisfying. He could cause even more humiliation to the Reniers, satisfy Aria and enjoy himself in the process. It would be the work of minutes to seduce her once the setting was right.

He muffled a groan. No matter what she thought she wanted, he was still responsible for her. And in spite of recent lapses, he was still a gentleman.

He closed his eyes and concentrated on the roar and rattle of the train, the stale and smoky smell of the air, anything but the woman beside him.

His all-too-vivid imagination haunted him all the way to Sacramento.

"WE'RE LEAVING."

Babette shot Yuri a quizzical glance. "Of course we are leaving," she said. "Isn't that the plan?"

Yuri cursed as he hurried her toward the Ferry House. The boat was filling quickly, and the raised hairs at the back of his neck refused to lie flat.

"We are leaving California," he said. "Permanently."

She stopped. *"Excusez moi?"*

He tugged her into motion again. "You heard me."

Her strength was far greater than her petite frame suggested. She dug in her heels and refused to be budged again. "What madness is this?" she demanded.

"No madness." He looked right and left, his unease stronger than ever. "We have no time to waste."

"We have time, *mon ami,*" she said, "for I will not go one step farther until you explain yourself."

With an explosive breath, Yuri took her arm again and led her away from the surging crowd. Only once they were situated in the shade of the overhanging roof of a dockside building did he let her go.

"It is simple," he said, striving to calm both his voice

and his racing heart. "I do not believe that Brecht has given up."

Babette peered into his eyes. "You make no sense, Yuri. Monsieur Renier said you told him that Brecht was only a mercenary and would cause no more trouble."

"Cort may believe he knows everything, but that arrogance will be his downfall."

"His downfall?" Babette seized his arm. "Yuri, what do you mean?"

Yuri shivered involuntarily. Ever since he and Aria had staged their fight with Cort, he had been considering how much he dared tell Babette. That she still felt affection for him was beyond doubt. As tough as she was under that beautiful facade—and in spite of his poor treatment of her in the past—he knew he could easily manipulate her by showing her even a little affection in return.

But she was not stupid, nor would she accept an implausible explanation. It was too late to tell himself now what a serious mistake he had made in inviting her to be a part of the scheme he and Cort had devised.

"I knew Brecht," Yuri said heavily. "I had some dealings with the less savory side of New Orleans society, as you may remember." He hesitated, then made the leap. "He is the man who kidnapped Lucienne Renier."

It was not easy to shock Babette out of her practiced poise, but her face went pale, and she backed closer to the wall as if he had shouted in her face. "You knew, and you said nothing?" she whispered.

"Yes. But when I recognized Lucienne, it never occurred to me that Brecht would be in San Francisco. I had not seen him in eight years."

Babette pressed her hands to her bodice. "I cannot believe this," she said. "You knew the man who had kidnapped the girl, and yet you never thought to tell—"

"I never expected to see Brecht again. Cort said nothing to me until after the attack, and that was the first time I so much as suspected that he might be in town. Even then, I wasn't certain."

"Certain or not, you should have warned Cort! And Anna! *Mon Dieu,* the poor child."

"She has no memory of her past with him. Brecht must have lost her years ago. How was I to guess that he was still looking for her?"

Babette covered her mouth with her hands and shivered. "Why did he kidnap her? No ransom was ever demanded for the girl. She has clearly not been abused. What could he have wanted with her?"

"I do not know his thoughts," Yuri said. "I met him mere months before the kidnapping, and he disappeared immediately after he abducted Lucienne."

"Why in God's name did you not go to the authorities?"

"Brecht was gone, and any involvement on my part might suggest to the police that I knew of the crime before it took place." He gripped her arms. "Would you have wanted me arrested? Questioned, possibly tortured, by the Reniers, who have such influence in New Orleans? Tried for a crime that would surely have seen me hanged? You know they are capable of it!"

"You cared nothing for the child's welfare?"

"I made inquiries. I did what I could to learn more. But Brecht had covered his trail so well that no man could hope to find him. Not even the *loups-garous.*" He put on an expression of profound regret. "You know they searched for her. They failed. How could *I* succeed?"

"Oh, Yuri." She closed her eyes. "You could still have told Cort. It would have been so simple."

"Far from simple. I was considering how to tell him when he suggested this plan of escape. That convinced me that I no longer wished to be a party to his plans for the girl."

"If you had warned him as soon as you heard the name, he might not have suggested this plan! He would have known that Brecht was a more dangerous enemy than he—"

"I need not explain my reasons to you, Babette. It is enough for you to know that I…" He looked down at his boots. "That I wished to protect you above all else."

She opened her eyes and searched his face. For deception. For cowardice. She was right to suspect both those things.

"You must trust me, my dear," he said. "Though we met only briefly, Brecht may remember my name. If he knows that I am involved with Cort, he might attempt to use us against him. Cort will never allow Brecht to take her. He would throw away all our lives for the sake of his pride and greed."

"Are we speaking of the same man?" Babette's face had become flushed, and he realized he was once again treading on dangerous ground. "Yes, I know that both of you expected to be well rewarded for restoring the girl to her family. I came to San Francisco in full awareness of this, and I saw no harm in it, given the benefits to the girl. But to suggest that Monsieur Renier would go to any lengths to obtain this reward…"

"You do not know him as I do." He softened his gaze and touched her cheek. "What's done is done. What Cort does with the girl is no longer my concern. He will no doubt get away safely, and it is my intention that we do the same."

He had hoped for capitulation and found himself sadly disappointed. "You know we cannot, Yuri," she said. "*I* cannot."

"Brecht's men may be following us even now. We must board that ferry."

"You go on," she said. "I will—" She broke off and looked over his shoulder. Yuri turned and followed her gaze.

A man was threading his way toward them through the crowd, feigning deep concentration on his own affairs. Too *much* concentration.

"Come quickly," Yuri said, taking Babette's arm again.

This time she didn't balk. They set off at a fast pace toward the Ferry House. They were far less likely to be accosted once they were in the midst of a dozen or more passengers, and by the time they docked on the opposite shore of the Bay, he would have made some kind of plan to get away from Brecht's minions. Or so he prayed.

Only a few more yards, and then—

He bumped hard into a slender man, who grabbed his arm and stuttered an apology. Yuri shoved the man aside, swung Babette clear and reached for the Derringer in his pocket.

He wasn't fast enough. The slender man drew a pistol from inside his coat and jammed it into Yuri's side. Yuri chopped down on the man's neck with the side of his hand. The man staggered, and his pistol clattered to the pavement. Several passersby paused to watch the skirmish, less alarmed than curious.

"Do you require assistance?" one of the male observers asked.

"*Nyet,*" Yuri snapped. He turned to pull Babette away, but the observer's fingers were already digging into his shoulder.

"I fear you may need medical attention, sir," the man said. "I am a doctor. Please, come with me. I must insist."

Yuri cataloged the man with a desperate glance: well dressed, pleasant-featured, in every way a respectable gentleman.

Di Reinardus had been clever. The men who'd actually confronted Yuri looked nothing like the typical hatchet men Cort had described.

Fool. You miserable fool. But no recriminations would save them now. All his fears had been realized.

There is still a way out, Yuri thought. The very way he had hoped to avoid. Babette would likely never forgive him. But if it was a matter of their survival, he was willing to pay that price.

And the price of despising himself for the rest of his life.

CHAPTER TEN

THE DUKE WAS WAITING for them at a nearby warehouse, perched on a crate as if it were a throne. He slid to the floor, bowed to Babette and gestured for her to remove her veil.

Di Reinardus nodded with appreciation. "A brave attempt," he said. "I will admit that we followed the wrong scent. I also made the mistake of believing that you would understand my warning. Those errors, however, will be quickly corrected." He nodded for his men—now joined by much bigger and more threatening minions—to escort Babette out of hearing.

"Let go of me," she said, digging in her heels.

"You had best cooperate, *madame*," di Reinardus said. "I would not wish you to suffer…an indignity."

"Go!" Yuri said hoarsely.

The duke's men dragged her away. Di Reinardus gestured Yuri to another crate. "I see you have made your choice," he said mildly. "It seems to have been the wrong one."

Yuri settled on the crate as if he had not a care in the world. "You mistake me, my dear duke," he said. "I am done with Renier."

The duke smiled. "Do not pretend with me, my friend. Such blatant mendacity does not suit you."

There was no profit in suggesting that he had planned to come to the duke all along. "I agreed with Renier's plan only so that Babette and I could leave San Francisco," he said.

"Leave? When I so politely asked you to stay until I required your services?"

Yuri shrugged. "You never contacted me, so I assumed…"

"Renier proved more troublesome than I expected." Di Reinardus folded his hands behind his back. "Did you warn him, Yuri?"

"No," Yuri said. "I did not."

Di Reinardus nodded. "You appear to have kept some of your sense. A pity that you have underestimated me in so many other ways."

Yuri prayed that the duke's keen hearing hadn't detected how frantically his heart was beating. "I have never doubted your resolve," he said. "But I must once again warn *you* not to underestimate Renier. He has powerful reasons for keeping the girl."

"The same reasons as yours."

"He wants more than money. He wants revenge against the New Orleans Reniers."

"Oh? Very interesting. Why did you not see fit to tell me this before?"

"Do you wish to hear the story?"

The duke waved for him to continue. When Yuri had finished, di Reinardus smiled.

"How very intriguing. I had suspected he was not entirely a gentleman. A pity he is so stubborn. I might have offered him a chance to take his revenge without the fatal consequences of opposing me. You, however, may yet preserve your life." Di Reinardus removed a cigarette from a gold case tucked in his coat and held it out to Yuri.

Yuri took the cigarette with trembling fingers.

"Perhaps I would prefer to die rather than serve you again."

Di Reinardus shook his head as if he were admonishing a recalcitrant child. "Are you so certain that your fair companion feels the same?"

As desperate as the attempt might be, Yuri had to make it. "Why should I care how she feels?"

"I believe you care a great deal, Baron. I was not unaware of your dealings with Babette Moreau in New Orleans."

"That was over long ago."

"And yet here she is." The duke blew a smoke ring. "Allow me to make the decision easier for you."

He snapped his fingers, and one of his armed attendants left the room. The men who had taken Babette away returned, one keeping a firm hold on Babette's right arm. No one would guess that she was frightened, but Yuri knew she was far too intelligent not to understand how badly things were going.

The duke gestured for the men to bring her closer. He bowed to her with a click of his heels.

"Madame," he said. "Permit me to introduce myself. I am Duke Gunther di Reinardus."

Babette hid her surprise well. "How very interesting," she said. "I had not realized we were to be honored by the attention of someone so distinguished."

Gunther's face darkened. "If you have any influence with the baron, now might be an appropriate time to make use of it."

She met his gaze. "In what way, *monsieur le duc?*"

"Persuade him to tell us where Renier and the girl have gone."

"I doubt he will listen to me, sir," she said.

"I doubt that Monsieur Chernikov would enjoy seeing

that pretty face of yours marred because you failed to convince him to cooperate."

"Leave her alone!" Yuri snarled.

"That is entirely up to you." The duke drew an ivory-handled knife from inside his coat, unsheathed it and held it up as if to admire the finely etched blade. His men pushed Babette closer to him. She flinched but held her ground.

It was more than Yuri could bear.

"Very well," he said, almost too sick to speak. "Let her leave, and I'll do better than tell you what you want to know."

Di Reinardus stared at him for a moment and then nodded to his henchmen. "Take the lady outside, but keep careful watch on her." He returned his attention to Yuri. "Do not waste my time, Baron. I am done with your games."

And so Yuri bargained as he had never bargained in his life.

SACRAMENTO, ARIA THOUGHT, was not nearly as over-whelming as San Francisco. The streets were much wider, the buildings not nearly so tall and the crowds less daunting. It felt odd to be in such a flat place after the steep hills of the coastal city.

She kept close to Cort as he checked them into the hotel, glad for the pretense that allowed her to hold his arm so tightly. While they were staying in the hotel, she would be Miss Anna Reynolds, his younger sister. He had not even considered two separate rooms; he had said he wouldn't let her out of his sight until Babette and Yuri joined them.

Still, they might as well have been miles apart. As soon as they entered the two-room suite, Cort set their bags in the corner of the sitting room, locked the door and went to the window. He stared out for a long time without speaking.

"Is it all right?" Aria asked. "I didn't smell anyone following us."

"Nor did I," he said. "But we will not let down our guard until Yuri and Babette arrive."

And she could tell that he wasn't going to let down his guard with her, either. She sat on the small sofa and yanked off her gloves. She had come so close to admitting on the train that she couldn't possibly be Lucienne Renier. She had hoped he would tell her that it didn't matter if she ever went to the Reniers, that he wouldn't be upset or disappointed if she failed to become what he wanted.

But he hadn't said that. And once again she found that she couldn't bear the thought of his anger when he learned how completely she had deceived him. He would see a backward, treacherous child who had turned on a man who had only been trying to help her at some cost to himself. He wouldn't believe…

Aria twisted her hands in her lap. He wouldn't believe how much she cared about him. More than anything else in the world.

"It's late," Cort said. "I will go down to the dining room while you prepare for bed."

Aria glanced toward the door to the other room. That was the bedroom, and Cort had already made clear that she would sleep there while he would stay in the sitting room.

"You don't have to go out," she ventured. "I can get ready in the bedroom."

He didn't look at her. "I'll order dinner for us," he

said. "You haven't eaten since morning." He paused, frowning. "You're not still worried about Babette?"

She shook her head. "It's only…I wish…"

"What do you wish, Aria?" he asked, as if he were inquiring about her preference in tea.

"I wish all this were over with."

"I've told you there is nothing to be afraid of. Everything is proceeding just as we planned."

Her frustration boiled over. "You can't wait for me to go to the Reniers, can you?"

"You know what I want for you."

"But what do *you* want, Cort? Not just for me. What do you want for *yourself?*"

Cort strode to the door. "I'll be back soon," he said. The door banged shut behind him.

Aria leaned her forehead against the cool wood. She always seemed to say the wrong thing. Nearly everything she did made him angry, and then she ended up feeling just as angry with him. Or hurt, as she felt now.

She had thought that Cort had been hurting when he'd spoken of his family, that he could feel lost and alone, too. But he seemed to be able to push those feelings aside in a way she couldn't. He was always the one in charge, making decisions, deciding what her future was to be.

Ignoring her and how she felt about him.

What would it take to make him *see* her?

Cort returned with dinner on a tray, set it down on the table and left her alone again. She picked at the food, ate what she could and pushed the rest aside. Cort didn't even chide her. He went out again a little while later, ordering her to get ready for sleep, and didn't come back until after she was tucked under the covers.

She lay very still, listening to him pace back and forth in the sitting room. It was a long time before he stopped. Finally Aria drifted into sleep, but she woke many times that night, thinking about Babette and Yuri, and wondering what Cort was feeling.

The next few days were exactly the same. Aria spent the long daylight hours in their room, reading the book she had brought with her and pretending nothing was wrong. Cort paced the sitting room every night, his soft tread drumming in her ears.

On the fifth morning he informed her that they could wait no longer.

"They must have been held up," he said, gazing at the wall over her head as they sat opposite each other in the sitting room. "We'll go on to the mountains. Yuri and Madame Martin will find us there."

His voice was expressionless and remote, but Aria could feel his worry almost as strongly as she felt her own. He'd been so certain that Brecht had given up, and now he was thinking he'd been wrong.

Something bad might have happened to Yuri and Babette. And it would all be his fault.

And hers.

Aria hugged herself, and rocked back and forth in her chair. If he didn't have to take care of *her,* she knew Cort would have rushed right back to San Francisco and searched for Yuri and Babette until he found them. If they were in trouble, he would have found a way to get them out of it.

If it hadn't been for her, none of this would have happened in the first place.

"We should go back," she blurted out.

Slowly he met her gaze. "You know we cannot, Aria."

"I don't care if it's dangerous. I want Babette to be safe."

"As I do." Cort leaned his elbows on his knees and put his head in his hands. Aria couldn't bear it. She jumped up from the sofa, pushing her skirts out of the way, and put her arms around him.

He was so stiff that he felt as if he might break apart, yet he didn't try to get up. He simply sat there as she pressed her face into his shoulder.

"It will be all right," she whispered.

Without a word he took her into his arms. It was just what she had wanted for so long, but she wasn't thinking about herself now. She was only comforting and being comforted, sharing Cort's sadness and guilt. When he found her lips with his, it felt like the most natural thing in the world.

The kiss was nothing like what she'd expected. It was far more wonderful. His mouth was gentle, moving softly over hers. His fingers brushed her cheek as lightly as snowflakes. She followed his lead, stroking him as she would a kitten or a newborn lamb. The rigidity went out of his body. Her eyes filled up, and she had to stop to wipe them before Cort could see.

He pulled away. "Tears?" he murmured. *"Non, non, ma petite."* He stroked her cheek with his thumb and smiled. "We will wait one more day."

AS IT TURNED OUT, they didn't have to wait even that long. The next morning, while Cort was down getting their breakfast and Aria was at the window, watching as always, she saw a familiar man and woman crossing the street. She ran to the door, barely able to contain her excitement.

Five minutes was all it took. Cort nearly bounded

into the room, grinning the way he used to when they'd first met.

"They're all right," he said, closing the door behind him.

"Where are they?"

"They've checked into another hotel down the street."

"I want to see Babette right away!"

"Not now, Aria. It would be better to let them rest a while."

"*Did* someone follow them?"

"Yes. But their pursuers were only humans. They were not difficult to evade, but Yuri preferred to take no chances." Cort frowned, and the light went out of his eyes. "If anything had happened…"

"But it didn't," Aria said. She moved closer to him and touched his hand.

He took a sideways step, stopping out of her reach. "It didn't," he agreed, his gaze fixed on something she couldn't see. "There is no reason to delay any longer. I've hired a wagon to carry our supplies to the lodge. I'll leave for the mountains before dawn tomorrow. You, Babette and Yuri will follow by train in two days' time."

"You mean you'll be going alone?"

"There is no reason to subject the rest of you to an uncomfortable journey."

But she knew that wasn't really what he was worried about at all. The way he had moved aside when she'd touched his hand told her the real reason. He wanted to pretend the kiss last night had never happened.

But she wasn't going to let him forget it.

"I'm going with you," she said.

"No," he said with a brief, distracted glance in her direction. "Babette will be spending the next two days buying clothing and other necessities for you. You will almost certainly arrive at the lodge before I do, and that will give you and Babette a chance to settle in. It's best this way."

Best because he didn't want to be with her.

"I stayed in your ugly city and did what you told me to do," she said, "but this time I'm going to do what *I* want."

"Aria," he said, very low, "it would not be wise."

"Because you don't want to kiss me again?"

His jaw tightened. "I don't think it would be wise to yield to your animal instincts."

"You mean become a wolf. I know how much you hate it, and I know it wasn't safe in San Francisco, but why can't I do it when we're far away from the city?"

"You must get in the habit of restraining that part of yourself," he said in a rough voice. "The New Orleans clan are not in the habit of frequent Changes, and they never do it casually. They know the danger as you do not."

"I'm not in New Orleans yet."

"Aria…" He sighed, his eyes going distant again. "If I take you with me," he said, "will you promise to Change only when I give my permission and stay within my sight at all times?"

It was almost an easy promise to make. Almost. "Yes," she said. "I won't Change unless you say it's all right."

"We leave before dawn. Get your things ready."

That was the end of the conversation, and Cort left a short time later to take care of business. She hardly saw him for the rest of the evening. A few hours after midnight he returned, packed his own bag and took her downstairs.

No one came out to see them off when they left the hotel and walked to the livery stable a few blocks up the street. The wagon was waiting in the yard behind the stable, loaded up with bags and crates of supplies.

The horses tied up near the wagon snorted and bobbed their heads, curious and uneasy around two people who weren't quite human. Cort quieted them with a few soft words and hitched them up with deft, practiced hands. He helped Aria onto the seat, climbed up beside her and clucked to the horses.

The streets were not quite deserted in spite of the hour. Less than savory characters were out and about, looking for potential victims staggering out of the noisy saloons on the outskirts of town, and thin, unhappy-looking women huddled under streetlamps, pulling shawls tight around bare shoulders. Cort's eyes were constantly moving, missing nothing, but he drove them straight out of town without any sign of real concern.

They continued well into the next morning before they stopped for breakfast. Aria had been near to jumping off the seat from the moment they had gone beyond the edge of town and into the farmlands east of the city. She stayed obediently in the wagon until Cort drew it to a halt beneath an enormous oak with gnarled branches that bent nearly to the ground and roots as wide as she was. Cattle grazed peacefully in a nearby field, and Aria could smell water on the other side of a low hill.

"We'll rest the horses for a few hours," he said, "and continue slowly until evening. They have a long away to go."

Aria stared longingly at the silhouette of the distant mountains, seeming so close and yet still days away. The nearer they got to the foothills, the more she could feel the wolf blood stirring in her veins, longing for freedom.

Soon, if Cort was reasonable, she would be able to run free again.

Because soon, too soon, she would have to become someone she didn't want to—and perhaps couldn't—be.

That knowledge preoccupied her for the rest of the evening. Cort kept his distance from her most of the time and spoke to her only when he gave instructions or commented on some aspect of the journey. Their meals were made up of bread, cheese and dried meat. Cort ate as if he hardly tasted the food.

Aria didn't mind the simple fare, even though the wolf inside was hungry for good, fresh meat. She'd survived on so much less. But when they stopped for the night, even she lost her appetite. Cort still wasn't speaking to her, and she knew he was trying to avoid her. He spread her bedroll beside the rear wheel of the wagon and carried his own blankets to the front, where he sat staring into the darkness.

Aria knew he was watching her in spite of his deliberate isolation. He probably thought her "animal instincts" would overcome her sense and send her flying off into the night. She would have welcomed a lecture from him now, even an outright scolding—anything but this awful wall he had put up between them.

By the third day they were well into the hills, tawny as a roe deer's coat now that summer had come to dry the grasses and shrink the streams. The wagon road had become a series of curves, winding and doubling back on themselves, and the horses slowed even more.

The mountains were close now; the live oaks that dotted the hills were interspersed with stands of pines, and the air was crisp with promise. The only stain on the beauty of the wilderness was the scent of machinery and torn earth from the mining camps that sometimes reached Aria on the wind.

At night, when even the faintest sounds rang loudly in her ears, she listened to Cort's breathing and tried to match her own to the same steady rhythm. It seemed the only way she could be close to him.

When they reached Placerville, a dusty mining town crouched against the mountains, Cort took the wagon to the livery stable, bought a fresh pair of horses and secured a room for them in a hotel. As soon as Cort saw her up to the room, he turned back to the stairs.

"Wait!" Aria said, following him onto the landing. "Where are you going?"

He stopped without turning, his hand on the bannister. "Go to bed, Aria."

"I'm coming with you!"

"You'll only be in the way."

"In the way of what?"

"Earning money."

"But I thought…you said in San Francisco that you had enough to pay for what we needed."

"It's always better to have more than we need."

"Where are you going to find money here?"

"In a card game, of course." He half turned toward her and smiled, though there was an edge to it that removed any sense of humor. "Miners are notorious gamblers." He took a step down. "Don't wait up for me. I'll be back before dawn."

"Cort!" He stopped again, and Aria could feel his temper growing short. She didn't care. "Why don't you talk to me anymore?" she asked.

Aria heard the groan of cracking wood. "What would you like me to say?"

"Anything." She felt her own nails cutting into her

palm, digging painful crescents into her skin that healed almost as soon as she made them. "What have I done wrong, Cort?"

The railing began to split. Cort removed his hand and dropped it to his side.

"You've done nothing wrong," he said in a harsh voice. "Once we get to the lodge, you'll be under Babette's instruction. We won't be seeing much of each other. You might as well get used to it now."

"But I don't *want* to get used to it!" She went down several steps so that she was standing right behind him. "There are still things only *you* can teach me. About the Reniers, and New Orleans…"

"Babette can tell you anything I can."

"Not everything."

All the muscles in his body seemed to turn to stone. "Go to sleep. We'll be leaving early tomorrow morning."

She laid her hand on his shoulder.

He turned so fast she could barely catch her breath. "Stop this, Aria. It's no good."

And then he was down the stairs, taking them three at a time, and gone. Again.

Cort didn't return to the room that night, and came back only briefly in the morning with breakfast. Though he claimed to have won what they needed, he seemed almost haggard and refused to discuss anything that had been said the night before.

After hitching up the fresh horses, he drove them out of Placerville through denuded hills and the scars of mining, new and old. They began to climb at an even steeper angle, following an ever-narrowing path along a rushing river, and in a few hours they had left the mixed forest and were among the pines.

Aria made no attempt at conversation. When they stopped for the night, she lay down, closed her eyes and waited patiently. When she was certain that Cort was asleep, she stripped, concealed her clothes among a tumble of boulders near the camp and let herself pretend they no longer existed, that nothing human existed.

The Change was glorious. She ran on four swift feet higher into the mountains, filling her lungs with clean, fresh air. Her paws found purchase on slippery rocks and needle-strewn deer paths, splashed through streams and over fallen trees thick with moss.

She hadn't intended to go far. She had only wanted to get away from Cort for a little while, leave behind the sadness and frustration she had felt every minute of this journey. She wanted to remember what she really was, that her whole life didn't depend on a man who seemed to think she was a doll he could put aside when he was tired of her.

But no matter how far from the camp she went, she couldn't shake off the slender thread that bound her to Cortland Renier. He was always there, in her breath, in her racing limbs, in her heart. She chased and killed a rabbit, tearing into the warm flesh and gulping down the stringy meat with the efficient single-mindedness of a predator.

Nothing helped. It was only an hour before dawn when she turned back, tired to the bone and wondering what she would do tomorrow, and the next day, and all the days they were at the lodge.

A familiar scent and the faint vibration of running feet brought her to a halt. Her hair stood up along her spine, and she laid her ears flat. Joy and fear mingled in her chest.

A red wolf burst out of the nearest stand of pines,

looking even bigger and more imposing than he had when they had fought side-by-side in San Francisco.

Aria knew why. He wasn't going after bad men this time. He was coming for her, and he was furious. She braced herself, expecting his full weight to crash into hers, but he stopped at the very last second, bumping her lightly but just firmly enough for her to feel it. His jaws seized her ruff, teeth pressing on her skin but not breaking it.

Cort was all wolf now. He shook her as if she were a pup. His breath was hot in her fur, and he growled in a continuous rumble. Aria made herself as small as she could, a little frightened in spite of herself, and whined in her throat.

Shaking her one last time, he let her go. He put a little space between them, shook his bristling coat and Changed.

CHAPTER ELEVEN

IT WAS NOT AS IF ARIA had never seen him naked before. It hadn't been so very long since the last time. But something was different since the fight. Cort looked larger, stronger, more muscular, than before.

She Changed, as well, and as she did her feelings became fully human again. She felt weak in a different way now, and her mouth had gone so dry she couldn't speak.

"Merde," Cort swore. "Damn it, Aria! Where in hell do you think you're going?" He took her by the shoulders and shook her again. "Did you think you could run away from me?"

Part of Aria wanted to rail against him, fight him, swear at him in return. He deserved it for making her hurt so much inside.

Instead, she moved until she was flat against him and wound her arms around his shoulders, kneading his back with her fingers. "I'm sorry," she murmured.

His heart thudded inside his chest, booming in her ear. Her breasts, crushed against the hollow beneath his ribs, hummed and tingled. She felt a difference in him, in that part of him she'd never had a chance to examine too closely. It grew very hard, wedged between her stomach and his.

She touched it, more than merely curious. She knew right away that her touch affected him deeply by the way he groaned and closed his eyes. She had begun to ache in between her thighs, and she didn't have to think very hard to realize what it meant.

She wanted to join with Cort. She wanted to be so close to him that there was not so much as a hair's breadth of space between them. She wanted him to—

Cort pulled away almost violently, stumbling back and striking his foot on a rock. He hardly seemed to notice the pain. He stared at her, his breathing louder than the wind in the tree tops.

"Non," he whispered. "You don't know what you're doing."

"Yes, I do," she said, starting toward him. "From the first time you brought me into your house."

He swore again. "Do you think…what you want will help you with the Reniers? If they were to learn—"

She was almost touching him again. He sucked in his breath. She leaned her forehead against his chest.

"You never told me why they should care."

"A proper lady—"

"I know you want to do it just as much as I do," she said.

Cort leaned his head back, the pulse beating fast in his throat. *"Dieu du Ciel,"* he said. "God help me."

Aria kissed the base of his neck. He stopped breathing completely. Slowly his hands curved around her waist, stroked up her back. She tilted her face toward his, and he kissed her.

That first kiss in Sacramento had been nothing like this one. He didn't even try to be gentle. His lips were demanding, forcing her mouth open so that he could push his tongue inside. It felt as if he wanted to devour her.

But her hunger was just as great. She cupped the back

of his head and kissed him every bit as hard. Everything
was right, slipping into place like a key into a lock. She
licked his chest and his small, tight nipples, delighting
in his ragged gasps of surprise and pleasure.

But then he set her back again, cupped her face between his big hands and looked into her eyes so deeply
that she almost became afraid.

"This cannot change anything, Aria," he said
hoarsely.

His words meant nothing to her. She put her hands
around his shaft and rubbed it against her belly. When
he shifted his grip and swept her off her feet, she knew
she would finally have what she wanted.

She tucked her face into his shoulder as Cort carried her into the trees and found a place where the pine
needles were thick under his feet. He laid her down
with such care that she didn't even realize she was on
the ground until he stretched out beside her.

There were no words after that. Cort began by touching her cheek, stroking her skin in gentle circles. Aria
closed her eyes, matching the rhythm of her breathing
to that of his fingers. If her body hadn't felt so alive, she
might have fallen asleep under his caresses.

But sleep was the last thing on Cort's mind. His hand
moved down from her face to her neck, dipping into the
hollow at the base of her throat. He leaned over her,
and his tongue replaced his fingertips. The sensations
that radiated out from that one point of contact were
indescribable. Aria squirmed, and Cort kissed each of
her shoulders and then the top of her chest.

Aria had quickly learned how good kissing Cort's
chest had made him feel, and she thought his doing
the same to her would feel just as nice. But she wasn't
prepared for the shock of his mouth moving down over

her breast, his lips drawing her nipple inside and his tongue swirling over the tender tip. He began to suck, tugging and nipping, until her breath came in ragged gasps and she couldn't help reaching for that very wet place between her legs.

Cort put his hand over hers and pulled her arm above her head, holding it there as he cupped her other breast in his palm and kissed her lips. She strained upward, longing to put her arms around him, but he wouldn't let her. He kept on kissing her while his hand moved down and down, stroking her belly, her hips, her thighs.

And then coming, at last, to the wetness. His finger barely grazed her, but she jerked almost violently when he touched the swollen little nub between the soft folds of flesh.

This was what she had wanted. No one had ever told her about it. She had never been sure that women, like men, could enjoy this so much.

Now she knew it was more than possible. It was astonishing. Cort teased the nub with little flicks, and Aria gasped again and again. He knew exactly what made her feel good, just as if he was in her body and felt it himself. The wetness became a flood, and she felt like a flower opening its petals to the sun.

She almost didn't notice when he let go of her arm. Only when he drew away did she open her eyes and begin to protest.

Cort wasn't listening. He was too busy kissing every place his hands had gone, all around her navel and along the tops of her thighs. She was almost ready when his tongue slid over the nub.

But she wasn't ready at all.

She cried out, sending birds flying from the trees above them. Cort didn't stop even for an instant. It was as if he were drinking from her as he would from a cup full to the brim, as if she were a fountain that could never run dry.

But there was a vast empty place farther down, deep inside her. That was the entrance to her body, the opening where babies emerged into the world. But Aria wasn't interested in babies now. Something very powerful was building inside her, getting bigger and bigger, until she knew it wouldn't stay still much longer.

Cort felt Aria shaking, moving closer and closer to the moment of release. He hadn't believe it was possible, after so many years of sleeping with beautiful, jaded women of energetic skill and experience, to feel as he did now, trembling with the desire to give this innocent girl a kind of pleasure she'd never known.

It was wrong. He knew it in his head, where the gentleman still ruled over the beast.

But his head wasn't strong enough. Not against the demands of his body. The feel of her slick, quivering flesh against his tongue drove him to want more…more of her sweet taste, her little whimpers of excitement, her surrender.

No, she had never known anything like this before. He was the first man to touch her naked skin, just as he had been the first to kiss her lips.

He kissed her other lips now, sliding his tongue deeper, lifting her hips and spreading her thighs so that he could go deeper still. Her entrance was hot, tight and wet. So wet and ready that he could have lain over her and entered her without feeling the slightest resistance.

The weeks of self-restraint, the longing, the frustration, seemed to vanish as if they had never happened.

Aria arched against his mouth as he thrust his tongue inside her, crying out again.

She had started this. Perhaps she didn't know exactly how it would end. But he knew she would accept him into her without a moment's hesitation, joyfully and without regret.

Nor would *he* have anything to regret. He had made a plan his "honor" had forbidden, but he was well beyond the reach of such strictly human constraints. He would mark Aria as his own, and when he took her to New Orleans…

He realized he had stopped his caresses when Aria reached down to tangle her fingers in his hair. Her arms were strong, pulling him up, all but forcing him on top of her supple body. She rubbed her thighs along the outside of his hips, oblivious to how her movements drove him beyond any hope of sanity.

There was no time to ask her if she was sure. He braced himself on his arms and fitted his body to hers. His cock was trapped between their bellies. He moved again, making ready, pressing his lips to hers so that he could swallow her little gasp of surprise when he took her. She clung to him, her pale lashes thick against her cheek, her golden hair like an angel's halo.

It wasn't honor that made Cort stop. It wasn't even the distant thought that he might get Aria with child when he had never imagined himself a father.

It was Aria herself. Her purity, her honesty, the fearless trust that shone in her eyes when she opened them to meet his gaze.

It was the love he saw in them. The love that strangled his desire and made him choke on his own hypocrisy.

He rolled away from her, slid down her body and put his mouth to her again, working with lips and tongue until she bucked beneath him, rose up like a cresting wave and fell gently back to earth.

"Cort," she whispered, stroking his sweat-damp hair. "Oh, Cort."

THE EARTH STOPPED spinning, and Aria remembered to breathe again. The sunburst of overwhelming pleasure was gone, but a warm humming filled her body from head to toe. She reached for Cort again, desperate to hold him, to stroke his back, to hear him murmur gentle words in her ear. To tell him how much she loved what he had done.

How much she loved *him*.

But he didn't fall into her beckoning arms. He sat up, his shoulders hunched, and shuddered like a horse shaking off a stinging fly.

Aria got to her knees, gazing at his back in bewilderment. After a little thought she began to guess what was wrong. He had done so many wonderful things to her, but never once had he asked for anything in return.

The picture came clear in her mind. She had wanted to feel him inside her, and he had wanted the same thing. He had deprived himself of pleasure when he had stopped.

But why? What had gone wrong?

Nothing but his insistence that they should never be alone together. He had kept away from her after they had kissed the first time, too.

But Aria knew she could make him finish what he had started. A touch was all it would take. A hand on his rigid back, her lips on his chest.

Only one thing kept her from acting on her impulse. He couldn't just pretend nothing had happened. Not after this. And there was something else she had to do now that the wall between them had crumbled.

She could explain everything. There would be no more secrets. Once Cort knew the truth about her, the real truth, he could let go of his plans for her and they could make new plans. Together.

She put her arms around his back and rested her cheek on his shoulder. "Cort, there is something I have to tell you."

He stiffened. It was only a small change in his body, but Aria felt it jar her bones and knock the air from her lungs.

"Not now, Aria," he said.

"But…it's something you need to know. Before we get to the lodge."

Without a word he slipped out of her grasp and got to his feet. "Aria," he said quietly, "I told you nothing would change."

She tried to remember when he had spoken those words, but they were only a vague echo, like birdsong from a distant canyon. Her heart seemed to squeeze into a tight little ball, too small to push the blood through her veins.

"Cort," she said, rising to stand behind him. "When I tell you—"

"It's no use. I should have made it clearer. I am sorry."

Sorry? "What do you mean?" she asked, dreading his answer.

"I mean that you and I…we can never be together."

She didn't believe him. No one could do what they had done and not…

Her heart burst open, dying a little more with every breath she took. "Tell me why," she said.

He lifted his head, turning just enough that she could see the deep lines etched around his mouth. "I don't want to hurt you, Aria."

"I want to know the truth."

The breeze caught Cort's auburn hair and teased it with mischievous fingers just as she had done so brief a time before. "I…care about you, Aria," he said. "But I can't be what you want me to be. It isn't only because of your family and the things they will want for you. There was a woman, a…lady…I thought cared for me. When she left, I knew I could never let that happen again."

The part of Aria that could still think, the part that couldn't feel, remembered the day in San Francisco when she had wondered if Cort had ever been with a woman. She'd even thought it might be Babette, but she'd known for some time that they had never been together.

"You…you lay down with that woman the way you did with me," she said.

But it was more than that, and she knew it. He was talking about something even stronger than joining bodies.

He was talking about joining hearts.

"She must have been a very fine lady," Aria said.

"Yes."

Of course she was. A lady good enough for a gentleman like Cort. Someone who had hurt him so much that he couldn't care for anyone else the same way.

He had tried to warn her, and she hadn't listened. She hadn't been able to see what seemed so obvious now, the reason why he had always hesitated to touch her, why he always seemed to be one step beyond her reach. It was nobody's fault but her own.

And she wouldn't beg Cort for what he wouldn't give

freely. She no longer had any reason to worry about telling him that she wasn't Lucienne Renier. The only thing she had to decide now was if she wanted to leave—leave Cort and the silly dreams she'd let herself believe in—or go on with his plan.

If she didn't have Cort, she wouldn't have anyone. She would be completely alone. But if the Reniers believed she was their kin, they would offer her a home among her own kind. She could learn to be what they wanted. Maybe she could even make them love her.

And she could show Cort that she could be as "fine" a lady as the woman he had loved. She would be so good at it that he would never dream of treating her as he had done all these weeks. He would have to bow and smile and be polite just the way he was with Babette.

Then he would finally know what he had lost.

"Aria," Cort said softly, "it would be best not to mention any of this to Babette or Yuri."

Of course not. He wanted to forget this had ever happened.

"I won't tell anyone," she said coldly.

They returned to camp, stopping to pick up their clothing along the way. Cort was very polite. He made no special attempt to avoid her, and he smiled more than he had for days. They were sad smiles, though, telling her that he felt badly about what he had done. But it was all very formal, and she was just as formal in return. It was the only way to keep her damaged heart beating.

By the second day after their brief interlude, they no longer saw any sign of human habitation except the occasional small shack or cabin. On the third day, when the road had gone from a track to a set of wheel ruts overgrown with grass and weeds, Aria saw the lodge rising out of the trees. The horses snorted with relief and went a little faster up the final slope.

The lodge wasn't quite what Aria had expected. It was built all of wood and stone, like a Carantian mountain cottage, but it was much bigger and taller. As the wagon got closer, she could see that the walls weren't made of logs but of wooden planks, and the building had been painted a sort of grayish color that almost faded into the background of thick forest and rocky cliffs. The door was strangest of all; it was very fancy, carved and set with a big brass knocker. It seemed to belong in San Francisco instead of the mountains, where there was no one to appreciate just how fancy it was.

She would learn to appreciate it, along with all the other nice and expensive things her new life would bring.

She was doing her best to believe those things would be enough when Babette and Yuri emerged from the house. Babette, dressed in a much simpler gown than any Aria had seen her wear before, came toward her with hands outstretched. Yuri trailed after her, scowling as always.

Cort came up beside Aria, silent as only he could be, and watched Yuri stride toward them. Cort was smiling with his mouth, but his eyes were empty. "*Bonjour,* Madame Moreau," he said with a slight bow. "Good evening, Yuri. I trust you've made yourselves comfortable."

THE WORDS SOUNDED careless even to his own ears, but Cort felt anything but sanguine. His throat was hard and tight, and his skin was hot as if with fever.

Not that he hadn't been feeling those sensations for some time. They had been with him ever since he and

Aria had left Sacramento, when he had made the unforgivable mistake of kissing her.

Disaster.

"Bonjour, monsieur," Babette said, smiling warmly.
"And Anna. It is so very good to see you." She took
Aria's hands and led her away, chattering gaily about
the house. Cort was hardly aware of Yuri as the Russian
joined him.

"You took your time," Yuri said, glancing after Aria
and Babette. "Did you have trouble?"

Trouble. Trouble of the kind he certainly couldn't
confess to Yuri.

He had thought he was in control of himself during
the journey from Sacramento, even in the presence
of the one temptation he had seemed unable to resist.
During the daylight hours of traveling, he had been just
disciplined enough to shield himself against her intoxi-
cating scent and the warmth of her body. At night he had
maintained his distance, and distracted himself with the
thousands of sounds and smells that sang as exquisitely
as the voices of angels.

But it seemed all he'd done was deceive himself from
the moment he'd sat down at the card table to win a
shivering, half-naked girl. Listening to the voice of the
wilderness hadn't been a solution at all. It brought back
too many memories of drifting on a pirogue on Bayou
Gris, as much a part of the swamp as the bullfrogs and
gators, happily believing that anything was possible for
a boy who could dream.

Still, he might have managed to keep his head if he
hadn't Changed when he'd found Aria gone from the
camp. The wolf had taken him completely. Worry and
anger had mingled with the relentless savagery of the

beast, driving his human self to a state of uncontain-
able lust.

Even then, if Aria had rejected him, he might have
walked away. But she had wanted him. And where she
felt, she acted, so all hope was lost.

Aria had been everything he could have desired, completely without inhibition and utterly unselfish. It would
have been so easy, so very easy, to carry through with
the idea he'd had on the train.

But he'd remembered himself just in time. The dep-
rivation had been agony. He hadn't just wanted to be
inside her, he had wanted to be *part* of her. In every
way.

Cort heard Babette laugh, and he wondered how
much Aria was suffering. He didn't flatter himself that
she wouldn't get over it. He had hurt her, deeply, but she
had a rich life ahead of her. If he'd taken her, all her
chances of happiness would be gone.

He couldn't give up his need for revenge. But he also
couldn't go through with the idea of taunting the Reniers
with Aria's loss of honor at his hands. Better to have her
hate him than love him.

He laughed under his breath. Did she even know
what love between a man and a woman really was?
She showed no sign that the kind of ecstatic delirium
he had felt with Madeleine had ever been a part of her
life. Could anyone forget such emotions?

Regardless of what she had felt in her hazy past,
Aria would soon be too busy to brood over his rejec-
tion. And once she was in New Orleans, she would find
more deserving recipients for her affections. She would
undoubtedly marry some arrogant aristocrat who would
see only what Cort and Yuri and Babette had created.

Cort growled, and Yuri gave him a sideways glance. "You didn't answer my question," he said.

"We were hardly traveling light," Cort said. "And you? No further difficulties?"

Yuri looked off into the forest. "I said there would be none, unless by 'difficulties' you include being confined to a filthy railcar, followed by endless days on horseback with an equally filthy guide." He shrugged. "Well, we are here."

Here, and as sharp-eyed as ever. Yuri had never brought up the subject of Cort's possible attraction to Aria after that first day, but one slip on Cort's part might remind him of his earlier suspicions. He would be far from happy that his partner had put their scheme at risk after all Cort's protestations of disinterest in their protégée.

And Babette's feminine instincts would not be easily deceived. She had never suggested that there might be anything personal between Cort and Aria, but that didn't mean she hadn't considered it.

"I appreciate all you have done, *mon ami*," Cort said.

Yuri coughed and avoided his gaze. "The girl is ready to begin?

"She has been looking forward to it."

"Fortunate that she and Babette have become so fond of each other."

"Aria hungers for friendship and affection. Babette has given her both."

Babette and Aria came to join them, sparing Cort further conversation. Aria was smiling a little too brightly, her arm locked around the older woman's waist.

"You must be hungry," Babette said. "The kitchen here is quite adequate, and I will have something prepared within the hour. In the meantime—" she gave Aria's shoulder a squeeze "—we will heat water for Anna's bath." Her nose wrinkled. "And also for you, *monsieur,* when she is finished."

Cort bowed. "As you wish, *madame.* Far be it for me to offend your delicate sensibilities."

He regretted his boorishness immediately, but Babette seemed unaffected. She gazed at him for several moments, glanced at Aria and then gave a brief, almost imperceptible shake of her head. She and Aria led the way into the lodge. Aria glanced over her shoulder once, but there was no expression in her eyes.

The lodge was as rustic inside as it was without, but it was the sort of rusticity favored by wealthy men who preferred their brushes with the wild to be doled out in careful measures like sugar for coffee. The furniture was all handmade by fine artisans, and the carpets, plain as they appeared, were far too expensive to be trampled by dirty boots. Large paintings of stags and hunting scenes decorated the walls, along with a number of mounted heads.

The kitchen was well stocked with canned and preserved foodstuffs, as Babette had indicated, and the range was equipped with a large hot-water tank. There was no tap, of course, but a large pump had been fitted in the sink, drawing from a nearby spring. In addition to the kitchen, there were a study, a large living area and six bedchambers upstairs.

In short, it was ideally suited for their purpose. And for keeping two people apart.

While Cort and Yuri unloaded the wagon and saw to the horses, Babette assembled a cassoulet out of canned and preserved foods, while heating water for Aria's bath.

Afterward they sat down at the substantial kitchen table and ate in near silence. Cort was uncomfortably aware that Babette's gaze frequently moved from his face to Aria's, as if she were attempting to solve a particularly challenging puzzle. Aria hardly looked up from her plate. Later, while she and Babette cleared the table, Cort and Yuri carried buckets of hot water to the tub upstairs.

It was all too easy to imagine Aria in the water, head tipped back as the steam caressed her breasts and dampened the blond curls around her face. But it wasn't only her physical beauty Cort imagined. He pictured her expression the way it must have looked when he'd told her about Madeleine.

Aria had believed the lie that he'd been heartbroken over his lost amour and could never love again. He had learned to hate Madeleine long ago, but the second part was the truth.

Wasn't it?

The thought was so unexpected that he nearly tripped on his way downstairs with the empty bucket. Babette was starting up the steps as he caught himself. She stared at him in astonishment.

"What is it, *monsieur?*" she asked. "Are you ill?"

"*Non, madame.* I am perfectly well."

"You should rest."

Behave as if everything is normal, he told himself. "Surely you're fatigued, as well, Madame Martin."

"Perhaps a little." She smiled. "You must call me Babette. We will be working together closely for the next few weeks."

"I doubt I will be much involved, Babette, as I have no experience in training girls to be ladies."

Her smile faltered a little as she stood aside to let him

pass. He focused on the floor in front of him and didn't look at her again.

That night he left his shoes at the doorstep and went walking in the woods. The loam and pine duff were thick and pungent under his bare feet, and the air smelled heavily of resin.

The mountains were different from the bayous of Louisiana. Very different. Yet a few days ago he had felt just like the rough, naive boy he had been, running with his kin through the swamps and bald cypress woods, hunting deer and howling one to the other across the water.

He missed them, his cousins and nieces and nephews. Even his father, who had cursed him when he'd left the bayous for good.

And his mother, who had died of grief.

Clenching his jaw, Cort fought the urge to Change and outrun the memories. He sat at the base of a mammoth pine, an old patriarch that had never seen a saw or a meadow of broken stumps, and laid his head back against the rough bark. He half expected Aria to come looking for him, breathless and defiant, Changing from wolf to nymph in an instant.

But if she had ventured outside, she didn't wander in his direction. After a few minutes he headed back, in no better state than when he had left. He had come within a quarter mile of the lodge when he heard raised voices.

Yuri and Babette. He continued a few steps and stopped. Curiosity was not enough to put him into the middle of a lovers' quarrel when he was raw with guilt and self-disgust.

Turning on his heel, he returned to the forest.

"I KNOW YOU, YURI. You will not go through with it."

Babette stood with one hip resting against the massive oak dining table, her dressing gown pulled tight around her waist and her hair down about her shoulders. She had not been able to sleep; the masquerade she and Yuri had been performing since Cort and Anna's arrival had exhausted her, and she was in no mood to indulge the man she loved.

Yuri sat in one of the rustic chairs, his arms folded across his chest. "We have no choice," he said, his expression as glum as she had ever seen it. "If we fail to cooperate, Brecht—"

"Brecht!" she said with a laugh.

"—di Reinardus will not let us escape a second time. You have no idea how ruthless he is."

"But he is only one man! You said yourself that his former allies—"

Yuri cut the air with his hand. "He still has those who obey him, and he is the most dangerous man I have ever known. I have no wish to die, and I will not allow you to get yourself killed. The girl won't suffer. We will deliver a woman worthy of being a queen, and that is what she will become."

"As the bride of a traitor and regicide!"

"Why should you care what happened in a distant country twenty years ago?"

Babette leaned over the table, hands pressed flat to the polished wood. "It is not a distant country that concerns me. I tell you, Yuri…nothing is worth betraying her like this. Or betraying your dearest friend."

"I cannot afford such friendship now," Yuri muttered.

"Are you certain you can afford mine?"

His brown eyes, so full of the feeling he refused to

express, gazed mournfully into hers. He was little better than a villain himself, but always, always, she became weak and foolish in his presence. Even though he was weak and foolish himself in so many ways.

Babette could feel herself beginning to lose control. That would never do. She could still hardly believe what Yuri had told her after he had taken her out of the warehouse. It was a fairy tale of epic proportions. An infant girl born into royalty in a distant land, the child of murdered parents, swept away from those who might exploit her and brought to the thriving new nation called America to be raised by the distantly related Reniers, very few of whom knew her true background or name. The most absurd thing Babette had ever heard.

Or it might have been, had she herself not risen from a naive, ill-educated peasant girl to become the most celebrated whore in New Orleans. And regardless of her rank, Anna—Lucienne, Alese, or whatever name they called her—needed her now. A clear head was the only thing that would give Babette the slightest chance.

"There must be another way," she said. "You said yourself that the duke was exiled from his own country and has no current allies in Carantia. He will have to depose yet another king in order to claim the throne."

"You seem to forget, my dear, that the king in question is a weakling who lacks the support of the Carantian people."

"And di Reinardus will have such support? That I very much doubt. You said that the loup-garou nobility in Carantia, including the duke, prefer to oppress the human majority, which will hardly endear him to his subjects. And ambition blinds him. He will make a mistake." Babette bent closer to Yuri. "We must tell Cort everything."

"Out of the question."

His expression was unyielding. He had made up his mind. Perhaps if he had not been so bent on protecting *her*...

"You convinced di Reinardus that Anna needs further refining before she becomes his bride. That is the only reason he let us go. Perhaps if I were to leave now, you might not find it so simple a matter to achieve what he demands."

"That will not protect you, my dear." Yuri closed his eyes and waved his hand. "Go. Go if you wish. I will not stop you."

Because he knew he wouldn't have to. For all her bold words, she didn't doubt just how dangerous di Reinardus could be. She'd met his kind before. Even if she thought she could elude the duke's henchmen, she could never leave Yuri to face the man's wrath alone. Or abandon Anna to an equally unhappy fate.

Babette drifted away from the table, scarcely knowing where she walked. Anna had already lost so much, taken from the only family she had ever known and whisked away to a usurper's stronghold.

Naturally di Reinardus didn't think of himself as a usurper. He saw himself as the one who would set things right in the tiny sequestered nation of Carantia, where *loups-garous* ruled and humans—until the reign of Anna's more enlightened parents—had been less than second-class citizens, as they were again under the current king.

Di Reinardus *had* been exiled, to be sure. And now his foppish, ineffectual cousin ruled instead.

But Alese would change all that. He would keep her with him, isolated and friendless, and force her into marriage as soon as she came of age.

He might have done it years ago, if she had not escaped. Escaped to become Anna, strangely bereft of all the graces she would have learned among the Reniers. It was as if she were a different girl entirely.

A different girl.

Babette paused to touch the hard, dry nose of one of the poor dead creatures hung on the wall in the large drawing room. When Yuri had first identified Anna as Lucienne Renier—Alese di Reinardus—he had been unable to explain how she had fallen so far from the young lady she must have been. The girl had become a blank slate, her previous existence wiped clean, or so Yuri believed.

So *di Reinardus* believed.

With a little shake of her head, Babette wandered to the window. The night was very dark here. Her thoughts were no less so. Yuri was blind in so many ways. Had he ever for a moment considered the possibility that Anna had not merely lost her memory, but that she was not Alese di Reinardus at all?

"Babette," Yuri called, his voice impatient.

"Un moment," she murmured. So many bewildering possibilities. Anna could read Russian and speak French. According to Yuri, she readily Changed into a wolf, though the Reniers preferred to ignore their animal side. A well-bred lady's most thoughtless gestures were alien to her, and she despised the clothes a woman of culture wore with artless grace.

Such skills and preferences were not simply forgotten. They were trained into a child until they became a matter of instinct. Amnesia could not drive them into hiding.

But if Anna were not Alese, who could she be? Could two such identical girls exist?

They might. If they were twins.

CHAPTER TWELVE

THAT THOUGHT BROUGHT all others to a stop. It was a ludicrous notion. Babette knew far too little of Carantia and its royal history. Surely di Reinardus would know if there had been a second princess…a princess who had a wildly different background than Alese di Reinardus.

And Babette knew she had absolutely nothing to back her peculiar theory except the intuition of a woman who, even in her most cynical moments, had always recognized the possibility of miracles.

She glanced back at Yuri, who was pouring himself a glass of the vodka he'd found in the sideboard. He would only scoff if she shared her suspicions. For now, she must concentrate on what she could be sure of.

And she still intended to save Yuri from his own worst impulses. As she intended to save Anna, whoever she might be.

"I'm coming," she said, giving the words a subtle flavor of resignation. She joined Yuri at the table. "Let us go up to bed."

He downed the rest of his drink. "Are you sure you want me in yours?"

She laid her hand on his shoulder. "We have been friends too long, *mon ami*."

Yuri gave her a weary look. "Yes," he said. "A long time."

They went up the stairs together. And after they had

comforted themselves with each other, Babette went downstairs again and made herself a pot of tea.

"You can't sleep, either?"

Anna's voice was barely a whisper, but Babette could hear the strain in it. When she turned, she was not surprised to see a young face drawn with exhaustion, shadowed eyes and tangled hair that had not seen a good brushing in several days. Even those minor flaws could not dim such remarkable beauty, but Babette well knew that beauty wasn't enough.

Spirit was everything. And Anna's had been badly affected by something that had happened during the days when she and Cort had been traveling alone together.

Just as Cort's had been in ways he had been desperate not to show.

"Perhaps you would like some tea?" Babette asked, indicating a chair at the small kitchen table.

The girl sighed and nodded, allowing Babette to pour.

"Are you quite well, *ma petite?*" Babette asked after a long silence.

"I'm never sick," Anna murmured.

"But something is wrong, *n'est-ce pas?*"

Anna lifted the cup to her lips, set it down again and pushed it away. "I—" Suddenly she looked at Babette with that direct, guileless stare. "Do you like mating with Yuri?"

Babette nearly dropped her own cup. Tea sloshed over the rim. *"Excusez-moi?"*

"I know what you do at night." She hesitated, but there wasn't a trace of a blush on her fair skin. "I heard him call out your name."

Calmly Babette rose, found a towel and mopped up the spilled tea. "It is not polite to listen, Anna. At the very least you must never suggest that you have heard."

"I didn't think you would mind," Anna said. "You said we would be good friends."

Ah. That was the rub, balancing the lessons and Anna's need for firm discipline against her hunger for a confidante. If Cort had once served that purpose, he could do so no longer.

Especially since it was apparent now that Babette's intuition had not entirely deserted her.

"Yes," she said slowly. "And I meant what I said. But even between friends, some subjects…"

"Are you ashamed of it?"

Babette could hardly keep her countenance. "Do you think I should be?"

"No." Anna fidgeted in her chair, the unhappiness in her face even more bleak than before. "Why won't people talk about it, Babette? What is so bad about two people touching each other that way?"

This girl was not a complete naïf. Inexperienced, yes. Bewildered, to be sure. But in some ways she was as wise as any woman Babette had ever known. Wise in ways society was never likely to appreciate.

Wise…and perhaps more experienced than she seemed, in spite of the bizarre gaps in her education.

"Lying with a man is nothing to be ashamed of," Babette said gently. "But it must be done only in the right circumstances. *Par exemple,* for an unmarried girl to do so would be considered scandalous in most circles—including the one you will soon be rejoining."

"But why? What is so special about marriage? Why should that make any difference?"

Babette was amazed anew that even such basic matters were unknown to Anna. She could only have been living in some dim recess far from civilization. A mountain cave in China, perhaps, with monks who never spoke a word.

"It is complicated, *ma chérie*," she said, deciding to begin as if Anna had indeed been living in a cave all her life. "Marriage is one of the institutions that binds society together. I had intended to speak of the rules of courtship as we progress. Is there a reason you must have the answer now?"

Anna ran her finger through a drop of tea Babette had missed. "I just want to understand."

"Surely your parents were married. You have no memory of them at all?"

"No. And Fra—I don't remember anyone else ever telling me about it." She dropped her chin into her hand with a dejected look. "*Why* do people get married?"

"There are many reasons, Anna. It is the relationship most women and men seek when they become adults. It is a way for people to live together when they feel affection for one another."

"You're not married to Yuri, are you?"

Babette hesitated. There was no point in concealing the truth. "No," she said. "I am not."

"But that doesn't stop you from feeling affection for him or sleeping in the same bed with him."

This was turning out to be so much more difficult than even Babette had imagined. "One must carefully weigh one's obligations to family, station and society before making the decision to form such a relationship outside the bonds of matrimony," she said. "In the case of a young lady like yourself, such activities would be unwise for many reasons, not least among them the disapproval of one's family."

"But *why* should they disapprove?"

"The prohibition goes as far back as the custom of marriage itself," Babette said. "As a rule, few men enjoy the prospect of wondering whether or not a child is theirs or another man's. And the strictures against motherhood among unwed…" A sudden, alarming thought occurred to Babette. "Do you know how babies are born, Anna?"

Anna rolled her eyes. "Of course. The same way fawns and kittens are born. The male and the female mate, and in a few months the mother gives birth."

And, in truth, that was more than many a young girl knew. "Yes," Babette said, "but babies are quite different from fawns and kittens in one important way. No one thinks anything of a dog whelping a litter. But a young woman who has a baby without a husband is not regarded kindly. Her reputation is ruined."

"Don't people want babies?"

"Of course most women want children, as do most men. That is another important reason for marriage. We are not speaking of wanting, but of what society expects."

Anna pulled her cup toward her and sniffed the tea with a kind of indifference that didn't deceive Babette in the slightest. "Does a baby happen every time people mate?"

Alarm overwhelmed Babette's self-control. "No, but the risk cannot be ignored. An unmarried mother is considered a very bad woman, and her situation is very difficult. She is unlikely to have any means to support herself or her child, and supporting a child is very difficult without money."

"But people work to get money, don't they? Why couldn't she work?"

"Few would hire such a woman, even if she could find suitable employment."

"And no one will help her?"

"No man, not even the father, will feel obligated to assist her in any way. Even her family may choose to disown her."

"But it's all right for a man to help make a baby and leave the mother by herself?"

How clearly Anna pointed out the hypocrisy of "good society." "Unfortunately, that is often the case."

"And even the woman's family would hate her?"

This was definitely no longer a matter of conjecture. Anna was asking for very personal reasons.

"Is something worrying you, Anna?" she asked. "You know you may confide in me. About anything."

Anna was quiet for a long time. The tea crew cold. Babette was nearly convinced that the conversation was finished and she would never receive an answer when Anna spoke again.

"I don't want my family to be angry with me," she said. "I want to know what's right and wrong so they'll still want me."

But it wasn't only that, Babette thought, her heart aching for Anna's wretchedness. It was about Cort, and what must have happened along the trail to the lodge.

If Anna was with child...

"I'm certain they'll want you and love you," Babette said. "We will make sure of that."

Anna sighed. "Love," she said, as if the word were as foreign to her as the concept of marriage. "People get married because they feel...affection for one another."

"Most people, yes," Babette said carefully.

"But do men and women who love each other *always* get married?" Anna frowned. "Does Yuri love you?"

Babette rose. "I think that is enough for tonight, Anna. You must sleep if you are to be fresh for our lessons tomorrow. You do want the Reniers to be proud of you, do you not?"

Anna sat up straighter, her chin jutting with stubborn determination. "I *will* be good enough for them," she said. "I'll be good enough for anyone."

With her usual strong spirit restored, Anna went back upstairs. Babette was left to sip her cooling tea and think back on everything Anna had said.

Perhaps her first guess had been wrong after all, and Anna had not slept with Cort. The attraction between them had never been in doubt, but until their arrival at the lodge, Babette had been certain that Cort had kept firm control over his desire for Anna. He certainly would have considered the danger of getting her with child, and how that would ruin his and Yuri's plans.

Yet Anna's questions about babies had been alarming. And then there was her defiant statement: "I'll be good enough for anyone."

Did that, too, have something to do with Cort? Anna clearly loved him…or believed she did. When had she recognized her feelings? Had she declared them to Cort? He had obviously been avoiding her, but had he given her to believe that she was in some way not good enough for him?

Babette set her teacup down with a bang. Had she so badly overestimated Cort's sense of honor?

Honor. As if any of them possessed the slightest crumb of it. Nevertheless, in spite of her own obvious errors in judgment, Babette was determined to protect Anna from this moment on. No man was going to take advantage of her again—not Cort, not Yuri and certainly not Duke Gunther di Reinardus.

But first she would have to learn exactly what was going on between Cort and Anna. And until Yuri came to his senses, she would have to tread very carefully indeed.

"WE BEGIN WITH the undergarments."

Aria stared at the corset with dread. She had seen them before, of course—in the magazines Cort had given her, in drawings and advertisements that claimed "Perfection of Shape, Beauty of Finish, Durability in Wear and Moderation in Price." She knew nothing about price or durability, but there was nothing beautiful about it, and as for the shape...

"How can anyone fit into that?" she asked.

Babette smiled and turned the corset around. "You see the laces in the back? These adjust to the figure. The hooks in the front allow you to remove it without unlacing, which of course would require a maid."

Aria rested her hands on her waist. The magazines had made it very clear that ladies were supposed to be very small there, and wide on top and below. But Aria didn't think she was very big around the middle to begin with. Cort had seemed very happy with the way she looked when they...

No. She wouldn't think of that. She had made a mistake in asking all those questions of Babette last night. The answers hadn't helped. They didn't change anything at all.

But she did know a few things she hadn't before. What if she and Cort had made a baby? What if she were to become very big around the middle, so that no corset would ever fit her? Would Cort hate her even more if she did? The Reniers surely would.

It was too late to worry about babies now. "Why

would anyone want to wear something they can't put on themselves?" she asked Babette.

"No respectable young women can be seen without stays. It would be considered a sign of loose morals."

Everything Babette taught her seemed to be about good and bad behavior, and being "respectable." It seemed that "respectable" people had to have other people, servants, do things for them that they could easily do for themselves. Aria couldn't imagine why anyone would want to be a servant, or why *she* would want to have one.

"Will I need to have a maid, too?" she asked.

"You need not concern yourself with such considerations until you are with your family again," Babette said. "For the time being, I shall help you with your toilette."

Aria slumped on her chair.

Babette shook her head. "You must sit up, *chérie*. Your spine must never touch the back of the seat, no matter the state of your emotions or the weariness of your body."

Aria sat up again. "That would *make* you sit straight," she said, pointing at the corset in Babette's hands.

Babette smiled. "Indeed, there are some advantages to modern fashion."

Not any that Aria could see. But she had made up her mind, and so she listened obediently as Babette described the layers of undergarments, from the corset cover and various kinds of chemises to drawers, stockings, garters, petticoats and, finally, the bustle.

The last had looked ridiculous in drawings and on the ladies Aria had seen, but the one Babette showed Aria actually made her snicker.

"You may scoff," Babette said, "but only ten years

ago the bustle was considerably more pronounced." Her hands traced a bulging shape behind her back. "But of course, you do not remember."

That, at least, was not a lie. "I'm only glad that people don't dress like that anymore," Aria said.

"I should not be surprised if the larger bustle comes back into fashion," Babette said. "But we need be concerned only with this one. Shall we try on the corset?"

Groaning inwardly, Aria rose and allowed Babette to fit the horrible thing around her body and lace it over the chemise. She sucked in her breath as the boning compressed her ribs.

"Relax," Babette advised. "You will become accustomed to it. And since you are already so well formed, we need not lace it too tightly."

Any lacing at all was too tight, but Aria held her tongue until Babette was finished. She noticed right away that her breasts protruded much more now that they were forced up by the top of the corset.

"Que belle!" Babette exclaimed, clapping her hands. "It is an excellent beginning."

Only the beginning. Aria wriggled, imagining what it would be like to try to remove the corset if she had to Change in a hurry.

But that wouldn't be necessary, would it? No one here wanted her to Change, and from what Cort had said, the Reniers didn't do it very often. He probably hoped she would forget she was a werewolf completely.

As if in answer to her thoughts, Cort's warm, earthy scent came drifting into her room from underneath the closed door, and she heard his nearly soundless tread on the stairs. She hadn't seen him since yesterday before bedtime; he had gone out, and hadn't come down for breakfast.

She didn't care. It was better if she didn't see him until the lessons were complete. Then she would show him....

"Ah, Monsieur Renier!"

Babette had opened the door wide, stepping out of the way so that Aria had an unobstructed view of the landing. Cort stood framed in the doorway, his face caught in a moment of surprise.

"Will you not come see how delightful our charge appears?" Babette asked him. "She will turn heads everywhere in New Orleans!"

Cort looked directly at Aria, cleared his throat noisily and turned red. "If you will excuse me..."

He turned and almost ran down the stairs. Babette made a soft noise that almost sounded like a laugh and closed the door.

"Why did you do that?" Aria demanded. "You told me this morning that a woman who isn't married should never let any man but her husband see her in her underthings."

"I thought he should see how lovely you look. He has witnessed you in a state of undress on more than one occasion, has he not?" Babette asked, removing a pair of sheer stockings from a box on the table.

She meant the Change, but Aria found herself thinking again about what had come after that last time in the woods. A time when she hadn't had any reason to be ashamed. When Cort had seemed to feel...

She grimaced. How many times had she promised herself not to think about Cort's feelings for her, or her own about him? But the look on his face when he'd seen her through the doorway...

"Mademoiselle. Kindly pay attention."

Aria tried to do what Babette asked, and after a while she was buried in a bewildering array of garments that felt as heavy as a mountain pony. The dress Babette had brought from Sacramento had far too many ribbons and too much lace, and the skirt clung to Aria's legs like a deep snowdrift.

"A lady must always select the appropriate dress for every occasion," Babette said, adjusting the fall of the underskirt over the bustle. "This is a simple morning dress. The hem is cut so that it will not drag in the filth, should you wish to cross a park or a busy street. The weight of this gown is appropriate for warmer weather." She produced a pair of white gloves. "A lady must always wear gloves outside or at any social gathering. Please try them on."

Aria did her best, but they didn't want to fit over her hands, and her fingers felt like overstuffed sausages.

"Well, we shall learn," Babette said, patting Aria's shoulder. "Next, I will show you a selection of hats and bonnets, and describe their use. After luncheon, we will begin…"

Her words blurred together in a hum of meaningless noise. Aria did as she was told, took things off and put other things on, tried on this dress and that. Eventually she and Babette shared a quiet luncheon downstairs. Cort and Yuri were nowhere to be seen.

After luncheon, Babette removed another gown from the wardrobe in Aria's room. It was quite different from the other three the Frenchwoman had made her try on.

"This," Babette said with a satisfied air, "is a ball gown. You will see that the sleeves are short and the bodice is cut low, so as to reveal the lady's arms and the upper part of her shoulders. The lady, however, will cover much of her arms with long gloves. She will wear only the most subtle of jewelry."

Jewelry was a subject that Babette had touched on only briefly, and Aria was more interested in the fact that the gown seemed a little fuller in the skirt. She might even be able to move in it, though certainly not ride or run.

"Shall we try it on?" Babette asked.

Babette fussed with the dress until she was satisfied and stepped back. "Ah," she said. "*Parfaitement.* Once you have learned to walk properly in it, no man will be able to resist you."

She took Aria's hand, led her to her own room next door and made Aria stand in front of the cheval mirror near the wall.

Aria didn't know the woman in the glass. The face seemed the same, as did the hair—Babette had promised to show her how to wear it up "properly" later—but nothing else looked the way it had been before. The whole upper part of her chest was showing, and her skin looked like fresh milk against the pale fabric. Her waist was pinched in, and the skirt flared out from her hips, sweeping gracefully to the ground.

Cort had said she was beautiful. Now she thought she was beginning to understand.

"We will learn ballroom etiquette later," Babette said. "After I have taught you the basic forms." She smiled into the mirror over Aria's shoulder. "Tonight you will wear a gown to dinner. Not this one, of course. We shall see what Cort and Yuri make of you."

Aria's throat tightened. "You said no man would be able to resist me," she said.

"I have no doubt of it."

"But why would I want men to look at me and want to be with me if ladies and gentlemen are supposed to stay apart unless they're married?"

"There are many rules of conduct that permit unmarried men and women to enjoy each other's company in the public arena. In fact, no marriages could take place unless ladies and gentlemen met at balls and parties and similar engagements."

And fell in love, Aria thought. She smoothed her hands over the glossy fabric of her skirts.

"Will my family expect me to meet gentlemen?" she asked, praying for the right answer.

"They will undoubtedly introduce you to the most eligible young men in New Orleans."

"Eligible," as near as Aria could figure out, meant "good enough."

"Will they be *loups-garous?*" she asked.

"Another *loup-garou* would be better qualified to tell you that, *ma chérie.*"

But Aria had no other werewolf to ask. "Will they want to marry me?"

Suddenly serious, Babette turned her about and put her hands on her shoulders. "If they fall in love with you. And you are very much worthy of love. Never doubt it."

Not worthy enough for Cort. And Aria didn't want any other man to love her except the one who didn't want her. As for what the Reniers would expect…

She might have to go along with many tedious rules in order to make her way in the world, but there were some decisions, some choices, she would never let anyone make for her.

Not even Cortland Renier.

THE SMELL OF Babette's cooking was a siren song to Cort's empty stomach, but the rest of him took little pleasure in it. He knew he couldn't get away with avoiding Aria any longer; his behavior was becoming too obvious, and no matter how often he told himself that Babette's opinion was of no consequence, he knew it was.

Especially where Aria was concerned.

He had no idea why Babette had opened the door to him when Aria had been in her underclothes—unless the Frenchwoman had meant to gauge his reaction.

If that had been her purpose, he had certainly given her ample cause for suspicion. He'd gaped like a schoolboy glimpsing his first *belle de nuit*.

And that was the strange thing about it. He had seen Aria naked, every intimate part of her exposed, and yet the sight of her wearing a corset, chemise and drawers had had a very unexpected effect.

Uncomfortably aroused and feeling a fool, Cort made a final adjustment to his tie and went downstairs.

The others were already gathered in the drawing room. Cort saw Babette first, elegant as always in a muted red gown. She turned and smiled as he walked into the room. Yuri was so busy with his drinking that he didn't seem to notice Cort at all.

Aria pretended not to notice him. But he noticed her. And what he saw nearly knocked him off his feet.

CHAPTER THIRTEEN

ARIA'S GOWN WAS made of cream-colored satin, taste-
fully embellished with ribbons and lace. The color was
suitable for a young woman who had recently made her
debut, yet it was highly flattering, especially to a girl of
Aria's coloring. The bodice was so tight that even she
could not have fit in it without the aid of a corset, and
her breasts swelled full and ripe above the neckline.
Her hair was still down about her shoulders in a golden
cascade, but in no other way did she resemble the wild
young woman he had brought to the lodge.

Aria turned and caught him staring. She smiled with
perfectly courteous detachment, and Cort felt a chill.
There was a veil behind her eyes that he couldn't penetrate. For the first time since the day she had told him
her name, she was truly a stranger.

He became aware that Babette was watching him, and
strolled over casually to join her and Aria. He bowed to
them formally and waited for one of them to speak.

Babette nodded to Aria. "Mademoiselle Renier," she
said, "may I present Monsieur Cortland Renier. *Monsieur,* Mademoiselle Lucienne Renier."

The formal introduction was a necessary part of
Aria's lessons, and they had all agreed that Aria ought
to be called Lucienne when they were at the lodge. Cort
simply hadn't expected it to feel so wrong.

"Mademoiselle," he said with a shallow bow. "I am honored to make your acquaintance."

Aria met his gaze and swept into an equally shallow but quite proper curtsy. *"Monsieur,"* she said, "I am pleased to meet you."

Babette nodded approvingly. Cort locked his hands behind his back. "The gown is lovely, Madame Martin," he said. "Your taste is exquisite."

"Merci," Babette said, inclining her head. "But I cannot take credit for the beauty its wearer lends to the garment."

"Indeed," Cort said. "Mademoiselle, my compliments."

"You are too kind," Aria murmured.

"Would you care for a drink, *monsieur?"* Babette asked.

Cort did, but he didn't dare risk losing control of his senses now. He felt as if he had walked to the very brink of a great chasm. A step in one direction would take him away from disaster. A step in the other would send him plummeting.

"Thank you, but no," he said. "If you will forgive me…" He bowed to Babette and Aria, and escaped to Yuri's side just as Babette began to explain the finer points of formal introductions to Aria.

The Russian had, from the look of him, already consumed half a bottle of vodka. He looked up blearily.

"Renier," he muttered. "You look much too sober." He lifted his half-empty glass. "Have a drink."

"No. And you might reconsider having another yourself."

Yuri laughed and emptied his glass in one swallow. "This is a night for celebration, is it not?" He waved in Aria's direction. "She is already halfway to being everything we had hoped."

"You exaggerate, *mon ami*," Cort said abruptly.

"Do I?" The Russian grinned. "She's the most… beautiful thing I've ever seen."

A rush of pure, irrational jealousy buffeted Cort with the force of a hurricane. He knew Yuri couldn't have any personal interest in Aria beyond what money he could get out of her, yet that fact didn't mollify him. It didn't help that he'd been sensing something wrong with Yuri ever since they had arrived at the lodge. The Russian had always tended toward brooding and pessimism, but now his moods were black instead of gray. Cort's were hardly better.

He turned back to Babette, who was speaking very softly to Aria.

"I shall instruct you as we eat," Babette was saying. "Do not feel self-conscious, *ma chérie*. Poise and confidence are just as important as which spoon one uses for the soup."

Aria nodded and glanced over Babette's shoulder at Cort. He quickly looked away.

"Shall we go in to dinner, *monsieur?*" Babette asked.

Without thinking, Cort started for the dining room.

"Perhaps you would escort Mademoiselle Renier?"

The Frenchwoman's gentle prodding was a reproof to a man who had forgotten his gentlemanly duties. Cort retraced his steps, bowed again to Aria and offered his arm.

"Mademoiselle," he said.

Aria laid her hand lightly on his forearm. She didn't lean or cling, but floated at his side as if he weren't even there. Though her arm was covered with a long glove, her scent, warmed by the heat of her body, drove every other smell from the room. Cort found himself breathing much too fast.

As befitted Yuri's higher rank and Babette's maturity, the two of them preceded Cort and Aria into the dining room. The table had been set as well as one could manage in the hunting lodge of a wealthy man, which was to say quite handsomely. Babette indicated that Cort was to take his place at one end of the table and Yuri at the other. She and Aria would sit opposite each other at the sides. Since the table was large enough for a party of twelve, the seating arrangement left considerable space between diners.

Cort moved quickly to pull back Aria's chair. Yuri did the same for Babette, who waved him away and went to the sideboard.

The fragrance of rich soup penetrated the haze of Aria's scent just long enough for Cort to remember how hungry he was. He offered assistance as Babette approached with a tray, but she deftly declined, laid a bowl at each place and then took her own chair. Aria waited, hands demurely in her lap, and looked to Babette for instruction.

Babette demonstrated laying her napkin in her lap and selecting the soup spoon from among the carefully arranged utensils. She dipped her spoon delicately into the soup, raised it and took a small sip. Aria mimicked her, an expression of intense concentration on her face.

"The soup is always first," Babette explained. "Ordinarily this course would be followed by fish. After that come the roast and other dishes, but we are necessarily limited in what we may serve here."

"It's very good," Aria said.

Babette inclined her head, looking pleased. "We have

plenty of time to learn the proper etiquette and particulars of dining," she said to Aria. "Tomorrow we shall discuss the use of the various implements in greater detail."

She continued to speak in a low voice as the meal progressed from soup to canned meat. "As a rule," she said, "one would not speak directly to someone seated across the table but focus one's attention on the guests to either side. However, these being extraordinary circumstances, such niceties are not practical."

In fact, Cort thought, given that no one else was talking, it wasn't even possible. That suited him very well indeed.

"On any occasion," Babette went on, "prolonged silence is an indication of an awkward gathering." She looked pointedly at Cort. "Wouldn't you agree, *monsieur?*"

"Of course," Cort said. He cut a small piece of canned beef, the metallic taste of which Babette had skillfully masked with some kind of sauce. "You have done wonders tonight, *madame.*"

"You compliment me too highly, sir," Babette said.

"Tomorrow I will bring fresh venison," Cort offered, "and dress it for you."

Aria turned to Cort. "You're going hunting?" she asked.

"That would seem to be the best way to acquire venison in the forest, *mademoiselle,*" he said, aware of the unreasonable sharpness of his voice.

"I assume you will use a rifle," Aria said sweetly, "given how much you despise Changing. You would not wish to rely on bestial instinct."

Babette shook her head. "Lucienne," she chided, "one must never be confrontational at mealtime."

Aria's eyes widened. "I am sorry, Madame Martin. I did not realize I was stating anything but fact."

Yuri snorted. "Give them both a drink," he said. "That will settle them down."

"Let us save that for another time," Babette said. She smiled at Aria. "It takes practice to drink properly, as with everything else."

"I don't want to drink if it will make me clumsy and bad tempered," Aria said.

No one could mistake her meaning, but Yuri seemed not to notice. He simply poured himself another glass of vodka.

The rest of the meal was completed in relative peace. When everyone was finished, Babette rose with a nod to Aria.

"The ladies will retire to allow the gentlemen to enjoy their port and cigars," she said. "When they have finished—"

"Why should the ladies go out?" Aria interrupted. "And why would any *loup-garou* want to smoke a cigar? They stink."

Babette gave Aria a reproving look. "Whether or not a man chooses to smoke, this is the way things are done."

"I think it's foolish," Aria said.

Cort stifled an unwilling grin. Only a moment ago he'd been angry with her, but suddenly he was glad. The old Aria wasn't gone after all.

"Unfortunately," Babette said, "we do not make the rules. Come, my dear."

"Yes, *madame,*" Aria murmured, and glanced at Cort. He remembered to pull her chair back, and she quietly left the room with Babette.

"I spoke too quickly before," Yuri said, slopping

liquor over the rim of his glass as he poured another drink. "The girl still has far to go before she is ready to join civilized society."

Cort snatched the bottle away from him. "Your judgment is hardly to be trusted, Baron."

"*My* judgment?" Yuri chortled and leaned back in his chair until the front legs were well off the floor. "What of yours, *tovarishch?* Sometimes I wonder if you really want her to become Lucienne Renier again."

"Why should I want anything else?"

"Perhaps you are not ready to let her go."

Cort laughed shortly. "What in God's name gave you such an idea?"

"The fact that you have been so careful to avoid her. I have always known you had some personal interest in the girl, even a certain affection, but it seems you are almost…" He hiccuped. "Almost afraid to be in the same room with her."

"*Absurde.*"

"Is it? The girl seems angry with you. A little too angry, considering her former attachment to her benefactor." He sneered. "What happened when you were traveling alone together, eh?"

Cort glared at the nearly empty bottle of vodka in his hand, regretting that he hadn't accepted a drink when Babette had offered it. "I fear for your mind if you continue to indulge yourself as you have been, my friend."

Yuri's chair banged to the floor. "You assured me that there is nothing between you and the girl, and I was fool enough to believe you. What have you done?"

Cort was careful to set the bottle down gently instead of smashing it as he wanted to do. "What is wrong with you, Yuri?" he demanded. "You've been like a bear with a sore head ever since we arrived."

Wiping his mouth with his sleeve, Yuri reached for the bottle. "I want it over with," he said. "Over and done."

"Then we are in perfect agreement."

Cort didn't wait for Yuri's reply but went directly into the drawing room. Babette was sitting alone on the sofa.

"Lucienne has gone upstairs," she said when Cort joined her. "In spite of her questionable behavior at the table, I believe she has made considerable progress. Do you not agree?"

Her words suggested that she had overheard at least part of his argument with Yuri and was courteously pretending she had not. "You have worked a miracle, *madame,*" Cort said.

"No miracle. Once Lucienne has set her mind on a thing, she is not easily turned aside from it." Babette ran her hand over the heavy brocade fabric of the sofa cushion. "You have spent much time away from the lodge. May I ask why?"

Cort had already prepared a plausible explanation, though he had been too angry to use it with Yuri. "A precaution," he said. "I have no doubt that you and Yuri threw off any pursuit, but it seems wise to keep watch for intruders, particularly as we are uninvited guests in this house."

"*Bien sûr.* One cannot be too careful. Nevertheless, it would be most helpful if you could remain closer to hand. I will need your assistance in teaching Aria how to behave with a gentleman of her own class. I can think of no better example of a true gentleman than yourself."

Cort parsed her words for mockery and found none.

Yuri had known better than to speak of Cort's true origins, and Babette's opinion of him was better than he deserved. He found he wanted to keep that good opinion as long as possible.

And if this were yet another test…

"I am honored by your confidence, *madame*," he said, "and am happy to oblige."

"Excellent." She rose. "If you would make yourself available after luncheon tomorrow…"

"It will be my pleasure."

He waited until Babette had gone upstairs, and then went outside. The mountains were filled with night noises, hoots and calls and distant howls. True wolves still roamed the Sierra Nevada, though the encroachment of man and his resentment of any predator other than himself had thinned their numbers.

Still, they persisted. And Cort felt their song pierce his very being and tug at the other self that was becoming more difficult to control with every passing day.

The wolf would not be silenced. The wolf wanted his mate. These mountains had become a trap, and the only way out was through the complete and total transformation of the girl he had known into a lady who would be forever beyond his reach.

ARIA WAS FURIOUS with herself.

She had been so certain that she could be indifferent to Cort. He had made it easy enough for her by staying away from the lodge for most of the past several days. Even when they'd been in the same room together, he'd barely glanced at her, let alone acknowledged how much she had accomplished.

Accomplished exactly what he'd wanted. Shouldn't

he be glad? As *she* should be, because it was what she wanted, too—wasn't it?

Then why was she anything but happy? Why did she keep wondering what Cort was doing, what he was thinking, how he felt when he—

"Are you ready, my dear?" Babette asked.

No, she wasn't ready. She didn't want to see Cort again so soon. Even a restless night's sleep hadn't lessened her self-disgust. Or her silly, childish anger. But she couldn't admit any of that to Babette.

"I am ready," she said, and followed Babette to the stairs. As she had feared, Cort was already in the drawing room. He scarcely looked at her as he bowed and waited for the women to enter.

"Thank you for attending us, Monsieur Renier," Babette said. She held out her hand to Aria. "Lucienne is eager to begin today's lesson."

Aria smiled mechanically. "*Merci, monsieur,* for your assistance."

Cort's glance flickered to her face. "*De rien, mademoiselle.*"

Nothing. That was exactly what it was.

"We discussed introductions yesterday," Babette went on. "One does not simply introduce oneself to strangers, nor should one introduce one's friends to just anyone. An introduction is a social endorsement." She smiled as if with secret amusement. "One addresses all but one's closest friends and family members by their titles. Were Monsieur Renier your brother or fiancé, for example, you might call him 'Cort' in private. As an unmarried woman, however, in public you should address him in only the most formal way."

That's fine with me, Aria thought. *I doubt I'll be addressing him at all once we get to New Orleans.*

The thought raised a lump in her throat that refused to be budged.

"As a gentleman," Babette continued, "Monsieur Renier would never introduce one of his acquaintances to you unless he was certain that you would find the connection agreeable."

An odd expression crossed Cort's face. Aria wondered if he was thinking of people he might have introduced to her if things had been different. His mysterious family, perhaps?

"If you should wish to avoid further dealings with one to whom you have been introduced," Babette said, "you may avoid meeting that person's eyes when he or she approaches you."

Just the way Cort was avoiding *her* eyes.

"As a lady, you must not give your hand to a gentleman unless he is a friend of a member of your family or an intimate acquaintance. A gentleman never offers to shake a lady's hand unless she offers first." She gestured toward Cort. "Let us try it."

Hesitantly, Aria put out her hand. Cort was slow in taking it. Though both of them wore gloves, the spark Aria felt was immediate. Burning heat penetrated deep into her skin.

Cort snatched his hand away much too quickly. He dropped his arm to his side, and his fingers worked as if he were trying to rid himself of her touch.

Babette pretended not to notice. "The kiss is another form of greeting that must be used only among family and dear friends," she said. She took Aria's shoulders and turned her around, kissing the air to either side of Aria's face. "This is how it is done among Europeans. In America, it is considered somewhat vulgar to greet even a friend this way in public."

Aria felt Cort's gaze on her back. She was remembering a very different sort of kiss. Was he remembering, too?

"Of course, a lady never leads a man to believe he should be permitted a greater familiarity than society deems correct," Babette said, her voice growing dim in Aria's ears. "Formality is seldom an error with any male acquaintance. True intimacy should exist only among close family members, or between a husband and wife."

Or two people who lie together without being married, like Babette and Yuri, Aria thought.

Babette turned Aria to face Cort again. "You must continue to practice such formality with Monsieur Renier and Baron Chernikov," she said, "so that you do not lapse into bad habits when you are introduced to New Orleans society."

If only she'd been enough of a lady to begin with, Aria thought, none of this would have happened.

"I understand," she said. "I will practice very hard."

Babette smiled approvingly. "I am certain you will. It will also be helpful to remember that a lady should never reveal too much, or discuss personal or controversial subjects, with strangers or recent acquaintances. A certain frankness is admired, but it must be tempered with discretion. For instance, you should not gossip or introduce subjects such as the intimate relations between a man and woman."

Aria knew Babette was referring to their conversation at the kitchen table and wondered why she had mentioned it in front of Cort. Cort seemed to be wondering, too. He was looking straight at Aria again, his dark brows drawn into a frown.

Was he afraid that she'd spoken to Babette of what they'd done on the way to the lodge?

"A true lady is modest in all things," Babette said. "She always strives to maintain her poise. Too great a show of any emotion is discouraged."

"Is the same true of a gentleman?" Aria asked, meeting Cort's gaze.

"It is even more true for them. Is that not so, *monsieur?*"

Cort didn't answer, but he looked very uncomfortable. Aria was glad.

"If you have other business to attend, Monsieur Renier," Babette said, "Lucienne and I will continue our discussion of dinner menus. Will we see you at luncheon?"

He looked slightly startled at the dismissal. "Yes. Of course."

They left Cort standing alone in the drawing room. After a moment Aria heard him walk out the door and close it with a slight but noticeable bang. She found herself shaking as she joined Babette in the dining room, and even Babette's praise at the end of the lesson didn't make her feel any better.

For the next week Aria practiced and learned everything from how to manage a conversation to making social calls. Babette placed particular emphasis on the specific obligations of an unmarried woman of good breeding, though she never again brought up their talk on the subject of mating. And neither did Aria.

Aria's encounters with Cort were coolly formal, just as Babette had advised. She gave him a shallow curtsy every time they passed each other, and he bowed in return. Their eyes, if they met at all, did so only briefly.

By the end of that first week, Aria felt as if she had turned to ice, as unfeeling and transparent as glass.

At the beginning of the second week, Babette mentioned a ball.

"Naturally we cannot have a real one," Babette said, "but we can make two couples and imagine the rest."

"Are you going to teach me to dance?" Aria asked, a sharp stab of worry catching her under her tightly compressed ribs.

"That is a rather essential part of a ball, *n'est-ce pas?*" Babette said with a smile.

"So I will dance with you?"

"The entire point of the exercise is that you learn how to dance with a *man*."

"Yuri is a man."

"The Baron is not a very good dancer. Monsieur Renier, given his nature, must be graceful as a matter of course. As you will be."

There was no getting away from it, Aria thought. And when Cort joined her, Babette and a slightly unsteady Yuri in the drawing room, she could see he hated the idea as much as she did.

"First, the host or hostess will generally see to introductions," Babette said. "A ballroom acquaintance seldom extends beyond the ball itself, unless the individuals meet frequently on other occasions. Therefore a young lady cannot accept more than two dances with the same man, or others may misconstrue their relationship."

No one could misconstrue my relationship with Cort now, Aria thought bitterly.

"A true gentleman will always accommodate a lady's reasonable request, whether it be to take her into the ballroom when she is without an escort or retrieve a glass of punch." Babette nodded to Cort. "I am certain that Monsieur Renier has been in much demand as an escort at those events he has attended."

"You do me too much honor, *madame*," Cort said.

But Aria could hear something wrong in his voice, as if Babette had said something that made him want to laugh.

"A ball usually begins with a waltz," Babette said, "so that is what I will demonstrate first. Though we have no music, I will endeavor to hum a tune. Anna, watch me and Baron Chernikov."

Her heart sinking even lower than before, Aria watched Yuri place his right hand rather clumsily on Babette's waist and take her hand with his left. They both wore gloves; Babette had been firm in explaining that bare hands must never touch at a ball.

Humming softly, Babette nodded to Yuri. He took an awkward half step, caught himself and then slowly swung Babette in a circle. He was certainly not graceful, but when she glanced at Babette's face Aria could see that Babette didn't mind at all. She was smiling faintly, and her eyes were half-closed in pleasure. Even Yuri looked happier than he had in days.

Aria didn't want to think about what they felt when they touched each other. But trying to avoid those thoughts only brought her back to Cort and *his* touch.

She glanced quickly at his face. He, too, was watching Yuri and Babette, avoiding Aria's gaze with such determination that she knew he was thinking of her, too.

You're made of ice, remember? she told herself.

Imagining herself as an icicle helped a little when Babette and Yuri stopped dancing and Babette indicated that Cort should take Aria's hand. Even when she felt his heat through her glove, she told herself that she was in no danger of melting.

But when he put his other hand on her waist, all the layers she wore, from her chemise to the ball gown itself, seemed to peel away and slide to the floor.

Cort didn't look at her. He only smiled stiffly and waited until Babette indicated that they should begin. The other woman counted out the steps as Cort guided Aria with his movements. It didn't take very long for her to catch on. The speed of Babette's humming increased, and so did the pace of the dance.

"As a rule," Babette said, as Cort swung Aria around the room, "there would be much more space for dancing. A ballroom can generally accommodate anywhere from a few couples to several dozen, perhaps more. The dancers take care not to bump into each other, and once a rhythm is established the effect is quite beautiful."

It *felt* beautiful, Aria had to admit. Her body seemed to be flying, her feet barely touching the ground.

And Cort was flying, too. He was just as graceful as a man as he had been as a wolf, each effortless motion sweeping her along until she could barely remember what it was like to walk. It was magic, just like in the fairy tales Franz had read to her when she was a child.

And just like magic, something happened on the fourth circle around the room, something Aria hadn't dared expect. Cort looked down into her eyes. And smiled.

It wasn't a distant smile, like before. His body had lost its rigidity, and the tension had gone out of his face.

"You dance very well, Lucienne," he said softly.

"I…I do?"

"Yes. I should have told you before how much I… admire you for what you've accomplished."

"I've done my best," she said, trying not to let him see just how confused she was.

"I know you have." He squeezed her hand. "I am proud of you."

Aria could see much more than pride in his eyes. And then the ice cracked. It sloughed away from Aria's soul and left her warm all the way through.

He still wanted her. He could pretend and pretend, just as she did, but his eyes didn't lie. Neither did his hand holding her waist so tightly, or his body brushing hers. She could feel his arousal when the dance brought them close, could hear his breath coming faster than such mild exertion would cause. The wolf was there, barely hidden, and her own wolf howled with joy.

The wolf she was afraid to trust.

"Tell me," she said, smiling up at him, "did that other woman, the woman you loved…did she dance as well as I do?"

CHAPTER FOURTEEN

CORT'S STEP FALTERED. Babette's humming stopped suddenly, and the dance came to a halt. Cort seemed to shake himself, and soon there was nothing left of his smile but a shadow.

He released Aria and bowed. She returned the courtesy, and when she straightened again, he had already stepped away.

How could she have been so stupid?

"Very good," Babette said with forced cheer, "but I can see that you will need a little more instruction, *chérie*."

"Yes, *madame*." Aria looked out the window, where the late-afternoon sun was casting the woods in shadow. "May I...speak to you privately?"

Cort took the hint with alacrity. Once he and Yuri had left the room, Aria took Babette's arm.

"I would like to take a walk in the woods," she said. "There is something I'd like to discuss."

"This sounds most serious," Babette said, peering into Aria's eyes. "Has this anything to do with our previous conversation?"

"In a way."

Babette sighed. "Very well. Let us go upstairs and change into something more suitable for walking."

For Aria, "suitable" meant the shirt and trousers Cort had reluctantly bought to replace the clothing that had been destroyed when she had Changed for the fight in the alley. Babette clearly didn't approve, but she agreed to let Aria wear them when Aria promised she would never consider donning such garments in New Orleans.

"It would be scandalous," Babette said. "And a terrible blow to your reputation."

Neither scandals nor reputations were of any interest to Aria now. She couldn't even bask in the freedom of an unencumbered stride and lungs that could expand all the way.

There was far too much at stake for anything else to matter.

She listened carefully when she and Babette stepped out the door. The usual woodland noises and scents were evident, but Aria couldn't hear or smell Cort at all. He, too, had probably left the lodge.

Nevertheless, she led Babette some distance away from the building, moving downslope as fast as Babette's dress would permit.

"Please!" Babette called out behind her. "I beg you, let us rest. I am neither *loup-garou* nor machine."

Aria stopped and looked back. Babette was leaning heavily against the trunk of a tall pine, bent at the waist and breathing hard. It was the first time Aria had ever seen her perspire.

They had gone far enough, in any case. Aria looked around for something to sit on and found a small cluster of boulders a few yards away. She took Babette's hand and led her to the rocks, waiting as patiently as she could for the other woman to sit and catch her breath.

"Mon Dieu," Babette breathed, dabbing at her forehead with a handkerchief. "I trust what you are about to say is worth such exertion."

"I think you will find it interesting," Aria said. She sat beside Babette and watched a small beetle meander its way through the rocks and pine duff. "I just don't know how to begin."

Babette was paying full attention to her now. "This is to do with Monsieur Renier," she said.

"Yes," Aria said. "But there are other things…" She hunched her shoulders. "Promise me you won't tell anyone what I'm about to say until I…until we decide what we should do."

Solemnly Babette laid her hand over her heart. "I promise."

"Cort and Yuri told you that I lost my memory?"

"Oui."

Aria could feel Babette's tension and hear the unease in her voice. This would not be easy.

"That was a lie," Aria said. "At first, I was afraid to trust Cort. I didn't want to tell him anything about myself after what those men had done to me. Later, when I knew he wouldn't hurt me, I still couldn't tell him. He thought I was…someone I wasn't, and I was afraid…"

"Ah," Babette sighed. "I begin to comprehend."

Aria refused to let her courage falter. "I am not Lucienne Renier. I am not even Anna. My real name is Aria, and I grew up in the mountains in a place called Carantia, on the southern border of Austria. I—"

"Did you say Carantia?"

The question was so sudden and urgent that Aria was taken off guard. "Have you heard of it? When I first came to America, no one I spoke to had heard of it."

Babette nodded. "I have heard of it. Please continue."

"I never knew my parents. A man name Franz raised

me. I didn't realize other werewolves existed for most of my life."

She told Babette how she had grown up in the mountain cottage, ignorant of her origins and family.

"Franz never seemed to want to answer my questions, and after a while I stopped asking. Then, a few months ago, he decided to bring me to America to meet other werewolves who had come from our country. He said he would explain everything when we got to San Francisco." She swallowed. "He died in New York before he could explain much of anything. I came to San Francisco by myself, hoping I could find the people he wanted me to meet."

Babette covered her mouth with her hands, muffling laughter. "Ah, *chérie*. The world is indeed a marvelous place."

"You're not angry that I lied?"

"Angry? *Non, non.* Doubtless I would have done the same." She lowered her hands. "Did you always go by the name 'Aria'?"

"That was what Franz always called me, though he never wanted me to tell anyone else."

"Do Cort and Yuri know?"

"I told Cort after he rescued me, but I asked him not to tell anyone but Yuri. I went by Anna when we met the other people who lived in the village." She smiled weakly. "I seem to have a lot of names."

"More than perhaps even you can guess." Babette released a long, quivering breath. "If you are not Lucienne," she murmured, "you cannot be Alese."

"Who is Alese?"

Babette seemed not to hear. "Have you heard the name di Reinardus?"

"No. Is it important?"

"Non," Babette said, and hurried on. "If I understand correctly, you knew from the beginning that you could not be Lucienne Renier."

"Not always. I didn't know until you told me that she was a baby when she was kidnapped and had grown up in New Orleans."

"And you were afraid to disappoint Cort?"

Aria nodded. "He wanted so badly for it to be true. And after he…after he didn't want to be with me anymore, I thought having a family, even if it wasn't really *my* family…"

"Cort no longer wished to be with you? What do you mean… Aria?"

She met Babette's gaze. "On the way here, we did what you and Yuri do every night." She lowered her eyes. "I know it's rude to mention it."

"I am not offended." Babette took another deep breath and let it out again. "Is this why you asked me so many questions the other night?"

"Yes."

"Is it possible that Cort got you with child?"

"I don't think so." Aria touched her stomach. "Wouldn't I be able to tell?"

"If he entered you—"

Aria swallowed. "He didn't. I wanted to, but…"

"Then it is very unlikely you are pregnant."

Babette seemed relieved, but Aria was almost sad. "He told me that we couldn't be together," she said. "I was angry. I thought it would be easier to ignore him the way he ignored me if I really did become a lady."

"Do you know *why* he ignored you, Aria?"

That was a question Aria didn't want to answer. "He has been staying away from me and treating me as if we don't know each other. Until today. Today, when were dancing, he told me that he was proud of me."

"And that makes you unhappy?"

"I…"

"Aria…do you love him?"

Aria couldn't make herself answer.

Sliding down from the rock, Babette began to pace. "This is not unexpected," she said. "Your attraction to each other was clear to me from the first moment I saw you together, but I did not realize how far it had…" She kicked at a pile of sticks with one small booted foot. "I have been blind, but Cort is an even bigger fool."

So am I, Aria thought. *And I can't seem to stop being one.* "He can't love me," she said. "I know that now."

Babette turned to face her again. "Do you remember when I said that gentlemen must hide their feelings, too? Cort may fear what he feels for you."

"I don't believe he feels anything for me, except maybe for wanting to lie with me again."

"And what does that mean to you, Aria?"

"It means I'm never going to tell him that I am not Lucienne. I'm going to go to the Reniers just as we planned. But before I do, I want to make Cort see that he has made a mistake. I want to make him forget that other woman."

"What other woman, child?"

"I don't know her name. It doesn't matter. I'm going to make him want me so much that he'll never be able to forget *me.*"

Aria had expected Babette to disapprove of her plan, and it was clear that the other woman was distressed from the way her brows drew together and her full lips tightened.

"You're speaking of revenge," Babette said softly. "Are you sure you know what you're doing, Aria?"

"Yes."

"Do you think this will make you happy?"

"Yes." Aria lifted her chin. "I want you to help me, Babette."

"How can I possibly help?"

"Can you…can you teach me how to make him unable to resist me?"

"You wish to seduce him?"

Aria wasn't quite sure what the word meant, but she could guess. "Yes," she said. "Can you show me how?"

Babette turned away and was silent for several long, agonizing minutes. "There are things I must think about. We will speak of this further tomorrow."

It wasn't what Aria wanted to hear, but she knew she should be grateful that Babette might be willing to help her at all. And it was a relief that at least one person knew her secret.

"Let us return before the men begin to worry," Babette said. "Behave just as you have been. Nothing must change until we are ready."

For the first time in days, Aria felt in control of her life again. The word *revenge* didn't sound very nice. But it seemed that getting it was the only way she could go on with her life and forget Cort once and for all.

"SHE CANNOT BE ALESE."

Yuri stared at Babette, certain that he couldn't have heard her correctly. *This* was what she had made him swear never to reveal? He knew her to be a sensible woman who was usually free of the pleasant illusions that imprisoned most of mankind, but she could be as irrational as any female under the right circumstances. Their frequent arguments were a testament to her lack of judgment where Aria was concerned.

Or perhaps this was only a new tactic in her subtle war to convince him to defy di Reinardus.

"It is true," Babette said, coming to sit in the chair near the bed. "She never lost her memory. Though it appears she was ignorant that other *loups-garous* existed before she came to America, nor did she know how to find her countrymen here. She does not recognize the names Alese or di Reinardus. She left her home only a few months ago, and thus could not have lived with the Reniers or been stolen by the duke."

It was a ploy, surely. A ploy to throw him off guard and sow doubts in his mind. But he refused to be baited. He folded his arms across his chest and shook his head.

"Give up this game, Babette. It will do you no good."

"It is no game." She looked at him from under half-closed lids. "Of course I understand why you do not wish to believe me. It must be difficult to accept that Aria has deceived you all this time."

Yuri snorted. "I had my doubts about her claims of amnesia from the beginning. That hardly means that she is not—"

"Think, *mon ami!* Think of what this could mean if we use this information wisely. It might be possible to trick di Reinardus, fool him into—"

"Trick him?" Yuri felt his skin flush, and he realized that Babette's conviction was beginning to have its effect. "The *trick* is how this girl appears identical to the princess and happened to be born in the same country!" He got up from the bed and paced across the room. "Perhaps you have noticed the birthmark on her back?"

"Of course. What of it?"

"It is the mark of the Carantian royal line."

"Why did you not tell me before?"

"It would have made no difference. The point is that it is very likely the girl is lying *now*."

"But why?" Babette held out her hands. "Only think, Yuri. She would have had to perform an astonishing masquerade to appear the bumpkin if she was raised a lady as the real Alese was. The fact that she was apparently brought up in strict isolation explains so many things. If she escaped di Reinardus four years ago, why did she not attempt to return to the Reniers before? She knows nothing of your original plan to seek a reward for returning her, much less your intention to offer her to di Reinardus. Why should she go along with all these lessons and submit to so many rules and restrictions if she already knows everything I can teach her?"

"Why should she submit to them if she knows she cannot return to the Reniers as their lost cousin?"

"The man who raised her is dead. She wants a family, Yuri. That was reason enough to continue the masquerade."

"Then why would she tell you the truth now?"

"The deceit had become too great a burden for her."

Yuri returned to the bed and stared unseeingly at the mismatched patchwork of the quilted bed cover. "If you are so certain of her honesty," he said, "how do you account for her identical appearance to Alese di Reinardus?"

"There is only one way to account for it," she said. "There are two princesses."

Yuri had already been prepared for just that answer, but it still jarred him like a billy club to the back of the skull. "Two princesses," he muttered.

"It makes perfect sense," Babette said. "A queen desperate to save her children from a ruthless enemy. One child sent to America. The other raised in obscurity in the mountains of Carantia, with no knowledge of the existence of her own kind or kin, forbidden to venture into the more populated areas where someone might recognize her…."

It did make sense, he had to admit. Clever to send one heir to the opposite side of the world, leaving the other hidden under the very nose of her potential enemies. Di Reinardus had certainly never suspected there might be more than one princess. There had never been even a single rumor to that effect.

"But why did her guardian bring her to American now?" Yuri asked. "Alese disappeared years ago. Did *he* know of her? Could there have been some new movement from the loyalists to regain the throne, perhaps among these Carantians she was to meet?"

"Aria certainly can't tell us," Babette said. "She has never indicated that she knows anything of Carantian royalty, past or present."

"And these Carantians were obviously not in San Francisco. Cort is aware of every werewolf in the city, and he never mentioned foreigners."

"Perhaps they had moved to another location."

Perhaps. Di Reinardus had never mentioned anything about them, either. The Reniers had hidden the princess for years; di Reinardus had told Yuri of their connection to the Carantian di Reinardii before the abduction, which explained their willingness to conceal and protect the true heir to the throne.

But they could not have restored her to her rightful place without the aid of the Carantians themselves, and Yuri had never seen any sign of such men in New Orleans. They could hardly be a threat if they could not be found.

In any case, their existence was not at issue now. Gunther di Reinardus's ambitions were all that mattered. How in hell did Babette think they could use Aria's existence to trick di Reinardus? Yuri would still have to deliver a girl with a certain birthmark to the duke at the proper time.

Oh, di Reinardus would be surprised, perhaps even shocked, to learn the girl was not Alese, but he would quickly overcome such feelings and forge ahead with his plans. He might have lost one princess, but a twin sister would do just as well.

"Yuri?" Babette said. "Are you listening to me? If we could stall di Reinardus and find these Carantians, it might be possible to stop him. Together with the Reniers, we could—"

"Stall di Reinardus? He has men in Placerville even now, waiting for me to send the signal that we are ready to turn Alese over to them."

"Hear me out, Yuri. If we were to tell Cort the truth about di Reinardus and make Aria understand who she is…"

"You are insane, woman!" Yuri swung toward her and took her by the shoulders, digging his fingers into her tender flesh. "If you value our lives, say *nothing* of this to Cort. Do you know what he would do if he even suspected the deal I've made with di Reinardus? He would kill me and take Aria straight to New Orleans."

"Knowing that the duke would surely follow?"

"You expect rationality from a man driven by passions

you know nothing about. When he first agreed to return Lucienne to the Reniers, he did not do it merely for the reward we would claim. He did it for a far more primitive reason. Revenge."

"Qua?"

"You heard me. Eight years ago he had a lover from within the family, a woman he believed would marry him. She rebuffed him instead."

Babette gave him an incredulous look. "That is all?"

"How can you, with all your vast experience, doubt how far jealousy and hatred will drive a man?"

"But why hatred? *Why* did this woman reject him? He is a gentleman, very handsome and *loup-garou*. He is, to be sure, not a wealthy man, but…" She rubbed her bare arms. "Did she have another suitor?"

"Doubtless she did, but that was hardly the issue. He was not one of *them,* Babette."

Her expression cleared. "Of course. He belongs to one of the other Renier clans. And that was enough cause for this woman to reject him?"

"More than enough."

"And yet in all this time, Cort has never indicated…" She shook her head. "I can scarcely believe a man of his obvious stature would let himself carry a grudge so violent that he would still be seeking revenge after so many years."

A man of his stature. Yuri chuckled. "Your ignorance of *loups-garous* blinds you. The New Orleans Reniers have little to do with any of the other clans, but there is one branch they despise above all others. Cort Renier was born in the bayous, one of the "mud Reniers," as the city Reniers call them. They are said to be more wolf than human. Cort—Beau, as he called himself then—was an unlearned, unwashed boy when Madeleine Renier amused herself by dallying with him."

"Cort was…not a gentleman?"

"No more than you were a lady. He looked above his station, and the New Orleans clan could not forgive him. They beat him and threw him out on his ear when he dared offer marriage. He is not one to forget such a humiliation."

"But his behavior now…his manner, his speech…"

"I made him into what he is today. Though I admit he was an extraordinarily good student. He came to despise his low origins as much as those who rejected him. He even turned away from the werewolf in himself, just as the New Orleans clan have done. He was determined to become in every way their equal, and the ignorant world would doubtless say he has succeeded."

It took Babette several long moments to absorb this shocking new information. "So Cort intends to flaunt the fact that he found the girl when none of the Reniers could do so, as well as demand money for her return," she murmured.

"He intends to force them to acknowledge him as an equal," Yuri said.

"And he believes that will make him happy?"

"What is happiness? He can never return to what he was. Revenge is all he has left."

Babette turned in a slow circle, head bent in thought. "You speak of passions, Yuri, but there are others just as powerful as hatred, as *I* have cause to know. Have you never noticed the attraction that exists between Aria and Cort?"

Yuri stared at her. He had made a stab in the dark when he'd accused Cort of "dalliance" with Aria on the way to the lodge, but he hadn't really believed that any such thing had happened. Cort knew what was at stake. Oh, he might lust after the girl and seek to avoid her for that reason, but he would never ruin their scheme because he couldn't keep his cock inside his trousers.

Or would he?

"I've noticed it," Yuri said shortly, "but Cort would never jeopardize our plans by—"

"Why should he consider it jeopardizing your plans?" Babette asked with a mocking quirk of her lips. "He could hurt the Reniers even more by making Aria his lover."

"Are you saying that they—"

Yuri struck the bedpost with his fist. Cort would not have made such a decision on his own. He and Yuri were partners. They were…

Friends?

But are you not ready to betray him? he asked himself. *Why should he not do the same to you if his self-interest demands it?*

"Could he have made the girl pregnant?" he demanded.

"I do not think it has gone quite that far," she said.

"I will speak to Cort," Yuri said. "I'll make him tell me—"

"You are too angry," Babette said. "You will not improve the situation by attacking him."

Yuri had to admit that she was right. Oh, di Reinardus would be furious if Cort had taken Aria's virginity, but there was no reason Yuri had to tell him, *or* confront Cort about it. Even if the girl *was* pregnant, Yuri had no intention of being anywhere on this continent by the time it became obvious. The whole matter would soon be out of his hands.

"I will wait," Yuri said.

"There are some things that cannot wait," she said. "I would not have become a part of this if I had known that Aria was to become a tool for vengeance. I am not proud that I was prepared to take money to teach her so that you could sell her back to the Reniers. But I thought then that she was Lucienne Renier. Nothing is as I believed it to be." She met his gaze. "It has gone too far, Yuri. We must tell them."

Yuri got up, strode across the room and seized Babette by the shoulders once again.

"It's too late to back out now," he said, giving her a hard shake. "Do you understand me, Babette? Say nothing to Cort or Aria, not a single hint of anything we have discussed."

She blinked, and he knew she understood how very serious he was. "I will say nothing," she whispered.

Yuri let her go. "Good. Now you are being sensible. You must give me time to consider all you have told me." He tucked his chin into his chest. "Perhaps there is a way."

It was hardly a promise, but Babette offered no further argument and left the room without a backward glance.

He was glad of that. He had not controlled her nearly as well as he had hoped, expecting that her love for him would be enough. He should have remembered how incredibly stubborn she could be.

Still, she would not betray him. However strong her feelings for Aria, she was not prepared to abandon him. No matter what he decided to do next.

CHAPTER FIFTEEN

THE NEW LESSONS began the next evening.

Babette had considered the situation long and hard, but in the end there had been only one possible decision.

In spite of her promise to Aria, she had felt compelled to reveal some of the other woman's secrets to Yuri in hopes that he could be persuaded to turn against di Reinardus. Now she was glad she had. Yuri had said he would reconsider his plans, and she had learned a few essential facts that gave her a new and very vital perspective on the entire situation.

The entirely unexpected information about Cort's desire for revenge had altered everything. In spite of his cold behavior, Babette was no longer in any doubt that he felt far more for Aria than he was willing to reveal, and she was equally sure that it was not merely a question of lust. Whatever he and Aria had done together in the past, Cort had chosen to reject her rather than use her as he so easily could have done.

Gentleman or no, he was *not* without honor. And that gave Babette hope. If there was any way out of this grotesque mélange of greed, competing schemes, revenge and hidden identities, there was one emotion that made life worth living.

Love.

People in love made sacrifices for their loved ones.

A man in love would protect his lady against anyone who would harm or use her for any purpose. He would do whatever was necessary to see to her happiness.

Cort might not be an aristocrat. He was certainly not without his own considerable flaws of character. But he could save Aria from Yuri and di Reinardus or anyone else who sought to use her. Once he understood who and what she was, he alone might give Aria the chance to choose her own future.

And Aria would have to make such a choice, a choice that would define her life forever, once she learned the truth.

Babette knew in her heart that Aria would be better off if she were never to meet the Reniers or these mysterious Carantians—if di Reinardus were to vanish, and she never had to deal with the ambitions and desires of those involved in the politics of a country divided. Aria clearly had no knowledge of royalty, nor could she possibly conceive of what the life of a princess might be like. She hated the bonds of formality and ceremony, and loved her freedom almost too dearly—freedom she would surely lose if she ever became a princess in truth.

Yes. It would be better for Aria, far better, if she rejected such a future. And if she were willing to forgo the dubious privileges of royalty—if Cort loved her enough—he would also be free to forget old wounds and become who *he* was meant to be. Not a man desperate to assume the very image of his enemy, but one at peace with himself, his past and his future.

But first Cort had to recognize the depth of his feelings for Aria. If desire was the only way to make him acknowledge such feelings, then Aria's own plan for revenge could become a means of reconciliation.

And so, after the next day's regular lessons were finished, Babette began to teach Aria the ways of seduction.

"YOU ARE READY," Babette said at the end of the seventh day. "We might refine technique, of course, but there is no more I can teach you. Your instincts will do the rest."

Aria closed her eyes, took a deep breath and let it out again. It had been a strange and exhilarating week. Neither Cort nor Yuri was aware of what went on when the women retired to Babette's room. Cort stayed away except when Babette expressly asked for his assistance, and Yuri continued to drink. If they saw any change in Aria, it was only because she put extra effort into her "lady lessons."

Sometimes Aria was astonished by what she learned about sex. Nothing really upset her, though she was sometimes puzzled by the various things a woman did to arouse a man.

But was it so different from what Cort had done to *her?* She could still recall every moment of their time together in exquisite detail. He had made her feel very, very good. And she quickly decided that the "tricks" Babette taught her would be pleasurable for her as well as for Cort. After the first few days she had found herself squirming from the constant ache between her legs and envisioning everything Babette described with eager anticipation.

It made less sense to her than ever that any woman would be ashamed to do these things, as Babette had suggested more than once. But she took Babette's word that she must always be cautious about whom she spoke to about her newfound skills. Her "family" would certainly never know.

Now, as Aria contemplated the night to come and the sweetness of revenge, Babette stood by the window, very quiet and oddly subdued.

"You must understand," the other woman said, "that there is no guarantee of success. It may be that Cort will not respond."

Aria pulled her hair forward over her face and looked through the golden veil. "You said that no man would be able to resist me."

"What you are about to do may hurt you as well as Cort."

But Aria had already faced the worst that could happen. "Once it is over," she said, "he can never hurt me again."

"Very well." Babette sighed. "You will borrow my nightdress. It is far more...provocative than yours. It will certainly catch Cort's attention. After that..."

It would be up to Aria.

That night at dinner Aria was far too excited to eat. Once or twice Cort glanced across the table with a slight frown, as if he wondered what was going through her mind. She had been very careful with her table manners and everything else Babette had taught her. She wanted Cort to see her as composed and elegant and flawlessly correct.

She wanted Cort to be surprised when he found her in his room.

As usual, Cort went out into the woods after dinner. Aria had often wondered what he did when he wasn't hunting for fresh meat, but she knew better than to follow him. He would not welcome her company.

Tonight, that would change.

Near midnight, at the time when Aria usually heard Cort return to the lodge, she bathed and put on Babette's sleeveless nightgown. The sheer silk and lace flowed over her body like a second skin, a single layer that was as soft and light as her own nightgown was thick and heavy. It made her feel daring. And irresistible.

Careful to make sure that Yuri didn't see her—though she doubted he could see anything, since he had drunk too much again—Aria crept down the hall and into Cort's room. His scent was everywhere. She wandered around the dark room, touching the few objects that belonged to him: the two good suits he wore when he was indoors, his shaving kit, his traveling bag. Then she lay facedown on his bed and drank in the smell of the sheets, burrowing as deep as she could and squeezing the pillow against her chest.

Her nipples grew hard, and she moaned. The sound of the front door brought her out of her wonderful dream. Her heart began to race like a wolf on a rabbit's tail. Taking a deep breath, she got off the bed, smoothed her gown and listened as Cort climbed the stairs.

She heard him pause outside the bedroom door. He could smell her now; perhaps he thought it was only the scent drifting from her room or lingering in the hallway. She held her breath. The door handle turned.

Cort took a step into the room, saw her and froze. Aria tried to smile seductively, but all she could do was look at his face, at the way it changed from shock to uncertainty to something she had wanted very badly to see.

But he didn't come to her. He didn't open his arms and embrace her and kiss her. His expression closed, and he backed away, bumping hard into the door frame as he fumbled his way out of the room.

No. Aria stared at the empty doorway, sick inside. It couldn't end this way. She wouldn't let it.

Clenching her fists, she started toward the door. She was nearly there when Cort strode back into the room. Without a word he seized her and kissed her with bruising force. She laced her hands in his hair and answered with a kiss fully as ferocious as his own.

HE SHOULD HAVE seen it coming.

Cort drew back, licking Aria's sweet taste from his lips. His mind was in a daze, his body entirely out of his control. Only a small part of him was sane enough to realize how stupid he had been.

All his efforts to escape his desire had failed. There was no way to outrun it. There was no forgetting that day on the way to the lodge, even if he'd really wanted to.

Aria was far more than merely beautiful now. He had seen her naked, but in the sheer nightdress she was a wanton goddess, blond hair sweeping over her bare arms, brown nipples pushing against the silk like emerging buds in spring. She was every man's dream of the perfect lover, eager to give him all he could possibly desire.

"Cort," she murmured.

His name was an invitation, a whisper of seduction. He had known for weeks that she was no longer the girl he'd once thought her, but in his mind he had refused to let her become fully a woman.

Now there was no doubt. She was a woman, and she had become a lady. A lady she had left behind in the drawing room, as she had discarded her ladylike garments for the wisp of fabric that left almost nothing to the imagination.

Cort took a step back. Aria murmured a protest.

"Let me look at you," he said, hardly aware of the growl in his voice.

Aria blushed a little, but her bold gaze never left his. He let himself look his fill, taking in the lush fullness of her lips, the column of her graceful neck and the pulse beating so fast under her velvet skin, the strong but unmistakably feminine slope of her shoulders.

And below, where her breasts swelled and peaked, revealing her own desire just as her shining eyes did. Her slender waist, which had never needed a corset. The shadow between her thighs, as pale as her hair.

Aria ran her hands over her body, molding the silk to her belly and hips and thighs. "Do you like it?" she asked.

"What?" he asked, trying to catch his breath.

"The nightgown," she said.

"It's…lovely," he said hoarsely.

"I thought you'd think so," she said.

Laughter lodged in his throat. Was that what concerned her? Whether or not he liked her nightgown?

He closed his eyes. He had one more chance to walk away. A thread of discipline, more fragile than a spider's web, still stretched behind him through the open doorway.

Why was she doing this? Had she abandoned pride entirely? Was she trying to trap him into something they would both regret?

Even if she was, he knew he was fighting a losing battle. He heard Aria move, felt her hands brush his chest. He never wore a collar, tie, vest or coat when he went out to the woods; there was no one there for whom to play the gentleman. Aria's small fingers began to work at the buttons of his shirt, undoing the uppermost and tracing the exposed skin with her fingernail.

Cort ground his teeth as she replaced her fingers with her mouth, kissing his skin as she worked at the second button. As she undid each one she left a trail of little kisses, and when the placket was open she reached inside and cupped his pectorals, rubbing her thumbs over his nipples in slow, deliberate circles.

Cort swallowed, not daring to watch what she was doing. Where in hell had she learned all this? The first time they'd been together, he'd taken charge, and she had accepted what he had to give without trying to return the favor. Her few attempts had been tentative and awkward, though she had enjoyed his attentions with shameless abandon.

There was nothing awkward about her now. She tugged the tail of his shirt from the waistband of his trousers, pushed it up and kissed him again, first under the arch of his ribs and then lower, stroking her hands up and down his back.

He had been at full attention the instant he'd seen her in his room, but the pain became more acute with every caress. When she began to unbutton his trousers, he was too stunned to stop her. There were no undergarments to contain him, and in a blistering moment of shock he felt her hands on him, closing around him, working up and down with exquisite gentleness.

The thread of discipline snapped as she took him into her mouth, enfolding him in warmth and wetness. She knew exactly what to do, though he had been certain she'd never been with another man. Her tongue danced, and he could feel himself edging closer and closer to completion.

But he refused to let himself go. Instead, he stepped

back, though it nearly killed him to do it, and swept Aria up in his arms. She clung to him, burying her face in his neck, licking the perspiration from the hollow of his throat. He could smell her arousal, an aphrodisiac as potent as her mouth on his cock.

It would have been the work of seconds to part her thighs and take her. But the instant he had her on her back she slipped away, supple as a mink, and somehow ended up on top of him.

"There's no hurry," she purred into his ear, her hair sweeping over him. "I am not finished."

No words from any woman's lips had ever seemed so exciting. She quickly followed promise with action, beginning with a deep, lingering kiss and an eager welcoming of his tongue into her mouth.

But she didn't let him get any further. Her small, strong hands pressed down on his shoulders as she proceeded to caress him with her lips and tongue in a manner almost identical to the way he had pleasured her in the woods.

It was quite a different experience, however, to be on the receiving end. Women had done such things to him before, but not with such complete devotion. Aria treated every inch of his flesh as if it were the rarest delicacy. She found his nipples, teasing them with her teeth, and then continued to the hollow beneath his ribs and the ridges of his stomach. Each little bite left a delicious sting in its wake.

Again he tried to roll her over, very much afraid that he wouldn't be able to control his body much longer. Aria proved just how well she could resist him when she'd set her mind on it. Lower and lower with lips and tongue and teeth until she sucked him in again.

Aria didn't need anyone to tell her that Babette's training had succeeded. Cort groaned as she took him deep into her mouth and did what she had done before, this time kneeling over him with her hair tumbling over his stomach and her breasts stroking his thighs.

Babette had told her what might happen if she moved too quickly or Cort became too excited, but he stayed very still and hard while she explored the part of him Babette had called a "cock." It didn't remind her of a rooster at all, except perhaps in its pride. It felt very smooth and pleasant in her mouth, and she liked even better how helpless Cort was to resist. He didn't even try. Not until he reached up to spear his fingers through her hair.

"Aria," he gasped, "if you don't stop now…"

So she stopped. She slid up his body, propped herself up on her arms and offered her breasts to his mouth.

It was as wonderful now as it had been in the forest, but once again she was in control. She moved up and down, stroking her nipples over his lips, pinning his arms with her thighs so that he couldn't pull her closer. He strained to devour her, and she doled his sweets out to him as her own body protested her restraint.

There were many other things she could have done after that to please him and herself, but she had nearly run out of her own patience. The joining she had wanted so badly before was so close now. All she had to do was…

Cort freed his hands and locked them around her waist, and she realized he was going to do it before she could.

"No," she said, staring into his eyes. "Let me."

Rising up, she straddled him, moving down until she was positioned right over his cock. She eased down with a sigh until she felt his hardness inside her, pushed lower until he filled her completely.

She had understood what the physical act involved, but what she had imagined bore no resemblance to the reality. It was as if she were finally whole. Babette had warned her that there might be pain, but she felt quite the opposite. She felt glorious.

Cort shuddered as she began to move up and down, pulling away and then impaling herself again. Cort grasped her waist as if he were afraid she might stop.

But Aria never wanted this to end. That feeling was building up in her again, that humming that would soon become a roar and send her flying into the heavens. She closed her eyes and flung back her head, waiting for the moment when Cort's body would tell her that he was ready, too.

Suddenly Cort moved, dragging her off, rolling her to her side and then to her back. They were apart only for a few seconds, and then he thrust into her.

Aria was far past caring who was in charge now. She wrapped her legs around Cort's waist and let him set the rhythm. When the moment came, she could no longer tell where he ended and she began. Cort stiffened, trembled and gasped. Aria felt his muscles relax as her body quivered, and she wept with joy.

Cort kissed Aria's damp forehead, her lips and her chin, sated and grateful beyond measure. She smiled dreamily, her eyelids heavy as she gazed at him with love.

"Did you like it?" she murmured.

He laughed in his chest and stroked a damp strand of golden hair away from her lips. "What do you think?"

She grinned, stretched her arms high above her head

and squeezed her thighs around his waist. "Do you want to do it again?"

Cort's body might have been tempted, but his mind had other ideas. There was no question this time of getting up or turning away from her as he had in the forest. He was no longer capable of such an act.

He rolled onto his back and pulled her against his side, sighing deeply as she rested her head on his chest, entwined her leg with his and curled her arm around his shoulder.

The situation he'd wanted to avoid had come to pass, and he couldn't regret it. Aria had bound herself to him, and he to her. It was no longer a matter of simply presenting her to the Reniers, and forcing them to acknowledge him and pay him for her return. The prospect of hurting them further by revealing how he had taken her virginity was even more impossible to contemplate.

He could see only one solution. He had a chance to make things right once and for all time. Even if he didn't want to do it.

But he *did* want it. That was the great irony. Aria had never made any real demands of him. He had given her shelter and clothing, and a chance to be with her family again, but he had taken far more. He wanted to give her something that couldn't be bought.

Not love. He'd told her the truth about Madeleine, and he had learned his lesson well. But he *could* surrender the purpose that had driven him when everything else had been lost.

And he could give her affection, belonging, the things she most hungered for. It would not be so difficult. He could settle down and provide her with a decent life.

If that was what *she* wanted.

"What are you thinking about?" Aria asked, tracing a lazy spiral across his chest with her fingertip.

Cort nuzzled her hair. "The future."

She went very still. "Whose future?"

"Yours. And mine."

Her breath stirred the hair on his chest. "You mean… together?"

"What else could I mean?"

With a little squeal of joy, she leaped on top of him and showered his face with kisses. He tried to hold her off, but it was a losing battle.

"Be calm, *chère,*" he said with a chuckle. He wrapped his arm around her waist, amazed to find that her weight on his body seemed to lift the burden from his heart.

Could it be that he was happy? Could she, this innocent wanton, have done this to him so easily?

No, not easily. Not easily at all.

He pulled her closer, and kissed her lips and nose and forehead, then lifted her with both hands and tucked her against his side again. "What do you want, Aria?"

Her eyes widened as if she couldn't believe he'd had to ask the question. "I want to be with you forever!"

How in God's name had he ever come to deserve such selfless devotion? She didn't even know what he really was, how much his determination to make her into a lady had to do with his own bitter transformation.

"Do you know what that means, to be together?" he asked softly.

She nodded with such force that her hair went flying. "Yes."

"It means…you won't be going to the Reniers."

"I'm glad," she said.

Only two words, but they were so earnest that Cort found it difficult to disbelieve them. Aria was willing to give up everything for *him*. Whether or not she'd once longed to be reunited with her family, she didn't care anymore.

Or so she said.

"Listen to me," he said, turning to rest on his elbow so he could see her face. "You would be wealthy, surrounded by family eager to give you everything you could ever want."

"But *you* wouldn't be there."

"No."

"Then I don't care what they could give me."

"And what of their loss? Will you be at peace knowing they'll go on believing you may have died eight years ago?"

She squirmed, avoiding his eyes. He could see she felt badly about letting them think she had vanished forever. But she finally shook her head, slowly this time, and met his gaze.

"They have lived without Lucienne this long," she said. "They must have accepted that she is never coming back. How can they be hurt if they don't know?"

Cort stroked a lock of blond hair out of her face. *They* wouldn't be hurt. Not by her *or* him. The New Orleans Reniers would never suffer the consequences of what they had done to him. What Madeleine had done.

The vivid image of Madeleine Renier's laughing face came back to him. Laughing at him as her brothers and cousins beat him to the ground. A worm who'd dared to look up at a butterfly. *Payson,* they'd called him. Peasant.

A shudder of hatred ran through him, plunging his soul into a bath of acid. The happiness he had felt for so short a time dissolved. He rolled onto his back and threw his arm over his eyes.

If he told Aria, would she understand? Would she forgive him for his deception, his plans to use her, his commitment to a vengeful cause that could never be hers? Could *he* forget so much of his life, or would his bitterness eventually overwhelm what he felt for her and she for him?

If he never confronted the Reniers, could he live with his own self-contempt?

"You're unhappy," Aria said, pulling his arm away from his face. "Why? Did I...do something wrong?"

God. Would she always be afraid of his judgment every time he fell into a mood? She didn't deserve that. *He* didn't deserve *her*.

"Non, chère," he said. "Never. But..."

"Tell me."

Her hair was like a shroud over his face, hiding the secrets he knew he wasn't ready to share. He sank even further into his cruel memories.

He couldn't simply walk away from them. They had to be expunged, and there was only one way to do it. He could still get his revenge. Present Aria as his wife. The worst that could happen was that they would turn on her for agreeing to marry him, but that hardly mattered. He would make it up to her. He would make her happy, even if it took the rest of his life.

"Aria," he said, "I think we should go to see your family."

"But why? I know you don't like them." She bit her lip. "You never planned to see them when we went to New Orleans, did you?"

He touched her cheek. *"You* need to see them, Aria, and they need to meet you. If we don't go, you'll regret it for the rest of your life."

Her silence was an accusation, as if she had seen

through his lies. But when she spoke again, she was resigned.

"I don't have to stay with them, do I?"

"No, *mon amour*. You will not have to stay." Cort held her face between his hands and smiled. "Aria, will you marry me?"

AT FIRST THE WORDS made no sense. Aria listened for their echo in the quiet that followed, repeating them to herself until she was certain she hadn't misunderstood.

She had won. Not revenge, but everything she had ever wanted.

"Yes," she said, the word starting as a whisper, growing louder with each repetition. "Yes, yes, *yes!*"

Cort pulled her down, pressing her face into his neck so she couldn't see what he was feeling.

But he must love her. He wouldn't ask her to spend the rest of her life with him if he didn't.

And she couldn't ruin this wonderful moment by telling him that she wasn't Lucienne Renier. If she had to go to New Orleans to make Cort happy, she would pretend. Just for a while. And *then* tell him, when it was over.

Even the guilt of deceiving him for a few more weeks couldn't mar her happiness. "When?" she asked.

"I think you're ready now." He sighed. "You've exceeded my greatest expectations. I—"

She pulled out of his embrace. "I don't mean when are we going to New Orleans. I mean when can we be married?"

He frowned in thought. "There must be someone in Placerville," he said. "A justice of the peace, or a minister of some kind."

It wasn't so terribly far to Placerville. And they would be together, truly together, before they ever went to New Orleans.

The laughter fizzed in her chest and bubbled out. "Can we leave tomorrow?"

He didn't answer, but she was satisfied. There were no more questions in her mind. Tomorrow, the next day… it would happen soon.

"Can I tell Babette?" she asked.

"Let me speak with her first."

"But how can I keep it a secret when I see her in the morning?"

"There are many things you'll have to hide from now on," he said gravely. "You must still be a lady with the Reniers."

"But why, if we aren't staying?"

"Do it for me," he said, his warm hand cupping her chin. *"S'il vous plaît."*

Anything. Anything at all for him, even if she didn't completely understand the reason.

"All right," she said. "But promise me one thing."

A guarded look came over his face, but she forged ahead. "You must learn to like being a wolf."

The sound he made was almost a laugh. "I promise to try," he said, and grew serious again. "It will be my wedding present to you."

It was the most natural thing in the world to kiss him and start the loving all over again.

"WE'RE TO BE MARRIED."

Cort's blunt statement came as a shock, though Babette should not have been surprised. She had hoped for this very result. Hoped, but not quite dared to believe.

She had certainly never considered revealing her hope to Aria.

But the young woman had done much more than what she had set out to do. She had captured a man who displayed all the characteristics of a perennial bachelor, a man who had never needed to worry about anyone but himself…a man so driven that he was half-blind to the world around him.

Was it possible that he really *had* fallen in love with Aria?

"Congratulations," Babette said, extending her hand. "I am happy for both of you."

Cort didn't look happy. He took her hand and immediately let go. "Thank you," he said. "We will be leaving for Placerville tomorrow morning, where we will be married. If you wish to accompany us…"

"Of course I wish it. It is a pity that there can be no real wedding, but…" She shrugged. "Someone must give the bride away."

"Then you will be welcome."

There was something in his tone that kept her on edge, and she knew she had to approach her next questions very delicately.

"What will you do afterward?" she asked.

He walked away from her, hands knotted behind his back. "We will go to New Orleans, as we planned."

Her heart sank. "May I ask why?" she said.

"She should meet her family."

That was hardly an answer, but Babette feared his honesty. She had speculated that Cort might make Aria his lover so that he could flaunt his conquest in the Reniers' faces. How much more terrible for them when he presented "Lucienne" as his bride.

But surely that was not why he had offered to marry

her. Surely he would not go through with his revenge once Aria was his wife. He could not be so cruel.

She had promised Yuri not to tell Cort what she had discovered about Aria, and the hope that Yuri would change his mind about helping di Reinardus had kept her quiet. But now it was time to admit part of the truth. The part that might convince Cort to abandon any idea of meeting the other Reniers.

She paused to assure herself that Yuri was still occupied with his bottle in the dining room.

"Let us sit down," she said.

Something in her tone must have alerted him, because Cort shot her a glance full of suspicion.

He had a right to be concerned. This would be much worse than he imagined.

"Please, *monsieur,*" she said.

He gestured toward the sofa, and she took a seat. He chose one of the chairs and sat on the edge, his body nearly vibrating with tension.

"I will get directly to the point," she said. "I have recently learned that Aria is not who we believe her to be."

To his credit, Cort did not become angry with her, or with Aria—at least not openly. He listened with his gaze fixed on Babette, revealing nothing of his feelings. She told him everything Aria had told her: about her childhood and youth in a distant European country, her guardian's plan to find others like her in America, his death and her journey to San Francisco in search of *loups-garous* like herself. And her false claim that she had lost her memory.

The one thing she didn't tell him was that Lucienne Renier had in fact been Alese di Reinardus, lost princess of Carantia…and of her certainty that Alese wasn't the only royal heir. It was far too much for one man to accept all at once.

But Cort was far from stupid. "If Aria isn't Lucienne," he said, "why did Yuri claim they were identical in appearance? Why does Brecht believe she is a Renier?"

Babette could not entirely avoid the subject, so she shared another small part of the truth. "It seems to me," she said, "that Aria must in fact be related in some way to the Reniers. Yuri has said that they have connections in Europe, though they may not have the same surname. It is possible that even distant relatives could share a certain similarity of appearance."

Cort stared at her, and she could see the thoughts working behind his eyes like the cogs of some intricate machine. "If that is so," he said slowly, "her guardian could have been looking for the Reniers all along. But why was she living alone in this Carantia if she had kin in America? What became of her parents? Why did her guardian plan to bring her to California instead of New Orleans?"

"Aria never knew these things, and her guardian failed to tell her before he was killed in an accident in New York. She doesn't know the names of those her guardian sought or where to find them."

"So she was prepared to go with us to the Reniers, unaware that she might be their kin?"

Babette nodded. "Surely you can understand why Aria kept the secret of her past. She did not wish to disappoint you. And she needed a family to go to." Babette met and held his gaze. "But now she has found something far better than distant relatives who might not even know she exists. She has found *you*. And you are all she wants."

Cort didn't reply.

Babette couldn't let the awful silence stand. "Can you understand?" she asked softly.

"She didn't trust me," he said. "She let me believe a lie."

"And you let her believe your only reason for helping her was pure gentlemanly concern."

He got up, took a few awkward steps across the room and turned around with the same uncharacteristic lack of grace. "Did Yuri know this?"

"I informed him after Aria told me about her real past. I was hoping to convince him—"

"That he should give up the idea of selling Aria to the Reniers? Why did you wait so long to tell *me?*"

"Perhaps I should have mentioned it earlier," Babette said without apology. "But surely you see that perpetrating such a deception on the Reniers would be a mistake."

His mouth curved in a harsh smile. "Why—if she *is,* essentially, one of them?"

"Why should you wish to put your own wife through such an ordeal?" Babette asked. She leaned forward. "Do you love her, Cort?"

The muscles in his jaw flexed. "I care for her."

"Then you cannot go through with this farce. I know you have had another reason for wanting to take Aria to New Orleans. What exactly is your revenge worth, Monsieur Renier?"

The boiling emotions he had held in check spilled over. "Damn Yuri," he snarled. "What else did he tell you?"

She decided against explaining that she knew about Cort's "low origins" in the Louisiana bayous. "I know that you were soundly rejected by a woman who is one of the New Orleans Reniers," she said. "And by her family. Yet I find it difficult to believe that mere spite—"

"Believe what you choose," Cort said. "Aria has already agreed to meet them, even though she has evidently known all along that she is not Lucienne. If she is prepared to do this—"

"She knows you were involved with another woman. Does she know this woman was one of them?"

"None of this is your business, *madame,*" he said coldly.

"But it *is* my business what you do with Aria when you are finished using her."

"She will not come to any harm."

"If you betray her, you will destroy her."

"Your part in this is nearly finished, Madame Martin. You will be paid as promised."

Like a whore who had performed her service and was to be dismissed without a thought. But *this* whore still harbored secrets that could change everything. If Babette betrayed Yuri now and told Cort who Brecht really was, surely Cort would have the sense to take Aria away immediately.

Or Cort might kill the human who had betrayed him, just as Yuri had feared.

"I do not want your money," she said. "I only want Aria's happiness. Can you promise me that?"

He turned to leave. "We will speak no more of this, *madame.*"

Babette followed him. "I promise you, if you fail to take proper care of Aria, I will—"

CHAPTER SIXTEEN

THE SOUND OF the door banging against the wall cut off her threat. Yuri staggered into the room, a bottle in his hand and a sneer on his face.

"You'll what?" he said, weaving his way toward Babette. "What can *you* do? You're nothing but a whore, after all."

In an instant Cort was between Yuri and Babette, his clenched fist half-raised. "I told you not to speak to the lady in such a manner," he said.

"I'm not calling her anything but what she is," Yuri said. "He took another swig from the bottle. "She gave herself to every man who wanted her in New Orleans. She ran the biggest brothel in the Vieux Carré." He giggled. "What d'you think about that? A whore teaching Aria to be just like her."

Cort hit him. The bottle flew from Yuri's hand, and he struck the nearest wall with a grunt of pain and surprise.

"No doubt you think yourself very clever, Baron Chernikov," Cort said. He turned back to Babette. *"Madame,"* he said quietly, "is this true?"

There was no point in denying it now. "It is."

"And did you…teach Aria how to—"

Babette looked away. "Yes."

He didn't ask her why. He merely stared at her as

if she were a cockroach he planned to smash beneath his boot.

"I congratulate you, *madame*. You convinced me that you were a true lady."

The blood seemed to rush out of her head to pool at her feet. No insult had ever seemed so awful to her, and for a moment she hated him as much as she hated Yuri.

It was on the tip of Babette's tongue to tell him then and there what Yuri planned. She was no longer thinking clearly, and Yuri deserved whatever punishment Cort gave him.

But she said nothing, and after a while Cort turned and left the room. Yuri lay slumped against the wall, his chin on his chest and saliva dribbling down his chin.

She went to stand over him. "Are you satisfied?" she asked.

He lifted his head. His eyes were bloodshot, but she could see no sign that he had been seriously injured. "Why…didn't you tell him?" he croaked.

Kneeling was no simple matter in the dress she wore, but Babette had done far more challenging things in a bustled and corseted gown. "Because I didn't want you to die," she said.

He tried to laugh, but the sound was a horrid mix of cough and groan. "I overheard all of it," he said. "I wasn't quite as drunk as you thought."

"Then you know they are to be married."

"I never would have believed it. He must think it will make his revenge all the more satisfying."

"There is no certainty that he is still intent on revenge," Babette said, clinging to her last fragile hope.

"He's waited eight years for this."

"I refuse to believe he would go to these lengths for

such a purpose. Would he be so eager to take Aria to Placerville if he were not sincere?"

Yuri braced his hands on the wall behind him and pushed himself to his feet. "Hmm. That does present a problem."

The bile rose in Babette's throat. "Di Reinardus's men?"

"*Da.*"

She remained on her knees. "And you plan to let Aria and Cort go to them like lambs to the slaughter?"

He gave her a pained look. "Did I not say I would consider the information you had given me?"

"Do you mean you won't betray them?"

"My dear girl." He took one of Babette's hands and lifted her to her feet. "Have a little faith. I have thought of a way to misdirect di Reinardus and his men while the four of us to go to Placerville. I will, of course, be placing our lives at risk, but…"

"Oh, Yuri." Babette embraced him and kissed him on both cheeks. "I knew you could not go through with it! What will you do?"

"Leave that to me. If you truly believe Cort will marry the girl, you must spend your time preparing the bride-to-be." He turned her hand and kissed her palm. "I, too, must prepare. There is one thing you can do for me…."

"Tell me."

"I will be gone the rest of this day and possibly into the night. Give any excuse you can think of, but do not let him look for me."

The tension in his voice gave Babette pause. She almost wondered if he might be lying to her.

It couldn't be so. She refused to accept that even her

love-blinded eyes could fail to recognize such blatant treachery.

"I will do all I can," she said.

He kissed her hand again. *"Spasibo, moia lubov."*

My love. Babette's heart fluttered like that of a girl given her first compliment by a young man. Yuri had never once used that word before.

But the pleasure didn't last.

Yuri let go of her hand, glanced around the room and started for the front door. He didn't even pause to pick up his bottle.

Babette shook out her skirts and returned to the sofa. For a long while she sat there, thinking, going over every one of Yuri's expressions, movements, words.

She could not be mistaken. He had chosen to do the right thing. And yet…

Babette felt carefully under the cushions for the object she had hidden there when they first arrived. The tiny pistol fit her hand perfectly. It was small, but it would be just as effective as a much larger weapon if the time ever came to use it.

THE JOURNEY TO Placerville took years.

That was the way it felt to Aria. She would have been happy to run as a wolf, carrying her clothing and necessities in a pouch around her neck, but Cort had been stubbornly opposed to the idea. Rather than take the wagon, which he rejected as too slow, he and Yuri rode the two horses Yuri had brought from Placerville when he and Babette had first arrived, while Aria and Babette rode the stolid wagon horses.

Babette had advised Aria to pack her simplest dress for the ceremony, since it was near-white and suitable for a young bride, even if she was no longer a virgin.

Aria wore her trousers for the journey, while Babette had produced a riding habit that had obviously been made for a different kind of saddle. She smiled frequently, though sometimes she seemed a little nervous. Aria felt a more than a little nervous herself.

As for Yuri, he was completely different than he had been for the past weeks. He didn't bring a bottle with him, and he observed everything with the sharp gaze she had become accustomed to before they'd arrived at the lodge. He didn't seem happy, either, but Aria hadn't expected him to be. In a way he was losing Cort to a woman he had never really liked. She could almost feel sorry for him.

It was Cort's behavior that puzzled her the most. He spoke to her with affection and smiled often. That was the problem; he smiled *too* often, and Aria glimpsed strain in his expression on more than one occasion. He rode as if he had lived in the saddle since childhood, but his body never quite lost the hint of stiffness she had seen the night after he'd told Babette of their plans.

Of course, *he'd* never been married, either, and he had lost the only other woman he had ever loved. Aria was determined never to let him regret his proposal, no matter what she had to do to make sure of it.

The first night was difficult, because she had to be close to Cort without being able to touch him. She knew it wouldn't be polite to kiss in front of Yuri and Babette, and Babette seemed to think it was important that she be on her best behavior now that she was to be a bride. The older woman sat up with Aria when she couldn't sleep, and explained the simple ceremony that would bind Aria and Cort together forever. Even that seemed silly to Aria, but it was a small enough price to pay for such a wonderful result.

On the second day Yuri fell ill. He leaned heavily over his horse's neck, swayed in the saddle and would have fallen off if Cort hadn't caught him just in time. The Russian collapsed against a tree trunk and clutched his head as if his hands were all that were keeping his skull in one piece. He resisted every effort to move him, and Cort seemed resigned to stopping early to let him recover.

Strangely enough, it was Babette who made light of Yuri's condition. "It's because he has stopped drinking," she said to Cort. "You mustn't let him delay you. I'll remain behind and see that he recovers."

Yuri chose that moment to fall unconscious, and all discussion of Cort and Aria riding on came to an abrupt end. Cort threw a blanket over the Russian and asked Aria to gather wood while he made a fire. Aria could hear him talking to Babette, and it almost seemed that they were arguing.

She wanted to listen, but she had promised Babette she would behave like a lady. When she returned to the clearing where they had made camp, neither Cort nor Babette acted particularly upset. Yuri seemed to recover very slowly, and every time it seemed that they might continue the journey, he got sick again.

On the third day Cort lost his patience. "I begin to think you are right, *madame,*" he said to Babette. "We must tie Yuri to his horse. We will run out of provisions if we don't move on."

We could hunt, Aria thought. After all, Cort had promised to try to accept the wolf side of himself.

But he wasn't ready. She needed time to teach him. And she didn't want to stay here one moment longer, anyway.

"I can ride behind him and hold him up," she offered.

Babette and Cort turned to stare at her as if they had forgotten she was there. Babette frowned.

"No," she said. "It will not do. I will remain behind with Yuri."

"I wouldn't leave you alone here," Cort said. "It is not safe."

"What possible harm could come to us?" Babette gave a little laugh. "Surely you do not suggest that these woods are inhabited by man-eating wolves."

"There are bears, *madame*. And men worse than any beast."

"I can handle that kind of beast," Babette said. "I also know how to shoot, if you'll leave me a gun."

"Cort is right," Aria said. "We can't leave you alone."

"I assure you that I can—"

"Out of the question," Cort said. "If Yuri can't travel, we'll wait another day."

Babette glanced at Yuri, who lay wrapped in his bedroll under a tree, and for a moment she looked as if she had been caught in a mountain blizzard wearing nothing but a thin gown, with no provisions and no hope of rescue.

"Aria," she said, "if you don't mind, I would like to speak to Cort alone."

"That will not be necessary," Cort said. He knelt beside the fire and pretended to tend it, though all he did was poke at the ashes with a stick. Babette stood over him, her fists clenched in her skirts.

"I would prefer to be discreet," she said, "but I will do whatever is necessary to make you see reason."

Cort threw the stick in the fire and looked up at her.

Aria could feel his anger, the dangerous kind of anger she'd seen in him when he had fought Brecht's men in the alley. After a long silence Cort turned to Aria. His eyes were as bleak as Babette's.

"Aria, please watch Yuri while we're gone," he said.

"Whatever you have to say," Aria said, "I think I should hear it."

"Forgive me," Babette said, "but it is a private matter between us."

There was nothing Aria could do but stamp her feet and behave like a child, and she had no intention of sinking so far.

"Very well," she said, with as much dignity as she could muster. "But please don't make me worry by being gone too long."

Neither Cort nor Babette smiled at her attempt at a joke. Cort got up, came over to her and laid his hand on her shoulder.

"This won't take long," he said, and kissed her forehead.

Aria grabbed his hand and tried to hold him, struck by a sense of something terribly wrong. But Cort pulled away, nodded to Babette and escorted her into the trees.

Aria crouched, picked up the end of the charred stick Cort had tossed into the fire and drew a word in the dirt at her feet.

L-o-v-e. Love. Cort still hadn't told her that he loved her. She knew that would come in time, but it was difficult to be patient. Why couldn't he talk about what he felt?

Because he was a man.

That was what Babette had said. Aria cradled her

chin in her hands and stared into the flames. Her eyelids grew heavy. She didn't want to sleep. She wanted to be awake when Babette and Cort returned. She knew very well that they were talking about *her*. This time she would make them...

An unfamiliar scent brought her out of her doze. It didn't belong to Cort or Babette or Yuri, who was snoring in his bedroll, but it definitely belonged to a man.

Before she could wake up enough to wonder who else could be in this part of the mountains, the first scent was joined by another, and another, still at a distance but approaching in a circle around the clearing. The horses tossed their heads and snorted. The sharp stink of sweat and fear seeped into Aria's skin.

She sprang to her feet. Her body quivered with the need to Change, but she couldn't afford to be without her voice. She spun and raced in the direction Cort and Babette had gone.

She found Cort running back toward camp, looking like a shepherd whose entire flock had been killed by bears or mountain cats and left to rot on the hillside. He came to a stop when he saw her, and his skin seemed to lose all its color.

Aria didn't have time to wonder why. "Someone has come," she said. "Several men. They're all around us."

Cort lifted his head to sniff the air. His face went from pale to dark in an instant, and his pupils dilated until the yellow was nearly swallowed up by black.

"Where is Yuri?" he asked.

"Still in camp. Who are they? Could they be—"

Babette ran up behind Cort, panting heavily. "Aria? What has happened?"

"Keep her here, Babette," Cort snapped, and broke back into a run.

Aria turned to follow, but Babette stopped her. "We must stay here," she said urgently. "Cort will return with the horses."

"So that we can run away?" Aria said. "Cort knows who these men are, doesn't he? Are they the same ones who followed you and Yuri?" She shook her head. "If you couldn't fool them before, nothing will stop them. We have to fight!"

"Cort won't let you," Babette said. "He cares only about getting you to safety."

"But there are so many of them, and he's alone!" Aria jerked free of Babette's hold. "I'm going!"

"Then I am coming with you."

Aria didn't wait. She stripped out of her clothes, ripping her shirt and trousers, and Changed. Sound and smell sharpened, and she could count exactly how many of the enemy had found them. Eight men, ready to attack. How could Yuri and Babette have been so wrong?

The report of a gun burst in Aria's ears, and she flung herself through the trees like a mad dog. One of their horses galloped past her as she reached the clearing, and she quickly saw that only two of the animals remained where Cort had secured them to a sapling. They were snorting and rolling their eyes in panic, straining to get away.

Cort and Yuri were facing each other over the fire, Yuri with a gun in his hand. Cort's lips were peeled back in a snarl.

"*Batard*," he said. "When I kill you, it will not be because you have betrayed our friendship, but because you meant to hurt Aria."

"I mean no harm to her," Yuri said, his voice shaking. "No more than you. She will have everything her heart desires."

"Because di Reinardus will treat her well in order to gain what he wants?" Cort shook his head. "Yes, I know his plans. Babette told me. He'll keep her in a gilded cage for the rest of her life—if he doesn't get her killed first."

Aria stopped, fur bristling. The scene made no sense to her. Why was Yuri aiming a gun at Cort? Who was di Reinardus? Babette had mentioned the name once, when Aria had told her that she couldn't possibly be Lucienne.

"Do you think *you* can provide for her?" Yuri asked. "You, with your miserable origins, and a woman of her blood?"

"I can make her happy."

"You will never get the chance. They will be here any moment."

"At least I'll take you down first. Your gun won't stop me."

"It will if I shoot you through the heart," Yuri said.

Whatever they were talking about, Aria knew there wasn't a minute to lose. She flung herself into the clearing and charged straight at Yuri.

The Russian was taken off guard just long enough. As he shot wildly in Aria's direction, Cort leaped over the fire and barreled into him, smashing the gun out of his hand. Aria jumped at Yuri's chest, forelegs stiff, and knocked him to the ground.

"Aria," Cort said, breathing heavily, "take the horses and go back to Babette. I'll keep the others occupied while you escape."

He was already beginning to remove his clothing.

He clearly realized he would have to fight as a wolf to have any chance at all. But Aria knew there were too many for one man to defeat, and that she and Babette had no chance of escaping if Cort lost, even if she were willing to leave him.

Aria Changed into human form again, knowing she had only seconds to pose the questions she needed to ask.

"Why was Yuri pointing a gun at you?" she demanded. "Who is di Reinardus?"

Cort flung his coat into the shrubbery. "There is no time for this now. Take the horses and go."

"No. You have no chance if you fight them alone."

He bared his teeth at her. "One of the men about to attack us is Brecht. He'll do everything possible to take you without injuring you. I can't protect you while I fight them."

No blood had flowed, yet Aria's senses were choked by a phantom scent of death. Brecht had come all this way after all this time to take her. Why? Just because she was beautiful and he wanted to lie with her?

And why would *he* be willing to give her everything her heart desired?

The only thing in the world she desired was Cort. If she lost him, she would lose everything. Including the will to live.

"Aria!"

Babette ran into the clearing, her face damp and flushed, and her hair half-loose. "I'm sorry, Cort. I couldn't hold her." She saw Yuri lying on the ground and gasped. "What has happened? Is he—"

"He's all right," Cort snapped. Aria knew he wouldn't tell Babette of Yuri's treachery even if there were time to do so. By now the scent of the approaching men had been joined by the sound of their heavy human tread.

Cort stepped in front of her. "Would you put Babette in danger?" he asked softly. "Brecht could take her and use her against us. You're the one who has to protect her now."

A thick ball of tears clogged Aria's throat. Cort had given her an impossible choice. But he was right. There was no one left to protect Babette. Yuri was still unconscious, and he was a traitor, as well—though she didn't know why. Had he known about Brecht coming here all along?

"Promise me," she whispered to Cort, pressing close to his warm, naked body. "Promise me that you won't die."

He took her in his arms and kissed her hard, as if this were the last time he would ever hold her. She didn't let go of him until he pushed her away.

"Follow your instincts," he said. "Find a place to hide until you can get to Placerville."

Where they were to have been married. There would be no wedding now. Perhaps not ever.

The tears spilled over. "Cort…"

"You must go to the Reniers. They *are* your family, Aria. Promise me you'll listen to Babette and do as she says."

She didn't understand him, but she had no chance to ask what he meant. A snapping twig told her that the enemy had arrived. She hugged Cort once more, turned and ran for the horses. She helped Babette mount, then flung herself up into the saddle. When she looked back, a red wolf was crouching in the clearing, ready to kill.

Or die.

YURI HAD BEEN RIGHT.

As Cort waited, his heart leaping behind his ribs, his ears pressed flat, he remembered every devastating word Babette had spoken.

Yuri's betrayal had been the least of it. Even the fact that Babette had gone along with the Russian's scheme could be forgiven, especially since she had confessed her part in it and warned Cort that Yuri might still betray them in spite of his recent promises. Cort couldn't afford to doubt her willingness to make up for her betrayal. Whore or lady, he needed her too much.

But as for the rest…

A woman of her blood. Royal blood from a tiny country Cort had never heard of until Babette had told him all the other things she and Aria had kept hidden from him.

From the first time he had met her, Cort had felt pity for the girl who had lost her memory. He'd seen her as a tool in the beginning, and then as something more. Something he didn't want to lose.

But he'd always thought of himself as her superior in every way that had mattered to him: experience, sophistication, an understanding of the world as it was. Even when he'd come to respect her intelligence and courage, he'd never doubted that he held the advantage.

Now he knew how wrong he had been. Yuri had mocked him with his miserable origins, and he'd had reason. Everything Cort had believed about Aria, about himself, was false. In that world of privilege and power Cort had so long coveted, he could never be her equal.

Oh, she didn't know it yet. She had been told nothing of her true heritage. But she would find out soon enough. Babette would explain everything as soon as they were on their way to New Orleans.

And then? Cort couldn't laugh, but he could see the humor in the situation. Aria would do what they had always planned: go to the New Orleans Reniers, who had once sheltered a girl whose real name had been Alese. Aria's twin sister.

Ironically enough, Aria's arrival among the Reniers would be a far worse shock than Cort had anticipated when he'd planned his revenge. But they would accept her in the end; that telltale birthmark would ensure it.

And then she would never want for anything again— not family, not money, not shelter, nor any of the other things that made life better than mere existence. And, one day, she might hope to find a mate worthy of her.

The thought was unbearable, but Cort took some comfort in knowing *he* was worthy enough to die for her. And he was more than willing.

Because he knew now that he loved her. Now that it was too late.

He flung back his head and howled a challenge to the one who was coming. He knew that Brecht—Duke Gunther di Reinardus—would not fight as a man. He was evidently done with leaving his vital work to human henchman. There were at least two other werewolves with him, and though there were humans, as well, Cort knew they would be used only as distractions and decoys. Once di Reinardus discovered that Aria had fled, he would go after her himself, and set his *loups-garous* and humans on Cort.

Leaves rustled and tore from their branches. Cort braced himself. A blond wolf burst out of the trees, thick coat erect and ears pricked in challenge. He went straight for Cort's throat.

His followers crowded after him, a pair of humans with guns and two werewolves, one brown and one gray.

Cort had no time to locate the other humans he sensed encircling the clearing. Di Reinardus was the most powerful *loup-garou* he had ever encountered, and soon he thought of nothing but teeth and claws and blood.

Voices called, and bullets whizzed past Cort's ears as he danced and lunged, snapping at any part of di Reinardus he could reach. Powerful jaws closed on his foreleg, and he felt the bone break. In turn he sank his teeth into the other werewolf's flank. He felt bone pop, and nearly choked on the gouts of blood his bite released.

And then, suddenly, the blond wolf was gone, and the gray and the brown had taken his place. They were neither as swift nor as powerful as the duke, and in spite of the raging pain in his leg Cort was able to hold them at bay.

All he could hope to do was prevent them from following di Reinardus in his pursuit of Aria and Babette. A bullet grazed Cort's shoulder, and the gray wolf sank his jaws into his ruff. Cort tore away, leaving a hunk of fur in the gray's mouth, and turned on the brown. There seemed little hope that he could win.

But he was desperate, and his enemies were not quite desperate enough. He beat them down one after the other, leaving them whining and whimpering with debilitating injuries, and then went for the humans. Without the *loups-garous* to protect them, the humans lost their nerve. One got off two more wild shots before he died. The other lasted a little longer and managed to shoot Cort in his left hind leg.

When he was finished with his attackers, the full pain of Cort's injuries broke through the wall he had built against it. He collapsed, gasping for breath, his broken foreleg useless and his hind leg dragging behind him.

If he remained as he was, the odds were stacked

against his survival. If he Changed, he might heal himself almost instantly, but the Change itself, in his weakened condition, could kill him.

He had no choice. If he had any chance at all of reaching Aria, he had to take it. He turned his head to look for Yuri.

The Russian was gone. Cort didn't give a damn. He bent his muzzle close to the ground, preparing himself for agony.

CHAPTER SEVENTEEN

FIRE EXPLODED IN his heart, eating its way through bone, muscle and flesh. His body twisted grotesquely, caught between two shapes, striving to Change and heal itself at the same time. Cort struggled to hold on to consciousness, but the fire had reached his brain. Aria's eyes, shining like the bright Pacific, were the last image he saw in the depths of the holocaust.

When he came to his senses again, he was human. And whole. The Change had worked its magic. He got to his feet, stretching limbs stiff and clumsy from his time spent curled on the ground, and took stock of his surroundings.

The two dead humans were still where he had left them. One of the *loups-garous* had died in wolf shape, unable to complete the Change. The other had fled, and there was no sign of di Reinardus, or the human he had smelled but never seen.

Cort knew he had wounded the duke badly enough to force him to Change and submit to a period of healing just as Cort had done. But he almost certainly wasn't dead, and Cort's preternatural senses told him that a full day and night had passed. Cort might pray that the women had outwitted the duke and gotten safely to Placerville, but as long as di Reinardus was alive, he would never stop pursuing Aria.

Cort Changed and began to circle the clearing, sifting

one scent from another until he found the right set of paw prints in the churned earth. Not far outside the clearing he discovered a bloodied depression in the dirt where di Reinardus had lain, first as a wolf and then as a man.

But it was as a wolf that di Reinardus had left after his recovery. Nose to the ground, Cort tracked the spoor into the woods, and soon he was running full out toward the west, following the trail of the man he hated most in all the world.

The two men he hated most, for after several hours of pursuit he picked up Yuri's scent, mingled with the smell of horse. Yuri and di Reinardus had not been traveling together, however; Yuri had appeared from a side trail and followed di Reinardus. Apparently he had scuttled after his master like the cur he was.

But when Cort reached another place where the ground was stained with blood, both human and were-wolf, he knew he had made the wrong assumption. There had been a struggle here, and gunshots. Two blood trails led away from the area, Yuri's first and then the duke's. One of them had decided to end their alliance.

Di Reinardus must have been badly wounded if he hadn't been able to kill Yuri outright, but he hadn't Changed this time. He'd gone after Yuri trailing blood and violent rage.

Cort burst into a run again, ears flat and tail stream-ing behind him. Soon he heard the thunder of fast-moving water, and scented wet rock and earth.

It was the river, the same one that ran alongside the wagon trail he and Aria had followed into the moun-tains. Cort sped toward it—and the lone figure who stood on the high, steep embankment overlooking the rushing water. He skidded to a stop just short of the edge of the cliff.

Yuri looked at him, his eyes blank and his body bent in pain. He held one arm cradled against his chest, and one trouser leg was shredded and soaked with blood. A gun lay discarded at his feet.

"He's dead," Yuri croaked. "I shot him."

"You wounded him," Cort growled.

"I got him…through the heart when he chased me here. He—" Yuri waved toward the cliff.

Cort Changed, watching the Russian out of the corner of his eye as he moved to the edge of the precipice. Puddles of congealing blood painted a crimson path to the rocky brink and flowed over it. The river was white with foam and choppy waves beating at massive rocks worn down by the relentless current.

"He fell," Yuri said, coming up behind him. "He hit the rocks and was carried away."

There was no reason that Cort should believe him. No reason but the evidence of his own eyes, the blond hair caught in a crack in the rocks at Cort's feet, the sunburst of blood on the stones far below.

He turned on Yuri. "If you're lying to me…"

"I didn't do it for you or the girl," Yuri said, tears in his eyes. "I hated him."

Cort bunched his fist, raised it and let it fall again. If Yuri had claimed he'd done it out of loyalty or concern for Aria, Cort wouldn't have believed him. Perhaps he had a good reason for hating di Reinardus and wanting him dead. But whether the Russian was lying or not, Cort knew he could never be sure of the man again.

"I should kill you," Cort said.

Yuri's shoulders slumped, and he looked almost longingly at the river. "Make it fast."

Cort laughed. "I *should* kill you, but I won't. You were a good friend for many years. But I warn you. Never let me see your face again."

He turned his back on the Russian, Changed and raked the earth with his hind feet as if he were covering offal. Then he ran west toward Placerville. He would look there first, but if Babette had done as he'd asked, she and Aria would already be halfway to New Orleans.

And Cort would follow. Not to propose to Aria again, or to tell her that he loved her. He would remain in New Orleans just long enough to be certain she was safe, now and for all the years to come.

GUNTHER PULLED HIMSELF out of the water, gasping with the pain of his wounds. At least he was no longer bleeding; his werewolf blood had already healed the most dangerous of his injuries. Now that Yuri was alone again, a simple Change would take care of the rest.

He tore off the sodden remnants of his clothing, tossed them on the nearest rocks and Changed. Chernikov looked on from above, looking far more the drowned cat than Gunther felt.

The man had done his job, and he would still be useful for a little while longer.

Choosing the easiest course up the steep bank, Gunther scrambled to the top. Yuri backed away and raised his hands as if to ward off death himself. He'd had enough sense to leave the gun in the grass where he'd dropped it.

Gunther Changed again. "Well done, Baron," he said. "You may very well have convinced the peasant that I am dead."

"Da," Yuri said, swallowing several times. "I think he believes."

Gunther didn't bother saying that Yuri's life depended upon Cort's belief. He didn't need to.

"You have one more task to perform," he said. "Continue on to New Orleans. I have deposited a substantial sum in the Merchants National Bank in Sacramento. Use as much as you require to hire as many *wehrwölfe* as you can find. I have my own man with strong connections to the Reniers already in place. I will give you a message for him." He sniffed the air. "I will be following very soon. Do not make any mistakes, Baron."

"I will not fail you."

"Then get your horse and make speed to Sacramento."

Yuri dragged his sleeve across his forehead, turned and started for the woods.

Di Reinardus grimaced. God grant that his ally in New Orleans would be of more use to him. Though *he* might not be quite so easy to kill when this was over.

THE BREATH-STEALING humidity struck Aria in the face like a bucket of boiling water. The train had been bad enough, but now there was not so much as a cabin wall between her and the relentless heat.

"Anna?"

Aria started at Babette's voice behind her. She stepped down from the train car, ignoring the porter's offered hand.

It was summer in New Orleans, and the temperature was high enough to drive even a werewolf to madness. In San Francisco the fog kept the air cool, clearing away in the afternoon to bless the earth with gentle sunlight.

There was nothing gentle about this place—or Aria's

thoughts. Her mind insisted that Cort must be dead or he would have caught up with them by now.

Her heart didn't believe it. If she and Babette had been able to get away from their enemies, Cort would have done the same. No matter how smart Aria had been in evading Brecht and his men, she and Babette could never have escaped and reached Placerville if Cort hadn't stayed behind and won the battle.

After reaching Placerville, they'd sold their horses and gone on to Sacramento, where they stayed hidden away in a seedy hotel in one of that city's poorest neighborhoods. Babette had been very quiet, and Aria had known she was thinking about Yuri. The last time they had seen him he'd been lying unconscious on the ground.

Had Yuri been working for Brecht all along? Why would he have done such a thing?

When she thought back, Aria realized that she had never been quite sure why Yuri was helping her and Cort find her family. She'd come to accept that Cort was doing it because he wanted to help her. Because he *cared* for her.

But Yuri *didn't* care for her. Still, whatever his reason for helping her, why would he betray Cort? And why didn't Babette know anything about what he'd been planning, when they had spent so much time together?

Aria didn't have the heart to ask her. Better for Babette to believe that Yuri had fought with Cort, not against him. At least Cort wouldn't hurt Yuri—or Aria didn't think he would, anyway. He would never forgive himself if he did.

But they didn't see Yuri again, and finally, after three days in Sacramento, Aria was certain that Cort had stopped their attackers for good.

Babette wasn't mollified. She urgently reminded Aria that Cort had wanted them to go straight to New Orleans. When Aria asked what Cort had meant when he'd said "they *are* your family," Babette told her something that didn't seem nearly the shock it should have been: that she must be directly related to Lucienne and the Reniers.

Babette explained that when Cort had come to tell her about his plan to marry Aria, she had admitted that Aria had feigned her amnesia and could not be Lucienne. Aria didn't blame Babette for telling him; she knew *she* should have done it long ago.

But it did seem odd that Cort hadn't been so much angry as puzzled and thoughtful. True, Aria had come from across the sea, but so had the Reniers many years ago. Kin long separated by time and distance could unexpectedly share a resemblance.

Whatever he had thought, Cort hadn't felt ready to speak to her about it before they left for Placerville, or along the way. That didn't bother her. She didn't care what he had kept from her. She cared only about making sure he was all right, no matter how long she and Babette had to wait in Sacramento to do it.

But Babette would not be swayed. "It was Cort's wish," she said. "We must delay no longer."

And so, after paying the hotel bill and buying the train tickets, they had purchased new clothes and necessities with the money they had left over from selling the horses in Placerville, saving the small amount of cash Babette had been carrying hidden in her clothing. Two fine ladies had boarded the Southern Pacific bound for New Orleans, one blonde and one dark, both beautiful enough to catch the eye of nearly every man they met.

How Aria had hated it.

Now, as the heavy Louisiana air stole her breath, she snapped open her parasol and indifferently watched as the porter brought their small trunk and bags from the train. Babette came up beside her.

"I have asked the porter to summon a carriage," she said. "Come into the station, Anna."

Numb with despair, Aria followed Babette inside. Travelers sat on the benches, talking or simply sitting, the men reading newspapers and the women idly plying their fans. Aria waited, unmoving, until the porter came to fetch them.

Everything about New Orleans was new and strange, even after all she had seen in San Francisco. The streets were full of people of every color, including some she hadn't seen in San Francisco. Even the simply dressed women Aria presumed were servants carried themselves with unconscious grace and elegance. The shops and buildings were festooned with delicate ironwork, pretty as the women's gowns, and the crowded markets were vibrant and colorful.

None of it left any impression. Aria stared blankly at the fancy upholstery on the opposite seat of the carriage as they rode to the hotel Babette had chosen for their first night in the city. Babette quietly reminded her that she should remain as quiet as possible and volunteer nothing about herself to anyone they met, even if someone should seem to recognize her. If it became necessary, Aria would share only a few "facts" that Babette had devised, a story that had very little to do with what had really happened since Aria had left Carantia.

"But why?" Aria had asked. "If I'm *not* Lucienne and they don't know me, why should I lie about where I came from and how I got here?"

"It will make things easier in the beginning," Babette

had said. "But it is only for today, in any case. There
are things I must tell you before we go to the Reniers.
Things I should have said before we—" She looked
down at her gloved hands. "Everything will undoubtedly
seem very strange to you, *ma chérie,* but you must trust
that Cort believed this course was best for you."

Believed. Aria found she could not even be upset at
Babette's use of the past tense. She paid little attention
as the coachmen drove along Royal Street and into the
porte-cochère of a hotel that rivaled the Palace in its
grandeur, if not its height. She stepped down to the
street, adjusting her skirts without thought. Babette took
her arm.

"This is not the finest hotel in New Orleans," she
said, "but it is quite respectable. We have just enough
money to stay a night or two if circumstances require
it, but I do not believe it will be necessary."

Aria followed Babette into the lobby, trailed by
porters with their trunk and bags. Like the Palace, *La
Court des Palmes* clearly catered to wealthy clientele.
The women were beautiful and seemed well aware of
their own worth. The men were dapper and handsome,
reminding her painfully of Cort.

He would belong in a place like this.

Almost as if she expected to find him waiting for
them there, Aria began to study the faces of those who
passed by. Many men returned her glances. Some stared.
Several smiled as they lifted their hats to her.

Babette seemed to notice the lingering stares, too.
She seemed increasingly nervous, especially after she
looked toward a particular group of men who were holding an intense conversation at the far side of the lobby.

"Let us check in and go directly to our room," she

said. "You must be hungry. We'll order a tray to be brought up as soon as we are settled."

Aria began to shake her head, but she never finished the gesture. One of the men from the group across the room, an older gentleman with a short beard, was staring in their direction with obvious interest.

"Mon Dieu," Babette whispered.

"Do you know him?" Aria asked with a spark of curiosity.

"Yes. Years ago."

"Why are you afraid?"

Babette didn't answer. The man began to walk toward her, accompanied by a much younger blond gentleman with longish hair and a suit much finer than anything Aria had ever seen Cort wearing.

"Madame Moreau!" the older man said, tipping his hat. He had an accent very different from Cort's lilt, but it still had a hint of the French in it. "What a surprise to see you in New Orleans after so many years."

Babette bowed and smiled. "Has it been so long, Monsieur Duplessis?"

"It seems an eternity."

"I have been in Denver, *monsieur.* I was married to Mr. Clive Martin four years ago."

"Married?" Duplessis raised his brows. "My congratulations, Madame Martin."

"Mr. Martin died a year ago, *monsieur.*"

"I am sorry." He cast a bemused glance at Aria, and then at the young man beside him, who had been staring at Aria all the while.

Babette seemed deeply flustered. Aria sensed that it had something to do with the etiquette of introductions, and realized that for some reason no one knew quite what to do. The seconds stretched into minutes.

"I see that we have interrupted your business, *madame*," Duplessis said. "If you will forgive us…"

"Forgive *me, madame*," the younger man cut in. "I must be unforgivably discourteous in introducing myself." He bowed. "My name is Benoit Renier. I am delighted to make your acquaintance."

Renier. Aria felt as if all the heat had been sucked out of the room. Babette inclined her head as if she were perfectly comfortable with the breach of etiquette. "It is my pleasure, Monsieur Renier," she said.

At once Renier's attention returned to Aria. "May I beg to know the name of your fair companion?"

Aria couldn't help but stare right back at him. The young gentleman's hair was only a shade darker than her own, his eyes a glacial blue. But there was nothing cold about his expression when he looked at her.

Was she actually related to him? Did he think he saw Lucienne, all grown up and magically restored? His curiosity was obviously eating him up, but Babette seemed to choke on her answer.

Aria didn't care what rules she broke. "My name," she said, extending her hand, "is Aria. Aria Renier."

CHAPTER EIGHTEEN

THE BLOOD RUSHED from Babette's heart into the soles of her shoes. This was not at all what she had planned. She had never known the Reniers or their associates to frequent the *Court des Palmes,* which was precisely why she had chosen it. Nothing in the world could have prepared her for this unexpected meeting—or Aria's response.

That response provoked such obvious shock in Benoit Renier that Babette was almost ready to call for a physician. His eagerness for an introduction had made it clear that he was too young to recognize Babette as a former courtesan.

But he was not too young to remember Lucienne—or to believe he had seen her across a crowded room.

"Mademoiselle," Benoit said, bowing unsteadily. "Your servant."

Aria curtsied. "Thank you, sir."

"Have we…have we met before?" he stammered.

"I do not believe that can be possible, *monsieur,*" she answered in a voice so cultured that no one could ever doubt that she had been born to wealth and privilege. "I have only just arrived in New Orleans."

"But…" Benoit's expression relaxed as he struggled to regain his poise. "If you are a Renier, we must be cousins, *n'est-ce pas?* Surely this cannot be coincidence?" He didn't wait for Aria to answer. "May I ask from whence you have come? Are you perhaps one of those Reniers who settled in the West? Texas, perhaps, or Arizona?"

The abrupt questions were just as rude as his forced introduction, but Aria was quick with a reply. "From even farther afield than that, *monsieur,*" she said demurely.

"Farther afield?" He leaned closer, breathing in deeply. "Surely you have not sprung from the ocean like one of Neptune's daughters?"

"I have been…separated from my family for some time," she said, lowering her gaze.

Babette knew she had let the situation get out of hand, and she had no intention of permitting further interrogation in such a public place. She had to take control, and quickly.

"We have come a long way, *messieurs,*" she said. "If you will forgive us…"

"Madame," Benoit said, pretending not to understand, "your manner of speaking…you are perhaps from New Orleans yourself?"

Babette glanced warily at Monsieur Duplessis. "I am."

"And have you known Mademoiselle Renier long?"

His behavior was unforgivable, but Babette knew where he was leading. "We were acquainted in San Francisco," she said.

"I see. Are you aware, perhaps, of the case of my cousin Lucienne Renier?"

No, this was not at all what Babette had planned. "I am, *monsieur.* A tragic loss to your family. I am sorry."

He stared at her for a moment longer and then turned

back to Aria. "Your family, *mademoiselle*...you said you were separated from them. Have you—"

"I never knew them," Aria interrupted. "My late guardian brought me to the United States from Europe to meet my American relations, though I did not know of them until we arrived."

"Europe?" Benoit repeated. "How remarkable! And you have come to find us?"

"Thanks to Madame Martin. I—"

"It is a complicated story," Babette said, "best told under more congenial circumstances."

The Reniers of New Orleans were not accustomed to being treated as they liked to treat their "inferiors," and Benoit was no exception. "If it is congenial circumstances you prefer," he said coldly, "I will be delighted to introduce you and Mademoiselle Aria to my family."

And that would be catastrophic. Benoit might not recognize Babette as New Orleans's former reigning Queen of Courtesans, but he would learn her identity soon enough. And Aria was lacking crucial information she must know before any further introductions could be made.

Whatever Benoit might believe—even if he thought that Aria was actually Lucienne but for some reason felt compelled to conceal her true identity—Babette strongly suspected he knew nothing of Lucienne's birth as a princess of Carantia. That fact would surely have been hidden from all but a few of the elder Reniers.

His ignorance was perhaps Babette's only advantage.

"I fear I must insist that Mademoiselle Renier be allowed to rest," she said. "Her welfare was put in my hands by her late guardian. If you have any concern for her, you will permit us to retire."

"The lady is quite right," Duplessis said, breaking in for the first time since Benoit had spoken. "All will be revealed in the morning."

He gave Babette a secret smile, and she wondered just how much he intended to say. But she would not borrow trouble. *"Merci, monsieur,"* she said.

Thus chided by his elder companion, Benoit had no choice but to give in. "May we escort you to the reception desk?" he asked.

So it was done. Like it or not, the first part of the introduction was over. The most difficult was yet to come.

The moment Aria was inside their room, she yanked off her gloves and hat, and flung herself down on the nearest chair. "I wish we had never come," she said.

The vehemence of Aria's declaration hardly surprised Babette. The young woman had done a marvelous job of presenting herself, almost making Babette believe that she had been pleased to meet someone she could finally claim as family.

But Babette had known better. Aria was far from ready to be pleased about anything. She was still very much in a state of shock. And grief.

Babette sat in the chair opposite the sofa and met Aria's gaze. "You are doing very well," she said. "In light of the fact that you ignored my advice to avoid speaking and gave them your real name, of course." She sighed. "I did not expect to meet any Reniers here. It could have been a disaster."

Aria's chin jutted like the prow of a Spanish galleon. "I'm certain he thought I was Lucienne when he first saw me."

"It was what we expected. He may still believe it."

"I don't care what he believes. I don't like him."

In this matter, Babette felt that Aria had exquisite judgment. Still, he *was* a Renier, so…

"You have only just met him," she said, "and there are others—"

"I always knew Cort didn't like them," Aria said. "But he never said why. Now I think I understand."

"You judge too quickly, Aria. He was rude, to be sure, but that is hardly reason to dismiss the entire family." Babette leaned forward, trying to make Aria listen. "You have come so far. Cort would be proud."

"I don't care about how proud anyone is of me." Aria sat up straight, fists clenched against the arms of the chair. "I'm only here for one reason. If Cort doesn't come soon, I'm going back to look for him. Once the Reniers accept me, they'll help me find Cort if I ask them to."

Oh, Lord. Was this why Aria had been so cooperative? How could Babette tell her that the New Orleans Reniers were not likely to help her find Cort under any circumstances, even if they never knew her true reason for asking?

How could she bring herself to suggest again that Aria face the reality of Cort's likely death? The young woman would never believe Cort was gone until she had absolute proof.

Babette herself had come to another conclusion during the train trip from Sacramento. Cort might not come after them even if he *had* survived. The news of Aria's identity had struck him hard, driven deeply and cruelly into the soul of a man who had reinvented himself to become a false reflection of those he hated.

Aria was a reflection of *him,* transformed from backward child into elegant lady. But there was one major difference. *She* had been born to nobility. No matter how thoroughly he altered himself, Cort would never be anything but a backwoods peasant boy rejected and spat upon by those who deemed themselves as far above him as an eagle from a swamp rat.

Aria believed Cort would come for her and marry her as he had promised. But he was proud, very proud, and Babette hadn't had the chance to ask him what he intended to do in light of his new knowledge. She hadn't been able to remind him that Aria's feelings for him weren't likely to change. Their conversation had ended when she had hesitantly admitted that Yuri might not keep his promise to her. That he might go through with his plans for betrayal.

Babette closed her eyes. If only *she* could have faith, like Aria. Faith that Cort was alive, and that he would come for Aria. Faith that Yuri had had no part in the attack, despite all her fears to the contrary. Faith that at least one person in their troubled quartet would find real happiness.

Soon, one way or another, Aria would have to make some very difficult decisions.

Well aware that such decisions—along with painful confessions—were not to be made on an empty stomach, Babette insisted that Aria eat the fresh seafood that was soon brought to their room. Well after night had fallen and Aria had gotten ready for bed, Babette called for a bottle of red wine. She poured a glass for herself and one for Aria when the girl returned to the sitting room.

"Drink," Babette said, offering one of the glasses to Aria. "It will help you to relax."

Aria sniffed the wine. "You didn't want me to drink before," she said dully, "and the way it made Yuri act…"

"As with many pleasures, it is perfectly acceptable in moderation. No harm will come of a drink or two."

No indeed. All the harm would come from the words Babette was about to speak. She waited while Aria finished the wine, almost gulping it down as if she hoped its effects would drown the fears she refused to acknowledge.

When the younger woman had finished her second glass, Babette began.

THE NEXT MORNING, bathed and freshly dressed, they sat across from each other in the dining room, pretending to enjoy their sumptuous breakfast. Aria's expression was that of a porcelain doll, presenting a pleasant aspect to everyone she met but devoid of any real feeling.

And no wonder. She had suffered shock after shock. First Babette had told her the easier truth: that the lady she knew as Madame Martin was no lady at all. Babette had once dared to hope that the time would never come when she would be compelled to reveal her past to Aria; it had always been her plan to leave before Aria went to New Orleans, where "Madame Moreau" would be recognized.

Keeping the secret had become impossible once she had become responsible for escorting Aria to her kin. She had to make Aria understand why she had to go to the Reniers alone. Once Benoit knew who Babette was, he would be horrified that he had offered to introduce a whore to his family.

Aria had begun to protest that she would never leave Babette, no matter who she had been once upon a time. Babette had stopped the argument by revealing the more difficult truth: Aria was no mere orphan seeking her prominent kinfolk in America; she was a princess royal.

Brecht was not simply a villain obsessed with a girl his agent had lost in a card game, but the distant cousin and murderer of the king her father and the queen her mother, a monster who intended to marry the princess and use her to take the throne from the current, barely legitimate ruler.

Some in Aria's position might have laughed at such absurdities. But Aria hadn't laughed when Babette told her how she had learned such incredible facts. There was no way to sugarcoat Yuri's villainy.

"From the beginning, Yuri recognized you as the princess Alese—raised in New Orleans as Lucienne Renier," she had told Aria. "He'd had dealings with the Reniers and knew the story of Lucienne's kidnapping. But he was also one of the few who knew that Lucienne was only an assumed name. He concealed this fact from Cort while assisting him in preparing you to meet the Reniers. It was his aim to demand a generous reward from the Reniers in exchange for your return."

It had been difficult then for Babette to keep the tears from her voice. "It was the birthmark, you see," she had said. "The birthmark on your back. It is the mark of the Carantian royal family, the rulers who were deposed by the rebels, distant cousins of the American Reniers. But Cort knew nothing of this. He had no idea that Yuri had decided to take Duke di Reinardus's part and betray us."

She had gone on quickly before Aria could speak, explaining how Yuri had finally admitted his scheme to her shortly after Cort had expressed his intention to marry Aria. Yuri had known Brecht—Duke Gunther di Reinardus—in New Orleans; it had been the duke himself who had first taken Alese, then lost her years later.

"The Reniers eventually learned that it was di Reinardus who had taken Alese, but they were unable to find either one of them, despite years of searching. They assumed Alese was gone forever.

"When I told Yuri that you could not be Lucienne, he was convinced that you must be closely related to Alese. More than closely related—that you must be sisters, both of you spirited away in infancy to be held in safety until the time came to restore you to your rightful places.

"Yuri said it would make no difference which princess di Reinardus married. The duke's men were waiting near the lodge for him to deliver you to them as soon as your training was finished. I appealed to him, Aria. I begged him not to go through with it. He finally agreed to turn against di Reinardus and make certain that we got safely to Placerville. He promised to tell Cort everything then. I thought… Oh, Aria, I am certain he tried to do what he said he would, but something must have gone terribly wrong."

Somehow Babette had stumbled through the rest of the explanation. Aria had listened quietly, staring into her empty wineglass. Afterward, she had simply gone to bed. She had asked a few questions that morning, but hardly enough, considering that her world had just been turned upside down.

"One thing has not changed," Babette had said to Aria before they went down to the dining room. "Your guardian clearly meant for you to be reunited with your people."

"Then why did he keep so much from me?" Aria had asked in a voice as weary as an old woman's. "Why didn't he tell me that the king and queen were *loupgarou* and that there were many more like me in Carantia? And why plan to take me to San Francisco instead of New Orleans? He said it was humans who would want to hurt me because of what I am. Did he know about my sister? Why was she sent to the Reniers, while Franz kept me hidden in the mountains?"

"Franz must have been loyal to the true king," Babette had said. "He wanted to protect you from the usurpers, and those who would harm or use you, like di Reinardus. He wanted you to be safe, as Cort did."

"I would have been *safe* if di Reinardus had taken me. If I had gone to him, Cort would still be…" Aria had choked on the unspoken words and changed the subject. "You don't think my sister is still alive."

"I do not know, *ma petite*. Di Reinardus was unable to find her after she escaped, and she never came back to New Orleans."

It was all the wildest speculation, of course. Babette knew that Aria had no reason to trust her or her opinion about anything. But the young woman would require advice and guidance now more than ever, even if she herself could not stay at Aria's side.

Without Cort, Aria needed somewhere to go. Someone to love. She would need a purpose, something to fight for. As the heir to a lost throne, she might find that purpose.

So Babette had forged on. "The loss of your sister gives you an even greater reason to try to understand your place in this remarkable story," she had said. "Do you not owe it to Alese, and to the man who raised and protected you? To your mother and father, who were so loved by their people and must have loved you just as dearly? To Cort, who fought to give you the chance to discover who you are?"

"Why should I trust the Reniers, when they weren't even able to protect my sister?"

"We do not know the circumstances of what happened all those years ago. And you are strong, Aria. You have nothing to fear. You can be anything, anyone you want to be."

Aria's eyes had filled with miserable tears. "I don't want to be anything but what I have always been."

And that could never be. Aria's life of anonymity and unchecked freedom was over and could never be restored.

Babette stabbed at an inoffensive slice of ham on her plate. "Benoit Renier sent a message that he will be meeting us here in an hour," she said as they lingered over their uneaten breakfasts. "They may have doubts at first when we reveal your identity, but the proof of your birth is clear. I have written a simple letter of introduction that we will say your guardian passed on to me before his death. It will be easier if you continue to play the role we agreed upon, that you are a distant relative, until you know them well enough to reveal more of your past and the circumstances by which you came to be here. Given what became of your sister, they will understand your reticence."

"More lies," Aria whispered, smiling blankly at a young man who bowed as he passed the table.

"It is only for a little while." Babette set down her fork. "I will excuse myself before you go to the Renier mansion."

"Because you once did things *they* don't approve of? Because they make you ashamed?"

"It is best this way, Aria."

Steel glinted beneath the softness of Aria's cheek. "I won't let them make *me* ashamed."

"You promised that you would say nothing about Cort or your future plans. At least not yet. And keep an open mind about the Reniers. You are too intelligent to do otherwise."

Aria fell silent again. A waiter refilled Babette's coffee. Aria hardly moved until another half hour had passed, when she lifted her head, sniffed the air and grew even more still than before. Babette knew then that Benoit had arrived.

"Bonjour, madame," the young man's voice said behind her. "Mademoiselle Aria, it is a delight to see you again."

Aria looked up at him, a beautifully painted smile on her face. "Good morning, Monsieur Renier." Her gaze shifted past Benoit's shoulder, and Babette turned in her chair. An older, taller man, also blond and blue-eyed, was standing just behind Benoit.

"Madame Martin," Benoit said, "Mademoiselle Aria, may I have the honor of presenting to you my brother, Henri Renier."

Babette inclined her head. "Monsieur Renier," she murmured, wondering why she had been so foolish as to think that Benoit would come alone.

Unlike his younger sibling, Henri Renier was clearly acquainted with Babette's former profession. He didn't smile as he bowed, and she could feel the disapproval in the stiffness of his shoulders.

When he turned to Aria, however, his whole manner changed. "It is remarkable," he murmured.

"I am most pleased to make your acquaintance, *monsieur,*" Aria said, offering her hand to Henri.

He looked a bit startled by the familiarity, but it seemed to please him. He took her hand and bowed over it, holding it longer than was strictly proper.

"I was told that you were beautiful, *mademoiselle,*"

he said, "but Benoit's description hardly does you justice."

Aria produced a very convincing blush. She smiled warmly at Benoit. "I am afraid that we told your brother very little yesterday and left him in a state of great curiosity."

"Not at all, *mademoiselle*," Benoit said. "There will be plenty of time to talk. In fact, my brother has come to second my invitation to our home."

"I have," Henri said. "No Renier is permitted to remain in a hotel while Belle Lune stands."

"But she is *not* a Renier."

Aria's face paled and then blossomed with joy. Babette caught her breath. Benoit and Henri turned to stare.

Cort strolled toward them, dressed as handsomely as always, and tipped his hat to Babette, Aria and then the gentlemen.

"Forgive me for the interruption," he said, meeting Aria's gaze. "I regret that I was delayed in joining you, *mademoiselle*."

"You're…" Aria grinned like the wild girl she'd always been. "How did you…?"

"You need have no further concern. Our little difficulty has been dealt with. I—"

"*Monsieur*," Benoit said, a very unpleasant expression on his face. "What do you mean by saying Mademoiselle is not a Renier?"

Cort looked at him, smiling with an insolence that the younger man could only have found infuriating. "I have not had the honor of your acquaintance, *monsieur*, but as it seems that you have been assisting the ladies, I will not take offense at your tone."

"*Monsieur*," Henri said, shooting a warning glance

at his brother, "as it appears you are acquainted with *mademoiselle,* I will—"

"Please!" Aria said. "Gentlemen, let us not quarrel." She smiled impartially at everyone, and only Babette could see how her eyes lingered on Cort with barely contained joy. "Messieurs Henri and Benoit Renier, please allow me to present Monsieur Cortland Renier."

Henri gave a visible start. Benoit frowned. Babette watched their faces carefully, trying to decide whether or not they recognized Beau Renier, the bayou boy who had once dared to court their sister.

But they seemed more annoyed than angry, as if it were only the mention of the shared surname that disturbed them.

"I am honored, gentlemen," Cort said with another slight bow.

The Reniers did not respond in kind. "May I ask, *monsieur,*" Benoit said tersely, "what is your connection to Mademoiselle Aria?"

Cort's smile was both charming and deadly. "I am her friend, *monsieur.*"

A finger of ice traced up and down Babette's spine. Cort would not be here if he hadn't seen to di Reinardus once and for all. Had he come to take Aria away? Had he realized he loved her? Did he hope to make a life with her in spite of the obvious obstacles?

Or did he still want the revenge that Babette had hoped he had given up forever?

"Monsieur…Renier," Benoit said, interrupting her thoughts, "I asked you why you claimed that Mademoiselle Aria is not a Renier, when she herself has told us that she is?"

Cort glanced at Aria and smiled. "I only mean to say that she is far more than merely your cousin, though she is too modest to speak of it in a public place." He turned back to the Reniers. "*Messieurs,* may I present Mademoiselle Aria di Reinardus, Crown Princess of Carantia."

CHAPTER NINETEEN

ALL HELL BROKE LOOSE.

Or, Cort thought, perhaps not quite hell. Only its vestibule.

Benoit's eyes opened very wide, as did his mouth. He clearly had no idea what Cort was talking about.

Henri was another matter. "Di Reinardus?" he repeated. His face hardened, and Cort guessed that he was one of the few Reniers aware of Lucienne's hidden identity. Cort knew that the two men had only met Aria yesterday evening. Even if they had initially believed she was their lost "cousin Lucienne," that misconception could not have persisted long. And now Henri had just been presented with something he had never expected.

If he believed Cort's claim.

And why shouldn't he? It would be difficult to doubt the evidence of his own eyes. Aria appeared in every way a princess. Cort had tried to prepare himself for the inevitable completion of her transformation, but he hadn't succeeded. Despite the warmth and animation in her eyes, her bearing and manner were impeccably aristocratic. Her beauty had always been astonishing; now it was but a single exquisite element that made up a radiant being of angelic perfection.

And to think he had actually been worried about her. Every moment during the run to Placerville, throughout the game that had won him enough to complete the journey from Sacramento to New Orleans, and then during the journey itself, he had prayed that she and Babette had made it safely to their destination. He'd wondered how well she would accept the incredible story Babette had shared with him.

Apparently she had accepted it completely. He felt her staring at him, and it was all he could do to pretend he didn't notice. He hadn't planned to interrupt these fine proceedings. He'd almost convinced himself that he could watch from a distance without becoming directly involved. It would have been so much simpler for both of them if he'd let Aria believe he was dead.

But he'd allowed his emotions to rule him, to drive him to confront his enemies and see Aria again. That had been a mistake, but not because he still intended to take revenge against the Reniers. When he'd come face-to-face with Henri and his brother, he'd quickly realized, with some shock, that he was able to lock his hatred away in a corner of his heart where it could not affect him.

No, the danger lay in the fact that they might recognize him too soon. He had changed so much that Henri didn't know him yet. But it was only a question of time before they realized that Cortland Beauregard Renier was the Beau Renier they had known, and Cort didn't intend to put Aria through the unpleasantness of the inevitable unmasking.

Because he knew now that he had done the right thing in sending her to his former enemies. Seeing her among her blond, blue-eyed, aristocratic kin had sealed his conviction. Wild she had been, and wild she still might be, but she would soon realize, as he did, that this was where she belonged: with her own kind.

And he need not fear that they would destroy her independence or the very qualities that made her so much finer than they could ever be. She would never again allow herself to become anyone's pawn, no matter what the Reniers and her countrymen might want from the sole remaining heir to the Carantian throne. Her future was as wide-open as the Western prairies. The future Cort had imagined for himself was no more than a flimsy stage set that had never been meant to withstand the end of his self-deception.

The game was nearly over. But before it ended, he had to speak with Aria alone. He had to make her understand.

"Princess?" Benoit said, cutting across Cort's grim reverie. "What is this?"

Henri touched his arm. "We will speak of it later, Benoit." He met Aria's gaze. "Mademoiselle, do you confirm this man's claims?"

Aria managed a perfect imitation of flustered modesty. "I… Monsieur Renier is no dissembler," she said.

Cort nearly laughed at the irony of her words. "I apologize profoundly for not having been here to see to your comfort, Your Royal Highness," he said to Aria. "But as you have found your family…"

"Ah!" Benoit said, brightening. "Of course! I remember Father mentioning a place called Carantia." He turned eagerly to Henri. "Di Reinardus…that was the name of the ruler, wasn't it? Father said there was a connection between the Reniers and the di Reinardii. Our distant cousins, are they not?" He bowed deeply to Aria. "Your Highness, please forgive my stupidity."

Aria blushed again. "Please do not call me 'Highness.' I was not told of my birth until my…my late guardian brought me to America."

Henri nodded, and Cort could almost hear his thoughts clicking against each other like poker chips. "Am I to understand that your guardian is no longer among us?"

There was nothing feigned about Aria's sadness. "Yes," she whispered.

"I am sorry," Henri said. "May I assume he intended that you come to us?"

"He died before he could make his intentions entirely clear, but Madame Martin and Monsieur Renier..."

"Forgive me," Babette said quietly. "The princess's guardian gave a letter to me before his passing." She withdrew an envelope from a pocket hidden among her skirts. "If you will be so good as to read it—"

"And just what is your part in this, *madame?*" Henri asked, dropping even the pretense of courtesy. Cort had wondered if the Reniers had recognized Babette, and now he had his answer. Had Babette already told Aria what she had been in New Orleans?

Aria's quick response didn't enlighten him. "Madame Martin and Monsieur Renier assisted Franz and me when we were in difficulty," she said. "They have been loyal friends, and I could not have come to New Orleans without their help."

"The details are unimportant," Cort added. "The princess honored us with her trust. We have sought to fulfill her guardian's request and to assure her safety while—"

"Safety?" Benoit echoed. "What do you mean?" He frowned and then turned to his brother. "Of course. Didn't Father mention some sort of revolution in Carantia? Is that why...?"

Henri looked sorely tempted to strangle his younger sibling. "Enough, Benoit," he said sharply. "The princess may tell us what she wishes when she is at Belle Lune, and has had time to rest and meet our father."

"Thank you," Aria said with a perfect balance of gratitude and dignity. "I am honored by your offer to receive me at your home, and I am certain that Monsieur Renier and Madame Martin shall be equally honored by your hospitality."

Cort bit back another laugh. He doubted that Henri had wanted to invite an unknown and undoubtedly inferior Renier and a whore to the family seat, but Aria had just made it impossible for him to refuse.

Impossible for *him* to refuse, as well, if he couldn't get Aria alone beforehand. Cort cleared his throat. "I thank you, *messieurs,*" he said to Henri, "but Madame Martin and I would not wish to impose. If I may speak to the princess before your departure?" He turned to Aria, keeping his expression remotely polite. "If you will be so kind, Your Highness…"

Aria sighed and closed her eyes. "I am so very weary," she said, touching her forehead. "And you must be, as well. Can we not speak later?" She smiled innocently up at Henri. "I am sure my American cousins will wish all of us to be comfortable. *N'est-ce pas, monsieur?*"

No, Aria would never be anyone's pawn. And she was making it clear to everyone that she would not go to the Reniers alone.

Henri had also recognized defeat. "As you wish, Your Highness," he said flatly. "Benoit and I will wait outside so that you may finish your meal without further interruption." He stared pointedly at Cort. "Perhaps you will join us, *monsieur.*"

So that you can ask a few more questions of your own, Cort thought.

But Aria folded her napkin and made as if to rise. "I am finished," she said, folding her napkin.

"As am I," Babette said, glancing at Cort with worry in her eyes.

"Our carriage is waiting," Henri said. "When will you be ready to depart, Your Highness?"

"Give us but a moment to collect our things," Aria said.

"I shall send a porter to your room," Henri said. He bowed and left the dining room with a final probing glance at Cort, who chose to ignore the other man's "request" to accompany them. Benoit moved behind Aria's chair and prepared to draw it back. Aria looked up at Cort.

Swallowing a growl, he stepped away from the table. He might not be leaving her just yet, but he would do nothing to encourage the idea that things could be as they had been before the ambush.

Whatever Aria thought of his failure to press his "claim," her gracious demeanor never faltered. She accepted Benoit's hand and swept past Cort with only the most impersonal smile.

Babette lingered. "Are you well?" she asked, touching Cort's arm.

"Yes."

Her eyes said how little she believed him. "And di Reinardus?"

"Dead."

"Dieu merci." Her fingers trembled on his sleeve. "Yuri?"

"He killed di Reinardus."

She closed her eyes and swayed. Cort caught her elbow.

"He's unhurt."

Her eyelids fluttered. "I hoped..." She collected herself and let go of his arm. "Is he coming?"

"No."

She nodded. It was the only answer possible, even if she believed Yuri hadn't betrayed them after all. "Aria was sick with worry over you."

"She seems to have done well enough."

"Yes." Babette touched her throat. "They have accepted her. But now that you are here, she will—"

"She doesn't need me now."

Babette didn't look startled by his statement. They'd had no time to discuss what his new knowledge would mean to his plans for Aria, but somehow Babette had known what he would say. She, with her knowledge of men and their foibles, had glimpsed something in him that he had never intended for anyone else to see.

Still, she was obviously not prepared to let his words stand unchallenged. "I don't understand you, Cort. You said you wanted revenge against the Reniers, yet you have not asserted any relationship with Aria other than as a friend and protector."

"What other relationship is there? I was scarcely able to protect her, and I was never a very good friend. Now I am even less."

"And what makes you so much less? How have *you* changed since we left the lodge?" Her eyes sparked with fury. "Can it be you still don't realize how much she loves you? Has always loved you?"

"Did she say so?"

"*Mon Dieu!* Men are such fools! She told me she intended to go looking for you if you failed to come after us. Isn't that proof enough?"

"She doesn't know what she's saying."

"You are wrong." Faces turned toward them, and

Babette lowered her voice. "What you saw here…it's all an act. Exactly as we planned. Only an act."

"An act to which she will soon become accustomed."

"I understood the necessity of encouraging her to come to New Orleans and accept her heritage when there was a chance you would not defeat di Reinardus, but he is dead and you are here. And you are all she wants."

"Surely you wouldn't rob her of a chance to discover who she really is."

"It is you who would rob her. You promised to marry her."

"You still believe that is possible?" Cort laughed softly. "There is much you still don't know about me, *madame*. Aria is a princess. I, however, am no prince. I offered marriage out of pity, because she was alone. I have no right to pity her now, and she is alone no longer."

"I thought you despised the Reniers!"

"And I was led to believe you wanted the best for Aria."

"I do."

"Then do not interfere. Give her time to decide what she wants without our interference."

"How can she make such a decision when she doesn't know how much you love her?"

Cort didn't bother to deny her assertion. He knew there would be no point. "Say nothing to her, Babette. I'll speak to her myself."

"And what will you say? She does not deserve more lies, Cort!"

"I will be speaking the truth."

"What you believe to be the truth!" More faces were turned in their direction now, but Babette seemed not to care. "Yuri told me you were not born a gentleman. Is that what you will say to her?"

Now Cort knew why Babette saw what was inside him so clearly. "Did Yuri tell you why I hate the Reniers?" he asked. "What I did to earn their contempt?"

"Yes. And I tell you it makes no difference!"

"It will not seem so trivial when the Reniers recognize me."

"And you think she will scorn you as they did?"

"It doesn't matter. I'll be leaving as soon as I've spoken with her."

"What makes you believe she won't simply announce to the world that you are engaged?"

"She would already have done so if she intended to."

"Tell her the truth, Cort. I beg you. If you ever cared for her—"

She broke off as Aria approached them from the doorway, smiling gaily. Benoit trailed after her like a devoted puppy.

"Are you ready?" she asked.

Babette seemed to shrink in on herself. Cort felt the moment of decision slipping through his fingers.

"Come!" Aria said, linking her arm through Babette's. "The carriage is waiting."

And so Aria had her way. But Cort didn't meet her gaze, and he kept his distance from her as they joined the others in the lobby. It was the only way he could maintain his own composure. The carriage arrived, servants secured Aria's and Babette's baggage, and Benoit handed the ladies inside. Only one seat remained.

"I have business to conduct," Henri said, standing back from the carriage and waving Cort ahead. "I will follow you."

Cort bowed. Their eyes met, and Cort was reminded how little time he had left before Henri remembered just where he had met this particular Renier before. He followed Benoit into the carriage.

The ride was spent in a tense silence. Babette was clearly uncomfortable, Aria's smile was too fixed and Benoit kept strictly to his side of the seat, as if he thought rubbing elbows with Cort would somehow contaminate him. The carriage wound its way through the streets of the city and passed onto River Road, the thoroughfare that stretched west alongside the Mississippi, and carried traffic to and from the various great houses and sugar plantations of Orleans, Jefferson and St. Charles Parishes.

Many of the plantations had fallen on hard times since the War, and few remained the vast and profitable establishments they had once been. Still, many maintained an outward grandeur, the shadow of gracious living built on an institution Cort's own people had always despised.

The New Orleans Reniers, however, had once benefited considerably from that institution, and as the carriage pulled into the long, oak-shaded drive that led to the great white-columned mansion, Cort was reminded just how successfully they had clung to their antebellum wealth. Adaptability had always been necessary to the survival of the werewolf kind. But Cort doubted that Aria had any knowledge of this region's past. She would never have accepted a world where anyone, human or *loup-garou,* was held in unwilling captivity.

"The house was built by our family nearly a century ago," Benoit said with obvious pride as they drew close. "I believe you will find Belle Lune the equal of any residence in this country, Your Highness." He hesitated. "Of course, you have lived in Europe. Perhaps the castles and châteaus are more impressive."

"*Mais non,* Monsieur Renier," Aria said. "It is lovely. Most charming."

Benoit leaned back in his seat, relaxed and confident again. After a few more minutes the carriage rolled into a circular drive before the immense, pillared portico of the mansion. Servants arrived to assist the passengers and see to the luggage. A butler waited at the door. Benoit offered his arm to Aria again, and they preceded Cort and Babette into the house.

Enormous doors opened into an atrium and the wide, open hall that ran through the center of the house. Decorative marble columns mirrored the much taller ones outside, and ancestral busts sculpted in the Greek style stood on pedestals between them. A grand staircase swept gracefully to the second-story landing. In every way the house was a monument to pride, power and the bluest of *loup-garou* blood.

Though Aria didn't show it, Cort knew she was impressed, perhaps even a little in awe of so much private luxury. For Cort himself, the place loosed a violent eruption of memories. He'd been in this hall only once, on the day Madeleine had rejected him. He'd come openly, hat in hand, to propose to the most beautiful woman in the world.

His last view of the place had been as Madeleine's elder brothers, including Henri, had dragged him out of the house, taken him into the shrubbery and beaten him senseless. He might have died if he hadn't Changed, availing himself of the healing power inherent in the transformation, and crawled back to the bayou in disgrace.

He felt like that boy again, terrified and furious,

forced to acknowledge his low birth with his face ground into the dirt. After all the years that had passed, all the things he had learned about being a gentleman, he had never left that Louisiana mud.

But, like the poised woman Aria had become, he was good at concealing his true feelings. He smiled, offered the appropriate compliments and waited with the others in a grand, gilded drawing room while bedchambers were made ready for the new guests. Servants brought refreshments, tea and cold drinks, which Cort didn't have the stomach to sample. Benoit fawned over Aria incessantly. She was unfailingly polite, if a little reserved. Babette hardly moved in her seat.

Soon a maid appeared to escort Babette and Aria upstairs. Aria looked directly at Cort, and he couldn't mistake the pleading in her eyes. *I must see you. Come to me.* Then she followed the maid up the stairs without a backward glance.

Benoit suggested that Cort join him in a drink, and they proceeded to an unmistakably masculine study, where the sideboard displayed a very fine array of expensive liquors. The young man revealed no further sign of the distaste he had shown in the carriage.

"Am I to understand correctly, *monsieur,* that you have been assisting the princess since her arrival in America?" Benoit asked, pouring Cort a glass of bourbon.

Cort refused to drop his guard, even in the face of Benoit's apparent friendliness. "I have," he said carefully.

"It is truly remarkable how closely she resembles my poor lost cousin."

"As you said before, *monsieur,* there are ancient connections between the Reniers and the di Reinardii."

"Hmm." Benoit picked up a second glass and examined it with a pensive air. "You have the look and the sound of New Orleans about you, yet surely you can't be from our fair city. The West, perhaps?"

"I've lived in many places. I prefer to move as the wind takes me."

"Ah." Benoit splashed bourbon into his glass. "A man of the world." He sipped appreciatively. "My father is out, but he will return presently. I'm certain he'll wish to speak with you."

"Presently" was too soon. The Renier patriarch was a sharp-eyed old wolf, however much he had suppressed his animal nature and those of his dependents. He was bound to recognize Cort, even if the others didn't.

And where is Madeleine? Cort thought.

Married, no doubt, and settled in some wealthy *loup-garou*'s home. Her choice of mates would have been severely limited in New Orleans; she might have left the city.

Cort was grateful to be spared meeting her again. He knew now that he'd never loved her as a woman, only as a graven image of celestial perfection he had created in his own mind. She wasn't worth the effort hatred required.

After today, no woman would ever engage his emotions again. His heart would truly be dead.

"If you have no objection, *monsieur,*" he said, setting down his glass, "I will look in on the princess and inquire as to her comfort."

"Of course," Benoit replied. "You are our guest. And I have certain business of my own to conduct."

With a bow, Cort left Benoit in the study and started for the grand staircase. He knew Aria was waiting for him. She would be bursting with questions about what had happened to him after she'd left with Babette, questions she'd had sense enough not to ask in the presence of her Renier kin. She would doubtless want to share her feelings about suddenly becoming a princess, and weep over gaining and losing both parents and a twin sister on the very same day.

It was even possible, as Babette had suggested, that she would remind him that he had promised to marry her.

When he was finished, she might mourn losing him. With luck, she would hate him. That would be best for her. Best for both of them.

He had reached the landing of the first floor when the massive front doors opened behind him and five men, three unknown to him, walked into the hall. One of the scents was all too familiar. Cort froze.

Xavier Renier, patriarch of the New Orleans Reniers, was an imposing figure, a powerful bewhiskered gentleman who ruled his domain with an iron hand. With him were Henri and three other men Cort had never seen before, one near Cort's age and the other two much older. The elderly men were *loups-garous,* the younger man human. They were engaged in a low-voiced, urgent conversation and didn't notice Cort on the stairs.

"If it is true," one of the elderly men said in heavily accented English, "it will be our salvation and the restoration of Carantia. We will have a real chance at overthrowing the usurper, and reinstating our good king's laws of justice and tolerance." He brushed gray hair from a high forehead. "If only we had remained in San Francisco, we might have found her much sooner."

"She is the very image of Alese," Henri said. "And yet you never knew—"

"She must have been well hidden indeed, most

fortunately for all of us. But it will be easy enough to be sure who she is. And once we are sure, we can begin our work."

"You ask much of a young girl," Xavier said in his deep, gruff voice. "She is not Alese. Henri says she was raised unaware of her heritage. How do you know she will be what you hope?"

"If she is the child of her parents, she will be."

"We have no time to waste," the second older man said, pushing at his spectacles. He glanced at Henri. "Our original agreement will still be in effect, provided there are no further complications, and assuming the princess is amenable. When may we meet her?"

Xavier stared at each of the men in turn. "Gentlemen," he rumbled, "the lady is a guest in this house and a stranger in this city. Permit me to speak with her first." He gestured to a servant waiting in the hall. "Rufus, see that our guests are made comfortable in the Rose Salon."

The servant bowed and indicated that the three strangers should follow him. They went, gesturing and muttering amongst themselves in a foreign language that Cort recognized as a quaint form of German.

"You should have come to me before speaking to the Carantians," Xavier said to Henri as soon as they were gone. "I will not tolerate such insubordination."

Henri lowered his head. "Forgive me, sir. I was eager to learn if the girl is who she claims to be."

"And you have sent for Madeleine? Why?"

"There are no Renier women in the house now that Aimée has gone to France," he said quietly. "It is only proper that the princess has a female companion other than—"

"You will get that whore out of my house by tomorrow

morning," Xavier growled. "I am not pleased, Henri. I would expect such unthinking behavior from Benoit, but—" His nostrils flared, and he turned toward the stairs.

"Who is this?" he demanded.

Henri followed his father's gaze and hesitated. Introductions were hardly necessary. Unlike his sons, Xavier clearly recognized the man who stood on his stairway. His face flushed deep red. The silence was like the stillness before a killing storm.

Without a word, Xavier strode toward the study where Cort and Benoit had shared a drink. Henri stared at Cort a moment longer and then fell in at his father's heels.

Cort knew his time had run out. He turned and entered the first-floor corridor, looking for Aria's room. He'd gone only a few steps when she walked out of the third room down. She stopped when she saw Cort, and Princess Aria di Reinardus vanished before his eyes.

"Cort!" she cried, rushing to meet him.

He raised his hand to ward her away. "Remember where you are," he said.

She stared at him, shook her head and laughed. "You can still worry about that now?" She bit hard on her lower lip. "Oh, Cort, I was so afraid you wouldn't…that di Reinardus…"

"He's gone."

"I knew you would do it! I wish I could have been there. He deserved—"

"Yuri killed him."

"Yuri?" The sparkle went out of her eyes. "But why? He betrayed us. I haven't told Babette. Do you think—"

Wearily Cort shook his head. "That isn't important now. We must speak of other things."

"Oh, yes!" She glanced toward the stairs and continued in a breathless rush. "When I saw you with the Reniers, I could see how much you didn't like each other. But you never told me why. Now that we're here, don't you think I should know? Babette told me what she did in New Orleans before she was married, but I don't care. If anyone—"

A servant appeared on the landing, and Aria paused until the woman was out of hearing.

Cort spoke again before Aria could finish. "Let us go to your room, Aria," he said.

She hesitated, then let him in and stood watching as he stopped just inside the door, arms folded across her chest.

"You're angry," she said softly. "I know I lied to you. I told you that I'd lost my memory. I let you believe I really was Lucienne. But I'm finished lying, Cort. I promise, when we leave here…"

"You have no need to make me any promises," he said, standing against the door like a coward waiting for the right moment to escape. "What happened in the past isn't important. What you are now *isn't* a lie. You're becoming who you were meant to be."

Her fingers bit into her arms. "What are you saying, Cort?"

"Aria…"

"You *wanted* me to come here. I did as you asked. I've met the Reniers. But now…" She searched his face, and he saw her begin to understand. "Is it because you think I'm different, just because my father was a king? But I'm *not* different. Can't you see?"

Cort's heart clenched. He'd spoken to Yuri of a gilded cage when the Russian had mocked him for daring to believe he could make Aria happy. He'd been referring then to di Reinardus's plans for Aria, but the men he'd overheard, the Carantians, had their plans, as well. Aria would be their "salvation." They assumed she would be ready and willing to help them reclaim the throne.

A woman of Aria's courage and spirit could do anything she chose to do. She would make her own decisions, but only if she fully understood what they would mean. Only if she were truly free to decide.

Cort couldn't free her from Carantian ambitions. But he could make her choice just a little easier.

"I see someone who has surpassed all my expectations," he said slowly. "I see a wise and gracious woman who will make choices based on facts and reason, not emotion. And reason suggests that you must think carefully about what you are about to do."

"What I'm about to do?" She sucked in her breath, and Cort could see tears welling in her eyes. "I thought I was going to marry you."

He looked away. "The Carantians are here, Aria," he said. "The people your guardian wanted you to meet. *Your* people."

"The Carantians? But I thought—"

"I don't know why they weren't in San Francisco to meet you, but they're here now, in this house. You must speak with them. Hear what they have to say about your family and your country."

Her chin jutted. "I don't want to talk to them." She took a step toward him, the first tear rolling down her cheek. "I want to leave. Let's find Babette and go. Right now."

He reached behind him for the support of the door. "You've come too far, Aria. You must finish what you've begun."

"But you will stay with me."

"I can't, Aria. When I tell you what I've done, what I really am—"

But he had delayed too long. The door opened behind him, and he had only a second to move out of the way before Xavier pushed into the room, followed by Henri.

"You blackguard," Xavier snarled. "How dare you defile the princess with your filthy presence?"

CHAPTER TWENTY

EVERY ONE OF CORT'S senses heightened to painful sharpness. He felt the wolf stirring, longing to shed the limitations of his other self. This time he wouldn't be thrown into the dirt. The Reniers would never expect him to Change. No peasant would dare...

Aria moved to stand beside Cort, tears gone, face coldly regal. "What is this, gentleman?" she demanded. She looked at Xavier. "I presume you are the owner of this house."

The patriarch bowed shortly. "Xavier Renier, at your service."

"Why are you addressing my friend in such a manner, *monsieur?*"

"Your *friend?*" Xavier echoed, his lips curling as if he wanted to spit. "How much do you know of this man, Your Highness?"

"I know he has helped and protected me when no one else would," she said.

"Protected you?" Xavier sneered at Cort. "But of course he must have deceived many with this pitiful masquerade. That is over."

The wolf howled, clawing at the inside of Cort's skin. Aria was too loyal to believe anything bad of him simply because the Reniers said it. She might even let her mask slip and defend him in a way no lady would, and he could not permit that.

No. It had to come from his own lips. Here and now.

"Messieurs," he said, facing the Reniers. "If you wish to respect Her Highness, you will allow me to tell her what occurred here eight years ago."

"Why should we give you the chance to lie to her further?" Xavier snapped. He bowed to Aria. "Forgive me, Your Highness, but you must hear an ugly truth. This...this *man* is—"

"I have been aware that there is no liking between you and Monsieur Renier," Aria said. "And I am eager to hear the truth. But it will not be under these circumstances." She looked steadily at Cort. "I understand that my countrymen are waiting to speak with me. I will meet with them first, and then we will continue this conversation."

Xavier was clearly taken aback by her assumption of authority, accustomed as he was to giving the orders. But he respected strength, at least when it came with rank, and he inclined his head.

"As you wish," he said. His eyes promised Cort that he would get no further time alone with the princess.

"I wish Madame Martin to join us," Aria said.

"Your Highness..." Xavier began.

Without waiting to hear his protest, Aria swept out the door. Xavier and Henri stood back to let Cort precede them. No doubt they were not about to let him out of their sight.

Cort was too numb to care. As he walked out into the corridor, Aria emerged from the adjoining room with Babette, who cast him a desperate glance.

"Shall we go down, gentleman?" Aria said.

They descended the stairs, Aria and Babette in the lead, with Cort and Henri behind them and Xavier bringing up the rear. Cort heard voices beyond the door of the Rose Salon as they reached the foot of the stairs; the three Carantians were speaking with hushed urgency.

"The people will rally behind her when we reveal that a royal heir still lives," the first elder was saying. "Once they are committed, it will surely not be long before the old laws are reinstated."

"And my people," the young human said, "will have full equality again."

Aria stopped halfway across the hall, listening. Babette paused with her.

"All will have the freedom to live as they choose," the young man continued. "No position or profession will be barred to humans if they show merit and ability."

Henri hurried ahead of Aria and opened the door. Cort waited until she began to move again and followed her into the salon.

The Carantians were already on their feet, staring at Aria. She chose a chair near the foreigners and sat, indicating that Babette should take the seat beside her. She showed no more emotion than the Venus di Milo.

The eldest Carantian found his voice. "I...I beg your pardon," he said, dropping his gaze.

Xavier watched Cort take a position at the side of the room and then went to stand with his son. "Gentlemen," he said with great formality, "I am honored to present Her Royal Highness, Aria di Reinardus. Your Highness, Graf Leopold von Losontz, Freiherr Sigmund von Mir and Herr Josef Dreher."

The three Carantians remained frozen. Aria smiled.

"*Meine Herren,*" she said. "It is an honor to meet you."

The youngest Carantian, Josef Dreher, dropped to one knee. The elder *loups-garous* glanced at each other and bowed to Aria.

"Your Royal Highness," von Losontz said, straightening. "We did not know. We were told that one of our king's old retainers was coming to San Francisco with word of the resistance in Carantia, but he said nothing…" The old man cleared his throat. "There was never even the slightest rumor that a second heir existed. If we had been aware, we would never have returned to New Orleans on what we believed was urgent business with other supporters of the former king."

Aria nodded graciously. "I myself was unaware until very recently, Count von Losontz. I am certain you have many questions. So do I." She looked at Cort. "May I introduce the two people responsible for my safe arrival in New Orleans…Madame Babette Martin and Monsieur Cortland Renier."

The Carantians had obviously not been warned about Babette. They bowed to her with exquisite courtesy and then turned to Cort.

"We are grateful beyond words, *madame, monsieur,*" von Mir said, adjusting his spectacles. "There is no recompense we could possibly offer for such a service."

Cort's mouth was almost too dry for speech. "Her Highness does us too much honor," he said hoarsely.

Aria was about to speak when a woman's voice sounded from the doorway.

"I beg your pardon. Papa? Am I intruding?"

Everyone looked toward the newcomer. Madeleine had hardly changed. Her figure was perhaps a little fuller than it had been eight years ago, her skin less dewy, her eyes more weary. But she was still beautiful.

Almost as beautiful as Aria.

Her gaze went instinctively to her only rival in the room. Aria stared back at her.

"*Bonjour,* Madeleine," Cort said.

Like her brothers, she didn't know Cort at first. She smiled, responding to the challenge of a possible new male conquest.

But then, slowly, her expression changed. Her eyes widened, and her face froze in disbelief.

"Beau Renier!" she cried. "What are *you* doing here? How dare you come back?" She spun to face her father. "Papa! You know what he did to me! How can you let him into this house?"

A dreadful silence seemed to suck all the air from the room. Aria's fingers clenched around the arms of her chair. The Carantians looked at each other in bewilderment.

"He presented himself to us as a gentleman named 'Cortland,'" Henri said, spitting out the words as if he couldn't bear the taste of them. "He has become quite the play-actor. If it were not for the princess—"

Madeleine turned toward Aria again. "The princess? Are you—"

Xavier introduced the women to each other, though he stared at Cort with undisguised hatred. Madeleine— Madame Madeleine Rivette, as she was now—pink with anger and confusion, curtsied to Aria.

"Please forgive me, Your Highness," she said. "It is only that I…this man…"

"*Messieurs* and *mesdames,*" Aria said, "I had hoped to have a civilized conversation before dealing with this unexpected contretemps, but I see that will not be possible." Her gaze swept about the room, stern and regal. "It appears that my friend and companion, Monsieur Cortland Renier, is not welcome in this house." She turned to Madeleine. "Especially not by you, *madame*."

"Oh!" Madeleine flushed a brighter red, her lip trembling with anger she dared not show. "Can it be...do you not know who this man is, Your Highness?"

Cort flinched in spite of himself. Not because of Madeleine, who was no more to him than a fly buzzing and blundering against a window, struggling to find a way out. But he couldn't allow her to control what was about to happen.

He bowed to Aria. "Your Highness," he said, "you have on occasion inquired as to my birth and relations. I have never answered you honestly. Now, however, I will speak only the truth." He swallowed, forcing himself to face his own vulnerability. "It is the truth that my family and theirs have had no dealings with each other. Except once." He nodded toward Madeleine. "Madame Rivette wonders why I am here because she is the woman who rejected my suit eight years ago."

"Your *suit?*" Madeleine sputtered. "How dare you call it—"

Aria made a cutting motion with her hand, and Madeleine held her tongue. "Please go on, *monsieur,*" Aria said to Cort, her voice revealing nothing but calm interest.

Cort's heart was a blackened husk in his chest. "My family," he said, "are indeed Reniers. But they do not live in this city. I was born in a *cabane* on Bayou Gris, far from what these people call civilization. My father was illiterate, and my mother cooked over a woodstove brought to the bayou fifty years ago. We had nothing... no fine houses, no education, no impeccable reputation, no money. We were not permitted to walk the same ground as the New Orleans Reniers, let alone court their women."

"Animals," Madeleine hissed. "Tell her what you tried to do to me, all because you wanted my fortune. You and your kind, worthless beasts wallowing in the mud, imagining yourself good enough—"

"You thought I was good enough for a few months' diversion," Cort said. "Until your father discovered your low tastes. That was when you chose to lie about me to save your own reputation."

Henri lunged toward Cort, hand raised, but he came to a quivering stop as Aria rose from her chair.

"Arrête!" she cried. "Stay where you are, *monsieur!"*

"Your highness," Henri said in a low voice, "I cannot permit this *chien* to insult my sister."

Aria ignored him. "How did she lie?" she asked Cort.

"She said he abused her," Babette said, speaking for the first time. "Forced her to lie with him."

Henri groaned. Xavier shook like a man struck with palsy. Aria simply looked at Cort.

"You didn't do it, did you?" she asked.

"No," Cort said. "I proposed to Mademoiselle Madeleine. I believed she loved me."

"Loved *you?"* Madeleine shrieked. "You thought you could make yourself into a gentleman, but you can never remove the stink of the swamp. Never!"

"Monsieur Renier has always been a gentleman," Aria said coldly. "I believe you are the one who is lying, *madame."*

"Not entirely, Your Highness," Cort said. "I did believe I loved her and that she returned my affection, but I also wanted the privilege and wealth marriage to her would bring me. After the Reniers made it clear I wasn't welcome, I worked to become as you see me now." He smiled as if it were all a great joke. "Madeleine is right. The mud has never washed away."

"And you saw another opportunity to have your way when you met the princess," Henri said. "If you ever dared to—"

"I *did* dare," Cort said, before Aria could defend him again. "I intended to return to this house and have my revenge against all of you. Through her."

Aria sank back into her chair. "Cort?"

Meeting her gaze, Cort braced himself to tell the ugly mingling of truth and falsehood their audience made necessary.

"You must understand, Your Highness," he said. "I barely escaped this house with my life. I would have done anything to make the Reniers suffer for what they had done to me. When I met you, even before I knew your true name, I recognized at once how much you resembled Lucienne Renier. And when I learned who you were and realized how important you would be to the Reniers, I was eager to assist you and make myself invaluable to you. I didn't help you out of the goodness of my heart or from some noble sense of chivalry. I saw a perfect chance to take my vengeance."

Aria's skin went from white to red. "I don't believe you."

"Once you had bestowed your affection and trust upon me, I intended to ruin you so that these aristocrats would always have to live with the fact that I had taken something they valued even more than they did Madeleine."

"That isn't true!" Babette said, rising. "Aria, don't listen to him!"

Cort ignored her. "I courted you," he said. "I tried to seduce you. I even asked you to marry me, all with the purpose of causing the Reniers as much suffering as possible once we arrived in New Orleans." He laughed harshly. "A peasant, married to a princess. They could not endure it."

Aria stared at him, unspeaking. Babette trembled with horror. As if from a great distance, Cort heard the Reniers' angry protests and shocked exclamations. He shook them off.

"It was fortunate for you that the marriage never took place, Your Highness," he said. "But that did not stop me from planning to—"

"Why would he risk his life for you and come here only to be humiliated?" Babette said, cutting across his words. "Why should he confess such ugly intentions in front of those he hates?" She pressed Aria's arm. "He says these things because he loves you!"

"I love no one," Cort said. "I despise all men or women who think themselves better than—"

A hard fist smashed into Cort's jaw, knocking the words out of his mouth. He staggered. A growl rumbled in his ear. Another blow split his lip. A clear, ringing voice burst through the senseless noise.

"Enough!"

The grasping, striking hands withdrew. Cort straightened, shaking his head. The pain of the blow was already fading. His nose told him who had struck him: Benoit Renier, who had apparently slipped into the room when he wasn't looking. The Carantians were on their feet. Babette was speaking in low tones to Aria, who seemed in a daze, and Madeleine was leaning heavily on Henri's arm, trembling and pale.

"Get out," Xavier shouted, pointing at Cort. "You

foul the very air we breathe!" He advanced, death in his eyes. "This time you will not crawl away."

The three male Reniers were in perfect accord. Cort had done what he planned to do, and there was no reason to remain. He tore at his clothing, the fine gentlemanly garments he had purchased in Sacramento, scattering buttons and studs and shredded fabric at his feet.

The last thing he saw as he Changed were Aria's eyes, damning wells of misery and pain. He spun on his hind legs and raced into the hall and out the door, barely avoiding a servant sweeping the marble floor.

There were no limits on him now, no bonds to hold him. All the distaste he had felt for the wolf in himself was gone, cast aside along with his failed ambitions.

But he was only an empty sack of bones and fur. There was nothing to replace the man he had created out of foiled ambition and the hatred that had been his lifeblood for so long. Nothing to fill the vast, gaping hole where Aria had been.

You did what was right for her. She would be happy again. And he…

He had to return to the one place he had thought never to see again, to the people he had rejected. They couldn't offer him absolution. No one could. But at least he would face what he had done. Even if they turned their backs on him and cursed the ground he walked upon.

South and west he ran, leaving the civilized world behind. He plunged into the wilderness of the bayous, tortuous waterways choked with matted vegetation, swarming with mosquitoes, and thick with fish, birds and alligators. A few rickety shacks clung to the dryer ground, and intrepid fishermen plied expertly carved pirogues in search of their daily bread. Only the cleverest humans could find their way through the maze of forest and swamp; only the most experienced penetrated so far into the realm of gator, fox and ibis.

And of the wolf. Of the *loups-garous* who had ruled this wilderness for centuries.

Even after his fur was saturated with mud and his paws were heavy as tombstones, long after he had passed the last miserable habitations of men, Cort kept running. He stopped only when he heard the old familiar song Maman had sung to him nearly every day when he was a cub, long before he had learned that there were two kinds of Reniers. Someone was playing a fiddle the way his brother Armand used to do before he died.

Cort crouched in the wet grass, his chest heaving, a howl building in his throat. He could still turn back. They no doubt believed he was dead by now, dead or so far gone he might as well be. He had no right to disturb their peace.

But he had run from Aria. There would be no more running.

The song ended. Cort heaved himself to his feet. He Changed, and stood naked and trembling, gathering his last scraps of courage and will.

Then he walked through the palmettos, across a narrow, meandering stream and through a grove of live oak to the low hill that rose up out of the swamp, dotted with little *cabanes* arranged around a grassy clearing. Smoke puffed from a dozen chimneys, laden with the smell of meat and gumbo. A boy and girl played with a stained ball while two women gossiped under the washing they had hung to dry. A pair of young men, talking rapidly of a recent hunt, walked into one of the shacks. Their cheerful voices carried across the clearing. They had been little more than children when he had left the village.

Cort closed his eyes and breathed in deeply. The memories came thick and fast, nearly driving him to his knees. The little girl, clad only in a dress cut short at the knee, dropped the ball and ran to her *maman* under the drying laundry. The woman spoke to the child and looked in the direction her daughter was pointing.

Releasing his breath, Cort walked out of the trees. The children stared. The other woman dropped the shirt she had been about to hang on the line, her mouth open in surprise.

The girl ran down the hill, short legs nimble as only those of a *loup-garou* could be. She came to a stop a few feet from Cort and peered up into his face.

"Qui es-tu?" she demanded, wrinkling her nose. She couldn't have been more than seven years old. The boy, perhaps a year older, ran to join her, his stare challenging this stranger he had never seen before.

Cort managed a smile. *"Bonjour,"* he said.

The boy's mother approached, a slight frown on her face. She opened her mouth to speak and sniffed the air suspiciously. Then, all at once, she smiled.

"Alphonse!" she cried over her shoulder.

A man appeared at one of the cabin doors, shading his eyes against the glare of the setting sun. He didn't move again for a dozen aching heartbeats.

"Papa," Cort whispered.

The man broke into motion, still swift and strong even after nearly seventy years. He passed the woman and children, and only stopped when he would have bowled Cort over with one more step.

"Beau?" he asked hoarsely. *"Est-ce toi?"*

"Papa," Cort said. "I'm home."

Alphonse Renier opened his arms.

CHAPTER TWENTY-ONE

"WHERE HAS HE GONE?"

The tears had dried on Aria's cheeks, but the pain was still as fresh and as cutting as an icy mountain wind. The Reniers were speaking in loud voices on the other side of the room. Whatever their fears or concerns, the Carantians had known better than to interfere and had made a hasty retreat into some less public area of the house.

Babette stood quietly beside Aria, her hands immobile at her sides, her face as frozen as Aria's heart.

"Where, Babette?" Aria asked.

The older woman closed her eyes. "I do not know, Aria. I wish I could tell you."

But she *did* know something. Aria was sure of it.

"Why did he say those things?" she asked softly. "You said they weren't true. But I think some of them were."

"He…" Babette bowed her head. "He did mean to use you at first. He was full of hatred. It blinded him. Until he began to see you, Aria. Until he recognized you for the extraordinary woman you are."

But did he ever really see me at all? Aria thought. Why should she believe Babette, when Cort's confession had made so much sense? No one could doubt how much he hated the Reniers, and they him. He had never really been a gentleman, helping Aria out of the goodness of his heart. And he'd denied only one part of Madeleine's accusation. He had tried to use her just as he'd tried to use Aria.

She didn't believe he had hurt the other woman. But he had always been so intent on "ladies" and "gentlemen." Sometimes it had seemed as if that was all he thought about. Being good enough. Making *her* good enough.

And he had never said he loved her.

"I wasn't extraordinary enough to see what he was doing," she said. "I let myself believe—"

"Oh, my dear." Babette laid her hand on Aria's shoulder. "When he told me that he had asked you to marry him, I had my doubts at first. But I was certain that what he felt for you was real. He wanted to marry you, Aria. Not for revenge, but because he loved you—even if he refused to admit it to himself."

The knot in Aria's throat was so big that she could hardly breathe. So many people had deceived her. Everyone seemed to want her to be something other than what she was. And she was beginning to feel she could hate them for it.

All she had to do was walk out of the house. Leave the Reniers and the Carantians. Leave Babette. Leave Cort. Live free, perhaps in the Sierra Nevada. She'd spent most of her life virtually alone anyway. She didn't need anyone.

But then she remembered the things Cort had said to her before they had come downstairs. He'd said she had surpassed all his expectations. He said she'd come too far not to finish what she'd begun. He'd said he couldn't stay with her because of what he'd done and what he really was.

But he *hadn't* tried to take advantage of her since he'd

arrived in New Orleans, though he must have known all he had to do was crook his finger and she would come running. Instead, he'd kept his distance. And Babette was right about one thing. There had been no reason for him to let the Reniers accuse him in front of everyone, and then admit that he had behaved like the dog and bastard they had named him.

Not unless he wanted Aria to believe things that *weren't* true. If he thought her loving him, staying with him, would prevent her from finishing what she had begun, wouldn't he want to make her hate him?

He hadn't given her a chance to really think about what he had said or make a decision based on "facts and reason." He had obviously hoped she would simply let him go.

Aria bared her teeth. One way or another, he had made a mistake. Either he had used her as he'd said, or he'd thought he could manipulate her into choosing the life *he* thought she should have.

But he wouldn't get away with it. The choice was hers, not his or anyone else's. *She* would decide whom to believe and what to do. And no one, human or *loup-garou,* could stop her.

She turned to listen to the Reniers, who had reached some agreement and were looking at her expectantly.

Xavier approached her, his eyes as hard as granite chips.

"We are going after him, Your Highness," he said. "He must pay for what he has done to you."

She faced the old man squarely. "It remains to be seen what he has done to me," she said. "It is not your place to punish him, *monsieur.*"

His hand came up as if he intended to strike her, but

he let it fall again. "It *is* my place to protect you," he said. "Whether you wish it or not."

"As you protected my sister?" She glanced at Babette. "Go back to the hotel, Babette. I will come for you later." She started for the front door.

"You'll never find him!" Xavier shouted. "You know nothing of our country. We will not be responsible for—"

"No, you won't," Aria snapped. "And you will *not* follow me."

"Aria," Babette said, rushing up behind her. "Remember what Cort said about his family and the bayous. Perhaps he has gone home."

Home.

Aria squeezed Babette's fingers and let her go. She stripped there in front of them all and raced out of the house. A thousand scents assaulted her, but she found the one she wanted just as she had picked it out from among so many others that eventful day in San Francisco.

Nose close to the earth, she flew away from the house and through the carefully tended gardens, leaping the southern fence that separated the tended grounds from the fields. Her golden fur was a beacon even in daylight, but any humans she passed would never be sure that they had seen anything but a large dog on the hunt.

She almost lost Cort's scent when she reached the swamp. The smells of decay and lush growth, water and wet earth, overwhelmed her. There was nothing of the clean mountains here, only a crushing hunger almost greater than her own.

Still, she went on, half drowning in deceptively lazy streams and catching her fur on snags of rotted wood. When Cort's trail finally vanished in the mud and murk, she lay on a low hill blanketed with relatively dry grass, and bit at the ground in rage and frustration.

He was here—somewhere. But this was *his* country. If he didn't want her to find him...

A rustling among the tangled bushes caught her attention. Her fur stood on end, rising from ruff to tail. She had never before seen the golden wolf who emerged from the undergrowth, but she recognized him well enough. She stood to face him and Changed.

"Benoit," she snarled, "I told you not to come. Go back, or I will—"

Another yellow wolf, bigger and heavier, appeared behind Benoit and shouldered him aside.

Aria's legs turned as soft as the mud under her feet. Cort had been wrong.

Duke Gunther di Reinardus was very much alive.

THE CARRIAGE RATTLED at reckless speeds over the dwindling roads, wheels striking stones and squelching in ruts that never dried even in the hottest weather. Babette stared out the window at the increasingly wild landscape, praying that the sun would delay its setting. Graf Leopold von Losontz huddled in the seat opposite hers, his silence loud with fear and worry.

The Reniers had not been silent in the moments after Aria's departure. "I will go after her," Benoit had declared, shouting for a servant to ready his horse.

"Let her go," Xavier had said. "She's made her choice."

Henri had stared at his father in disbelief. "We cannot, father. Our bargain..." He signaled to another servant. "Tell John to prepare the phaeton at once!"

That was when Babette had realized just how averse to Changing the Reniers were, preferring a slower, man-made vehicle or a horse to the swiftness of a *loup-garou*. As the Carantians rushed into the hall, drawn by the angry voices, Henri had run out and Xavier had simply disappeared.

It was left to Babette to explain what had happened. The horrified Carantians had seemed incapable of action until Babette had the presence of mind to ask if the Reniers had a second carriage.

The stable attendants hadn't argued when she and the foreigners had commandeered an older equipage, one clearly reserved for leisurely drives in the country. But in spite of the groom's quickness in hitching the horses, it was a full half hour before the carriage was ready. Babette used the time to tell the Carantians why Cort had spoken as he had. Whether or not they believed her, they had seemed willing enough to let her come along.

While Herr Dreher took the coachman's seat, Baron von Mir Changed and plunged ahead, grizzled ears flat to his head and gray-tipped tail like a plume of smoke behind him. His nose, apparently still keen in spite of his age, kept them traveling in the right direction. Soon it became a mad dash of foam-flecked horses and jouncing wheels hurtling through the waning afternoon with only the Carantian *loup-garou* to show the way.

Once they were well past the plantation boundary and the cultivated lands, it became more and more difficult for the carriage to negotiate the increasingly rough ground. Von Losontz muttered to himself and shook his head.

"She has gone too far," he said.

As if to confirm his words, von Mir appeared in the carriage window, keeping pace and panting heavily. "The wetland lies ahead," he said. "We must go on foot."

"Is there no sign of Henri and his carriage?" Aria asked.

"There are recent tracks that lead into the marsh. It appears he drove beyond this point."

"But if it isn't safe…"

Von Mir shrugged and fell back. Von Losontz looked at Babette, brow deeply furrowed.

"I will Change and go on with the baron," he said. "Josef is human and will not be able to keep up. He will stay with you."

As worried as she was, Babette knew the count was right. "Please," she said. "When you find them, remember what I have told you."

He reached for the door handle. "I pray all you have said about this Cortland Renier is true, *madame*."

"It is, I assure you. He would never allow anyone to harm her, or interfere with whatever fate she chooses."

Von Losontz nodded brusquely and jumped out of the carriage.

Babette leaned back in her seat and closed her eyes. It had been a very long time since she had asked anything of heaven. She bowed her head, made the sign of the cross and began to pray.

CORT STOOD ON THE LOW HILL amid the patch of summer wildflowers, the place where his people had brought their dead for a hundred years. There were no burials here, where the water rose so near the surface. None of the fancy marble vaults and crypts favored by the rich in New Orleans for their "cities of the dead."

The only trace left of those who had passed were

the wildflowers themselves, growing so abundantly on this little hill. Cort knelt and picked one of the flowers, cradling it in his hands.

Maman.

She couldn't hear him, of course. She had died not long after he'd left Louisiana. She'd always been against his courtship of Madeleine Renier, of his ambitions to become a "real gentleman." On the day he'd gone to propose, she'd begged him to stay home and forget Madeleine.

"No good will come of it," she had said. "We are your kind, your people. You can never run from what you are."

He'd ignored her, the beloved matriarch of the bayou Reniers, thinking only of the life he would have with Madeleine. After the city Reniers had thrown him out, he'd crawled home. Not to admit she was right—never that. He'd thought only of leaving Louisiana, making himself the equal of the Reniers so that one day they would regret what they had done.

He hadn't listened when Papa had told him that Maman couldn't bear losing him. He'd barely spoken to either one of them, except to tell them that he was through rooting in the mud like a pig and living like a savage. Humiliating them, rejecting them, despising them as he despised himself.

Papa had cursed him when he'd finally walked away, and that curse had rung in his ears long after. A few months later the awkwardly scrawled letter had found its way to him in Houston. Maman was dead. She had begged for her only surviving son with her last breath.

Cort dropped his face into his hands, crushing the flower against his cheek. *Forgive me, Maman.*

The evening breeze caressed his hair like a gentle

hand. He lifted his head. Papa was coming up the rise, barefoot and shirtless, his frayed trousers rolled up to his knees.

"*Mon fils*," he said. "I knew you would be here."

Cort swiped at his face and sat up. The night chorus had just begun, the buzzing and humming and croaking and crying of the thousands of creatures that made this wild land their home.

Alphonse crouched beside him. "I have spoken with the elders," he said.

"Do they still want me here?" Cort asked softly. "After all the things I...?"

Papa laid his hand on Cort's shoulder. "Everyone is glad you are back."

"They shouldn't be."

Alphonse Renier's hands were as strong now as they had been when he'd lifted Cort's beaten body onto his shoulders decades ago. His fingers bit into Cort's skin.

"You were young and foolish. No one blames you for a boy's mistakes."

"I killed Maman."

"No." Alphonse dropped his hand and sighed. "Yes, I blamed you at first. I swore I would never speak your name again. But time passes and wounds heal. She never stopped loving you, and neither have I."

Cort turned to lean against Alphonse, the tears scraping his throat raw. "Everything I've done has turned to poison," he said. "I've learned nothing. I've hurt—"

"Who is she?"

Slowly he met his father's eyes. "I don't—"

"Who has sent you running here with your tail between your legs? It is not Madeleine again?"

Cort tried to laugh. "No. Not Madeleine." He sobered,

slipping from his father's embrace. "I didn't come back because of a woman. I came to remember who I am."

"But there *is* a woman."

How could he ever explain Aria to Alphonse? She would be as alien to him as Madeleine was.

But that was a lie, a lie he told himself to justify what he had done. Aria had come from the mountains, from a world utterly unlike the bayous. But she loved being a wolf, just as his clan and kin cherished the wolf in themselves. She flourished in the wild places and scorned what men called civilization.

Or she *had*. That was already changing. She couldn't come to this little village and see what he had seen during the happy years of his childhood, before the corruption of wealth and position had lured him to disaster. She couldn't understand what he saw now, how much affection had survived in some tiny fragment of his heart, cherished and protected when the rest had turned to stone.

"Did you love her?" Alphonse asked.

"Yes."

The old man rose. "I will not ask you to speak more of this, my son. You have come home. I only hope that it is what you truly want. And that you find your peace." He cuffed the side of Cort's face affectionately. "You will hunt with us tomorrow."

"Yes."

With a slight shake of his head, Alphonse started down the hill. Cort stood where he was for a long time afterward, watching the sun sink into the cypress swamp in the west, giving himself up to the night.

But there was no peace. There could never be peace so long as he could remember Aria's eyes searching his as he told her how he had betrayed her.

He'd lied to his father just as he'd lied to so many others. He *had* run away. If he'd also come back to remember who he was…well, now he remembered. And that was the reason he was afraid.

I've never stopped running, Maman.

A hunting owl squeaked, and rodents rooted in the grass. Cort drew in a deep lungful of the richly scented air, and for a moment he thought he smelled *her.*

An illusion. But it seemed she was there with him, beside him, her small, firm hand in his.

"You will stay with me," she had said.

He closed his eyes. *You would have liked her, Maman. She is strong, like you.*

Sabine Renier's dark eyes smiled at him from the shadows of memory. *You will need someone strong, mon fils.*

Aria, stubborn and courageous, determined to face down her fears. Aria, who had never been less than loyal, not even when she had deceived him.

What if, after all he had told her, after all his mistakes, she still wanted him, just as he was now? What if *she* would stay with *him?* What if he went back to her, asked her…begged…

Cort bared his teeth. No begging. Only the simplest statement.

Come with me. That was the only way it could be possible. No discussion, no apologies. He could never live in the world she was about to join. The choice was still hers. If she loved him as Babette said she did…

He would be doing what he had sworn not to do. But the gentleman was gone. The wolf had taken the idea between his teeth and refused to relinquish it.

She is yours. Take her.

There on the hill of memory Cort removed the

homespun shirt and trousers, folded them and laid them
neatly among the flowers.

I will bring her back to you, Maman.

He Changed and ran down the hill to the village,
sweeping past the cabins and the people going about
their daily work. Papa was there, in conversation with
two of the village men. He paused when he saw Cort
run by.

When he heard the wolves behind him, Cort didn't
slow down. Apparently Papa had an idea that he should
keep an eye on his prodigal son. If the people of Bayou
Gris wanted to follow Beau Renier all the way to Belle
Lune, he wouldn't stop them. And if the New Orleans
Reniers tried to stop them, he knew who he would bet
on.

THERE WERE TOO many of them.

Aria fought. She brought Benoit down within a minute and almost got away from di Reinardus before nearly
a dozen men and wolves surrounded her and the net fell,
tangling her paws and catching on her teeth. She snarled
and struggled, but each frantic movement only tightened
the ropes. Rough hands seized her neck, while others
forced the muzzle over her jaws, and soon the humans
were dragging her away, di Reinardus trotting alongside
and Benoit limping behind.

She had long since lost track of time, but the sun had
set and the moon was peeking above the trees when they
stopped. The smell of the swamps had receded, and
there was a narrow, rutted road stretching away among
the trees. North, Aria thought, though she couldn't be
sure. Her body was bumped and bruised, and her mind
dark with despair.

"You have what you want," Benoit said, human again.

"Cursed bitch. You're welcome to her." He held out his hand to di Reinardus.

"Pay him," di Reinardus said. She heard him moving behind her, heard the rustle of bills and the clink of coins as the duke's human lackeys counted out the money. Then di Reinardus was crouching beside her, lean and muscular and powerful in his nakedness, peering through the heavy netting.

"My dear Aria," he said. "How remarkable you are. Just like your sister." He reached through the ropes and removed the muzzle, letting it fall to the ground. "I think you will do very well. Very well indeed."

Aria Changed, ignoring the protest of her cramped, sore muscles. "You should be dead," she said.

"Is that what your 'protector' told you?" he asked. "He has been clever in his way, but he has a fatal flaw. He believes his friends even when they betray him."

Yuri. Cort had never told her how the Russian had killed di Reinardus or what had happened afterward. But he had let Yuri go. He must have believed…

"Where is Yuri?" she asked.

"You will see him soon enough. For now—"

"How did you find me? Was it Benoit?"

"Sniveling puppy," di Reinardus said with a curl of his lip. "Jealousy will drive a man to idiocy as surely as love."

"Jealousy? Because of me?"

"Because of your sister. Twenty years ago, when the Carantian loyalists sent Alese to live with the Reniers, they promised that one of the Renier sons would be permitted to court the princess when she came of age. No guarantees, mind you, but there was a chance that a Renier might become the consort of a future Carantian queen." The duke reached through the net again and touched Aria's hair. "Even though he was hardly more than a boy and she only a girl, when the final decision was made, Benoit already believed himself in love with Alese. He was enraged when Xavier chose Henri as the prospective suitor. Better to let anyone else have her than the brother who would steal what he believed to be his."

Then Benoit always knew Lucienne was a princess, Aria thought, remembering how the young man had pretended shock when Cort had told him and Henri who she was. *He knew all about Carantia and what happened to the royal family.*

She pulled away from di Reinardus's stroking hand. "So he decided to help you kidnap her?" she asked.

"Yuri, who was a frequent guest in the Renier household, recognized a potential ally. His gamble paid off. A door left unlocked, a distraction…" He shrugged. "When Alese…escaped, Benoit was, like many younger sons, in need of funds to support his taste for luxury. He kept watch for me over the years. And he was ready when Yuri informed me that you were on your way to New Orleans."

Aria turned her face away. She had known nothing of treachery when she had left Carantia. Now it seemed impossible to escape its reach.

"Take heart, my dear. Your trials are nearly over. I will take good care of you. In time—"

She twisted and sank her teeth into his hand.

He pulled it back and laughed. "I admire your spirit. I may even permit you to keep some of it—within reason." He rose. "The carriage is only a short distance away. Unfortunately, I cannot let you loose until we reach it."

He snapped orders to his men, who lifted the net and began to trot along the path. The *loups-garous* remained in wolf shape, ranging to either side. It took them far less time to reach a main road than it had taken Aria to get to the place where they'd captured her. She had been well and truly lost, but not quite lost enough.

A closed carriage was waiting on the road, one meant for long-distance travel and large enough to carry four inside and several more outside. A man was waiting with the carriage, wan and drawn and seeming ten pounds lighter than when Aria had last seem him.

Baron Yuri Chernikov.

He didn't look at Aria as the humans carrying the net pinned her down and cut it away, quickly binding her hands behind her. While Yuri climbed up the driver's perch, the men pushed her through the open door and set her on the rear-facing seat.

Aria lay still, trying to think. She knew it was possible that other members of the Renier family might have come after her when she'd left Belle Lune, but she couldn't assume they would ever find her. Cort could be anywhere in the swamps, oblivious to what was happening. And even if he did know, would he come for her?

Her moment of doubt shamed her. But her faith in Cort, a faith that refused to die, wouldn't help her now. Di Reinardus, fully dressed, climbed into the carriage and took the front-facing seat, settling comfortably. The carriage rocked with the weight of several men as they clambered up to the roof. Di Reinardus's *loups-garous* milled around the wheels.

"We will be going directly to the port," di Reinardus said, removing a pair of gloves from his coat and pulling them on. "A captain there is prepared to take us to New York, where we will board a ship bound for the Continent." He turned his hands about, examining the fit of the gloves. "You may be uncomfortable for a short while, my dear, but it will not last long. You will have your own cabin—at least until the marriage can take place."

Aria sat up. "You can't force me to marry you," she said. "Or make me tell the Carantians to obey you."

He sighed. "I assure you that I have considered all these obstacles, and I am not in the least concerned. We shall both be making sacrifices." He smiled at her. "Bedding you will not be one of mine."

As he finished speaking, the carriage began to move. Aria flexed stiff fingers and worked carefully at the bindings that held her arms behind her back; they were thick and strong enough to foil even a werewolf, but she picked at them stubbornly. Changing, bound as she was, would prove not only painful but dangerous.

Di Reinardus was no longer watching her. He leaned his head back against his seat and closed his eyes. The carriage moved on through what remained of the night. The *loups-garous* broke away, doubtless to Change so that they could enter the city in less conspicuous form. Aria smelled dawn before the sky began to lighten. She knew they were close to New Orleans now. The port would not be far.

The Reniers might eventually learn what had become of her. Perhaps Cort never would.

Aria clenched her teeth and set her bleeding fingers to the ropes again.

CHAPTER TWENTY-TWO

Aria had been here.

Cort circled around the trampled grass, every hair standing straight up from his spine. He had underestimated her badly. He had let himself believe that she would never follow him, that pride and hurt and anger would stop her. He had never considered that she might lose herself in this land he knew like the back of his paw.

But she had. And someone had come after *her*. Benoit Renier. A dozen humans and *loups-garous*.

And Duke Gunther di Reinardus.

There was no time for shock or self-recrimination. Cort was moving again before his kin caught up with him, a streak hurtling through the swamps like a devilish apparition.

Babette sat up in her seat. The unmistakable rattle of another carriage drew her to the window.

It had been a long night. The sky was beginning to lighten, bringing with it the renewed hope that the Carantians would return with Aria. Josef Dreher stood by the carriage, staring south in the direction of the swamp.

There was no reason to think that the oncoming vehicle had anything to do with them or posed any threat, but Dreher briefly stepped out of Babette's sight and returned with a rifle held loosely in his hands.

Babette felt inside her handbag for the tiny pistol. It was still loaded. She opened the door and climbed out. The approaching carriage was large and heavy. She could see several dark shapes riding on the outside: two men sitting on the top and two others clinging to the sides. The rising sun illumined the man perched on the high coachman's bench.

Without a thought, Babette ran into the middle of the road and raised her hands. The coachman pulled sharply back on the reins, drawing the horses to a sweating, trembling stop.

She walked slowly toward the carriage. The men on the top were already climbing down, and she glimpsed the flash of metal.

A man's voice rose from within. "Curse you, Yuri," di Reinardus called. "Why have you stopped? We must get to the port!"

So the duke was alive.

Yuri looked down, meeting Babette's gaze. She felt nothing. Nothing at all.

"Why, *mon ami?*" she asked him.

"Get out of the way, Babette!" Yuri snapped.

Dreher came up beside her. "Who is this?" he demanded.

Before she could answer, di Reinardus jumped out of the carriage. He looked from Babette to Dreher without the slightest trace of surprise or worry. Dreher paled in shock.

"Carantian, if I am not mistaken," di Reinardus said. "Where are the others, boy? Did they send you and the whore out alone?"

"*Ich bin*...Josef Dreher," the young man said. "You are—"

"You have one chance to stay alive," di Reinardus said, cutting him off. "Take this woman and leave."

Dreher's hands trembled as he lifted the rifle. "Not until I kill you, traitor," he said hoarsely.

The other men, all armed, had reached the ground and were pointing their guns at Dreher and Babette.

"There will be another time," Babette whispered. "Herr Dreher, put down the—"

"Run!" a woman's voice called from inside the carriage.

Aria!

Babette had no sooner grasped that fact than Dreher fired at di Reinardus. The armed men were quick to respond, and the Carantian fell, mortally wounded by a dozen bullets.

"Young fool," di Reinardus said. He stared at Babette. "A pity you hadn't the good sense to escape when you had so many opportunities." He gestured to his men. "Make it quick."

With a cry, Yuri flung himself from his seat and fell on di Reinardus. The startled humans swung toward them as Yuri hung on to the duke's back and clawed at his face. Babette pulled out her pistol and ran back to the meager protection of the Reniers' carriage, frustrated by her helplessness. She couldn't hope to get near Dreher or Aria without being shot down. And Yuri couldn't possibly win.

She had nearly lost herself to despair when a low shape leaped into view beside the duke's carriage and struck di Reinardus with stiffened forelegs, knocking Yuri away and sending both men tumbling to the ground. Within seconds four more red-furred wolves appeared, going straight for the armed men.

Babette didn't know these *loups-garous,* but she knew Cort, and the others were fighting alongside him. One of them yelped as a bullet struck, but he only fought all the more fiercely. One by one the humans were disabled or had the good sense to run. It seemed that it would be a swift victory until six more wolves of varied colors raced out of the trees to the east of the road.

Whose side they were on was quickly apparent. They attacked the red-coated wolves, and soon all Babette could see was a flurry of fur and flashing teeth. She caught the briefest glimpse of di Reinardus climbing back into the carriage. There was no sign of Aria.

As if he had nothing at all to do with the fight, Yuri stood to the side, in obvious pain and nursing an injured arm. All the old habits urged Babette to go to him, comfort him, care for him until he was well again.

But she had done that once too often. As the vicious growls and cries of pain began to subside, she became aware of the forgotten pistol clenched in her hand.

Slowly, as if the hand belonged to another woman, Babette raised the weapon. Yuri's gaze flickered down to the pistol and then returned to her face. He smiled.

Babette aimed and fired.

CORT'S KINFOLK GATHERED around him, all wounded, one limping badly. A notch had been bitten out of Papa's ear, but he was still as vigorous as a man twenty years his junior. Di Reinardus's *loups-garous* were all down; three had already Changed to heal dangerous wounds, but they showed no interest in getting up again. One of the humans wasn't likely to move ever again; a second moaned over a shattered leg, and the others had fled.

Babette stood over another body, a pistol dangling from her fingers. Yuri lay at her feet, quite dead. Josef Dreher was also dead, his body riddled with bullet wounds.

Cort would have gone to her, but there was no time. The most dangerous enemy of all was still inside the carriage with Aria. It had been all he could do to make sure the duke didn't escape or try to take Aria away during the confusion of the fight.

Now she was his hostage, and Cort knew that threats would be of no use at all. He Changed, and spoke quietly to Alphonse and his cousins. They set to watch over the captives while Cort approached the carriage door.

"Stay where you are," di Reinardus said.

Cort couldn't see the man, but he could smell sweat and a dozen subtle odors that spoke of fear as well as anger. Di Reinardus was afraid. He had been hunted down and cornered at last.

And he was desperate. Desperate enough to take Cort's world with him when he fell.

"Cort!" Aria cried, the word instantly muffled.

Cort lunged for the door.

"Stop, or she dies."

Cort froze. "You have nothing to gain by killing her, di Reinardus," he said, struggling to steady his voice.

"Perhaps not," the duke said. "But I have much to gain from the threat of it."

Alphonse gave a warning growl behind Cort. A pair of wolves were running toward the carriage, their scent altered by their shape but still familiar.

"It's all right, Papa," Cort said. "They're friends."

The Carantians came to a sudden stop at the edge of the road and Changed.

"Princess!" von Losontz cried.

"Stay back," Cort warned, then turned to face the window again. "What do you want?" he asked di Reinardus.

"That should be obvious," the duke said with an easy calm he could not be feeling. "Let me leave with the girl. That is the only way you can guarantee her survival."

A frightened moan rose in the darkness of the carriage. "Cort," Aria whimpered, "don't let him kill me."

Aria's voice, but not Aria's spirit. She would never give in to fear, or to di Reinardus. Not like this.

But the duke didn't know her quite as well as Cort did. "You would be wise to listen to her," di Reinardus said. "She has been brave, but she has the sense to know that courage is not enough. And that I will make her death most unpleasant."

"Let her go!" von Mir shouted. "We'll give you anything, pay any ransom…."

"Please," Aria sobbed. "I will marry you, Duke. I will do whatever you tell me." Her voice was closer to the carriage door now. "*You* asked me to marry you, and I refused!" she called out to Cort. "I want nothing to do with you." A portion of her pale face showed in the window. "Do what he says. I order you! Take all these men away."

"You heard Her Highness," di Reinardus said. "You have three minutes to decide."

Three minutes. Three minutes during which Cort would take a terrible chance.

"Where is Yuri?" the duke asked. "Have you killed him?"

"He's dead," Cort growled.

"It would have been better, for your sake, if you had

seen to him in California. Are any of my men still alive and capable of handling the carriage?"

"One."

"Let him up. He will drive us. And be warned…if anyone follows, the princess will die."

Cort backed away and gestured to his father. Alphonse Changed and jerked the man in question to his feet. The fellow scrambled onto the coachman's seat and gathered up the reins with trembling hands. Aria continued to whine and weep.

"Very well," Cort said. "You can go."

"No!" von Losontz cried.

"You have made a wise decision," di Reinardus said, ignoring the Carantian. "Tell the coachman to move."

Cort gave the signal. "Farewell, Princess," he said. "I am sorry it has come to this."

The carriage lurched into motion. Di Reinardus smiled through the window.

"Auf Wiedersehen," he said. "Though we shall not meet aga—"

His face turned crimson, and he gagged. His hands clawed at the rope biting into his throat. Aria's face appeared behind his, her expression grim with purpose.

Running beside the carriage, Cort yanked open the door. Di Reinardus fell forward, Aria clinging to his back. Just as the duke recovered and was turning on Aria with his fist clenched to strike, the carriage shuddered to a stop. Cort seized di Reinardus's collar and dragged him out the door. Aria jumped out after him, throwing the rope aside. The driver had jumped from his seat and was running as fast as his two human feet would carry him.

If there was anything civilized left of Cort in that moment, it was too deeply buried to matter. Di Reinardus had no chance. He died as a man, his last expression one of utter disbelief that he had been defeated at last.

When he was done, Cort turned to look for Aria. She had gone to the other carriage and was standing with Babette, supporting the older woman as she sobbed uncontrollably. Von Losontz waited a short distance away, while von Mir knelt beside Josef Dreher's body. Alphonse and the villagers still stood guard over di Reinardus's men, but it was clear the captives were bewildered and anxious to understand what had happened.

Cort went to join them, pausing to look at Yuri's body. His treachery had caused so much suffering, and yet he had paid the ultimate price for his mistakes. Just like his master.

At least Cort had not been forced to kill him. Someone else had done the job. But *he* still had to face the consequences of his own unforgivable errors.

He met Freiherr von Mir halfway to the other carriage.

"Di Reinardus?" the Carantian asked, his face pinched with grief for his fallen friend.

"Dead."

Von Mir hurried past him toward the body, undoubtedly to confirm Cort's assertion.

Aria was helping Babette into the Renier carriage. She straightened when she saw Cort.

"Are you all right?" he asked, searching her face and body for injuries. "Did di Reinardus…?"

"He didn't hurt me." She met his gaze directly, but there was nothing in her eyes but deep sadness. "I'm sorry I didn't stay to help, but I knew you didn't need me."

Need her to kill di Reinardus, she meant. He must

366 LUCK OF THE WOLF

have looked like a monster, likely to turn on anything or anyone who got in his way.

He swallowed. "Aria, I didn't know you had come after me. I am responsible for this. My mistakes have—"

"We have all made mistakes," she said quietly. She closed the carriage door and turned to look at Dreher's still form, which von Mir had arranged into gentle repose and covered with his own coat. "That young man is dead because of me."

"No, Your Highness." Von Losontz joined them, naked as all the other *loups-garous* but clothed in a kind of dignity no human garment could give him. "We never dreamed that di Reinardus was still a threat, or that he was here in New Orleans. If we had suspected…"

"I believed he was dead," Cort said. "There is a great deal I didn't tell you about myself and how I came to be with the princess. If not for my stupidity—"

"Assez!" Aria cried. "Enough!" She faced von Losontz. "I am not who you think I am," she said. "I am as much a fraud as Cort ever was. I have brought you grief, *monsieur,* and I can never be what you want me to be."

Von Losontz's face creased with distress. "Your Royal Highness…"

"I was never raised to be a lady," Aria said. "My guardian never told me that I was of royal blood. Almost none of what I led you to believe is true."

As Cort's kin quietly gathered around to listen and von Mir rejoined them, she told the Carantians her story. She omitted the part about Cort winning her in the poker tournament and how close their relationship had become. Never did she suggest that Cort was to blame for anything that had happened, even his failure to make certain that di Reinardus was dead. He had been a perfect gentleman every moment he was with her, committed to protecting her and doing what he could to prepare her for her meeting with the family she had never known existed.

"Whatever he may have done in the past," she said, "he has more than atoned for it. And as for myself…" She looked beyond the Carantians, south and west toward the wilderness. "I may be Alese's sister, but I am nothing like her. It was all make-believe." She glanced at Cort, tears in her eyes. "Almost all of it."

Cort held his arms rigidly at his sides, knowing that if he let go of his self-control even for a moment he would take her in his embrace and carry her away, back to Bayou Gris, where she would never have to pretend again, never face the danger of fighting for a throne she didn't want. He was still ready to do it. If she would have him. One word…

"Your Highness," von Losontz said, his voice shaking, "I thank you for your honesty. I understand why you were driven to act as you did. I regret the circumstances that robbed you of your rightful privileges. But it changes nothing. You are still our princess by blood and nature."

Aria seemed not to hear. She met Cort's gaze, and he waited, his heart in his throat.

"Monsieur Renier," she said, "may I speak with you?"

She walked away, and Cort followed. They were still within earshot of the *loups-garous,* but Aria showed no signs of concern that the others might overhear.

"How did you know where I—"

"Why did you come after me?" Cort asked, speaking over her words.

They stared at each other. Aria almost smiled.

"You know why I came," she said.

Always honesty from her, even when her pride and heart and future were at stake.

"How did you know di Reinardus had found me?" she asked.

He offered a crooked smile of his own. "Because I was coming back for you," he said.

She took a step toward him. "Why?"

"You know why."

The rest of the world went away. Aria held out her hands, and he took them.

"Who are these people with you?" she asked.

"My kin. My father. My family."

"And you were coming to take me to them?"

"To my home. To the place I never should have left. The only place I belong."

"It is a strange world, your home."

"You could learn to love it."

"Is that what you want, Cort?"

"If you can forgive me."

"Can you doubt it?"

He opened his mouth to answer, but a firm hand on his arm stopped him.

"Monsieur," von Losontz said softly. "You do not know what you do."

Von Mir joined them, as grave and grim as his compatriot. "If we may speak to you alone…"

"Whatever you wish to say to Cort may be said in my presence," Aria said, her smile gone.

"Very well, Your Highness." The elder Carantian faced Cort again. "You have no stake in our country. You have no knowledge of it, or what the return of the true heir will mean to us. Before the deposition of our rightful king and queen, Carantia was on the path to becoming a modern country, free of superstition and feudal cruelty. Before König Wilhelm came to the throne, the *wehrwölfe* nobles were a law unto themselves, and humans like Josef were treated as little better than slaves. Wilhelm changed that."

"He gave the hope of equality to the humans of Carantia," von Mir said. "He introduced the sciences and medicine to cure human illnesses that could not be helped by the Change. He established just laws, standing firm against the aristocrats who would oppose them."

"Until di Reinardus fomented rebellion," von Losontz said. "He succeeded in murdering our king and queen. And when he was exiled, his cousin took the throne by default…a weak and unstable ruler who let the nobles have their way and returned the country to the dark, benighted place it had been before."

"But the people and some of the nobles will rally behind a true heir," von Mir said. "Carantia can be what it was meant to be. But only if the princess returns with us." He raised clasped hands. "I beg you to think of all those who will suffer if Her Highness leaves with you."

"It is not my choice," Cort said. But his throat ached and his stomach clenched with the knowledge that Aria, too, had heard every word the Carantians had spoken.

"She will be loved," von Losontz said. Tears leaked from the old man's eyes. "Fifty thousand people, humans and *wehrwölfe* alike, wait to adore her. To be free again. Give her back to us."

Slowly Cort looked at Aria. Her eyes, too, were wet. She was too good, too generous, not to be moved by the Carantians' plea.

And it was tearing her apart.

"Tell me," Cort said thickly. "What was your bargain with the Reniers regarding Alese?"

Von Losontz cleared his throat. "That Henri be permitted to accompany the princess to Carantia and pay court to her."

"Marry her?"

"Become her consort, if she would have him."

Aria made a choked sound. "*I* would never have married him," she said.

"That would never be asked of you," von Mir said. "Only think of what great good you can do for so many…."

Aria's eyes were full of anguish. She looked at Cort and then away. He knew that if he asked her, she would come with him. She would let him make the decision for her. And she would live with the guilt for the rest of her life.

He had told her that the bayou was the only place he belonged. And he had meant it. To go out into the world again would mean returning to his failure. Taking up the mask that had made a mockery of his life, and betrayed Aria time and again.

He could tell himself that he could let Aria go. He might eventually learn to live without her. And Aria would do her duty. She wouldn't ask him to come with her, knowing he had chosen his path. She would learn to become Queen Aria di Reinardus, because she could do anything and be anyone she chose.

But she would be alone. No matter what the Carantians said, she would always be alone.

Silently, he held out his hand to Aria. She took it. They stood for an endless moment without speaking, pinned beneath the curious and anxious stares of *loups-garous* from two worlds that could never meet.

"I never stopped wanting you to marry me," Cort said at last.

"Nor I you." She tried to smile. It was a brave effort. "I didn't want to let you go."

He cradled her hands in his. "But you will, for their sakes."

"They...they need me," she whispered. "I may be the only one who can make things right in Carantia."

"I know."

She pulled her hands away. "Thank you," she said. "Thank you for taking care of me. For..." She stepped out of his reach. "I'll never forget."

"How can you forget," Cort said, "when I will be there to remind you?"

Her body stiffened. "I don't— Cort, I can't—"

"I have no ambition to become the consort of a queen," he said with a wry smile. "I'm no prince. I'm not even a gentleman. But I can stay by your side. I can be whatever you want me to be, even if we never—"

"You would do that for me?" She glanced at Cort's father, at the other bayou Reniers who listened so intently. "But your home, your family..."

"They will understand. I turned my back on them once, but they know I'll never leave them again. Not here." He touched his chest. "My father would think I was mad to let you go. If you'll have me."

Her face lit up brighter than the rising sun. "I will. But only under one condition." Chin high, she marched back to the anxious Carantians. "You will have your princess," she said, "if she may marry whom she chooses."

Von Losontz had no need to ask what she meant. He shifted uneasily and glanced at Cort. "It is...most unusual...."

"You would have let Henri marry the Queen," she

said, all but bristling with wolfish challenge. "Cort is a thousand times the man Henri is. Henri or any one of those fine New Orleans Reniers."

The old man's face flushed. "But Your Highness…"

"You want Carantia to change, become what you call a modern country," she said. "I don't know anything about that. But if you want people to be equal, you can start with us."

The battle was brief, and in the end the Carantians recognized their defeat. "He cannot be king," von Losontz said gruffly. "At best, he will be your consort."

"I've no objection," Cort said, coming to stand beside Aria. "As long as I have all husbandly privileges."

Like the spirited girl she had been when he'd first brought her home, Aria flung herself into his arms and kissed him soundly. "I can't wait," she whispered in his ear. "I love you."

"And I love you," he said. "I always have."

The physical consequences of their embrace might have proved embarrassing had there not been a very timely interruption. A second carriage bearing the Renier crest arrived, coming to a stop behind the others. Henri Renier climbed out, his gaze taking in the scene with astonishment and chagrin. He stared at Aria.

"Your Highness?" he said. "Thank God you are safe! I followed you when you left Belle Lune, but the carriage was mired in the…" He noticed Cort. "You? What are you—"

"*Monsieur,*" Aria said with a little lilt of triumph, "may I present my fiancé, Cortland Beauregard Renier?"

Henri gaped. Alphonse approached Cort and Aria, trailing Cort's curious cousins.

"My father," Cort said hastily. "Alphonse Renier."

The old man bowed to Aria with courtly grace. "My son does not deserve a lady of such great courage, sense and beauty," he said.

Aria blushed, offering her hand. "I am greatly honored, Monsieur Renier."

Alphonse grinned and kissed her fingers. "I believe you may be the only one on this earth who can keep him honest," he said with a sly glance at Cort.

"I shall do my best, sir."

He squeezed her hand. "Perhaps you can spare a little time before you return to your home, *mademoiselle*. I would like you to meet the rest of Beau's kin."

"Beau," she said, giving Cort a sly glance of her own. "It suits you, *mon amour*."

Cort winced. "I've become rather used to Cort," he said. He swallowed. "Papa, will you give us your blessing?"

Alphonse held out his other hand. Cort took it and knelt. Aria knelt beside him.

"My blessing on these young folk," Alphonse said, as the other villagers bowed their heads. "May God watch over them and keep them in the palm of his hand."

Taking Aria's hand, Cort rose. "*Merci,* Papa," he said. "I only wish that Maman—"

"Do not think she will not see you," Alphonse said. He winked at Aria. "Is there any reason you cannot be married at Bayou Gris, *ma fille?*"

Von Losontz coughed loudly. "Your Highness!"

"None at all," Aria said, her eyes sparkling with mischief. "May I call you Papa, too? I never knew my own father."

"*Ma chérie,*" he said, "you make this old man very happy."

"What is going on?" Henri demanded as he burst into their little circle of happiness. "What have you done, Aria?"

"I will tell you," Babette said, very pale but steady on her feet as she came to join them. "If you will hear the story from one such as I."

Henri groaned. Aria pulled Babette close.

"You are coming to Carantia with us, of course," she said.

Babette smiled sadly. "I can be of no use to you there, Aria. Do not worry about me. Like a cat, I always land on my feet."

"Then you can land on your feet in Carantia," Aria said. "If you don't come, I might forget how to be a lady."

Babette's eyes filled with tears. "If you are certain…?"

"Don't argue with her," Cort said. "You can't possibly win."

THERE WAS ONLY a brief conversation after that, a discussion of practical matters that finally concluded when Aria refused Henri's stilted offer of lodging at Belle Lune, and insisted on accompanying Cort and his kin directly to Bayou Gris. After binding the prisoners, the villagers and Carantians stuffed them into the second Renier carriage, where they would remain until the Carantians arranged a more permanent solution. Di Reinardus's body was tossed into the nearest bayou for the alligators to devour at will.

Von Losontz and von Mir returned to New Orleans with Dreher's body, promising to come to Bayou Gris once the young man had been properly interred.

"IT *IS* BEAUTIFUL," Aria said, standing with Cort among the wildflowers on the hill of memories. She leaned her head against his shoulder and sighed. "I only wish we didn't have to leave your home so soon after you—"

"There is no reason we cannot return someday," he said, resting his cheek against her hair. "A queen must have some privileges, after all."

"And she will make use of them," Aria murmured, kissing Cort's bare arm. "I wonder if Alese is still alive somewhere. I would like to come back and look for her someday."

"If she is alive, we'll find her," Cort said.

"There are so many things…"

Cort kissed the top of her head. "I know. But we can live only one day at a time."

She looked up into his eyes. "I know Carantia will seem strange to you."

"No stranger than it will seem to you. But we won't be alone."

No. Never alone again. "There are places in the mountains I can't wait to show you," she said. "Places just like this, where we can run without meeting anyone else for miles."

"Once Carantia is free," Cort murmured.

She turned her face up to his. "It will be. You and I will make sure of it."

He looked into her eyes, and she felt the earth spin under her feet. "You set *me* free, Aria."

"I only helped you remember what you had forgotten." She stroked his chest, wondering how she should tell him. "There is one thing…one thing I haven't told you yet."

"What now?" he said, eying her askance. "Bad habits you haven't told me about? A secret lover? A—"

"A baby," she blurted out.

The stunned look on his face worried her a little until she saw the joy in his eyes. "A baby?" he whispered. "How long have you—"

"I think I first knew when you came to the hotel," she said. "It was just a feeling, but it got so much stronger when you were there. I wasn't completely sure until we got to Bayou Gris." She snuggled into his arms. "I think he wanted to see his grandpapa."

"Alphonse," Cort said in a slightly strangled voice. "He…he'll be…"

"Are *you* happy?"

With a whoop he lifted her off the ground and spun her around until she was dizzy all over again. When he set her down and she could stand by herself, she took his hand and lifted it to her lips.

"Our child will have so much to learn," she said. "But we're lucky, Cort, we *loups-garous*. We can see the world through two sets of eyes."

"Speaking of luck," he said, still grinning like a madman, "will I be permitted to play the occasional game of poker?"

"Only if you promise to play by the rules. And not win every time."

"How can I promise that? I found Lady Luck one night in San Francisco, and she can never desert me again."

Aria closed her eyes, thinking of the life that lay ahead of them. A life that would bring many challenges. A life that would be wonderful because of this man and his love and the child that was coming.

"You never taught *me* to play," she said gravely. "Perhaps if you only play with me…"

"Only with you," he said, "until the end of our lives."

With a laugh he pulled her down into the grass, and they played all night long.

* * * * *

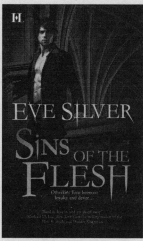

REQUEST YOUR FREE BOOKS!

2 FREE NOVELS
FROM THE SUSPENSE COLLECTION
PLUS 2 FREE GIFTS!

YES! Please send me 2 FREE novels from the Suspense Collection and my 2 FREE gifts (gifts are worth about $10). After receiving them, if I don't wish to receive any more books, I can return the shipping statement marked "cancel." If I don't cancel, I will receive 3 brand-new novels every month and be billed just $5.74 per book in the U.S. or $6.24 per book in Canada. That's a saving of at least 28% off the cover price. It's quite a bargain! Shipping and handling is just 50¢ per book.* I understand that accepting the 2 free books and gifts places me under no obligation to buy anything. I can always return a shipment and cancel at any time. Even if I never buy another book, the two free books and gifts are mine to keep forever.

192/392 MDN E7PD

Name   (PLEASE PRINT)

Address   Apt. #

City   State/Prov.   Zip/Postal Code

Signature (if under 18, a parent or guardian must sign)

Mail to **The Reader Service:**
IN U.S.A.: P.O. Box 1867, Buffalo, NY 14240-1867
IN CANADA: P.O. Box 609, Fort Erie, Ontario L2A 5X3

Not valid for current subscribers to the Suspense Collection
or the Romance/Suspense Collection.

Want to try two free books from another line?
Call 1-800-873-8635 or visit www.morefreebooks.com.

* Terms and prices subject to change without notice. Prices do not include applicable taxes. N.Y. residents add applicable sales tax. Canadian residents will be charged applicable provincial taxes and GST. Offer not valid in Quebec. This offer is limited to one order per household. All orders subject to approval. Credit or debit balances in a customer's account(s) may be offset by any other outstanding balance owed by or to the customer. Please allow 4 to 6 weeks for delivery. Offer available while quantities last.

Your Privacy: Harlequin Books is committed to protecting your privacy. Our Privacy Policy is available online at www.eHarlequin.com or upon request from the Reader Service. From time to time we make our lists of customers available to reputable third parties who may have a product or service of interest to you. If you would prefer we not share your name and address, please check here. ☐

Help us get it right—We strive for accurate, respectful and relevant communications. To clarify or modify your communication preferences, visit us at www.ReaderService.com/consumerschoice.

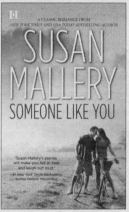

SUSAN KRINARD